LAND THAT I LOVE

This extraordinary story classically captures the mindset of the 1940s. Addie and her friend Kate reflect the voices women hear as they face confusing dilemmas 75 years later—my first read kept me up into the wee hours. I will refer my readers to *In Times Like These*!

Patricia Evans, author of

The Verbally Abusive Relationship,
Controlling People,
and other books listed at www.VerbalAbuse.com

Wartime brings out the best and the worst in people. I loved the way Addie and Kate, each in her own way, dug down inside to become more than either had ever dreamed. *With Each New Dawn* will inspire you toward resilience and personal growth even as it keeps you riveted with each page turn.

Sonia C. Solomonson, freelance writer and life coach
Way2Grow Coaching

In Times Like These clearly portrays the difficulties for women during WW2. First, there are the challenges of raising food, preserving it, making money stretch, wisely using ration cards and just plain living in fear of the war. But then the overlay of Addie's controlling husband made me instantly empathize with the main character. His verbally abusive and cold treatment of Addie unfortunately is not just a problem from another era. God's provision for her was intriguing. The value of faith, friendship and compassion are evident in this book. I personally enjoyed the food tips and recipes, as well as vivid descriptions of farm life. This may be my favorite book by Gail Kittleson. It is the first in the mini-series, *Women of the Heartland*. Be sure to read the books in order.

Cleo Lampos

Gail Kittleson introduces us to a small town community, under the strains of World War II. The everyday lives of the town folks unfolding their thoughts and concern for the husbands and brothers fighting for their country. The family and friends dynamics in this story keeps the reader wanting to turn page after page. The author knows how to keep the reader engaged. Looking forward to Ms. Kittleson's next book.

K Currie

Kittleson's writing style fosters instant empathy as her quiet heroine, Addie, struggles through daily living in Iowa during WW2. Readers are introduced to Addie through patriotism, friendship, and self-realization. "I've spent my whole life in fear instead of living each day," highlights Addie's growth in overcoming an emotionally abusive husband. Highest recommendation.

Carolyn Cobb

...the pages almost turned themselves. Great period piece exploring family dynamics and interpersonal relationships as well as the growth of self-esteem and the importance of friendship.

Lisa Lickel

Kittleson deftly writes strong female characters facing heartbreaking tragedies. *Until Then* features two: Marian, caught in the Blitz, and Dorothy, a surgical nurse whose work with the 11th Evacuation Hospital has taken her to North Africa, through Sicily and into France. Their stories intertwine in a narrative that touches then heals the soul. Highly, highly recommended!

Literary Soirée

Also by Gail Kittleson

Women of the Heartland Series
In Times Like These
With Each New Dawn
A Purpose True
All for the Cause
Until Then
&
Kiss Me Once Again
a Women of the Heartland story

In This Together
Catching Up With Daylight

With Billy Rae Stewart
Country Music's Hidden Gem

With Cleo Lampos
The Food That Held the World Together
A World War 2 Holiday Scrapbook

Land
That I
Love

a novel of the Texas Hill Country

GAIL KITTLESON

WordCrafts

Although a work of fiction, *Land That I Love* is based on actual events. The author has endeavored to be respectful to all persons, places, and events presented in this novel, and attempted to be as accurate as possible. Still, this is a novel, and all references to persons, places and events are fictitious or used fictitiously.

Published by WordCrafts Press
Cody, Wyoming 82414
www.wordcrafts.net

"I like living. I have sometimes been wildly, despairingly, acutely miserable, racked with sorrow; but through it all I still know quite certainly that just to be alive is a grand thing."
~Agatha Christie

Nottinghamshire England, 1936

They say tears and laughter remind us that lifeblood flows through our veins. After this night, I tend to agree.

Something pulled me from a restless sleep. Lace curtains shuddered in a wayward spring breeze as I cleared my head. Over Donnie's corner crib, moonlight undulated over the coverlet Grandmother had so carefully stitched to warm me in my youth.

Suddenly, I sat up and sniffed. Could that be smoke? I leaped from bed and peered into the hallway. My heart throbbed at the sight of hazy spirals encroaching over the sedate wooden bannister.

Turning back into the bedroom, I gathered Donnie in his coverlet and hurried out. Halfway down the stairs, William, alert as always, approached from below and caught my elbow.

"Sir, Mrs. Herring." He cleared his throat. "Some time ago, that is, just after a replay of Lawrence Gilliam's *'Opping 'Oliday* program, she slipped into the kitchen."

So like William, precise to the moment. But as he continued, my eyes began to sting from the foul air.

"I kept watch from my quarters as she made busy in there." He gave a violent cough. "I must have nodded off, and startled awake." His tone became a harsh whisper. "But it was too late. She had started a fire, and the smoke . . . . That is, sir, she . . ."

From the shadows, William's eyes glistened as he coughed again.

1

"We must get Donnie outside. Hurry!" He ushered us down the rest of the stairs, into the hallway and out the front doors.

Dew-drenched grass shimmered around us as I shielded Donnie from the coolness. Against a dark sky, smoke formed grey rivulets.

"Sir." William hunched closer. "Jeffries and I carried her . . . that is, Mrs. Herring's—er, your wife's body—to the carriage house." In a midnight mist, a shiver passed through William's tall form. "Please do stay here. I shall return soon."

With that, he strode away as ghostly events from the past few weeks paraded before me. Victoria's illness, the doctor's daily visits, caring for Donnie as best I could. Against my shoulder, our innocent toddler's breathing deepened as my own turned to nothing at all.

A few rods away, nightmarish flames leaped into a torrent that engulfed the only home I had ever known. During my childhood, the west section had housed the maid's entrance, cold cellar, storage room and servants' quarters. At this point, we required only a cook and a maid, who lived nearby, so William had moved his things there after Victoria and I married.

When he claimed the room next to the kitchen, I assumed his concern was for our privacy. But had he presaged trouble?

Separated from the house by an expanse of paving stones, the carriage house remained untouched by the fire. I pictured Victoria lying there alone, without even the wireless for company. My eyes burned, but held hostage by this inferno, my feet refused to budge.

A brazen belch from the blaze forced me back as a tinny bell clanged in the distance. Ah, the local firemen—William must have hailed them. Oh, the immense heat emanating from the conflagration, yet it failed to alter the icy river coursing my soul.

Never the same since Donnie's birth, she who bore this little one had risked killing us all. Victoria hated me, that I knew. My utter failure as a husband sat like a tumor at the back of my throat. This, I had come to accept, but to endanger her only son?

A frisson traced my spine as a heavy lorry rumbled onto the

drive, and a burly fellow—the village ironmonger, I supposed— descended from the cab. He loosed a thick rubber hose from its hooks aside the lorry as other workers toppled out into the night. Even the chemist from Holton Street lent a hand. Such a melee, this. Shouts and heroics poised against this tenacious monster that sizzled and flashed its eyes.

I could well imagine a medieval character from *Bows Against the Barons*, recently published by a local author, racing through the trees to save the day with Robin Hood and his band. Not far off, Sherwood Forest might have divulged them to strive against the King. Nothing could shock me now.

But the thought of this tale I recently purchased for little Donnie brought me to a sweat. Grandfather's books—oh no! His lovely library . . .

Not a great house like Wolford Manor closer to Nottingham, this structure possessed some such elements, including Grandfather's pride and joy, his mahogany-walled library. At the farthest point from the kitchen, this sanctuary boasted its own double doors leading into a garden.

Even as I panicked, those doors swung wide to reveal William and several workers hefting wooden crates. Relief washed me as he went about saving Grandfather's treasures.

A great crash shook the earth, and a nimble fellow scaled a corner, having found a foothold in a trellis Grandfather fashioned for his young bride long ago. This piece had served Grandmother well, and might have lasted another lifetime.

Four years ago, I had crooned, "From the past right into the present, my dear," before I gathered Victoria in my arms for our momentous step over the threshold. "And on into our bright future. All the love my grandparents shared will undergird our years here, too."

Her eyes reflected my passion, or so I believed.

Now Grandfather had passed from this world, and everything crumbled around me. The one place I cherished was fast turning to ashes. As if to underscore its demise, a cupola crashed onto the porch roof, broke through, and blazed where it fell. At the same time, a basement window burst out, to lie sizzling on the lawn in shards.

Suddenly, I remembered Victoria's warning a fortnight ago. During one of her rages, she shrieked, "It has never been as you think, Everett. This dream was all in your head, not mine, and soon you shall see it go up in smoke."

Gleaning nothing but metaphor, I replied like the schoolmaster I was, "Then why did you marry me?"

"For a roof over my head and a table set by others." She smoothed graceful fingers along her skirt. "And lovely gowns. Why else?"

Before I could reply, she stared at me with disdain and raced up the stairs. The door of the chamber she had adopted since Donnie's birth slammed with finality. Such behavior might have informed me of the state of things, but blinded by the physician's words, I had continued to hope. A few months ago, an alienist in a famed London hospital had concocted a new medication, he said, that would surely assuage her nervous condition.

But during the next weeks, that prediction proved false. No blame cast—our physician only performed his duty. 'Twas my dream alone that rendered me incognizant.

Dreams possess power to intoxicate to the detriment of reality. With our beautiful old home disappearing before my eyes, I finally succumbed to the truth. Victoria had been right—the fanciful portrait of our growing family existed only under my unruly hair.

Rude certainty faced me head-on. But even when the exhausted workers gave up their efforts to save this graceful building, I found the devastation impossible to embrace. Grandfather's precious house in ruins—how could this be?

Stone survives fire, but everything built upon it perishes. The night around me testified to utter demise, and these simmering remains reflected the undeniable state of my dream.

An automobile halted near the carriage house. My side vision revealed William hurrying that way. Grandfather's butler and reliable friend, as always, would oversee whatever procedure must take place.

Innocent Donnie sighed against my shoulder. The carriage house doors opened and the automobile backed down the drive and hastened away. How long I stood there, I cannot say, but at last, a great roar evidenced this debacle's closing chapter. Gathered in clumps on the lawn, exhausted workers stared. As the slightest wink of light appeared in the east, they wiped their weary brows.

Numb, I only knew the warmth of sweet Donnie against my chest until someone approached and pulled me aside. In the shadows, I scarce took in the fullness of his message.

"Your wife, Mr. Herring. We have removed her to the mortuary for an inquiry. 'Twas the smoke, no doubt. So young and lovely—such a shame." His gulp, as deep as the Channel waters, prickled the hairs on my arms. "Inhalation. Nothing could have saved her. P'raps, in mercy, her heart gave out . . ."

What he saw in my eyes, I shall never know. He pressed me toward the iron bench under Grandfather's laburnum tree. By day, deep yellow blossoms swayed in the spring sunlight, giving this tree its nickname—the golden chain tree. But in this dawn hush, the blossoms hung muted, a tenuous fog.

"Rest here now with your little one. Not as if you haven't suffered a terrible shock."

At last, our son's soft hair received my tears. Until this moment, I had still envisioned Victoria flitting out in a meadow somewhere, as was her habit. She would return with the dawn, William would ring up the doctor for more medication, and she would sleep away the day.

In the unforgiving chill, acridness laced the air. The men hauled their equipment to the lorry, and curious onlookers faded down the road.

Though I had given my all to bring her happiness, Victoria was no more. With this thought came another—no need to wonder what fresh distress would arise by day's end.

The steadiness of Donnie's breathing sustained me. Now, everything centered on this motherless child, this young heart beating next to mine.

Keep him safe. Whatever this required, I pledged myself to the task.

A few months later, William and I observed Donnie at play outside our neighbor's carriage house. The morning after the fire, Mrs. Tillman had taken us in and offered to store what the workers could salvage.

"Now, you just make yourself at home. With Mr. Tillman gone, this old house needs some lighter footfalls. Stay as long as you like."

Crammed into the back of this once-empty building, piles of boxes and crates blocked our way. William and I found seats, with an eye toward our young charge who left no leaf unturned on the drying lawn.

"Mrs. Tillman's rich milk has ruddied Donnie's cheeks. First thing in America, I shall find us a cow." William made this announcement as he leafed through some papers from his briefcase.

"What a rock she has proven for us. I can scarcely believe we have stayed so long—over a year."

"Quite. But she and your grandfather go far back. She always favored your father, and then you, of course. Nearly every afternoon, she brought her handiwork to pass the time with your grandmother, and during your grandmother's last weeks, she brought food daily and kept vigil beside her bed to spell your grandfather."

"Mmm." My memory of that time served me poorly. Grandfather's notification reached me at university just in time to say farewell before Grandmother took her final breath. "Always a kind and thoughtful neighbor, as I recall. But do you suppose I ought to offer something for all this time we have spent with her?"

"Indeed?" William's voice carried a warning. "I should think that might cause her pain, sir, for she sees you as family." He pulled open his briefcase clasp. "Shall we begin?"

"Yes. I cannot thank you enough for managing all the details."

"My pleasure, especially since your grandfather chose a solicitor above reproach. Mr. Firth bids us a hearty Godspeed."

"You are still certain you want to undertake this journey?"

"Unwavering, sir. To the very end, your Grandfather aspired to visit the United States. Tis almost as if we voyage in his stead. Many an early morning when the physician attended Mrs. Herring, we took tea together in the garden, and he spoke often of his comrade, who emigrated after the Great War.

"Their correspondence through the years has paved our way, for a letter arrived from New York this very day. Mr. Noelting has invited us to stay with him in the East as long as needful to locate a suitable homestead." William handed me two full pages in fine longhand.

"How excellent."

"As to the necessary funding, Mr. Firth assures me that all will be transferred to Mr. Noelting's reputable bank in New York, upon your signing several papers in this envelope."

"You have complete confidence concerning this?"

"Absolutely, as did your Grandfather."

"And you find the rest of our papers all in order?"

"Indeed." William patted his leather case. "Everything is at the ready, including our tickets for Tuesday next."

"Well then. What is left to do?"

Just then Donnie scooped up something from the grass. "Dada!" He stumbled crossing the threshold, and I caught him before he fell.

"What have you here?" A smile from William elicited one from Donnie, who held out an unhappy toad captured in his pudgy fingers.

"Oh my! Aren't you quick, though? Let us take Mrs. Toad out where she can hop about. Her babies might await under a plant somewhere, and she must fetch them food." I carried Donnie under a tree where he loosed his captive, and William joined us.

"Let me watch him while you read and sign everything, sir. We must return the financial information tomorrow. I shall take the early bus into Nottingham."

"Perfect." The papers seemed straightforward. Aware that, as usual, William had foreseen an approaching need, I applied my signature to a number of blank lines and folded the sheets back into their appropriate envelopes.

When I returned them to the case, something smooth and metallic met my touch. Ah, Grandfather's letter opener. William must have found this in the debris. The elegant piece had graced Grandfather's desk all these years, and one brush brought a rush of memories.

"Stay true to what you know to be true, and you shall be fine." A tear had fled Grandfather's eye as he bestowed this blessing upon me before he passed. "The Scriptures will guide you, and your schooling. 'Tis your gift to learn and teach. Always remember your calling."

At this instant, I sensed him here, surrounded by his own books. This vital connection, still intact beyond the grave, bade me linger. All around me lay the wisdom of the ages, and indeed, I would have continued teaching but for Victoria's actions.

Often at such momentous times, just the right bit of instruction arrived.

Grandfather experienced the same, he noted, throughout his days in the public works factory, centered on workers and production. When the plant was built, citizens sought him out as its superintendent, for no small amount of wisdom might blend various factions into a working whole to the community's benefit.

But in the evenings, Grandfather read, and saw to it that my father's education surpassed his own. No doubt about my future: "You are made for learning, Everett."

The first time Grandfather said this, we had recently laid Mother to rest in the churchyard. He repeated the sentiment through the years, and again on the day he saw me off to university. This vision spread over me like a mantle, yet now, things had changed, for Victoria had destroyed far more than our family home.

"But you also taught me to tend the orchard, Grandfather. Now is my time for this, but with Donnie as my sole student, I shall continue to teach."

A tremor ran through me and my teeth tingled. Was his blessing descending again?

Down on his knees on the far side of the yard, William gave Donnie a horsey ride. This dignified butler had shepherded my father through his youth, and chiseled his gravestone after the Great War. He had always performed his duty, but beyond that, Grandfather called William *friend*.

"Whatever happens, you may always count on William." Even in Grandfather's last words, he was pointing the way forward.

The sun dissipated a heavy morning haze as I crossed verdant grass to join William and Donnie. Like a beacon for sailors, sunlight penetrated through thick pine branches, and we were off to make a new beginning.

Chapter One

Summary 1938, Texas Hill Country

Acrystal blue sky intensified the morning's promise as I weeded our garden. With Donnie happily at play in a rocky rivulet, I set myself to my labor. As the heat increased, I recalled a wizened local's prediction. Daily, this tall, lanky fellow passed down our road afoot, and often launched a comment on the weather.

"Purty soon th' creek'll dry up. Y'ain't seen summer yet."

Near my growing weed pile, Donnie edged ever closer to our sturdy stone pump house. Silo-like and fed by a windmill, the water reservoir extended upward from the roof a few feet. An early settler's foresight created this reliable water source, so vital in a thirsty land.

After some time, Donnie paused in his play and pointed eastward at some clouds rising above our small orchard. Even as we stared, the bird chatter increased.

"Those clouds may bring us a summer storm. The birds are busy calling their young."

With a studied look over our hip-high corn, Donnie returned to his fence building, a miniature replica of the wooden posts and rails trailing the front of our yard.

Despite the long-faced forecast from our vagabond prognosticator, a rivulet still flowed in the creek bed, and best of all, the pump house offered plenty of water and respite from the heat. No matter the time of day, the air inside remained cool and moist.

Upstart willows formed a ragged line where Donnie carefully propped sticks with stones to ward off foxes intent on stealing his make-believe hens. His conversation with these imaginary creatures satisfied a father's heart, but now and again he stopped to listen to the birds.

Nothing so refreshing as a swig of clear flowing water from the pump house before returning to work with renewed vigor. We visited there twice, and soon, Donnie's had transformed his landscape into the great Atlantic, upon which he steered the Queen Mary from London to New York City. How easily he passed from one scenario to the next—time and change meant little to one so engrossed in the present.

With our bean rows freed from invaders, I turned to the squash vines. This fledgling patch hardly compared to Grandfather's, but little by little, spaces would fill in. William had ordered more flower seeds, and as each variety became established, our rocky earth took on the beginnings of a cottage garden.

Pulling out goat head stickers, or puncture vine, consumed a full half hour. As with most weeds, these fought to the death for their root systems. The next time I glanced up to check on Donnie, darker clouds threatened northward, beyond the corn patch.

The little fellow sent his pretend boat, a piece of mesquite branch, happily *chug-chugging* past the Statue of Liberty, a rock tucked into the sand. His oft-repeated "Liberty!" kept me informed of his whereabouts. From the pasture, one of William's cows mooed as if she agreed.

Often, Donnie re-enacted our passage to the States. Each time, he saluted Miss Liberty, as William and I had when we first sighted her in New York Harbor. But this afternoon, in tandem with Donnie's latest salute, sudden breathlessness followed an overall darkening of the sky.

Definitive restlessness entered the bird chatter now, drawing me to attention. Mesquite leaves turned listless and draped from their branches in distress, broad oaks stood immobile against the

11

closest hill. Seconds later, a foreboding bank covered the entire northwest expanse. Then came a rustle in the distance and a flash razed the cloudbank, now charcoal and ominous.

Donnie read my concern, and without uttering a syllable, dropped his earthy playthings and started toward me. I scooped him up, thunder rumbled down the vale, and we took off at a run.

Bouncing in my arms, he giggled—oh, the excitement of a storm! William's cows made their stately way to the barn. Soon after we arrived, he purchased them, and now plied his inherited cheese-making skill. The enclosed portion of our porch attested to the bacteria, yeast, and fungi required to transform bland curd into the squeaky delicacy we enjoyed every day.

Scarce under the shelter of the roof, Donnie slid down to gape at a closer flash. Thunder leapt from hill to hill, setting the floor-boards shaking as he clung to my knee.

Then, in a deafening roar from on high, the structure trembled once more. Thankfully, summer saw us thoroughly settled, and this old stone house had become our refuge.

"Time for tea. In we go for a bite of bread and cheese."

Donnie's eyes lit up like the firmament, once again scraped by lightning. Such joy in simple things—his every smile declared all was well.

Washed and seated at the table with pencils and sketch paper, he eyed the growing tempest as I prepared our tea. Then a great gust sent a veritable wall of rain through the crack between two hills where Cold Spring Creek carved its home.

All birdsong ceased. Pines branches sawed and shook. Donnie's dark eyelashes quavered. In the terse silence following the latest onslaught, we both hesitated, waiting out the storm.

Another close strike, and a reverberating roar. Together, we breathed once more. Our hillside grove turned to slate as a watery hedge descended. In a moment, the day's heat coalesced.

Again, I blessed the original settlers' attention to firm founda-tions. Their conscientious labor had placed giant oak timbers the length of the partial cellar beneath the kitchen. Carving that small space from the rock must have required gargantuan effort. But the end result—a sense of utter safety—grounded me.

The teapot whistled, and Donnie's eyes brightened as we ate our repast. "Nothing like Mrs. Tillman's lovely crumpets back in England, but this will do for us, eh?"

He smacked his lips. "Crumpets and tea!"

At the first pelt of hail, he bailed from his chair and took to his knees beside the open porch door. I hurried after him as a cool spray broke the sultry cloud hanging over our yard. At the post office the other day, a female patron had mentioned just this.

"Might could use an old-fashioned thunderstorm like we used to have up north when I was a girl."

As wild wind mashed the treetops together above our house, a veritable waterspout streamed to earth. Dry bark blackened against the wave, and I visualized beleaguered apple branches dripping unripe fruit on patchy weeds. Visible through the barn's wide south opening, William's patient bovines ruminated through it all.

And then, light arrayed the world in silver. Quickly, the great darkness dissipated, though rain still throttled our windowpanes.

"Shall we go for a walk?"

Donnie shook his head, but a smile teetered on his lips—he knew I was joshing.

"We would need to fetch our bumbershoots, wouldn't we?"

"Bumber—umbrellas?"

"Righto, old chap. But even they could not keep us dry in this deluge."

Meanwhile, our tea invigorated us. As William's homemade curd and toast filled the empty spots, we took to words. "Do you recall such a storm ever before?"

"No. I like it." Somber assessment accompanied the floating, downward motion of Donnie's fingers.

"As do I. Perhaps you might draw the storm for us? When William comes to milk the cows, you can show him, and he will be pleased."

While I put away the remains of our tea, Donnie set to his task. Through the window, every stitch of foliage dribbled rain, and an over-full eave spout gushed forth, along with one of my first memorized pieces:

"*Whan that Aprille with his shoures soote*
The droughte of Marche hath perced to the roote,
And bathed every veyne in swich licour,
Of which vertu engendred is the flour ..."

Hard at work, Donnie blinked at Chaucer's mesmerizing rhythm. "April, March. Every vein ..."

"Exactly right, my lad. 'Twas April in old England when Geoffrey Chaucer wrote these words. Here, late June has come, but with the same effect."

"Chaucer ... old England."

"Righto."

In Donnie's drawing, rain fell from the heavens in gluts. Through a glen, a stick figure father carried his lead-pencil child toward waiting shelter.

"Ooh, lovely. You have captured the rain." I kissed his forehead and he leaned in. "Now, shall we go out and check on everything?"

His nod sufficed, and he ran toward the porch. There, we donned our rubber boots.

"Shall we check on William, even though he will walk over this afternoon? This rain will prove whether our roofing efforts held water or not."

"Yes, and Lillian!" Donnie held up his forefinger as we took off through the orchard, exclaiming over the amount of windfall.

"Tomorrow we shall have to shovel all of this into buckets and carry it to our burn pile. That will keep the mud dobbers away."

"Shovel. Keep those dobbers away."

In the cool aftermath of our first storm, we made our way to a small house on the west edge of Loyal Valley and entered at a woman's call. This had required an adjustment.

During our first months here, William met a widow named Lillian at the Cherry Spring church. They caught the same ride to Cherry Spring. Lillian, accomplished in both German and English, sewed for people, so he arranged for her to make Donnie's clothes, and soon, they grew quite close.

Oh, the mix of bliss and astonishment on William's face when he spoke of their new friendship early in March! And then, over a fortnight, everything altered. One day, the judder in his voice alerted me.

"I say. That extra room we keep mentioning? We shan't be needing it, sir."

"Since when do you call me *sir*?" Before our journey to the States, he had finally agreed to drop the *sir* he had employed since my birth.

"Oh. Indeed. I must have slipped back—"

Until now, this quintessential bachelor made do in the upstairs without complaint. Virtually an attic, the space sufficed temporarily, though he took pains to avoid banging his head at the ceiling of the narrow stairway. He insisted we address other more pressing matters, but our next project was to be more suitable quarters for him off the kitchen.

"Rather—um—difficult to take in. Yet I have found . . ." Oh, the flush on William's face. "I had no intention . . ." He paused a second time. "That is, I never would have imagined . . ."

My inveterate mentor always knew his mind. Not like him to blunder around—he had garnered my full attention. Then came a third hesitation—what on earth was he trying to tell me?

"After all, a man of my age . . ." He deferred as Donnie ran past. "My, how this lad has grown over the winter!"

Standing on the porch near the ingenious washing machine William concocted during our first weeks here, I stared at the violent flush on his countenance. Using a gasoline pump, a pulley, and a washtub, he added an Anchor brand hand crank clothes wringer, and the result took hours from a tedious task.

15

When this conversation began, I was about to carry a load of clean items to the clothesline. This man might work wonders with mechanical objects, yet certainly was having trouble with his tongue today.

"Yes, who would have thought six months could change a small tyke into a youth? About time to order him a new set of play togs."

"Indeed." Eyeing Donnie out in the yard, William's forehead disfigured in distress, but words failed him.

"Do come out with it, old chap. Whatever are you trying to say?"

"Lillian—" The name issued like a painful belch.

"Yes?"

"That is, I have recently proposed m-mar—"

William, stuttering?

"Proposed?" I stood back. "Marriage? You and Lillian?"

He eyed me tentatively as the news seeped into my consciousness. I placed this woman in my mind. Average height, a rather angular face, a winning smile, and fully able to speak her mind.

"She seems lovely, mate. Do tell me how this transpired."

"Right off, she struck my fancy—so easy to speak with, so forthright. I looked forward to seeing her again, but assumed that at my age . . ."

William's hairline had been receding for years, but I rarely considered his age. He might be in his late forties or early fifties.

"Surely such a thing lay beyond my reach, I thought. But the last time I collected Donnie's new clothing, Lillian invited me in for tea." He threw up his hands. "You might ask how such a thing could transpire so quickly, as do I. The long and short of it is, we have decided to make our vows on the twenty-first."

As though he had survived a fierce battle, William wiped his brow. "You will stand as witness for us?"

Of course I would, although the concept of him marrying drained every spark of my energy. I had always looked upon him as inhabiting a realm removed from the things of earth, including the wiles of women. I pictured him always with us, an ever-present stabilizer.

But change showed its hand. My shock altered into acceptance, and Lillian and William married as spring turned to summer. This seasonal alteration became noticeable as Donnie and I helped William tote his things to his new home after their brief wedding ceremony following Sunday services.

In this climate lacking a severe winter, time would gradually teach me how to read its signs. Though the calendar designates a certain day to begin each season, those who have long experienced these changes simply know. For instance, they smell snow coming. As a newcomer, I claimed no such wisdom.

Still, as Donnie and I neared home, the evening breeze seemed rather subdued. On either side of the road, wildflowers exhibited more dust than vivid color. When a cicada revealed its surreptitious presence, Donnie glanced up.

"Da, what is that?"

"A cicada, I believe—an insect. They come out in hot weather, so I imagine they stay until September or October."

"Is he singing?"

"The male cicada makes the sound, most likely from that tree over there. He strengthens his volume by contracting and expanding organs called tymbals under his hollow abdomen."

"Like our lungs?"

I nodded, and Donnie reached for my hand. Moments after that first creature let forth, others joined in as we reached the curve in the path, where several trees line each side. In no time at all, a full-fledged chorus surrounded us, a veritable cicada serenade echoing from tree to tree.

"They sound like that round you sang at Sunday School this morning."

"Joy joy joy joy, down in my heart." Donnie beat a fist on his chest.

"What a quick learner you are!"

This exchange drove away whatever loss I might have felt. Picturing William at home with Lillian brought a smile. Plain and likeable, she might have lived in an ordinary English village. She welcomed us into her small home like family and sent us off this evening with a brown paper bag of homemade ginger cookies.

"Oh boy!" Donnie grabbed the sack and took a deep sniff. "Ginger!" Lillian touched his cheek, and he rested his winsome curls against her hand.

"Maybe you can teach me some new recipes from England."

"Umm—crumpets."

"He still remembers our neighbor in Nottinghamshire." William licked his lips. "She baked the most outstanding ones."

Lillian nodded, with Donnie still inclining toward her. Clearly, she filled some unspoken need. William patted Donnie's head then, and embraced them both. Something eased in my chest. We were family. This was the closest Donnie would come to it during his childhood.

From that day on, William's fresh frisson of excitement continued, although a seasoned butler's bearing never changes. But the silent glint in his eyes marked sheer delight—in a new way, he had come home.

On the evening of his wedding, the first star appeared as Donnie and I neared our stone haven, and Donnie murmured a bit of a tune Lillian hummed earlier. "Stars at night, big and bright, deep in the heart of Texas."

"William and Lillian. You and me."

"Righto, and we shall be just enough."

And so we were. Entering our cool abode, kept so by thick sandstone walls and a lovely live oak on the west side, we readied for bed and settled into our overstuffed chair. Ah, reading. The perfect activity to end a significant day.

On this Sunday, we ate with Lillian and William as had become our custom. After these meals, we spent many a genial hour. Lillian showed a lively interest in all things British, and relished having guests. Clearly, her quiet ways entranced Donnie.

Their first baking adventure a few weeks ago produced a tray of lovely cinnamon buns while William and I patched a leaky corner of the roof. Our elevated position provided a photographer's view. In the distance rose House Mountain, a granite edifice of about 1,700 feet. Between Loyal Valley and this protrusion spread nine miles of wild grasses and a vast array of wildflowers, many of them bluebonnets. What could be more beautiful?

Even though this land differed greatly from Nottinghamshire, we had been guided here. Wildflowers, rolling hills, even mountains! With Nottinghamshire's elevation at 150 feet, House Mountain indeed qualified.

Someone told William that Hickory Creek runs at its base, which covers Mason County's far southeastern corner. Closer to Loyal Valley, one crosses Marshall Creek, and then the one we claim as our own, Cold Springs Creek. East of Loyal Valley, its waters always run cold due to a deep underground source.

William's informant had climbed House Mountain many times, and mentioned a cave on the northeast side where a man named Oliver, still living, had been raised by the Indians. Stories about House Mountain thoroughly captured my attention. I could only imagine its grand vista. From there, one might see far and wide, including a lower hill called Prairie Mountain, just across the border in Llano County.

As William and I hammered and perspired on the roof, I set a goal to climb House Mountain. Such a venture would require adequate preparation, but Grandfather had passed along his penchant for always finding the highest point and a broad view.

The locals also told us that at one time, a fort had been built at Loyal Valley. One of them shared his grandfather's remembrances of those days.

The stagecoach drive around the fort left deep, lasting ruts, since drivers circled the enclosure a few times to get up a full head of steam when leaving for Fredericksburg. This way, the vehicle would be almost impossible to catch by anyone on horseback. I could almost hear the driver's whip flail and see the flash of hooves.

When Donnie heard this story, his favorite word became "Giddyap!" I took note—perhaps one might view those ruts from atop House Mountain.

True, the intense heat of summer still lay ahead. Leaves would soon curl and the wild grass turn brittle, but our first spring here testified that every year, this seasonal rhythm would replay. One day, we would again behold these glorious wildflower blooms as if for the first time.

From the kitchen, Donnie's laughter joined Lillian's. With such ease, she had entered our family. During our conversations, her emerald eyes flashed from time to time, but her generally placid demeanor dared anyone to truly upset her.

Exposed to culinary efforts limited mostly to jam-making, Donnie delighted in her bread baking. Their interactions produced hands, face, and clothes strewn with flour and dough, his usual questions, and plenty of chuckles. Always, I had felt him utterly safe with William, and now could say the same about another caring adult.

Otherwise, all things continued as before. William's offer to pay rent for the use of the pasture gave me opportunity to thank him again for his ever-present help.

"What if you bring us curds and cheese for a lifetime. Will that suit?"

He brooded. "'Tisn't enough, by far. Perhaps a weekly delivery of Lillian's bread as well?"

We agreed, so on Monday afternoons, he toted along cheese, curds, and three loaves of bread. Donnie relished all three, and we had plenty for toast with tea for the week.

Never was a young boy so enthralled with mucking out a barn—the dirtier he got, the better. A wash in the creek before standing under the pump for a good scrub made him almost presentable. On Saturday nights, a full soak in our copper tub returned the entirety of his freckles to their rightful places.

Thus, our life took on a regular rhythm, one thing leading to

20

another. Before dawn, the birds reminded us of the new day at hand. By twilight, a cicada symphony regaled us through our open windows. Often after tucking Donnie in, I collapsed in our big armchair with a book, and on the best nights, a heavenly breeze accompanied his quiet breathing a few feet away.

Chapter Two

Late April 1939

Next to the stoop, the branches of our Copper Canyon Daisy bush rustled. Springtime provided plenty of sunshine after winter's rest, and the bush added half an inch to its height each day. Its first leaves of the season prompted William to seek an apt description in a botanical journal, which led us to expect yellow blooms in late summer or fall.

All around, delicate magenta wine cups perched on beds of new grass as if placed by a genteel lady's hand. Brilliant blue spiderworts peered over the fence rail to observe our goings-on. Had I been Wordsworth or one of Grandfather's other favorites, I might have attempted a sonnet.

How to describe Nature's many marvels? Emily Dickinson wrote, "Bring me the sunset in a cup." When I shared this with William, he quipped, "Surely she meant a proper British teacup?"

As a newcomer to this country, I thought it best to spread my wings into American writers of late. Why not begin with Dickinson? Thoreau lay next in my reading pile.

But on this evening, today's Great Happening engaged me. Late this morning, Donnie and I had been weeding the garden when a couple appeared afoot. They must have passed through our nearest neighbor's grove and followed the lane.

"You must be Mr. Everett Herring? Toward the end of every school year, we pay annual visits to homes near Loyal Valley. No need for alarm, simply our normal regimen. Someone noted that your son would be ready to attend."

The man adjusted his hat. Clearly, he expected me to say, "Yes. Donnie will enter school in the fall."

But nothing of the sort issued from my mouth. In fact, no words at all came forth.

He fumbled with his hat again. "Surely you must have—"

The woman pushed back a heavy wave from her forehead, and something flitted through her eyes. A flash of concern, or perhaps anxiety? But I had long ago learned to avoid what might appear in a woman's eyes.

The man set down his leather briefcase. "See here," he began. "I ought to have introduced myself. Clyde Fletcher, county school supervisor." He held out his hand, and we shook. "And let me introduce Mrs. Bultmann, our new teacher."

Just then a lad of seven or eight came thrashing through the grass. The woman intercepted him as he bounded toward Donnie. "Anton, behave yourself now."

Donnie burst out, "Hello! Would you like to see my tree house?"

"Sure. Mom?"

"Just for a few minutes, and watch out for snakes!" High color traced his mother's cheekbones as the boys turned and ran.

"Could we possibly—?" Mr. Fletcher sent a longing glance toward the porch.

"Oh, forgive me, you must need a cool drink. Come over and have a seat." I led the way and went inside for some water. When I returned, Mr. Fletcher wet his whistle before continuing.

"Each spring, we like to acquaint our teacher with pupils for the coming year. Your son, Donal, should be ready for school by summer's end?"

He awaited my reply, but my jittery midsection vied for attention.

"Anton has met Donnie at Sunday school." Mrs. Bultmann attempted a smile. Could she guess I was berating myself? If only I had waited to take Donnie to the church in Cherry Spring

23

every fifth Sunday when the services were in English rather than German. But William and Lillian anticipated our company, and Donnie delighted in lessons with three or four other children.

"Our boys seem to get along well when Donnie comes." I must have winced, for she hurried on. "Watching our children grow up can be difficult, I understand."

The faintest breeze still toyed with our daisy bush as I sought some appropriate reply. At length, Mr. Fletcher broke the rather uncomfortable silence.

"We have made concessions over the years, Mr. Herring. For example, considering the dearth of male teachers in these parts, my predecessors let certain guidelines slide. After all, some rules are meant to be broken, aren't they?"

He smiled at his feeble joke, while Mrs. Bultmann paid undue attention to our rocky yard. I had no idea what rules Fletcher referred to—perhaps married women were not usually hired? That would have proven true in England, but this was the United States—the Wild West.

Like early morning cobwebs, quiet once again stretched across the porch.

Mr. Fletcher tried again. "So, Mrs. Bultmann can count on Donnie when school begins this fall?"

Finally, a cogent reply emerged. "I think we shall wait another year."

"Hmm. Born in thirty-three or four, I expect?"

Avoiding specifics, I countered. "Donnie has yet to turn five."

"Quite tall for his age, eh?"

His implication put me off, but I measured my reply. No need to start on the wrong foot with local authorities.

"Exactly right, as I see it."

Mr. Fletcher twisted his lips, and Mrs. Bultmann set about to ease the situation. "We really cannot compare children, can we? Well then. I shall look forward to having Donnie in class, but not until next year."

They rose to leave, and she called for Anton. Despite the age difference, these red-faced boys could not have looked more at ease.

"Here, drink some of my water." Mrs. Bultmann handed Anton her glass, and he gulped down what remained.

The whole time, Donnie's dark eyes flashed volumes. As soon as they left, he would bubble over, leading most likely to a chat about friendship. And that would inevitably bring us to Ratty and Mole in *The Wind in the Willows*.

As our visitors took their leave, Donnie waved to Anton and I mumbled appropriate sentiments. Before the three were out of sight, Donnie raved about the past twenty minutes.

"Anton likes my tree house."

"Good." A makeshift affair William and I cobbled together with materials left from reinforcing the barn, the small shelter in the live oak was Donnie's, all the same.

"He's eight. He goes to school."

"And so shall you. Next year."

That evening he continued to bask in his brief time with Anton. The joy of comradeship, I could accept. But the concept of elementary schooling was so different here, such an assortment of ages in one room.

The breeze quickened, wafting homey scents from the barn. In a few months, autumn would blend these daytime colors with bronze and gold. Summer wildflowers would fade, and wild sumac would redden in the sun. Always in the air, change instructed me once more.

Of course, we could not continue in this idyllic way forever. Donnie might be all I had, yet he must make his way out into the world.

May 1939

"Could I please, Da?" The pleading in Donnie's tone tugged at me. William waited, realizing my reticence paid obeisance to my old enemy, change. Lillian, however, may have taken my hesitation for mistrust.

"So, you really want to spend the night with William and Lillian?" I squatted to Donnie's level and observed excitement dance in his eyes.

"Oh, yes. William says we can play marbles and listen to a program on the radio, and in the morning, I get to help Lillian make breakfast. And bake cookies."

"Aha. That settles it."

He squeezed my hand. "You shan't be lonely?"

"We shall see—this will be our first night apart. Will you miss me?"

"Yes, but—" Donnie eyed our visitors. "Will you read to me at bedtime and tuck me in?"

Lillian and William answered in the affirmative. Donnie gave me a hug and ran to pack his nightclothes.

"You will be all right?" Disquiet showed in Lillian's eyes, blue-green at the moment, due to her azure jumper.

"Surely, but this does mark a significant outing." I glanced eastward and added, "Early in the morning, I think I shall trek up House Mountain. I often wonder how it looks up close, and what one can see from the top."

William nodded. "I shall check on everything when I do the milking. Donnie will be no bother at all."

Swinging a cloth bag Lillian had made for him, Donnie appeared with a massive grin. He took Lillian's hand, and William grasped his other one.

"See you tomorrow, Da." Then he was off on his first solo exploit.

Evening stars winked down as I sharpened my scythe on our whetstone. By now, William's seeds had sprouted and taken root as we embraced this land.

Our buildings, carefully fashioned three-quarters of a century ago by German settlers, still bore marks from the workers' tools.

These craftsmen bored holes in quarry rock in order to insert cedar or cypress poles. After a good dousing, the wood expanded and split the stone into manageable chunks. This process had produced the trim stones for our house.

Especially near doorways and windows, our sandstone revealed chisel markings from these tradesmen, parallel lines cut into the surface where the worker had applied pressure. Some might call these blemishes, but when viewed from afar, they added character and charm.

Perhaps they carried a message about the scars we bear.

Standing there with my sharpened scythe, I breathed in the evening air. No need to light the oil lamps—the moon supplied plenty of light for my needs. No reading tonight—straight to bed to prepare for an early rising.

A soothing certainty enveloped me. Regardless of how our move to the Hill Country had come about, William and I had made the right choice.

About halfway to House Mountain in the cool of the morning, the sun broke over the horizon. Dawn and sunset might have been created less spectacular, but season by season, they offered stunning beginnings and endings to each day.

On our ocean voyage, I witnessed these glowing commencements and closures reflecting on the Atlantic, and when we crossed from New York to Texas, our Pullman car revealed sunrise at high speeds. Hearing the Realtor quote the distance to Texas was one thing, but the seemingly endless passage amounted to another entirely. What an education we gleaned, and we often looked back on our discoveries.

Frequent stops at many small depots unveiled this great nation from city to county seat, to humblest village. Oh the sheer width and breadth of its expanse! Grandfather often exclaimed over this, and taught me equations by comparing distances between stateside cities.

As our train headed west, William's exclamations knew no end. "Eight-hundred miles, England's entire width, northeast to south-west. Even when we arrive, we will have covered only one-quarter of the way to the west coast."

Aboard the Cannonball from Chicago to St. Louis, a passenger strummed his guitar to Roy Acuff's famous *Wabash Cannonball*. We first heard these lines in a New York diner, but soon the tune appeared wherever we turned.

This musician shared the song's history. The Carter family had released it years earlier, but Roy—he spoke of the singer like a family member—had made it famous.

"Happens a lot. Got a friend by the name of Stewart. He writes the best songs, but they usually don't get recognized till somebody else records 'em."

"Who is Daddy Claxton in the song—a hobo?"

"Yeah, he's the make-believe hero. When hobos rode the rails looking for work, one of them was bound to die from time to time. So they made up a song about a special train that came along to take him to heaven."

Once the passengers in our car got used to each other, I allowed Donnie to traipse the aisles until he exhausted himself. "Hobo! Cannibal!" His exuberant cries won the hearts of many, though I kept correcting his pronunciation.

"Lest they think us uneducated," I whispered to William. Later, we repeated our favorite grammatical aberrations from the day. Most of them merely testified to this great land's variety, and several dialects reminded me London boroughs. Perhaps these Americans' ancestors hailed from there, Liverpool, or even Nottinghamshire.

What an opportunity to meet everyday citizens first-hand, taste new foods and view the country's great rivers. Near the mighty Mississippi, our conductor supplied a bit of history.

"In 1867, the St. Louis Bridge and Iron Company hired James Buchanan Eads, the man who built several Ironclad gun ships for the Union, to build his very first bridge. It depends entirely on cantilever construction, and its pneumatic caissons were sunk deeper than any other bridge in this country. A perfect example of American ingenuity."

William whispered, "Ah yes. Much more modern than our stone-arched London Bridge or its medieval predecessor."

"But I daresay that one lasted 600 years." I supposed that from now on, we would make all sorts of comparisons.

Through the hills and dales of Missouri and Arkansas, a smaller engine took us into Texas, where we split off toward Fort Worth. There, William spotted a massive, undulating mass of brown and tan—the livestock yards. When Donnie grasped that these were individual creatures, *cow* became his favorite word.

"Whoo—whoo! Cannibal! Miziippi! Cow!" Oh, how much he had matured in the months since then.

A less streamlined coach took us to San Antonio, and during our stay-over, we visited Fort Sam Houston, where civilian workers were expanding the cemetery. A laborer told us that a year ago, this burial ground had been renamed a national cemetery, and they were building a new flagpole base made of the same pink granite used for the state house in Austin.

Donnie learned to say "Lone Star State" as we witnessed the star being laid in the flagpole's concrete base. Interestingly, the workers used flagstone to create the lone star.

Asking, "Why is Texas the Lone Star State?" uncovered a rich vein of history from when Mexico ruled Texas and the flag had two stars. The top one stood for Texas, but after winning its fight for independence, Texas adopted a flag with one star and thus became "The Lone Star State."

All these months later, I felt quite American as I reached House Mountain and scrambled a short distance up for a better view. Already my perspective had changed. I peered back toward home and climbed higher, each step heightening my elation.

Whether the stagecoach ruts would be visible from the top made no difference at all. I moved forward knowing that whatever I did see would be instructive—such abundance here to explore.

Climbing House Mountain produced an inexplicable certainty. Others had left footprints at its base—and a recently used campsite. In due time, I would bring Donnie here to make this climb and camp near Hickory Creek, where huge granite boulders peeked above the water like the backs of pink whales.

On the way home, a rattler warned me in time to skirt him. Yes, it might be some time before I ventured here with Donnie. Local men described hunting snakes below the mountain late of an evening, but I had no such desire.

Chapter Three

O
n June 8, William heard on the wireless that King George VI and Queen Elizabeth were visiting New York City. Donnie's reaction struck me as worthy of note.

"Are they my queen and king, too?"

"Indeed. And the President your president, since we live here now. This marks the first time a British monarch has ever called on the leader of the United States."

"Ever?"

"Ever. Sometimes history occurs right before our eyes."

The next morning out in the orchard, Donnie spied a butterfly. "A Monarch, like the Queen."

"Indeed."

Our little chat spurred a recollection of our decision to emigrate. Although England held the highest number of immigration allocations of any country under the Johnson-Reed Act of 1924, the list of required proofs might have daunted less intent souls. But whatever the requirements, William and I determined to meet them.

Thankfully, Grandfather kept duplicates of all legal papers with Mr. Firth, and I simply followed suit. Had I not, the fire might have rendered emigration more difficult, or even impossible.

With my professional recommendation stolen away, a story hidden away, never to see the light of day, employment prospects in my homeland had been rendered minimal. But Grandfather's foresight prepared me in another way. When William learned that listing a trade made a difference with immigration officials, another piece fell into place.

I might honestly call myself a tree husbandman and cider maker. Since I was loath to declare myself a teacher, what better skill to offer?

Besides, caring for an orchard appealed to me—nature's companionship might assuage all ills. Mrs. Tillman, our closest neighbor, offered us shelter during those months after the fire, and often, I strolled back to Grandfather's orchard.

Perhaps each visit furrowed a fresh farewell to my old life. Something about seeing the house in its present demise brought needed closure. The original foundation, of magnesian limestone called the white freestone, revealed where outer and inner walls had once stood. All else had been cleared and hauled away.

Amid this devastation, I could scarce avoid another profound image, the shattered nature of my marriage. Still, these charred stones signified a strong foundation that had borne the weight of an entire house—the lower level, a distinctive wide staircase, and four full upstairs suites.

Once, Mrs. Tillman meandered over to stand with me. "Such a loss, dear Everett. Such a loss." Her simple remark underscored my reaction.

But what comfort those simple lines of aged apple trees afforded! They continued on as though nothing untoward had come to pass. Grandfather no longer tended them, the house had vanished, but they kept on giving fruit as always.

Now I had acclimated to this new world, a chap with two countries. This area's mellow, rust-colored sandstone had replaced England's white limestone. Both *God Save the Queen* and *The Star Spangled Banner* stirred me, and William shared these sentiments. Though we had not yet filed for our naturalization papers, this hill country had laid claim on us.

June 14, 1939

In Europe, tensions increased at a frenzied pace. William paid close attention, and his timely reports fed my curiosity. The visit of the King and Queen to America set my loyalties astir. What spurred them to visit now, after keeping their distance for more than a century? I had to wonder.

Then one morning, William strode into the yard carrying our mail. Posthaste, he explained that the Japanese Imperial Army had blockaded British trading settlements in the North China treaty port of Tientsin, a serious business.

This story headlined the newspapers on the fourteenth. To celebrate our first Flag Day here, we ordered the Stars and Stripes and set up a pole near our sign. Donnie helped me raise the emblem, and when the wind cooperated, the flag's gentle *flap, flap flap* carried to the house over the outrageous rose blossoms of a crepe myrtle tree.

"Why are there forty-eight stars?"

"It's been that way since 1912, I believe, when New Mexico and Arizona became states."

"Do you think someday there will be more?"

"Such a good question, Donnie. I really cannot say, but nothing would surprise me about this country."

In charge of caring for our new treasure, Donnie reminded me we needed to fetch it down each evening. We folded the stiff fabric to store just inside the porch. On one evening, I must have said "stoop" instead of porch, which perked up his ears.

"Do we have a porch or a stoop?"

"A stoop is uncovered, I believe, but a porch has a roof. So the steps and the area around them would be a stoop, technically, but the covered section a porch." Lately, he had become fastidious about meanings, and happily, my tentative knowledge satisfied him.

On ensuing days, William added more details about the international situation, finally noting the transfer of art from the National

Gallery to Wales. Until then, I had hoped many of the rumors were politically motivated. But the government was taking measures to protect national treasures in museums and government buildings?

Surely, war must be imminent.

A letter from a university chum living in London added more details. Though I had not yet responded to this fellow—Mrs. Tillman wrote that she had shared our address with him—now I did. On September second, even more radical news arrived via the BBC.

The day before, Germany proved its aggressive intentions by invading Poland, and France joined England in declaring war on Herr Hitler after he refused to reverse his actions. As if this were not enough, a terrible tragedy took place on the same day. The German submarine *U-30* torpedoed a passenger liner called the *SS Athenia*.

This, I kept to myself. Donnie would hear about these devastating events soon enough. Carrying over 1,000 civilians, including 300 Americans, the *Athenia* had just left Liverpool for Montreal when the torpedo struck. Ninety-eight passengers and nineteen crewmembers were lost.

The next day, the Royal Air Force raided German warships in the North Sea. We might have expected something like this. As when boiling down a cauldron of apples for apple butter, spillovers become unavoidable. One decision leads to another, one error results in more.

My foray into married life had followed the same route, and at times, regret concerning its harrowing course still overwhelmed me. But dwelling on the past amounted to sheer waste, when Donnie stood before me as incontrovertible proof that goodness prevailed.

William and I quietly agreed that all he need know about our life in Nottinghamshire was that the house had burned, and that his great-grandfather, a kind and learned man, would have loved him dearly. As for his mother, William would never divulge a thing about Victoria, and I might in all honesty attest to her beauty and charm.

What a gift, to have him with me through all of this—my

struggle and failure with my wife, and now, the war. How right Grandfather had been to call William *friend*. In this, he followed a line from one of his favorites, Samuel Taylor Coleridge: *Friendship is a sheltering tree.*

On this September morning, a knock at the back door called me from my thoughts as I tidied up our kitchen. Donnie, busy building a mountain with the wooden blocks William created from leftover pieces of plank, reached the kitchen first, for knocks came quite seldom and produced a stir.

"Good morning young fellow. How would you like to dine at our house today?" William appeared calm, yet his tone carried an unspoken message intended for me.

"Yes!" Donnie turned with anticipation in every feature. "Is it all right?"

"Of course. Put your blocks away before you go."

As he scurried about, William lowered his voice. "Down at the filling station, talk of war runs rampant. Go and peruse the newspapers, and bring me word. What a blessing that the local citizens gathered funds for our little facsimile of a library."

"And you joined for both of us—always thinking ahead."

He waved a hand toward the small building in town that housed a smattering of donated classics and various more modern titles. Grandfather's books, now situated along our back room walls, provided plenty of reading material, but the library's newspapers especially enticed us.

"Ah, our favorite lad, with everything quite in order!"

Donnie settled his hand into William's and they were off.

Though the news sounded dire, I could hardly wait to peruse official word. Under a friendly morning sun, great rumblings seized me—my country had just entered a war against a formidable enemy. Though German bombers might never whiz over this pleasant land, decisions made in London would make a difference even here, and alter Donnie's future, even as the Great War had transformed mine.

Grandfather often said the combined nations had learned our

lesson in that war, where the dreadful fighting along France's River Somme took my father's life. Not long afterward, the great influenza epidemic stole my mother's. In the seat of my soul, war and pestilence went arm in arm, and nothing good came of either.

Hurrying along the path as if my very life depended upon immediate arrival, I blessed William for this opportunity. How long had it been since I sat alone to read the news? Perhaps not since our stay in New York.

My intended half-hour became much longer. How could it not? The first report stated that the BBC's home service had broadcast Prime Minister Chamberlain's five-minute war announcement from 10 Downing Street to every household across Britain.

Families sat knee-to-knee in their parlors, listening with terrible intensity to this call to arms. Urgency pulsed the very drumbeat of the British Expeditionary Forces. Visions of Whitehall and the Queen's Royal Marines marching on the parade grounds flashed before me. During my university years, the marchers' precision always proved an inspiration when my mates and I attended.

The drums especially intrigued me. Hours and hours of practice created synchronized perfection, yet I still wondered that no member erred. After all, were not those drummers mere mortals?

But now, drums of war reverberated. One article said that twenty minutes after Neville Chamberlain's report, air raid sirens had sounded in London. Found to be a false alarm, the wailing surely had produced terror among the citizenry.

The Prime Minister immediately created a small War Cabinet, and named Winston Churchill as First Lord of the Admiralty. Ah, Mr. Churchill, whose ancestor, John, the first Earl of Marlborough, had won the fight against the Bavarians and Louis the Fourteenth at Blenheim in 1704.

Such history behind this choice. Surely destiny was having its say, and hope nestled in.

When the Loyal Valley school bell tolled the start of the year's classes. Donnie and I were out checking the orchard. During the past winter, we grew accustomed to this resonance, like hearing William in his chore boots crunch down the path toward the barn.

But on this morning, Donnie stared toward Loyal Valley for some time. I joined him, but held my tongue in check. No amount of sticking plaster could halt this change or slow its progress.

Nearly a full year lay behind us here, adding some months for our transit. Grandfather's friend graciously supplied all we needed in New York, and even shared some stories I had never heard, priceless insights into Grandfather's youth. At times, Donnie still reminisced his memories from that time, formed partially by photographs William developed and used as story fodder on the long train ride.

Oh, the tales he told. Leaving Donnie entranced, I wandered through the cars to stretch my legs and observe. Often when I returned, Donnie lay fast asleep against William's shoulder.

Twas near that immense city of New York, though, that the Realtor discovered this ideal locale. Hearing our inquiry, he formed a steeple with his fingers before turning to a large table heavy with maps and papers.

"Orchard land, you say. Washington state, or maybe Pennsylvania."

"Perhaps somewhere in the Southwest."

"Pretty dry there. Let me see—oh, I remember reading about a spot in the hills just the other day." He located a flyer and began to read aloud.

Mason County, Texas, sixty miles west of Llano River, eighteen miles southeast of county seat. Two-bedroom native stone house.

Water source on property. Three acres orchard, three pastureland, near one-room school in Loyal Valley. Live oak, mesquite, and high desert flora. Mature orchard (mostly apple, few peach, few pecan) and large garden plot. Stone pump house with windmill plus indoor plumbing/ septic tank. Part of Fischer-Miller Land Grant, nearly four million acres in Mason, Llano, Kimble, Menard, Concho, McCulloch, and San Saba Counties.

He glanced up and continued. *Plot surveyed east of Loyal Valley, founded by German immigrants. San Antonio one and one half hours, Austin, two hours.*

William leaned forward. At that precise moment, I did the same.

"Oh, this is interesting. In 1875, conflict erupted between Germans and English-speaking Americans, leading to the Mason County War. Twelve lost their lives, some in Loyal Valley. Referred to as the Hoodoo War because of masks the men wore. To this day, rival families still harbor animosity. More clashes occurred to the South, near Kerrville."

William raised his eyebrows. Donnie, occupied with a picture book, came alongside my chair.

"Da, I'm thirsty."

"There's a water fountain down the hall and around the corner." The Realtor shifted his glasses as William took Donnie out.

"Spritely little lad. You will all be living in this location?"

"Yes. Might I possibly see the flyer?"

"*Mature trees, creek with abundant water source . . .* "

This acreage had already gleaned my interest. When William brought Donnie back, his nod pronounced agreement.

We asked for copies of the descriptions and left with plenty of reading material, including the *Texas Agricultural Bulletin* from twenty years ago. On the way back to Herbert's, we visited the large city library, as well.

Donnie fell asleep under our table while we researched, and I checked on him as William gave forth. "Not to act in haste, but this Loyal Valley property seems to have need. Surely things have calmed down since those uprisings."

Later, we discussed the possibilities with Herbert, a well-read soul who had traveled some in the West. He agreed that past skirmishes only made for colorful history.

"People got testy over land or water rights, regardless of their nationality. Cattlemen against farmers, Norwegians against Germans, and so on. My relatives in North Dakota showed me certain roads that once divided land owned by Norwegian settlers from that belonging to German immigrants. If our ancestors had stopped moving west because of every potential conflict, there would be no United States at all."

In the end, Loyal Valley it was. The name itself endeared the location.

William revisited the real estate office and within a week we received a call. By month's end, the transaction was complete.

After the final signing, we hurried toward Herbert's, deed in hand. William chortled in Donnie's ear, "Young man, we are bound for the great state of Texas! During your great grandfather's last days, he said if he could live life over, he might be a cowboy."

"Cowboy! Texas!"

An uncanny sense of relief flooded me. "Thanks to Grandfather, we have plenty for this move."

"He left you a fine inheritance. And we still have my wages saved over the years."

"No, no. You earned that, and I would never have undertaken this without you."

Later, William rummaged in one of his trunks and handed me a large envelope. "Consider this an early Christmas gift."

Carefully wrapped packets of seeds emerged. Welsh poppy, hollyhock, columbine, foxglove, zinnias, and geranium, in addition to an array of vegetables.

"Your grandfather planted varieties tracing back to Dove Cottage and Thomas Hardy's Dorset home. You know how he treasured Coleridge and Hardy's works."

"Yes, but I had no idea he mimicked their gardens."

"Somewhere in his things, you will find a copy of Dorothy Francis Gurney's work. He often quoted her poem—*The kiss of the sun for pardon, the song of the birds for mirth, One is nearer God's heart in a garden than anywhere else on earth.* I believe Lord Ronald Gower's garden at Hammerfield Penshurst inspired her, and some of these seeds come from there.

"Your grandfather obtained a few from every garden he visited. He always sought ones that seed themselves again each year—or every two, as with the hollyhock."

Although our personal weatherman—the fellow who passed our property on most mornings—said autumn would bring moisture again, we had yet to receive a shower. "Might could rain b'fore then, but t'ain't likely."

But we were to discover yet another water source. One Saturday Donnie and I tromped toward the far southeast corner of our property. Soon, we were investigating a distinct gurgle. Midmorning found us wrestling with old fibrous vines twining down from a lacey oak branch.

"William says an Englishman named Howard Lacey named this species back in the 1870s. Who knows? Perhaps he came here from Nottinghamshire, just like us."

The bubbling led to what one might call a hedgerow. We scratched and scraped our way, stumbling on cedar and mesquite roots. When we broke through, Donnie squealed with delight, and I did a slow turn. Could this really belong to us?

In our first days here, the local Realtor, an affable fellow who took instantly to Donnie, had pointed out our fence line, so I searched for it in earnest. Soon it became clear that the line rose ten feet beyond this inviting spring. Better men than I would have walked every inch of their new property before now, but I had not yet visited this exact spot.

"We have to show William!" Donnie gestured with his hand. "Maybe fish live in here." Then, "Maybe we could get water for the garden from this pool."

"Why, yes." I considered what sort of engineering feat might embellish our water tank's supply. The regular gurgle testified to a source deep in the earth. The property description had not included a spring, but before our eyes, one bubbled up. In sight of several species of cacti growing on the surrounding hills, we possessed a veritable oasis.

Lately, I had been reading about John Meusebach, who founded this community. It seemed entirely possible that one day long ago, he might have happened upon this very spring. What had prompted his choice of Loyal Valley for a community? The soil, surely, and the creek. But exploring this wild area on horseback, had he seen from afar the difference in growth and color, and understood what this land was telling him about its possibilities?

"How old are you, Lillian?"

We were just finishing Sunday dinner, and I snapped to attention, but Lillian waved a hand in my direction. "Well, I'm nine years younger than William, and—Everett, how old are you?"

"Thirty-seven and one-half, to be exact."

"So, then. I'm about half as many years older than your father than I am younger than William. You're very good at mathematics, so I'll leave you to figure out the exact numbers."

On the way home, Donnie and I had a talk like one Grandfather had with me years ago. "Never ask a woman her age," he admonished.

"Why not?"

"Inquiring is simply improper. A woman's age is her secret."

"What about a man?"

"That is another matter entirely."

Chapter Four

In Nottinghamshire, summer temperatures rarely exceeded seventy degrees. But even with such a difference in the heat, each turn of the calendar called out to me.

On our first Sunday here, William visited the Tabernacle near the schoolhouse—a "brush tabernacle," they called it, made with four poles, a brush roof and sides. He returned with a wealth of resources. One family had harvested an abundance of sweet potatoes, another had ample cider and jam we might purchase, and yet another was about to butcher and had an extra hog.

This year, we produced our own cider and preserved peach jam. Potatoes, beans, onions, parsnips, turnips, and carrots filled baskets or barrels in our partial cellar. Tomatoes and greens and grapes, we dried on screens in the sun and stored upstairs, where the air stayed drier.

Every waking hour, birdsong and insect chatter, rooster crows and the hens' *cluck cluck* created a singular throb: *home...home... home.* Caring for trees and our fledgling garden made for productive, tiring hours. Unlike teaching, one observed instant results—clean vegetable rows, fences mended, sandstone walls caulked with care.

Through each day, a sense of belonging enveloped me. We had all we needed.

The birds chorused this melody before dawn each morning, and in the evening, the cicadas joined in. So much work in order to make the most of our property—an ever-growing list adorned our table, but as we attended to each item, satisfaction seeped through.

Lillian's copy of *Pioneers in God's Hills* reported a cholera epidemic in 1849. Disease had already taken many lives since the European influx in '46, but when cholera broke out, the *Leichenwagen* became a common sight in Loyal Valley.

Oxen pulled this two-wheeled, covered cart through the streets to gather the deceased. Their survivors, also fighting the disease, lacked the strength to build caskets, so they wrapped their loved ones in sailcloth and buried them in unmarked graves in the *Stadt-Friedhof*, the old part of the City Cemetery.

John Meusebach had made friends with Santanna, a Comanche chief. His people brought the settlers honey, bear fat, and meat. But the cholera swept the tribe and took Santanna's life. A couple named Fritze left behind their orphan children who were placed with other families, but no cemetery marker identified their resting place.

Not many lived to a ripe old age. A baby named Puryear born on August 20, 1888, died on the twenty-second. A child named Walter lived from 1883 to 1885. Another boy, *Our Little Amzic*, died at four years of age. A wife lived forty-four years.

"Surely this community might erect some sort of monument to those unknown," William commented. No doubt, he would submit this idea to someone at the church in Cherry Spring. When people gathered at the Tabernacle, so did we, but William saw the Cherry Spring church as an opportunity to improve our German, since all services except every fifth Sunday were *auf Deutsch*.

Somehow, John Meusebach survived the epidemic. Perhaps he employed natural remedies, since he leaned toward scientific ventures—in-breeding cattle, for instance. Clearly, challenges attracted him.

One Sunday when Lillian begged off, William and I packed a lunch and walked the three miles to Cherry Spring. In the Marschall-Muesebach Cemetery, we visited the Meusebach gravesite, just west of the church. Oak trees and a thick stone wall surrounded the graves.

On John's stone, mourners had etched TENAX PROPOSITI: *tenacity of purpose.* Or perhaps he had chosen these words for posterity.

After our luncheon, Donnie romped in the creek while William snagged a lovely fish for our supper. As we left, he remarked to Donnie, "I hope you have not worn yourself out, for we have several miles to go."

"I can ride in Da's backpack."

And so he could. This heavy canvas contraption had undergone major renovations to safely board a child, with leg openings that snapped shut when not in use.

A distance down the road, William hoisted Donnie up, and a pang niggled me at his comment. "Soon, young sir, you shall no longer fit."

Yes, and in a matter of years, he would outgrow much more than this old pack.

All the better to take advantage of each opportunity.

On summer evenings, Donnie and I often retired to the barn to fashion a wooden sign. After measuring, sawing, and sanding, we carved and varnished it with care. Seven simple letters proclaimed *H e r r i n g.*

Where our yard ended, as the road turned into Loyal Valley, we nailed our ten-by-fourteen inch plaque to a fencepost. As we returned, Donnie flitted from ditch to ditch, highlighting the straggly line our flowers and herbs were forming beside the fence toward our ordered vegetable rows. In the dip, perennials began to fill in as William had envisioned. One day, this scene would be positively picturesque.

The war accelerated by the moment. General armed forces mobilization had begun, and the signal "Total Germany" went out to all British ships. Parliament passed the National Service (Armed

Forces) Act on September third, requiring national service for British men aged 18 to 41.

What had become our old stone library exuded an appropriate hush, and typical odors—yellowed newspaper, well-seasoned dust. But was that a tinge of—could it be chicken feathers? Indeed, someone explained that this building had once served as a poultry house.

This conglomeration of shelves offered books from Loyal Valley citizens and former residents, and contained many donated by descendants of early settlers. I use the term *library* rather loosely—the woman who categorizes, dusts, and loans out these books volunteers her time.

Her family donated the small stone building, and she began cataloging the library's contents. I like to think that perhaps John Meusebach had a hand in its original construction—stones carefully chosen, scraped and shaped to fit well and last.

Several citizens joined together to order vital newspapers, and established a library *kitty*. William and I joined in, and on Saturday workdays when members cleaned or caulked, we brought Donnie along.

On this September morning, the aforementioned scents sifted around me. But as I noted the ages listed, panic evidenced its steely grip. All those chaps from my university years would be deployed in one way or another.

Upon reading again, a single comforting phrase stood out.

"All men . . . *in residence in-country.*"

Those several words calmed the fierce pounding in my chest. Had I been in England, my age qualified me. But *in residence* made all the difference.

Another article described the first RAF Bomber Command raid of Wilhelmshaven on September fourth by Vickers-Wellingtons, twin engined, long-range bombers. Recently designed at Brooklands in Weybridge, Surrey, they first saw action in this show of force against the German Fleet.

Unsuccessful as the raid had been, having achieved no significant hits even though carried out at a low altitude, the action impressed me. Perhaps some of the boys I had taught piloted these planes.

They called me Mr. Herring, and I referred to them as Mr. Culver or Mr. Wallace. But despite such formalities, we shared a bond not unlike a family. So many days together with insistent mist or pelting rain outdoors, discussing literature, and therefore, history. Fellows thrown together by necessity, one older than the rest.

Until now, I had put those years entirely out of mind, but now, found myself counting off the dates. Some of the older boys would be training by now, in Scotland's wilds or at one of the many air bases springing up all over England.

Alberts, Craven, Jenkins, Colman, Lewis, Milton, Potts—their names returned like scents on a breeze. At the Nottingham High School for Boys, I read this list at the beginning of each school day, and each student verbally confirmed his presence. Recollections washed over me. I might have been traipsing wood-lined hallways with young chaps jostling each other, but silently planning futures in business or medicine or education.

Now those fresh-faced, toothy fellows would be signing their names to military contracts, repeating their induction vows, and heading into battle. Like my father years ago, they would don British battledress or pilot's leather jackets. But this present enemy seemed far more formidable. Could they save our country?

When finally my mind could contain no more, I walked to William's. Lillian had their young charge in the back yard picking late raspberries, so we conversed over a cup of tea. As always, the steaming brew quieted my nerves.

"Will you have some toast?" William's offer sounded heavenly. "Was it not Wilkie Collins who said, 'My hour for tea is half past five, and my buttered toast waits for nobody.' We've a few hours yet until tea time, but this is America, is it not?"

He seized upon the air raid story. "Vickers-Wellingtons, eh?" His alarm came through in his expression, a pucker here, a twist there.

Oddly, his deep concern quieted me. My tight stomach whorl

unwound even as he sputtered, "Surely we require a new Prime Minister. May King George choose wisely."

The very thing I had been thinking.

William ran his hand through his thinning hair. "The Luftwaffe might have gained air control over Poland, but not over Old Blighty. Lot of fight left in her, yet we need a certain sort of leader to draw it out."

Before we left, William offered to watch Donnie the next day after milking. "By then, more news will have arrived. You can read and let me know what you learn."

I accepted, and the next morning, a fresh article appeared concerning the registration. On September fifth, two days after the declaration of war on Nazi Germany, Parliament's new National Registration Act was given royal assent. Sixty thousand enumerators were dispatched with forms across the entire Isle before the appointed Registration Day, September twenty-ninth.

On the following Sunday and Monday, these officials would issue identity card to members of each household. All this was due to the probable necessity of rationing, the article claimed, and because no census had been held since 1931.

Picturing those proper enumerators going door-to-door made my pulse rattle. No doubt, a similar canvassing took place just before the Great War, and our family had awaited it with trepidation.

Most likely, William answered the door, as Grandfather, at work, left the details to him. I could well imagine him informing Grandmother and my mother. Soon after, my father donned a wool uniform and went off to war. We never saw him again.

Visiting the tiny library on Moseley Street became a habit, and often, Lillian and William kept Donnie even after I stopped for him. Two or three times a week, he returned with William for the second milking. This change I could relish, for our humble library drew me. In the afternoon, I worked faster to make up for lost morning hours.

One day, a chap about William's age chatted with me near the library door as I was leaving. He introduced himself as Norman and suggested I join him down at the filling station, the local equivalent of a coffee shop.

Such a bitter taste—I much preferred tea. But some sacrifices must be made. Norman untied a grey mare from the hitching post, and she followed as we headed toward the station.

In this slat structure, lean-tos added charm, and cooking sounds came from the north side. Due to its inhabitants, the small interior exuded the same atmosphere as a back alley pub Grandfather had frequented. He felt entirely comfortable eating fish and chips at a small concern, and not once did I feel out of place as he conversed with the men of our town. If we arrived home around midday, we ate with Grandmother, but often as not, picked up a bite here or there.

My favorite stop served bangers and mash—even now, the aroma of that bracing vinegary concoction comes to mind with a mere thought. Invariably, someone Grandfather knew joined us, and friendly banter ensued. Thus far, this interaction had been lacking here, and I felt glad for this opportunity.

Still, entering the filling station gave me a rather odd sensation. Judging by the jerked heads and stares, others felt the same, although Norman introduced me around. At first, no one said much, but several nodded. Old wooden crates and a few metal lawn chairs supplied the furniture, set against shelves filled with oilcans, copper funnels, and all manner of tools and rags.

Norman told me he pastured cattle just over the creek, and his meaning eased over me as I took a seat on a grimy wooden bench. One or two of my Cambridge friends had kept in contact, but I had let our correspondence slip. Now, I had a neighbor, and this new alliance offered a different tone. Indeed, all of these men were neighbors taking in a stranger, and it was up to me to find common ground.

Norman knew them all by name, of course, and launched some pithy comment to make them chuckle. The second day was easier, with stares turning to grunts. After that, I added a tidbit here and there, and then one morning, the talk turned to the Neutrality Acts.

A wizened older man sitting in the shadows spoke up after an introductory spit that missed the spittoon. Until now he had seemed rather taciturn, but quiet. This morning, he spouted, "Make th' world safe for democracy, my foot!" He spat again and came relatively near the mark. "Wilson sent our boys to die for comp'nies that profited from th' war."

A horse whinnied, and Norman glanced out the window. Would what the books say about cowboys and their horses prove true— could he communicate with his mare without a word?

Meanwhile, the old fellow kept on. "Bankers and gun-makers connected to Europe, that's what. The, Neutrality Acts oughta stand. For once those Washington scoundrels did the right thing. Two years ago they made 'em stronger, on account of the Spaniards fightin' that civil war over there."

So he knew his facts. If looks told all, I might have guessed him illiterate in facts and figures.

"Fascists, the whole lot of 'em. I say we ignore 'em all. American ships oughtn't carry arms to b'ligerents, no matter where the arms was made!" He pounded his fist on the table for emphasis, and after a few moments, Norman stirred the pot.

"But Great Britain has always been our ally. Don't you think we should help them, with the Nazis breathing down their necks?" All eyes turned, while I kept mine on my tin cup. I daresay, some time had passed since it had been washed.

"We *are* helpin' 'em! The Brits're buyin' oil, but it's cash n' carry, th' way it oughta be. If they've got the money and the ships to haul it, then let 'em. They ain't always been our friends—my great-great-granddaddy fought 'em in the Revolution."

"We'll see what happens. They're debating it all right now in Congress."

"Congress, my foot! Roosevelt'll get his way—rich Northeast-erners always do. Don't know why we even bother 'lectin' senators."

"But they squashed the President in March, after Hitler overran Czechoslovakia. Quite a humiliation, don't you think?"

His sparring partner ignored this fact. "Jus' you wait. This confounded Democrat'll have us at war yet. If only Lindbergh woulda run for President, things'd be dif'rent."

"Would you have voted for him?"

"Sure 'nuff, and a whole lotta other folks would've too, 'specially them Sauerkrauts down in Gillespie County. Solid 'publicans. We got plenty a' problems right here—oughta stay outta the world's business. The *other* Roosevelt knew what he was doin'. A Republican like him's what we need right now."

"Teddy?"

"Who else? That Rough Rider busted the big monopolies, built the Panama Canal, even won that Nobel Prize stoppin' Japan and Russia from fightin'." He pronounced the prize *Noble*. "We need more men like him."

"Teddy was a great President. He saved the buffalo from extinction, too."

"That fella in there's spendin' taxpayer money barnstormin' the country, tryin' to control th' vote in local 'lections."

In the far corner, someone shifted his boots, and Norman peered in that direction.

"He's a socialist, I tell y'. Passed that minimum wage law, a quarter an hour. Whoever heared o' such?"

"But I suppose the workers appreciated it?'

"'If their bosses can't pay that much, what good did it do?"

"Still, the New Deal still put a lot of men to work. We've got the Lincoln Tunnel now, and they're working on the Blue Ridge Parkway."

"Th' WPA, th' CCC." Norman's adversary spat again. "Who needs parkways, anyhow?"

"People who live out East. And us, if we ever decide to take a trip that way. Anyhow, you saw where President Roosevelt's barnstorming got him!"

I had no idea. We followed the presidential elections back home, but this "barnstorming" must have occurred in the '38 election, during our travel. I could not even recall the name of the Kansan candidate who ran against President Roosevelt in '36.

"We showed 'im, sure 'nuff."

Norman swung the conversation in a new direction as easily as taking a sip of his coffee. People followed his lead like baby ducks trailing their mother.

"What do you think of the big New York World's Fair, Everett?"

William's descriptions of several attractions had stayed with me, so I offered a nondescript comment. "Those big companies created quite the outlay."

"I'd say Westinghouse beat them all, with that smoking robot. Seven feet tall, 250 pounds—and a 700 word vocabulary."

"Yes, and their time capsule. It's interesting they included an asbestos shingle and tooth powder." Funny how the appropriate trivia came to mind just when I needed them.

"Guess they wanted to give an overall view, from the everyday to that fancy Kodak camera and microfilm. A pack of Camels and a tin wind-up toy car, that modern Linotype machine and—"

The old fellow harrumphed. "And what? It's gonna sit unused for a hundred years? Sounds like a big waste t' me. Th' whole lot ain't worth a plug nickel. Oughta lock 'em all in the hoosegow."

Nonplussed, Norman squiggled his brow. "It's all progress, in my opinion. Even around here, we benefit from people's inventions."

"Progress, my foot."

Norman's rival seemed bent on conflict. For the first time in weeks, Victoria's face passed before me. This had been her way—always an argument. Did some people enjoy being miserable and do their utmost to re-create that image in others?

Soon a middle-aged woman came from the back with a second pot of coffee. "What would these men do without your cheery disposition, Mr. James?" She gave his shoulder a good-natured pat.

He shoved back his chair and growled toward the door she had left ajar.

51

Norman held up his hand as she poured. "Great coffee, Daisy, but I need to get home. Can't start acting like I'm retired, just because I've hired help."

"You have?" Daisy arched her brow.

"Good help. Bernardo's a hard worker and so's his wife."

"They live in your little house near the arroyo?"

Norman nodded, and Daisy faded into the shadows. I considered asking if Norman paid Bernardo a quarter an hour, but mused instead on the word *arroyo*. Like a gulch, the equivalent of a *dale* in England. But Norman turned my way again.

"Hear anything from back home lately?"

"Most of my family has passed, but William corresponds widely, and keeps me up to date."

"Afraid they're in for a tough time of it over there."

"I have to agree."

"The annexation in Czechoslovakia, I can understand. The Versailles treaty created Germany's lust for the Sudetenland. And Austria—the *Anschluss* expanded its borders no farther than where they were before the Great War. But now Poland—only a matter of time before Warsaw falls. I suppose your country had no choice when the Polish asked them and France for help."

"True. But calling on Hitler to back down would be tantamount to pleading with a mule to stop braying."

When he stood, Norman left a nickel on the old pot-bellied stove, so I followed suit. Outside, he eased his hand over his mare's muzzle. "Want a ride home?"

"No, thanks. I need to stop for Donnie and Lillian and William's."

"See you tomorrow?"

"Perhaps, if I accomplish enough today."

Tipping his Stetson and sitting tall and straight-backed in the saddle, he flashed me a smile like Gene Autry. Was it in San Antonio that we saw the poster of him on our train ride across the States?

Chapter Five

One evening, I went to fetch Donnie from a day with our friends. Out whacking at weeds near the fence, William welcomed me. "Lillian and Donnie are inside baking—probably raspberry pie."

"Mmm . . ." Most likely, the results would include *dodgers* made with leftover pastry. Sprinkled with sugar, these odd shapes melted in one's mouth and brought a smile to Donnie every time.

Taking a seat on a bench in the shade, William expressed dismay over some recent news. The British showing on September sixth had been dismal when a false air raid alert led to Spitfires and Hurricanes scrambling. In utter confusion, the very worst happened. The Spitfire pilots shot down Hawker Hurricanes.

"A terrible disaster, but none of the pilots involved had experienced battle before or even seen a German plane."

"How could they possibly have gotten so confused?"

"Chamberlain's appeasement policy has left our air forces unready. At first, I respected him, but then he signed the Munich Agreement, and Germany got what she wanted in Czechoslovakia. He thought that would be enough, but had no understanding of our enemy."

"At the same time, Hitler's Luftwaffe has waited at the ready, quite the feat in such a short time."

In addition to France and England, India, Canada, Australia and New Zealand had declared war on Nazi Germany, and no doubt, South Africa would follow. Almost the entire known English-speaking world, save the United States.

"Do you think President Roosevelt will succeed in leading this country into the fray?"

"Twenty years ago, Americans had more than enough of war, just like us. Over 100,000 killed, and all for Europe. I can't imagine it will be easy to convince them, can you?"

"Not at all. And I daresay that's the consensus down at the filling station."

As Donnie poked out his head to announce treats for us, William raised his brows. He would have thought this through already and have a clear response, one way or the other.

As we followed Donnie inside, my reflections brought a satisfied sigh. Such a pleasantry, to discuss matters in the absence of conflict. Dogmatic headmasters under whom I served clashed with some instructors and expected everyone to take sides. This, plus Victoria's quarrelsomeness wearied me. But William and I could discuss anything, including politics, without a stir.

Oh, the joy of eating dodgers and positively the most luscious warm pie ever baked. On our walk home, sleepiness overtook Donnie, so I carried him. Nothing like his steady breathing against my neck, in utter trust.

Moonlight revealed a raft of Copper Canyon daisies standing guard at our door. Their strong scent, distasteful to some, invigorated me. Also called Lemmon's Marigold, Mountain Marigold, and Mexican Bush Marigold, our bush now stood a good four feet tall.

Neither Hill Country heat nor deer on the hunt for tasty morsels affected its cheery blooms. How delightful to see them burst forth now, after watching and waiting all summer.

When we first arrived, all growth had died back and the bush seemingly had little to offer, but how wrong our first impression! This member of the Aster family could reach six feet in certain areas, William said, but the size of ours was perfect for Donnie to inspect its longish oval petals surrounding golden central orbs.

Like a thorny rosebush, this plant came packaged in protection.

Its odor kept the deer from stripping off the flowers, and its hardy nature ensured that blooming would continue until frost.

"We shall see what comes of it," William had said when we first inspected the plantings around the house.

I nudged open the door and lay Donnie on his bed. A wash of his face and hands and a quick change into his nightclothes left me ready for bed myself. No need to light the lamp at all tonight, for the moon shed light enough to see my way around.

October 16, 1939

Reports concerning the Battle of the River Forth arrived with William. This first Luftwaffe air raid on Britain involved twelve German bombers—Junkers. These Ju 88s flew over East Lothian to the Firth of Forth. Their target? Battle cruiser HMS Hood, the pride of the British fleet.

While William expounded just outside the barn, Donnie ran up and listened wide-eyed.

"German intelligence declared Scotland devoid of Spitfires, so when the Luftwaffe spotted the large British battleship in the river during a reconnaissance mission that morning, they attacked, taking the RAF by surprise. But British aircraft shot down second-in-command Hans Storp off Port Seton, the first German plane brought down over Britain since the Great War."

William punctuated the details with grand sweeps of his arm. "The final engagement occurred between a Ju 88 and two Spitfires over Portobello Beach. Flight Lieutenant Pat Gifford, who shot down the German aircraft, originally worked as a solicitor in Castle Douglas and had volunteered his skills to protect our nation.

"Pieces of anti-aircraft shells fell over Edinburgh, resulting in four civilian casualties. The enemy killed sixteen Royal Navy sailors and injured forty-four in this first bombing on British soil."

Donnie's question had nothing to do with the ships or planes.

55

"What is a firth?"

"An estuary—a long narrow inlet of the sea."

William and I silently agreed to see to his British vocabulary. But this was only the first attack—he would know too much about war at too tender an age. As if to prevent this, William changed the subject.

"Donnie, do you recall when we got off the train in Fredericksburg?"

"The depot was yellow."

"Right you are. And do you remember when someone drove us here?"

"It was dusty."

"Ah, yes, indeed. Our driver proved quite the tour guide. He started where the conductor left off, telling us about the railroads." William changed his diction, to Donnie's delight.

"Without th' railroad, towns disappeared. Th' iron n' copper book got Llano got their depot, but Mason lost out, n' Lole Valley, too."

I jumped in. "You memorized his words exactly, even through the engine's racket. In the back seat, phrases reached us like intermittent messages intercepting radio static."

"So true." William leaned down toward Donnie and mimicked the driver's accent once again. *"Snakes in these parts, betcher britches. Coral, Copperhead, Diamondback, Cottonmouth. Mud dobbers, too—stingin' wasps. Look sharp, 'specially with that young-un."*

"That's me."

"Righto." A sudden dip shot us heavenward, causing only a brief pause in his monologue. *"Got us bobcats 'n mountain lions, gophers that'll dig up your garden. Plug bugs t' plug up your gun barrel."*

I got into the action. "And Donnie, you kept asking, 'How far is it now, Da?' Finally, we turned right, onto an even bumpier road, and our driver slowed a bit."

"Lookee them fancy glass gas'line pumps! Even out here, vehicles is takin' over horses' work."

William took up the story once again. "Through clouds of dust, the faint outline of mesquite and live oaks appeared, and at one turn, our driver pointed out the brush tabernacle.

"Got brush arbor revivals where you're from? Travelin' preachers used t' baptize n' such here. Just b'yond, see that schoolhouse, young 'un?"

"I saw it, I saw it!"

"But our driver was not finished. *Happy Hills Coach Station used 't provision fresh horses from San Angelo t' El Paso. Stagecoach operator named Buchmeyer built this schoolhouse and the hotel 'bout 1870. Them ruins over yonder was the town Bawdy House. Burned down one Sunday afternoon.*"

"We craned our necks to both sides for a sketchy look."

"Betcha don't know Lole Valley once was bigger'n Mason, with the Gazaway General Merchandise Store 'n a cotton gin. Them stones next to that new house is what's left of Meusebach's house datin' t' th' War o' Northern Aggression. Couple o' years back, some fella built this new-fangled one."

Quite the pantomime William was presenting. Surely Donnie had forgotten about the battle on the River Forth by now.

"A distance further, we slowed again. *Up ahead's House Mountain*, yelled our driver. At last, he halted the big automobile. *Sandstone houses up here, but that's limestone trim 'round them windows. Good-sized Texas barn. Smaller'n the ones up north, with a lean-to you can drive right under.*"

Donnie gestured behind us, "This barn, right here. Our barn!"

"When the dust cleared, our new home sat not eight feet away. Your father opened the door for you to scramble out and up some stone steps. You called us to hurry as we paid our driver and removed our cases. Then the driver dipped his stained cowboy hat. *Much obliged, gen'lemen. Hope y' like it here.* After we hoisted our crates and trunks onto the porch, the back door lock responded to a big iron key the Realtor had sent us back in New York. We dragged our things inside, where someone raced around like a puppy released from captivity."

"That was me! Whoo-whoo—Lone Star State!"

William's efforts had worked. Donnie joined him in recollections of climbing the stairs together, with William bumping his head on the crosspiece.

"Now, then. Are you ready to help me with the milking?"

As they entered the barn, memories of those golden moments of discovery charmed me away from the Firth of Forth, as well. On our first day here, I had glanced around at rather modern wooden cupboards lining one side of our kitchen, where wide wooden planks steadied my feet. On the other end, German *Fachwerk* created an artistic effect with old slanted timbers, and spiders' webs added intricate masterpieces to each nook and cranny.

As William and Donnie clambered around upstairs, I circled the structure. Who had arranged these stones and hefted such mighty rafters? On closer inspection, chisel marks showed on the door and window casings.

I ran my finger along a rough mark. Each scar bore a story.

On the ride here from Fredericksburg, the vegetation had gradually changed. Here, a pine tree grew, and was that a spruce closer to the barn? Expecting a thin layer of topsoil over the solid rock of this countryside, I squatted to investigate. Ah, no—sandy with a reddish hue.

In Nottinghamshire, not far from Sherwood Forest, the soil had been sandy and quick draining. What I held in my hands right now contained some sand, silt, and clay, rendering it rich in minerals and nutrients, yet loose enough for roots to spread out and grow strong. This explained the grape arbors in town as we passed through. I bent to sniff, as Grandfather always did. No trace of ammonia or rottenness, and just a hint of sweetness.

We had come to a good land, a place to plant and reap.

Passing back into the kitchen, I opened the two tall windows to air out the room They squawked a bit, but soon gave way to my efforts, and the swelling in my chest rose with the breeze. The sensation relayed one essential meaning:

Home.

Hours later Donnie's breathing interspersed with intermittent creaks from the darkness. Did that one originate near the door, or perhaps in the small root cellar with its outside entrance? Soon these groans would become as familiar as the ones in Grandfather's house.

Over a year had passed since its demise. We had lived as vagabonds long enough, and even the timing of our departure seemed ideal. In the land of our birth, war had begun. Our hearts went out to our people, certainly, but often I looked up from working in the orchard and felt I had lived here since birth.

Joining William and Donnie in the barn, I glanced back at our yard. A fledgling cottage garden made its way along the fence. With patience and nurturing, it would grow and flourish—we need not have worried about our plantings.

The stone tank house, ever faithful through summer's heat, promised an ever-present supply, and nearby, our very own stone home graced the landscape, as sturdy a shelter as one might hope for. And I could still feel the texture of this earth in my hands from our first day here.

Things change. Despite our best efforts, they simply do. Unfortunately, people often fail to alter along with their situations. My stumble into marriage had taught me this, and though I had learned to merely glance back rather than stare in that direction, the temptation still lurked.

On an early Saturday morning when shadows seemed stronger than sunlight, Lillian invited Donnie to help her with her household duties. William issued the invitation, so after the milking chores, off he and Donnie went, hand-in-hand.

These days, I rarely allowed my lesser thoughts to lead me astray. Had not Grandfather admonished me time and again, "Keep your constitution strong'?"

Taking that to mean 'hold tight to your confidence,' I made every effort during my four years with Victoria. In retrospect, that particular confidence had been misaligned, for one person cannot, in effect, change another. Cajoling, attempting to manipulate circumstances, shielding another from harsh reality—the list goes on, and I had employed every possible tactic.

Had Donnie been here this morning, we might have chatted about the shadows on the west side of every building, bush, tree, and rock. But what characteristics divide shadow from sunshine?

Shadows remain flat and dull, without energy, while sunshine contains warmth and movement and spark. A shadow offers little of interest, while sunshine glints and glimmers, reflects and glistens, warms and cheers.

Donnie and I might have carried on for some time, noting other qualities. Without doubt, my spirits would have risen as we engaged in this topic.

Instead, gloomy thoughts about those old days invaded, and digressed at a steady pace until my outlook had skewed entirely. The trouble was, *if only* captured me. If only I had been less rigid. If only I had flexed more, been more realistic. After all, did not a healthy mental state depend upon a fine balance between these two?

Wisdom inserted, 'Yes, but Victoria would have had to be flexible, too.'

Still, my musings continued down the wrong channel—quite impossible to argue my way out. After all, my thoughts had brought me to this impasse in the first place, so how might I expect them to lead me out?

Thus, the *if onlys* continued. If only, earlier on, I had comprehended the depth of Victoria's dissatisfaction with life and with me personally. If only I might have intuited her motives, or gained a clearer picture of her intentions.

Staring at a peach tree in need of pruning, I shook myself.

No. No! I pounded my fist on my thigh. During the months after the fire, these never-ending queries had pummeled me raw. The same outcome always resulted: *what if* and *if only* always led nowhere.

Each time when I came to my senses, one valid fact remained. My alliance with Victoria, though fraught with misery, had brought

Donnie into this world. So very tangible and alive, our son's presence simply could not be denied.

And what a delightful presence. There, now! This was no time to slip back into endless speculation.

One thing Victoria had taught me—some people long for alteration. Wherever they land in life does not quite suit. Their very posture proclaims they had envisioned anything but *this*, and would leap at the chance for revision.

In an odd way, though, her very dis-ease had drawn me to her. I longed to make her comfortable, to provide whatever her happiness required.

As Donnie and I noted a year ago during our first full American autumn, even trees brace for modification. In those weeks, we began our first pre-winter orchard inspection.

At that point, he knew the significance of the closing school bell—another world opening up. For me, the sound symbolized an ending. Children grow up and forge ahead with their lives—if they have the chance, I reminded myself, as many in London would not.

After that soft clang wafted, we focused on signs of winter in the trees. The markers evidenced the next season—even as winter encroached, each lowly willow along the creek showed innate faith that warmth and growth would return.

Thanks to Grandfather, I recognized these ciphers, long, scraggly growths hanging from twigs. Some were fuzzy, but this usually occurred later in the winter.

As often happened, our lesson began with Donnie's question. "These things look like beans, Da. What are they?"

"Catkins. They're like a cluster of flowers without any petals. They help chestnuts and alders and hickory trees reproduce. The wind blows pollen from the male flowers, and the catkins allow the female flowers to be pollinated. Once seeds develop, the wind blows them away so they can find their own places. The willow, though, uses insects rather than the wind for pollination."

"Insects are like the fathers, then?"

I thought for a moment. "More like messengers, I would say."

For a few moments, Donnie seemed extra thoughtful. "Last Sunday, Anton told me about the night before his father left for Germany."

"His father went to Germany?"

"Yes. He had to, and Anton wants him to come home."

Donnie returned his attention to the catkins. "Why are they called catkins?"

"Perhaps because of the fine hair that often covers them. Soft, like a kitten's fur."

"To catch the seeds." He stretched his neck and peered upward. "Do pecan trees have catkins way up there?"

"I believe so."

"When did the apple trees first get them?"

"Hmm. These are at least seventy-five years old, and were propagated from seed or as seedlings. Wouldn't it be exciting to discover who planted them? It may well be that they brought the seeds from Merry Old England."

"William says so, too."

"Plenty of pioneers did, and from France, Ireland, Scotland, Germany, the Netherlands, lots of countries. Grandfather taught me to graft starts into a tree or grow them in containers, or plant bare-root upstarts. Imagine how carefully immigrants packed their starts, and how the life remained in them through long sea voyages."

"I remember our ship."

"Do you?"

"William showed me where the sailors stored the potatoes. It smelled like our root cellar, only stronger."

"A place I never chanced to visit. You had so much energy—we took turns walking with you all day long."

"And reading?"

"Yes, and meeting other passengers. What a journey that was! At any rate, these pecan giants look even older than our apple trees. I hear that one tree can produce pecans for around 300 years. Another thing—we call pecans *nuts*, but really, they are a kind of fruit called a drupe, like hickory nuts, cherries, and peaches."

"What makes them taste buttery?"

"Hmm. We must do more research."

If any further questions rose, Donnie let them go. Now, with him at Lillian and William's for the morning, memories of that day's conversation helped lift me out of my morass. Why waste energy on the past? All around me lay fertile soil, more fertile than I had imagined back in that New York City realtor's office.

Our stand of flowers and this year's garden stood as evidence. If long-ago immigrants could grow an orchard in this inclement country, anything was possible.

That evening, with dishes washed and comfortable in our over-stuffed chair, Donnie and I tended to our reading. The ring of each word told me all was well.

Those winter months saw us through *Oliver Twist*, *The Call of the Wild* and *The Hobbit*. Oh, the intricate questions we entertained in the flickering lamplight. From the East End's twisted alleys and lives to the frozen wilderness of Alaska, our minds and hearts wandered at will.

April 1940

Donnie and I had now become proud owners of our own Philco Radio in a handsome wooden case. We had not minded trekking to William and Lillian's to hear the reports, but William said having our own model made sense.

When the delivery truck drove down the lane a few weeks earlier, I let Donnie make the final decision as to our new treasure's location. While I went out to help port the thing in, he deliberated, and by the time the deliveryman and I entered the house, he made known his choice.

"Over here." He directed us like a professional. "Between the table and our big chair, don't you think, Da?"

"That looks a likely spot. Good work."

We settled the monstrous wooden object and plugged the cord into the wall socket. I pulled out my wallet to pay the deliveryman, but he declined.

"Delivery included in the bill, and your friend paid in full." He went on his way, and Donnie stood before our gift, running his fingers over the tan fabric insert.

"Could I turn it on?"

"Yes, but after this we shall listen only at certain times."

The electric fuzz issuing from the machine satisfied him that he was missing nothing, so he ran outside to play. As for me, I stood a minute to stare at the new addition, and as I did, the turbulence of the 1930s encroached.

How many hours had Victoria spent swooning over *Band Waggon's* Stinky Murdoch? The rest of her so-called stars had faded from memory.

With so many challenges at that time, I never could understand her obsession with their voices traveling over the wireless. Compared to reading a good book, what a waste of time this seemed. But Victoria soon became more involved with those voices than with our own, and in a feeble attempt to dissuade her by example, I gave up listening entirely.

After all, we were coping with a worldwide depression and massive job losses following the Wall Street Crash of '29. If that weren't enough, King George V died in '36, and his successor Edward VIII shocked us all by abdicating the throne at the end of the year. Unheard of—inconceivable!

When his younger brother George VI replaced him, we breathed a sigh of relief with our mates in England. Perhaps things might now return to normal.

But in this national hubbub, we neglected to ascertain the seriousness of the Nazis rising to power in Germany. How could the intelligent leaders of our nation have fallen for Adolf Hitler's wiles? Perhaps the *never again* mentality that enveloped us after the Great War put blinders over our eyes.

At any rate, war broke out, and here we were, standing alone against the vast *Third Reich*. Holland, Belgium, Norway, and France had fallen to the *Wehrmacht*. So far, we stood steadfast, but what was to become of our island?

As I touched the smooth varnished surface of our wireless set, ambivalence reigned. On one hand, having the evening news close at hand would be so convenient. On the other, I had observed Victoria turn the radio into her own personal thinking machine. I could tell by her eyes when she had absconded into some make-be-lieve world.

Nothing of the sort would happen in this house, I determined. War or no war, I would not allow this to occur with my son.

The next day after his afternoon milking, William followed Donnie into the house and straight to the set. Clearly, they had already discussed their next moves. He showed Donnie how to set the dial for the evening report, and Donnie's eyes brightened at the reappearance of voices from afar right here in our parlor.

Well aware of my angst, William said on the way out. "When the BBC comes through of an evening, what a perfect way to give Donnie a taste of proper English. How else shall he take on the finer nuances of our language?"

Not so sure this would amount to a blessing, I thanked him anyhow. As I walked him part way home, with Donnie behind us attacking tall weeds with a stick, William confided, "Lillian cannot get enough of the BBC broadcasts. She calls me a walking ency-clopedia about England and even speaks of visiting there one day."

For a few paces, he studied the dry grass. "After the war, of course. Her mother's side emigrated at the turn of the century from somewhere near Norwich, and she would like to find their origins."

Two hours later when Donnie and I finished supper and switched on the Philco, I laid aside my misgivings. Such vital news issued over the wires, I blessed William for seeing beyond my reticence. After the static dissipated, a male voice transcended all other considerations.

After Prime Minister Chamberlain signed the Munich Agreement, giving the Sudetenland region of Czechoslovakia over to German conquest, he promised this would bring 'peace in our time.' But that fragile peace fell victim to Hitler's invasion of Poland, and during the past eight months, Mr. Chamberlain's appeasement strategy has shown him ill equipped to prevent further invasions.

In recent weeks, Nazi activism has only increased, beginning with Norway in April and continuing with the Low Countries. As of May 10, Belgium, Luxembourg, the Netherlands and France have fallen to the Nazi regime. On that day, Prime Minister Chamberlain formally lost confidence in the House of Commons.

His resignation and a meeting with Lord Halifax and Winston Churchill informed the decision by King George VI to declare Winston Churchill, of late the First Lord of the Admiralty, our new Prime Minister. Our new Prime Minister has jumped right in, formed an all-party coalition and is fast gaining Britons' support.

After taking in every word, I gave Donnie the signal, and he flicked off the radio. Then he asked, "What does Prime Minister mean?"

"Something like a President, only in England."

"But not the King?"

"Correct."

"Do you know Mr. Churchill?"

"Not at all. He was born about twenty-five years before me, about the same time as your grandfather."

"Did Grandfather know him?"

"I doubt it, since he lived near Nottingham, and Mr. Churchill spent his boyhood closer to London. His mother was American."

"Are you joshing?"

"No, many old British families have sought American wives for their sons. But our Prime Minister grew up entirely in England and graduated from the Royal Military College. He has served in

66

the House of Commons and has known failure, too. It heartens me that he is off to a good start. England needed a new leader, someone brave and tenacious."

"Somebody who won't give up?"

"Exactly, like Sam Houston. Some day, we'll read about San Jacinto, the most decisive battle in Texas history."

"Like the Alamo."

"Exactly. Colonel Travis and the men who stood with him never gave up, even though they faced certain defeat."

The number of thought lines in Donnie's forehead increased. "And like Frank and Joe, too. They never give up trying to solve a mystery."

"The Hardy Boys?" I thought for a moment. "Right you are."

So *The Tower Treasure* was good for something, after all. I hesitated to delve into that sort of popular writing, but Anton had given Donnie a copy at church one day—nothing for it now but to read every word.

On May 24, Herr Hitler's forces surrounded the British Expeditionary Force, the French First Army, and the Belgian Army on the French coast at Dunkirk. All over England, citizens prayed for deliverance—and deliverance came. Churchill ordered all sea-going vessels to make across the Channel to bring back our boys. Donnie and I sat rapt at the news.

Had the enemy acted with speed, our boys would all have been lost, but German military action halted. The whole of England prayed, and for three days, the rescue took place. Hundreds of thousands were brought back to our shores. By Sunday night, churches in cities, towns, villages and hamlets were crowded with those thanking God for the deliverance of so many, and praying for the safe return of the few still being saved.

On June 4, we listened to the Prime Minister's speech at Lillian and William's, gathered in a tight little circle around their wireless.

"The British Empire and the French Republic, linked together in their cause and in their need, will defend to the death their native soil, aiding each other like good comrades to the utmost of their strength.

"Even though large tracts of Europe and many old and famous States have fallen or may fall into the grip of the Gestapo and all the odious apparatus of Nazi rule, we shall not flag or fail.

We shall go on to the end, we shall fight in France, we shall fight on the seas and oceans, we shall fight with growing confidence and growing strength in the air, we shall defend our Island, whatever the cost may be, we shall fight on the beaches, we shall fight on the landing grounds, we shall fight in the fields and in the streets, we shall fight in the hills; we shall never surrender, and even if, which I do not for a moment believe, this Island or a large part of it were subjugated and starving, then our Empire beyond the seas, armed and guarded by the British Fleet, would carry on the struggle, until, in God's good time, the New World, with all its power and might, steps forth to the rescue and the liberation of the old."

"Are we the new world, Da?"

"Yes, Son, indeed we are."

Chapter Six

September 8, 1940

*W**e find ourselves in the midst of a Blitzkrieg—a lightning war of devastating German bombing attacks over the United Kingdom that began on the seventh, after the RAF carried out a nighttime air raid on Berlin.*

Our valiant RAF heroes have prevented the Luftwaffe from gaining air superiority over the Channel. However, this week marks only the beginning of what we fear: a long and sustained aerial attack of immense proportions over our cities.

The Luftwaffe's onslaught of huge waves of bombs are part of a larger campaign attempting to devastate our infrastructure, wreak destruction on our people, and lower morale.

In London and elsewhere across our land, bombed-out buildings and mass casualties have become the norm. London's children have long been sent to the countryside for safety, but now the bombing strikes have moved inward. Is anyone safe anywhere on this Isle?

Night by night, we tuned in to the war report at William and Lillian's. At times, Donnie went to sleep to the reporter's voice, and William insisted on driving us home. While I dreaded hearing the terrifying news from London, it also magnetized me.

One day in late October, William heard from his friend in Oxford, the vicar of a small church. He penned the letter back in October after hearing a sermon at the University Church of St. Mary the Virgin.

The speaker, a don named Lewis, had posed an intriguing subject: With such horrific war news every day, why should students continue engaging in their studies? In such times, what good might come of studying ancient languages, history, or mathematics?

William read the conclusion aloud. "This Mr. Lewis assured his student audience of their purpose, even in the face of this ever expanding war. I find this oddly comforting for those of us too old to enter the fray by direct means. Perhaps our small daily efforts still make a difference, after all.

"Our flying boys have won the battle over the Channel—reporters speak of it separately as the Battle of Britain. But now, the Blitzkrieg continues. We volunteer as wardens to stand watch, raise funds for munitions and work in great truck gardens to feed the populace. By times, our efforts seem insignificant, yet taken together, they amount to some import."

On September 10, though, we shuddered through a description of a school bombing in the East End. The Hallsville School, in Canning Town, had become a haven for bombed-out families who used the basement for sleeping, but that day, the school took a direct hit and many were killed. Since the building fell into the basement, we heard no final count of deaths.

"Why should they bomb a school in a poor area?" Lillian asked the question that troubled me.

She already knew the answer. The men in the East End work at the wharves, and the Germans are set on destroying our shipping industry. Unfortunately, their families have no defense.

Christmas 1940

Through the holidays, the Blitz droned on. Such dreadful accounts of fires consuming vast areas of London, destroying homes and uprooting families. Through such unthinkable chaos and loss, the

70

determination of the British people shone bright, and we consumed tales of everyday valor like teacakes.

On Christmas Eve, we joined Lillian and William, and Lillian raved over a mock apricot flan Donnie and I concocted earlier in the day. He watched as she took her first bite, and her satisfied expression touched him.

"Mmm—oh, isn't this lovely! Did you and your Daddy make it together?"

"He let me help grate the carrots—a whole pound." As proof, Donnie held up his skinned knuckles. "You add six tablespoons of plum jam, and six tablespoons of water."

"That's all?"

"And four drops from a little brown bottle. What was that, Da?"

He turned to me and I hinted, "Al . . ."

"Righto. Almond essence."

"Will you show me how to make it one of these days?"

"And short crust pastry, too." Ah, Donnie was remembering how we devoured Mrs. Tillman's recipe yesterday, just the two of us. During these dark days, baking tidbits offset the radio's pessimism of an evening.

Lillian already owned a radio when William moved in, and they relied on this news source. He told us about the night horrors in London—he had actually taken notes when a newscaster read an American reporter's description of the bombings.

"We have so much to be thankful for this season. No bombs falling on us. A reporter named John Daly has a new show called *Report to The Nation*, and the specifics would make your hair fall out. I had read about incendiary bombs, but he gives such a vivid picture—I can almost see the bombs' white pinpoints as volunteers on the roofs watch for them and snuff them out with sand.

"Imagine, fire watchers in the darkness, on rooftops all over London. They hear the grind of approaching Luftwaffe planes and can only wait to see where the bombs fall."

Lillian clasped his hand. "But remember, Edward R. Murrow

saw German planes dropping bombs while your countrymen were flying the Union Jack from rooftops."

"Aren't they afraid?" Dannie's eyes widened with each new detail, and William launched in.

"Indeed they are. Anyone in his right mind would be, but Londoners have determined not to let Germany get them down! So they post the flags in order to send the Nazi pilots that very message."

Lillian added, "A perfect example of what my father always called *British pluck*."

"Will they win, Uncle William?"

"Absolutely. No question about that."

But a week later, for days on end, we consumed reports of the terrible firebombing that occurred on December 29. Like an Agatha Christie novel, this ongoing plot held us in thrall.

Late summer 1941

Those last months before school opened for the year, the idea of lumping boys and girls together bothered me a bit. I rather preferred the British method of separate classes—less distracting, more appropriate, more *right*. Then at a certain age, perhaps in university, they might learn together.

But I wondered. Had I experienced a youthful friendship with a girl, or grown up with a sister or even played with a female cousin from time to time, might I have entered adulthood with a better feel for the nature of women? Would I have seen more deeply into Victoria's person, regardless of her façade? Would I have developed skills to ascertain the real from the false, rather than being deceived by her beauty?

As Donnie tried on two new sets of school clothing, with William remarking how grown-up he looked, I noted the curve of his nose, so like his mother's. Could little boys in fresh plaid cotton shirts and little girls in flowered dresses learn well together? And why did I think they could not?

What superfluous concerns, these, for during the hot summer months, the radio announcer supplied far more reason to fret. In order to gain air superiority, the Luftwaffe intended to utterly destroy the Royal Air Force. Only in this way could the German military safely transport well-trained troops across the twenty-one-mile Channel.

The RAF alone stood between them and further conquest. Thus, raids of British ports intensified in August, to draw our planes into the open. August eighth saw the first increase, to the horror of city dwellers along Britain's coast. German pilots also began to bomb our radar defense system and fighter airfields.

With as many as 1,500 Nazi aircraft crossing the Channel each day, one might scarce glance up without spotting one. Grandfather's cousin wrote that at times, having so many airplanes in the air at the same time blotted out the sun.

But in spite of being outnumbered, RAF pilots relied on radar technology and lighter aircraft to resist this all-out invasion. Though we suffered many losses, our pilots destroyed two Luftwaffe warplanes for every British plane shot down.

And from London—the most recent report left us gaping. Engaged as an Auxiliary Fire Service watcher, William's acquaintance recorded sights impossible for radio broadcasters to duplicate.

Last night, I heard shrapnel hitting a building's iron guttering—ping, ping, ping. Some other workers and I rescued a teen-age boy hand-carrying a message to one of the Ministries. An ambulance worker attended to his serious wounds. One of many ARP messengers out every night, he was struck while riding his bicycle, and when I drew near to see if I might help, a Fire Service worker thrust a packet into my hands.

"Find this place, and quickly," he said. "Who knows how important this message might be?"

So I did, with great trouble. I knew better than to attempt to reaach the actual office. Even then, only a code defined the recipient. Finding a courier would have to do, and soon enough, I spied one making her way in the darkness between government buildings.

Scarce avoiding giving her a startle, I made known my request. Once I did, she accepted the packet and hurried off. How young she was—most likely, she worked by day as well, and slept a few hours in an underground refuge for government workers.

You would never believe how many like her we see these days. Some drive trucks, delivering who knows what to the air bases around the city, or work as mechanics. Who would ever have imagined this state of affairs? Our neighbor's daughter works in the kitchen on one of those air bases. Her parents fear for her safety, with troops brought in from all over the world. But what is to be done? Everyone wants to do their part.

Good thing I brought along a midnight lunch from a pie and mash shop, for it took an hour to return to my post. I was worn out.

This great drama entranced me, and equally magnetized William. At least one day a week, he absconded with Donnie after milking, making way for me to glean every word the newspapers offered. Later, we hashed over the reports and bemoaned the plight of our country.

By the time Mr. Fletcher and Mrs. Bultmann made their second pilgrimage our way, my question about male and female children attending school together seemed trite, and I kept this concern to myself. As for female teachers, I had read more history of Loyal Valley since their last visit. As far back as 1897, the town had hired women to teach their children.

The plight of Londoners, never far from my mind, instructed me to entrust Donnie's formal education to Mrs. Bultmann, who appeared amiable, yet firm, the ideal persona for an instructor, in my humble opinion.

During the past year, thousands of evacuated children lived in strangers' homes. These youngsters were forced to adjust to new schools and teachers, not to mention fill-in parents. Many a British mum sacrificed the joy of witnessing her child off to their first day at school.

Country schools like ours had been functioning for over a

hundred years. Instructors taught a smattering of children, all ages thrown together in one classroom.

Rather slapdash, but with so few students, what else could be done? And I had made the choice to bring Donnie to rural America. For the many benefits of life here, I had only to stand in the orchard and look east toward House Mountain. Such a stable sight—granite in a terrain of clay and sand.

Closer at hand, the great lacey oak guarded our very own spring. *Our very own*—the phrase itself warmed my heart. Often this summer, Donnie and I retreated there from the afternoon heat and daydreamed away an hour or two.

Something about this spot stirred the imagination. What if we had lived here in Civil War days? What if, at this very moment, we were Comanche warriors watering our horses, or early settlers, and a bear—or Indian raiders—stole onto our property to pilfer our provisions?

Recalling our musings made me smile. We had come to the right place, indeed. I could almost hear old John Meusebach say, "*Tenax propiciti!*"

Against all odds, this early pioneer commandeered the first real peace treaty with the Indians in present-day Mason County. Tenacity of purpose sufficed for his progeny, who made their living off this land. This same tenacity would see to Donnie's education, and would suffice for Old Blighty's challenges, as well.

Since Mr. Churchill became Prime Minister, so much had happened in such short order. Since the calamitous air invasion of Britain, France had signed an armistice with Nazi Germany. Charles de Gaulle, a new name to us, was now recognized as the Free French leader, with Marshal Petain, the Great War hero, Prime Minister of Vichy France.

France's quick collapse must have cheered Herr Hitler. I pictured him gleeful as Nazi troops occupied the great old city of Paris. Nazi troops occupying the country that had once been our ally only complicated matters.

General Petain earned elite decorations in the Great War, true. But he might leave much to be desired in a political role

Meanwhile, Norway also surrendered to Germany. Hitler and Italy's ruler, Benito Mussolini, had met in Munich, and the Soviets busily occupied the Baltic States. Next, the Vichy government broke off relations with Britain, and Italy occupied British Somaliland in East Africa.

By the moment, the war's scope increased. Last year, the third week of August brought the first air raids on Central London. Two days later, our pilots carried out a similar attack on Berlin. Now, word had it that Hitler was planning Operation Sea Lion, the land invasion of Britain.

These mind-boggling events meant a world of misery for so many. For Brits, the question was not *if*, but *when* Hitler would invade. Along the coasts, workers constructed thousands of pillbox defenses, for Operation Sea Lion focused on the southeast coast.

In addition, thousands more anti-tank stop-lines, heavy-gun emplacements, and anti-aircraft batteries were slated all over the British Isles. This stunning effort, unheard of since the building of the Martello Towers during Napoleonic times, was almost too much to take in.

Years ago, I visited the huge concrete "eyes" or mirrors built along the coast in the Great War to detect zeppelins and other incoming World War I aircraft. Now, chains of radar stations, invented by a Scottish physicist, peppered the area, forming a veritable fence to warn pilots of Luftwaffe activity.

On Donnie's first day of school, we set all of these concerns aside. We stood with other parents in the schoolhouse yard as Mr. Fletcher offered a few words to open the school year. Such an event would be impossible in London, as many schools had been forced to close their doors, and others bombed irreparably.

On the walk to town, Donnie and I practiced what would follow. "I pledge allegiance to the flag of the United States of America, and to the republic for which it stands . . ."

Under the American flag, I recited with the best of them. If anyone questioned my allegiance, they kept their doubts to themselves. Of course, everyone's eye trained on the students, especially the beginners, whom Mrs. Bultmann introduced by name.

Several other families recently moved here, so their children merited an introduction. Mothers' heads bobbed at the announcement of their offspring, and those who had always lived here listened with interest. Few fathers attended because of work, as would be the case in Nottinghamshire.

When Donnie's name was called, he stood stalwart, but managed to catch my eye.

As proud as natural grandparents, William and Lillian fixed their eyes on him, looking so tall in the shirt Lillian had stitched. Meanwhile, one wiry little fellow would have given anything to go back home with his Mum. He kept running off from his new classmates to cling to her skirts.

What a trial for that poor woman, beleaguered by two toddlers, as well. Though she had stationed herself in the brush tabernacle some paces south of the schoolhouse, her obvious flush turned even deeper each time her little son returned to her after Mrs. Bultmann had peeled him away. I breathed thanks for the readiness another year at home had provided Donnie, and for his intense eagerness to set out on this new adventure.

After Mrs. Bultmann's brief thank-you to the community and parents, our little man, head held high, carried his lunch pail into the schoolhouse. I walked with William and Lillian to their house on Dragoon Street, where we stood talking for a few more minutes.

I had done nothing to belong here, but a crystal clear thought struck me as I left for home. My son was now gleaning from living in this community. Perhaps the time had come for me to make a contribution.

Donnie's winning smile as he crossed the threshold set my pulse throbbing. A momentous day, this—a day of looking forward and expecting great things.

Great Expectations—Ah, best to wait a bit to read that one. Perhaps we might meet Mr. Scrooge first.

Back at home, the day's labor soon consumed me. In July, one of our trees evidenced the first sign of brown rot. Serious business, indeed. If a fungal disease overcame one tree, others might soon succumb. Our cider and jam business kept increasing, and recently the café owner had become a regular customer. That meant eight or ten more jars going out a month, so the trees must stay in tip-top condition.

This morning I headed for the peach tree upon which a grayish fuzzy spore mass had first appeared. At the orchard's edge, I clipped all growth near the area, burned all the matter I removed, and sprayed hydrogen peroxide on the bark. William believed this substance or copper hydroxide worked as well as the lime sulfur Grandfather always used, and could be obtained locally.

Still, it might be necessary to employ another remedy. Eternal vigilance made for a good orchard, Grandfather always claimed.

When I returned to the barn, William was fixing something, and shared his belief that Hitler would indeed invade Britain. Everything in recent letters told him so. The whole world held its breath for our native land, such a small isle amongst the nations.

Yet the British faced the terrifying night raids with courage. All across London, volunteers snuffed out incendiaries and kept a sharp eye for ones that smashed through rooftops, only to ignite and burn later.

Beneath every dire report ran a river of confidence, despite Hitler's bold malice. Old Blighty would prevail. Surely she would.

"Did you know our house is on the Pinta Trail the Indians used to use? The *conquistadors* and soldiers followed it too, all the way from San Antonio to—mmm—way up in the high Hill Country."

"*Conquistadors*? My, what big words you use these days!"

"That's 'cause I go to school, Da." Donnie allowed time for this statement to penetrate as we left the schoolhouse and turned onto the path leading home. Then he plunged in again.

"Did you know Loyal Valley was on the stage route from El Paso to San Antonio and pretty soon had a post office, livery stable, and saloon? But before all that could happen, that fella named John …"

"John Meusebach?"

"Yeah. He smoked a peace pipe with some Indians on the war-path. They were fighting the settlers, but he promised not hurt them. He sure was brave."

"Yes, he was."

"Do you think he was afraid?"

"I imagine so. What do you think?"

Donnie looked off into the distance. "I s'pose the Indians seemed scary. But John didn't let that stop him."

"Mrs. Bultmann told you all this?"

"After noon recess, she reads to us about Texas in the old days. 'Bout the Alamo—remember when we were there?"

"Indeed, I do, and we must go back again some day. We certainly have come to a place of rich heritage."

October 17, 1940

"Donnie and school go together well. He has always been a sto-ryteller, but can scarcely get the words out fast enough now. Jolly good to have such an imagination, with all the terrifying news these days."

Of course, I agreed. William and I were mending fence on a glorious autumn day, and the whole time, he had been spouting distressing statistics. His longtime friend in Cardiff wrote that beginning in July, hundreds of bombs had fallen on the Welsh city, one of the world's largest coal ports.

While I poured our homemade cement mixture, William posi-tioned and secured a fence post. "I understand why they would target the port, but why bomb civilian areas like Grangetown and Llandoff? The chap I know lives in Cathays, and his neighborhood has been hit as well. Can you imagine living with that fear, with Donnie being unable to go out and play?"

I could not. Meanwhile, the bombings continued.

"Mrs. Bultmann had us write a story about our family today, and we studied how the caterpillars molt. Did you know they grow a bigger skin under their old one? When they shed, the new one is already there. And today, Johnny Miller beat all the boys running around the bases, and I hit the baseball, Da!"

Without a moment's hesitation, he went on. "A girl was racing somebody and skinned her knee, so Mrs. B put a plaster on it. She calls it a bandage, and she told everybody to be more careful, and—"

"Oh my, such a lot of excitement!"

"Oops, I almost forgot—we talked about the 'lection, too. A guy named Willkie's runnin' as a dark horse against the President."

"What does that mean?"

"There's a race, and a horse comes up from behind and wins, but nobody ever heard of him before. Is Mr. Churchill a dark horse, too?"

"No, most Britishers had already heard of him."

"Anyway, we're all s'posed to vote on November fifth. S'posed to think it over really good, and when Mrs. B passes out some paper slips, we write down who we're voting for."

"How might one think it over really well?"

"Listen to the news and talk to our folks."

"Mmm—and I suppose we might read some newspaper articles, too."

"Yeah. Voting's real important—didja know that one vote made it so we speak English here instead of German?"

"Seriously? No, I didn't."

"Yup, in 1776. And Texas became a state because of one vote, and so did California and a couple other states, and in 1876, the president won by one vote."

"I had no idea. A good history lesson."

"Mrs. Bultmann knows a lot."

"Indeed."

Walks home from school provided such an avalanche of information, and when William sat milking his cows, Donnie repeated much of what he had told me. I looked forward to this time of day, and relished listening a second time.

We hardly found opportunity to interject a question. One day, between bites of a cheese sandwich—Donnie also came home ravenous—he emphasized the baseball games.

"I need to practice so I can hit a home run. Some of the other guys hit one 'most every day."

Heaven only knew how diligently we already practiced every evening. Together, we memorized Babe Ruth's advice: "You just can't beat the person who never gives up," and "Every strike brings me closer to the next home run." I borrowed a library book about the game's history and learned that its origins remained somewhat dubious.

Either it evolved from the British game of rounders, or, as some insisted, a fellow in the Civil War era invented the game. Historians had trouble settling on the facts, but one thing remained clear: modern-day baseball players displayed great determination.

"Like John Meusebach, right?" As often happened, Donnie provided the perfect summary.

"Exactly."

We listened to some games on the radio and were thoroughly hooked by the tension, as in a good story. Would that chap on third base get to score and change the momentum of the game? Would the center fielder be able to catch the hit and save his mate on the pitcher's mound from disgrace?

At school, the boys chose favorite teams. Donnie was hard put to choose between the Detroit Tigers and the Cincinnati Reds. We researched why they were called the *Reds*, and found that originally, they had been the *Red Stockings*. But why had they not worn blue stockings? This valuable information escaped us.

Both Hank Greenberg and Frank McCormick won Donnie's heart, and we made certain to be on hand for the World Series broadcasts. Somebody at school said the Reds had not won the Series since 1919, when their victory was tainted by a racketeer's "fix."

As Donnie put it, "They say somebody mucked up that Series."

Of course, we sought out the whole story and shook our heads at the high-stakes drama. But through it all, Donnie learned to hit the ball, which remained my one goal. I had a lot to learn about hitting, too, so we took extra pride in any show of progress.

Once the Series ended, reading filled our evenings again. But the other boys had shown Donnie their baseball cards, and he mentioned them to William. Suddenly, packets of gum with hand-sized baseball cards started showing up during milking times.

By the week, Donnie's collection grew, making the perfect hobby for stormy nights. What better activity than organizing players alphabetically and learning percentages and statistics?

One late October afternoon, I prepared our repast as William's long shadow faded through the orchard toward home. Donnie soon came bursting into the kitchen.

"Guess what, Da?" Such rosy cheeks—evenings had turned a bit cooler.

"What? And please wash your hands for supper." I poured our milk and readied myself for even more news from school when Donnie sat down.

"Yeah, okay." I had long since stopped correcting this to *Yes*. Oh, to be a fly in the classroom to see if Mrs. Bultmann retained her German *Yah* or used the correct English form.

"William told me a secret. I can tell you, but nobody else."

"All right. Mum's the word."

"Okay." Donnie angled his head for emphasis. "Lillian's going to have a baby."

Nothing could have astounded me more. In his early fifties, William was about to become a father?

"Ain't you pleased?"

82

"I—certainly. And since when do you say *ain't*?"

"Oh, sorry. Everybody at school—"

"Righto. Well, you sound like a real American, but there is a right and a wrong to English grammar."

"Do you think the new baby will be a boy?"

"Impossible to tell. Just think—William, who has been like a father to me and a grandfather to you, will soon swaddle his own infant."

"What does that mean?"

"Remember last Christmas when the mother in the nativity scene carried Baby Jesus wrapped in a blanket?"

"Oh, yeah. Swaddling clothes"

Still in shock, I marveled aloud, "A baby. The possibility never occurred to me."

"Because William's so old?"

"Yes. But how wonderful, since Lillian and her first husband had no children."

"How did he die?"

"In a hunting accident, I believe."

"What was he hunting?"

"I have never heard, but it happened during the Depression, when meat was scarce and people had to eat off the land. Perhaps he was climbing through some thick brambles when his gun went off."

During supper, Donnie turned thoughtful. "If William can get married and have a baby, so can you."

A swallow of potato nearly strangled me. After a coughing fit, I replied. "True. But I doubt I ever shall."

"Why?"

"My world seems so full already, with you and our work here." My stained shirt testified—the cider press had occupied me all day, and the sleeves pulled at my neck. "Having a wife means—"

His expectant look urged me on.

"It takes energy to—to care for a wife."

With a mystified expression, Donnie applied fresh butter from

Lillian's churn to the bread she had baked. As he added peach jam, he emitted a single word.

"Oh."

What would I have said if he noted that it didn't look as if William were caring for Lillian? Quite the opposite, she seemed never to tire of meeting his slightest need.

Chapter Seven

October passed into November, and Lillian became more visibly expectant. She and William kept her condition quiet, and in public, a sweeping trench coat hid her burgeoning middle. At this point, one could hardly have a decent conversation with William, so intent was he on making life easy for Lillian.

She stayed industrious as always, sewing baby clothes and two new sets of clothing for Donnie, one for Christmas and one for spring. When her sewing machine lay idle, she picked up her knitting needles. I offered to take over the bread making, but she scowled.

"By no means. I am merely preparing to give birth, not dying." She gave William a sour glance before turning back to me. "I suppose someone has made you think I've suddenly become delicate. Well, don't you believe it!"

In the evenings, William set his hand to creating a wooden crib. After much discussion, Donnie and I designed a tiny chair for the new infant, whom he tenderly referred to as "my new cousin."

One day on our walk home, the air had turned decidedly cooler, and absent of all insect chatter. I sought to recall last autumn—how had things gone, exactly? Back then, settling in filled our every moment, so I recalled little about the transition from autumn to winter.

Meanwhile, Donnie could scarcely contain his delight with occurrences at school.

"We're putting on a play, Mrs. B says, and I have a part in it."

"Oh my. Tell me more."

"It's all about the Pilgrims and the first Thanksgiving, Da! We need costumes, and she says we'll invite the whole community on the day before Thanksgiving, right after the noon hour. Our schoolhouse will be the Commonwealth of Virginia, and the Indians and Pilgrims will all be here. The big kids are writing our parts, and the third and fourth graders get long ones."

He paused for breath. "How interesting. The Pilgrims, eh? Where did they come from?"

"England?"

"Righto. From Lincolnshire, I believe. But they tried living in Holland before they set sail for America."

"On the *Mayflower*! And they got here in winter and had a hard time, so the Indians helped them out. I need to find feathers 'cause I'm gonna be an Indian. Can we make a headdress?"

"Absolutely. Biddy Hen and her mates shed a few each day, and we can save them. On Saturday we shall take a long walk and search for tail feathers from a quail or grouse."

As we rounded the curve into our yard, Donnie stashed his lunch pail and jacket in my arms and ran straight for the barn to tell William and launch his search for feathers. So began our plunge an American tradition that would soon become our own.

November 14, 1940

When the broadcaster announced the latest report from across the Atlantic, Donnie and I were hard at work. Using two extra-large needles threaded with Lillian's strongest thread, we secured feathers on Donnie's costume. This had become our nightly project. She stitched the canvas outfit, but Donnie claimed this task.

In our intensity, we often turned silent, so the announcement entered the room like a lightning flash.

As of last night, St. Michael's Cathedral in Coventry has fallen prey to the Luftwaffe. This Fourteenth Century Gothic structure, known and loved by many Britons, lost all but its spire and tower in the midnight hours. The tomb of its first bishop also survived, but irreplaceable artwork and sacramental objects are forever lost. On this day the city of Coventry mourns."

My gasp caused Donnie to look up. "Da?"

"A very large, very beautiful church in England has been bombed."

"By the bloody Germans?"

"Where did you hear that term?"

"William said it. Is it swearing?"

"Not exactly, yet impolite in some circles. At any rate, this church has stood for ages."

"Since the Fourteenth Century?"

"Yes. That was quite a tempestuous time in history, too. A Pope was poisoned, and the climate changed, bringing continuous rains to Europe. People thought the Old Testament flood had returned."

"You mean Noah and the Ark?"

"Righto. After all the rain, famines struck Europe and India. Robert the Bruce drove the British from Scotland, dynasties changed in India, and the shoguns revolted in Japan. I could go on and on."

"How do you know so much, Da?"

"Because Grandfather saw to my studies. At any rate, during that tumultuous period, the people of Coventry built this glorious cathedral. Quite the feat, long before men invented machines to transport materials."

"And it has lasted all these years?"

"Yes, for centuries."

"Like our house." Donnie rushed on to his next thought. "Were the Germans who built Loyal Valley related to the ones bombing right now?"

What a question, and how to answer it? I rarely chose to skirt a topic, but this might be an exception.

"I don't know. I would guess that some might be. But right now, I feel heartsick for the people of Coventry, and for all the people of England. Things will never be the same for them."

87

My mind may have retained a hoard of information concerning European history, but my knowledge of the First American Thanksgiving left something to be desired. I must admit that watching Donnie march over to Myles Standish, hold up his hand, and repeat his simple line created a thrill.

"How! We share our blessings with you and your people." Perfect diction, such a confident presence, and a smile tucked in at the end—his first public appearance left nothing to be desired.

Seated next to me, Lillian reached for William's hand. Her midsection had swelled beyond thought. I began to envision twins. She fashioned suitable dresses, but at this juncture, nothing could disguise her girth. She rarely ventured out these days, but Donnie's hand-drawn invitation, depicting an Indian chief bearing mounds of corn and fish, had wooed her. Or perhaps it was the curious turkey peering 'round a tree in the background.

William fairly beamed and often mentioned the coming birth. "A baby for Christmas—can you believe it?"

"Hardly. Coming to America has certainly turned out well for you, my man."

"Indeed, far beyond my wildest imaginings. Whoever would have dreamed I would become a father?"

The performance ended with an injunction by a prim little girl dressed in a fine navy and white dress, as clean and pressed as ever a dress might be. Linen, I surmised. Lillian's guidance in choosing fabrics for Donnie's latest suit provided me a lesson in yard goods.

"Ladies and Gentlemen, thank you for coming. The Indians and the Pilgrims invite you to join us for refreshments. This Thanksgiving, we hope your hearts will overflow with gratitude for all the gifts we have received."

Delivered with pomp, this lassie's instruction seemed fitting and simple to follow, for thankfulness indeed filled me. How could I not be grateful for this place, this time, these opportunities? Such a simple life we had adopted, and in such an isolated place. But people here had welcomed us, much like Squanto did the Pilgrims. Twas a bittersweet gratitude, however. Our hearts ached for the situation in England even as we gave thanks.

After Donnie fell asleep that night, I returned to his question about the pioneers who founded Loyal Valley. German to the core, but they laid lasting foundations in this new homeland and become American through and through. Were they related to some of today's Luftwaffe pilots? Quite likely, I daresay.

War made it impossible to split people up into good and evil. Some Germans did evil things, I might tell Donnie, yet those here stood for what was right. Take Mrs. Bultmann, for example. Of strong German heritage, who could fault her obvious loyalty to this country?

Over a hearty wild turkey dinner on Thanksgiving Day, we met Kenneth, Lillian's bachelor brother, who had bagged the fowl for the feast south of Llano. This marked his first visit since their marriage, which he took as a personal offense.

As it turned out, he harbored some strong views concerning President Roosevelt, too, and eagerly revealed them. In response to Lillian's "Happy Thanksgiving!" after William said grace, Kenneth took the floor.

"You mean Happy *Franks*giving? That's what they're callin' it now, 'cause Roosevelt changed the date again this year. Who does he think he is? Half the states are celebratin' today, and half did last week."

"Why is that?" William asked in complete sincerity, since he could hardly concentrate long enough to read a newspaper these days.

"'Cause Franky thinks he's a king. The shopping season before Christmas is too short, he says. Did the same thing last year to can satisfy them city slickers out East. Now we got *Republican Thanksgiving* n' *Franksgiving*."

William considered. "I guess we were awfully busy last year—we didn't even notice."

"That figures."

"Well, the idea is to give thanks today." Lillian squeezed William's hand and turned to Donnie. "What are you thankful for?"

"My new cousin! And school, and baseball, and pumpkin pie, and—"

"That's the spirit." William added his list and gestured to his brother-in-law. "Kenneth, what are *you* thankful for?"

"For once, Congress did somethin', and passed the Alien Registration Law. Lets us rest easier 'bout them Hun-lovers out East. Gotta keep our eyes open, 'cause German submarines can get right up to our coast."

His eyes narrowed to a slit, and for a moment, he reminded me of Jerrold down at the station. Thankfully Lillian bore little resemblance to Kenneth, either in facial features or outlook, but her retort proved one might push her too far.

"How can you say that?" Her tone turned scathing, and she jerked her head toward Donnie.

"Well, it's true. And them Frankfurters livin' up there is aliens. They'd as soon fight fer Germ'ny as fer the red, white n' blue. Our Gov'nor's inspectin' everybody down around here, too."

William touched Lillian's wrist. "It's all right, dear. We have—"

"No it's not. Kenneth, do you realize William and Everett had to fill out the paperwork required by the Smith Act, too? Do you include them as *aliens*?"

If only I had a camera aimed at Kenneth's face right then. His flush deepened to beet red.

"What're y' talkin' about? They ain't aliens—their English is way better'n ours."

"But they aren't citizens yet. And if you're any example, they ought to think twice about becoming one."

Kenneth sputtered. "They know I ain't talkin' 'bout them. An alien's them Japanese and Germans, n' them Italians."

90

"Oh, for Heaven's sake! If you had to give up all your customers of German descent, you'd be in big trouble."

Following William's lead, I held my piece. But Donnie burst out with something that made my blood run cold. "At recess, one of the older guys said Mrs. Bultmann's got no right teaching us."

Except for Kenneth, who started gulping down the best turkey dressing I could possibly imagine, we all stared at each other.

"He really said that?"

"Yah. One of the girls told 'im to shut up. Said, 'can't you see Mrs. B's teachin' us all about being patriots?' He laughed at her, and she said, 'You just moved here from up North—you don't know a thing, anyhow.'"

"Oh, my. I'm glad she stood up for Mrs. Bultmann."

"Me, too. Da, could a German sub really land on the Texas coast? If John Meuesebach's ship landed at Galveston, then—"

"It is possible, but the Coast Guard defends our shores, so we needn't worry."

Kenneth opened his mouth to say something, but Lillian burst in to ask about my gratitude list. Ever so quick to plunge into this pleasant topic, I waxed eloquent, and soon she bustled about, serving us pumpkin pie.

When school resumed after Thanksgiving, dialogue with Donnie centered around Christmas. He explained that during the Yuletide of 1777, George Washington and his 12,000 freezing troops spent a miserable time at a place called Valley Forge in the state of Pennsylvania.

"The men lived in tents the whole winter. They yoked themselves to carts to haul firewood."

"Why was that?"

"They ate all their horses 'cause they were starving, Da. It was awful cold—that valley's way up north of here. They didn't have coats or shoes and hardly nothin' to eat. Almost 3,000 of 'em were sick."

91

"Hardly *anything* to eat?"

"No, and the officers declared them unfit for duty, Mrs. Bultmann said. But even though some of them lived close enough to go home, they stayed with George Washington through it all, fighting for freedom."

"That sounds awfully miserable, indeed. They must have been convinced that he could lead them to victory. Do you know who they were fighting?"

Donnie's eyes burned. "The British. Them confounded British."

Obviously, the story captivated him, and so far, he had failed to connect William and me with *them confounded British*. Ah well, plenty of time for that. In fact, a distant ancestor on our family tree had fought under General Burgoyne at Saratoga. Against General Washington's troops, I might add. But why complicate matters?

Long after Donnie faded into slumber, the images of Washington's suffering men remained. Mrs. Bultmann certainly made history come alive. Over and over, Donnie brought home lessons like this, and often, we pored over our books seeking more information.

Why had that older boy accused this dedicated teacher? Though Donnie said no more, his Thanksgiving Day outburst kept reverberating. How could anyone get the idea that Mrs. B, as Donnie often called her, was anything but patriotic?

On December 27, 1940, Lillian gave birth to the most precocious child ever born. According to William, tiny Abigail Ruth, named after Lillian's mother, smiled and cooed during her first hour of life.

As privileged family members, Donnie and I were allowed to visit on the second day, but only for a brief time. Donnie seemed to comprehend the sacredness of glimpsing his newborn cousin. Suitably solemn and reverential, he refrained from reacting until we walked home.

"What do you think of tiny Miss Abigail, then?"

"She's awful small, and her face is as red as—that sumac over there."

"A fitting analogy. Quite the unique Christmas gift for us all, wouldn't you say?"

"Yeah, but William looks so tired, Da."

"He has lost some sleep. This marks quite a large change in their household."

"Good thing you offered to do the milking for him this week."

"With you to help, it goes quickly, and William and Lillian help us out, too. The next time we deliver their milk, remind me to take along some cider."

As we neared the barn, Donnie took my hand. "Thank you for our other surprise."

We stopped by to pet that surprise, a sturdy, amiable pony to pull the wooden wagon William built during the past few weeks. Having long ago finished his offspring's crib, he needed another project, he said.

This would aid in hauling milk and cheese back and forth to their house and to the customers he had amassed. The dappled grey came from Norman's stock. This winter, I had been far too busy to drop in at the gas station more than once or twice, but he stopped by one afternoon in early December, noticed the wagon taking shape, and allowed he had a pony for sale.

"Just right for that boy of yours. Come on over and take a look."

So I did. Sturdy and calm, this friendly fellow would make the perfect Christmas gift, I decided, and made the transaction post-haste. Norman agreed to keep the surprise until Christmas Eve, when he would make the delivery while we attended the evening service in Cherry Spring.

My homeland might be beset by dire distress, making this holiday sparse for many, but here, whatever we needed seemed to come along at just the right time. As agreed, Norman brought this new addition to our barn on Christmas Eve.

In the evening coolness when we returned home with candle flames still dancing before our eyes, I lured Donnie to meet this docile family member hidden in the barn's back stall. He could not have been more surprised or content. With the pony came naming privileges.

"Take your time. Names are important. Remember, yours means *world ruler*."

"But not like Hitler."

"Not at all, but overcoming whatever obstacles might hinder your dreams."

So far, what had Herr Hitler added to his destructive toll? The Luftwaffe kept pounding England, and on December twenty-ninth and thirtieth, firebombs started an inferno that might have swept London clean. But intrepid London firefighters showed incredible courage, battling blazes on every side.

The reports sickened me. It was all I could do to keep my mind on other topics. But on the afternoon of the thirtieth, when a newscaster reported that St. Paul's Cathedral still stood after a horrendous night, I let out a whoop.

Unused to such elation, Donnie startled up from his chair. "They didn't hit that one like they did the one at Coventry?"

"No. Right now, St. Paul's means a great deal to Londoners. Sort of like the Statue of Liberty to Americans, or maybe the Capitol in Washington, D.C. Last night, even though a bomb fell on St. Paul's, the firefighters kept its blast from turning into an uncontrollable fire. They worked all night long.

"Can you imagine—two nights of incessant bombing. Oh how it must have felt for people to view the Cathedral still standing this morning."

"Wow—just like *gave proof through the night, that our flag was still there*."

"Indeed." I drew Donnie close, grateful we were hearing about all of this secondhand.

January 1, 1941

The radio announcer relayed that the Luftwaffe had badly damaged or destroyed Old Bailey, the Guildhall, and eight churches designed by Christopher Wren. In response, the RAF attacked Bremen and made a direct hit on the Kiel Canal Bridge, which collapsed on a Finnish ship.

"But isn't Finland neutral?" Oh, how I loved Donnie's growing mastery of geography!

"Yes, but neutrality doesn't always provide protection during war. The sailors on that ship must have suffered greatly."

"The United States is neutral, aren't we?"

"So far, but we side with the Allies. Last September President Roosevelt announced a "destroyers for bases" deal with England. In exchange for a ninety-nine year lease to allow American military bases on British-controlled territory in Canada and the Caribbean, our government agreed to give England fifty old destroyers."

"We would never do that for old Hitler."

"Right you are."

"Lillian's brother said President Roosevelt hates Hitler."

"Yes."

"Do you think we'll get into the war, Da?"

"I don't know. I believe the President would like to do far more for Great Britain, but has no absolute power. The latest Neutrality Act prevents the interventionists from aiding England any more than they already are."

"But England's our friend. Why don't we help them out more?"

"Things take time. We shall see what happens—the isolationists and the interventionists are in a row. I certainly do not envy President Roosevelt."

After the next evening report, we found the city of Bardia on the Mediterranean coast of Libya. There, the Australian XIII Corps had taken 45,000 Italian prisoners.

"See how close the town is to the Egyptian border? Italy was colonizing this region earlier, and fortified Bardia with an arc of defensive posts to protect the town and its small harbor. Since the Italians have teamed up with Germany now, every single harbor is important."

"Wow, 45,000 prisoners!"

"Indeed, about ten times the population of Fredericksburg. This marks the Australian troops' very first battle—quite an illustrious start, wouldn't you say?"

Already busy drawing stick-man sets of thousands to equal forty-five, Donnie nodded. "The Australians are like cousins to England, aren't they?"

"Yes. Close cousins, I would say." I decided to stay with the mathematical side of things. No need to explain the term *penal colony* at this point.

Chapter Eight

J anuary days grew colder, but unlike Nottingham winters, where ample moisture fell all year long. The Hill Country's *dry cold* produced headaches. Thankfully, William bought plenty of our favorite remedy from a pharmacist in Llano. Someone told him this man sold formulas using native herbs, and so far, the concoction was working.

During this time, the nightly newscast moved to North Africa and the Mediterranean.

Tobruk presents the next target in North Africa, with the Greeks fighting to keep the Nazis out of Greece. But the German Luftwaffe has claimed air command of the entire Mediterranean. A long siege seems likely here. Indeed, this is quickly becoming a vast world war.

Indeed was right. It was all I could do to keep up with the geography and history lessons required for an elementary understanding of these events. On each front, British forces met desperate need, but how could they be everywhere at once? And so began this new year.

After walking Donnie to the semester's first day of school, I visited the library. Norman looked up and nodded as I settled in with the newspaper. So many details to catch up on, I hardly knew where to begin. Affairs around the world were so troubled, I declined a visit to the gas station, and discussed matters with William instead. He was busy with an infected udder, and had called out the veterinarian.

So much more palatable to deal with everyday challenges than the all-encompassing war, where gigantic obstacles cropped up by the minute. Still, we chatted about it after the veterinarian completed his ministrations and left his instructions. All the while, William brushed the poor cow.

The analgesic liniment the vet rubbed in seemed to work. William crooned consoling phrases, as though to little Abigail.

"There, now. You'll be better soon. Milking will still cause you pain, but there's no way out except *through*."

The larger metaphor was not lost on us. *No way out but through* for the world, as well. A dreadful set-to, and we fumbled to take it all in over a cup of steaming tea. Noting the increasing turmoil in England, William had ordered in an ample supply from the Twinings Company back in the summer of '39.

His cow's pain assuaged, he headed back across the orchard to the women in his life. Fortified by our tea, I felt I could face whatever came.

But what a winter this turned into. In mid-January, temperatures dropped far lower than normal, and early mornings found us shivering until I stirred up the fire. How glad I was for the dual kitchen stove William and I purchased shortly after we arrived. Featuring one electric side, but also a woodburning receptacle, it saw us through.

Even though the hardware owner in Mason spoke highly of this older model, I entertained some doubts. Why did it still inhabit a far corner of his shop after all these years? But the proprietor's apt reply convinced us.

"They sold great for a few years, but folks in bigger cities started to rely on electricity, all about progress and such. But I've heard several say they regretted tossing out this dual model. With it, you won't have to worry if the electric goes off."

William and I shared a glance. As yet, we had no electricity.

"You might not be used to the temperatures getting down into the low thirties at times. Can't go wrong with this stove. If worse comes to worse with the electric, you can still cook and keep the house warm. I could've switched to a newer model, but my wife still won't part with ours, and we've used it every single day." He scratched his scalp. "That would be since 1912."

William had experience with one like it, he said, and the low price convinced us. So each night, Donnie and I stoked up the fire before going to bed, and the water in the reservoir always stayed warm. In the morning, I built up the fire, and on these frigid days, Donnie smiled at me from the warmth of his bunk.

"Quick as you like, Da. I'll stay here a few minutes longer."

"Enjoy the warmth while you can."

With a thick wool sweater over my flannel pajamas, and wool stockings as thick as the sweater, the sight of me tickled his funny bone. I hoped he would tuck away this memory. We never know what will stick in our children's minds, but hope the good times nestle down.

In minutes, the stove blazed again and our full water kettle burbled with promise. Soon a sleepy sun blinked far beyond the fruit trees as we dressed and broke our fast. I dipped deep into our Twinings can this day—William had refilled it for Christmas. Nothing like strong hot tea on a frosty morning.

During this cold spell, Donnie wore a muffler and my old Bobbie cap. Lillian had offered to knit him one of his own, and no doubt she would, but for now, this worn specimen served well enough. With a wool scarf around his neck, he possessed the air of a sporty young bloke off to a polo match.

During the day, I checked each fruit tree—I would hate to lose one to this cold. Norman came upon me at my arboreal duties and assured me that the hill country had endured similar temperatures in the past.

"Wouldn't doubt but what it snows. The winter before you came, four inches fell. And if I remember right, Clifton had about two feet in twenty-four hours in '29. That's two hours north, but we felt the effects down here." He seemed to recall every winter from the day he was born, and some before that.

"Yep. That was a new record, but it'll pro'bly never happen like that again. Your trees are old stock, so they'll survive. Say, didn't England have record cold last year?"

"So we heard. The snow caused a significant problem, but rain and ice followed in Wales and the southwest Midlands. The longest lasting ice ever for the islands. The cold dislocated transport, and during the same period, a great storm struck the southeast, leaving snowdrifts well above fifteen feet."

"That's not usual?"

"We might get some snow, but never that much. A friend of William's said maybe Uncle Adolph has his fingers in the weather somehow, with a new technology. One more way to make his enemy miserable."

"Hmm. Uncle Adolph, is it? Guess those poor devils over there have to find a little humor. Nothing like that storm has ever hit here, far as I know. Sounds more like Montana, the Dakotas, Minnesota, Iowa. Anyway, we shouldn't have to worry."

A native's perspective—just the thing to calm one's fears.

On the twenty-second, we did have snow, enough to glorify our world with an elegant covering. Donnie and I popped in on William and Lillian after school, only to discover that William had developed a bad case of the sniffles. He had taken up the milking again soon after Abigail's birth, but I suggested we cover for him for a few days.

"You wouldn't want to pass that cold on to this little one."

Truly miserable, he agreed without argument. The next afternoon, we found him pale, weak and hoarse. He scoffed at my mention of the local physician, but the next morning after I dropped Donnie at school, Lillian said William's chest had hurt all night. I made haste to the medical office in the doctor's home a few blocks away. After the Thanksgiving play, we had met him briefly.

Fortunately he agreed to see William straight off. Turning his OPEN sign to BACK IN HALF AN HOUR, he started our conversation with, "You were right to come, with that newborn in the house."

Before issuing a diagnosis, he listened to William breathe and checked his heart.

"Pleurisy. Good thing we're starting treatment now, or this could turn into pneumonia." He turned to Lillian. "I'm leaving you with enough sulphapyridine tablets for fourteen days. One three times a day with a full glass of water, and make sure he drinks several more glasses during the day.

"They just discovered this medicine in '37. In England, doctors might call it M&B. Sulpha can affect the kidneys, so don't skimp on the water. If you see no change in three or four days, or if his condition worsens, let me know."

It took more than a week for William to recover his strength, and he memorized the news reports while resting. Every time I peeked in, he rehearsed the war's timeline. But stay in, he did. Anything to keep Lillian and sweet Abigail healthy.

Daily, Donnie watched for changes in her behavior. There, that must be a definite smile, didn't I think?

Oh, how that child loved her big cousin—her eyes lighted when he drew near, and she grabbed for his finger. His presence always produced smiles, while the sight of my face brought only tears. Perhaps it was my mustache, Lillian said.

How proud Donnie was to hold Abigail for the first time, and so careful, she might have been a fine crystal vase. I stayed in the background, with memories of his infancy surfacing. I could never get enough of holding Donnie, but Victoria—

The snow melted, temperatures rose, and one afternoon when we were feeding the animals, I had Donnie fetch the pencil we had set in a crack back in December. On the day of the winter solstice, we marked where the sun left its shadow on the wall.

"Watch from where the shadow starts, and see how it moves toward the vernal equinox in March. In the Southern hemisphere, just the opposite is happening."

"The seasons are switched around for them?"

"Yes. Or for us, from their point of view."

He recalled that lesson quite accurately. No surprise here—Mrs. Bultmann told me after school one day that he was studying several subjects with the second graders.

"You have prepared him so well, Mr. Herring. You must be proud."

Against the rosy blue of a winter sky, the sun burnished her dark hair. Until then, I had noticed nothing in particular about her, except her power to entice a young boy's imagination. Average height, average weight—nothing out of the ordinary. But framed by sunshine, her dark eyes seemed altogether soft and rich.

Donnie ran up then, so we started home. When we turned onto the road, I glimpsed Mrs. Bultmann, now surrounded by students—quite the feat to maintain control and teach so many different levels.

Donnie mentioned something and pointed back to the school-house. Perhaps I imagined it, but her gaze seemed to follow us.

April 1941

Aided by Italian forces, General Rommel's Afrika Korps forced a British retreat in their eastward drive against Tobruk, Libya. At the same time, a four-pronged Nazi attack was overwhelming Yugoslavia, Bulgaria, Austria, Romania, and Hungary.

Hitler's forces also attacked Greece from Bulgaria across the Pineios River in Thessaly, forcing 50,000 British soldiers to retreat. As Lillian's brother put it at our Easter dinner, "How kin that crazy Hun keep winnin'? He never wanted to attack Greece, is what I hear. It was only 'cause of that Mussolini fella . . ."

Discussing the war with Kenneth would never do, especially on Easter Sunday, so William took a brilliant tack. He posed a topic dear to Kenneth's heart.

"Tell Everett about this ham, won't you? I can hardly believe your family has been working with this breed for so long."

So we learned a great deal about the American Berkshire

Association, which Kenneth and Lillian's great grandfather joined in the late 1800s. The pedigree still hung in their family store, and living on the home place, Kenneth kept up the herd.

I longed to share what I knew about Berkshires, that Pig-Wig, the sow in Beatrix Potter's *The Tale of Pigling Bland*, most definitely boasted the same pedigree. Donnie caught my eye, and I could see he read my thoughts.

He shook his head *No* just the slightest. The message came across, and I settled back in my chair. A time for silence—we would rest content keeping this knowledge between us. Was that the slip of a grin on my son's face? Could he tell that Kenneth had likely never heard of Beatrix Potter?

As soon as we set out for home, he opined, "*Once upon a time there was an old pig called Aunt Pettitoes. She had eight of a family: four little girl pigs, Cross-patch, Suck-suck, Yock-yock and Spot; and four little boy pigs, called Alexander, Pigling Bland, Chin-Chin and Stumpy. Stumpy had had an accident to his tail.*"

"You remember the beginning word-for-word!"

"You read it to me a thousand times."

"You asked for it as many."

"I did?"

"Indeed. I wondered if you would ever tire of that story. Did you?"

"No."

"Perhaps because Pigling Bland was a wayfarer needing a friend."

"Yes, he was afraid sometimes."

"But always faithful and obedient. Your attachment to him told me the story was important, though eventually you grew beyond it."

"When did we read *The Secret Garden*?"

"Soon after that, I expect."

We walked in silence for a while, and Donnie's next statement declared he had passed onto some new plateau.

"Could I be a writer, Da?"

"I don't know why not. What would you write?"

"Stories about people. I bet Beatrix Potter knew somebody like

Pigling Bland, so she wrote about him. I would do that—without saying who they were."

"Anybody in particular?"

We had arrived home by then, and Donnie scuffed his shoes on the iron scraper. Then he almost whispered, "Anton."

"What would you write about him?"

"He gets so sad when the boys call him names. They made up a rhyme, too. 'Liar, liar, your panzer on fire.'"

"*Panzer?* As in a German tank?"

A nod was answer enough, and eyes filled as we entered the house. Once in the kitchen, he spouted, "Sometimes I'd like to punch them guys right in the gut."

What a mix, this lad. Reciting Beatrix Potter one minute, fighting his uncouth schoolmates the next.

Chapter Nine

Mid-May 1941

For the most part, Nottingham had escaped the ruthless Luftwaffe, but on May ninth, the "Nottingham Blitz" took 150 lives, injured several hundred people, and left over a thousand homeless. New descriptors emerged for the attack.

Savage. Uncalled for. Spiteful. Malicious. Vicious. Cruel. Hateful.

And for the perpetrators: *miscreants, malefactors, villains. Reprobates. Degenerates.* Suffice it to say, short of outright vulgarity, Donnie would suffer no lack of synonyms for the word *enemies.*

On the Sunday after the bombings, William rummaged for a map of the city and showed Donnie where the bombs had fallen. Donnie's reaction surprised us both.

"Is Mrs. Tillman all right? Did they hit her house?"

"Perhaps we shall hear from her soon to confirm our hopes for the best." William scanned the map again. "But it looks as if her area most likely escaped the onslaught."

"Good. When we go there, I want to eat one of her crumpets."

Where had he gotten this idea? We had never mentioned journeying back home.

"I'm going to write her a letter tonight."

"A wonderful idea. I shall post it tomorrow."

Most reports agreed that the toll would have been far greater if not for the Starfish decoy system at Cropwell Butler. *Starfish sites*, parcels of countryside designed to act as nighttime decoys, protected the actual targets of German pilots. These innovative projects called upon the ingenuity of local citizens in conjunction with the War Ministry Office.

William positively beamed as he shared details. "Workers waited until after the first wave of bombers. Then they set the decoy sites on fire to mimic burning factories and other city buildings. In the dark of night, the burning sites appeared to require more bombing, so German pilots honed in on them.

"Thus, of the more than 400 bombs that fell on Nottingham, many simply widened the bomb craters in the Vale of Belvoir."

He gloated as if this deception had been his idea. "You see, Donnie, this is what your forebears have been doing for centuries. The Vale has been the site of many a battle. You have heard of Norman the Conqueror?"

"The Battle of Hastings."

"Indeed. The Vale, a wide, shallow valley, takes its name from the first castle built there by a Norman lord, William the Conqueror's standard bearer at Hastings in 1066. He positioned Belvoir Castle, pronounced *beaver*, on the hills of Belvoir Ridge, at almost 500 feet high."

"Like House Mountain?"

"Comparatively, yes, but keep in mind that our Hill Country is much higher than the island of England. Belvoir means *beautiful view* in Norman French. A fitting name, for from that castle, the Nottinghamshire and Leicestershire countryside is visible as far as Lincolnshire."

"Lincoln?"

"Yes. President Lincoln's family hails back to England's King Edward Plantangenet. Your great-grandfather took great pride in this."

"Did Great-Grandfather tell you that, Da?"

Feeling like a criminal, I shrugged. "Surely he did, but memory fails me right now. We have so much history yet to learn."

William patted Donnie's shoulder. "The story goes on and on, but back to the Nottingham Blitz. Small villages and fertile farmland fill the Vale—the land has been farmed since the New Stone Age. In the 1400s, the castle was destroyed by the Wars of the Roses, and three others have been built since. The present one was erected during the first part of the Seventeenth Century for the Duke and Duchess of Rutland."

"Can we visit it when we go to Nottingham?"

I uttered a hearty "Absolutely" before William reclaimed the floor.

"How heartening to hear about our college students during this terrible time. Listen to this:

The attack originated shortly after midnight on the night of the eighth. When the all-clear siren sounded at about 4:30 a.m., eleven separate bomber raids had terrorized factories and industrial sites, including Raleigh and Boots.

Staff and students from University College had been volunteering for regular all-night fire-watching duties since 1940. They kept vigil at the city centre and University Park campuses in readiness for incendiary and explosives bomb attacks.

In the early hours of the ninth, the buildings on Shakespeare Street took a direct hit. Two of the firewatchers carried on with their duties in spite of minor injuries. They experienced good fortune compared to those at the Co-Op bakery on Meadow Lane. There, a direct hit killed forty-eight employees and a member of the Home Guard. Twenty others who had sought refuge in the air raid shelter in the basement suffered injuries.

At the College, bombs destroyed parts of the Gothic Revival building. Passersby viewed shattered windows and roof tiles blown off from the force of the blast, and walls still standing covered in shrapnel cracks and craters.

The west wing bore the brunt, as the Mining and Textiles Departments, including laboratories, were destroyed. The rest of the building was, in the words of the University Council 'scarred and heavily shaken'. Looking at the severity of the damage, one would never think that within a week the building would be repaired so that classes could resume."

"Who would have thought our ancient city would be struck like this?" A sick sensation filled me, and Lillian joined in.

"How old is the city?"

"In the Sixth Century, it began as a small settlement where people forded the River Trent. A man named Snotta owned it. The word *inga* meant belonging to, and *ham* meant city, so it was called Snotta inga ham, eventually shortened to Nottingham."

"So it was there long before the Norman Conquest."

"Yes, by then the Danes had conquered and turned the city into a fortification. When the English re-claimed the village in 920, the King built a bridge across the Trent. In 1067, William the Conqueror built a wooden castle to guard Nottingham, and it was rebuilt with stone in the Twelfth Century."

"When you say ancient history, you really mean it."

"Indeed. We could teach a year-long class on what happened after the Norman Conquest. The thought of those priceless buildings crumbling makes me heartsick."

Donnie, engaged with the apple pie Lillian set before us, perked up. "Do you think Norman's family lived in Nottinghamshire during the conquest?"

Much of the time, he seemed far older than his age, but was still a youngster after all.

Late July 1941

"How about you and your boy ridin' down to Fredericksburg with me to the *Schutzenfest* the first weekend of August?" Norman tossed a wooden coin in the air, landing it in his palm. "They mint a new one of these every year, or at least they did until last year."

"I imagine it's like the ones in the Old Country, although the coins in Switzerland and Germany are silver. Do they crown a king here?"

"Yep. And drink a lot of beer."

"Perhaps we could go. Thank you for the invitation."

"Best bratwurst around. Be good for you to see a little more of the country."

Gallivanting had little appeal, but perhaps Norman had a point. Though Donnie and I had read Texas history since winter—biographies of Sam Houston, Lorenzo de Zavala, Stephen Austin, Santa Anna, and of course, Davy Crockett and the battle of the Alamo—this state's topography remained a mystery.

The story of Colonel Travis, Davy and Jim Bowie defending the Alamo to the death magnetized us, and I was glad we had visited the site in San Antonio. Seeing places always brings them to life, and Donnie had a thorough foundational understanding of Texas history, as noted by Mrs. Bultmann on his final examination. Beside his A in social studies, she wrote, "Good work—someday you may be a history professor."

"What would you think of that?"

Donnie pondered as he wolfed down sausage and potatoes for supper. "Might not be so bad if everybody paid attention."

"Do some of the students give Mrs. B a hard time?"

"The older boys make trouble. The other day, one of them sassed her."

"Really? What did he say?"

"Somethin' I can't repeat. Mrs. B's face got all red and she took him outside. We could hear her ask him for evidence."

"And that was the end of it?"

"Nope. When they came back, he started talking about her husband being in Germany. You should have heard Anton yell, Da. 'You'd better be careful what you say about my dad!'"

"I thought they were gonna fight, but Mrs. B sent Bert home."

"Hmm. I started to carry dishes from the table, picturing Jerrold James about fifty years younger. But Donnie had more to say.

"Why would Anton's dad go to Germany?"

"I don't know about Mr. Bultmann, but I have something to tell you. Wash off the table for a look at our Texas map."

Soon, Donnie leaned in as I pointed out Fredericksburg. "Remember the depot there?"

"Sure do. Yellow and green."

"Righto. Well, most people there have a strong German heritage, and still celebrate some of the same holidays as back in Germany. Would you like to go to one?"

"Looks like a long way."

"Not really, compared to the expanse of our whole state." His reaction sealed my decision to accept Norman's invitation—life was too short to foster a narrow view of the world.

After walking through the orchard and reading more Texas history, Donnie returned to the subject of the older boys. Although I had never mentioned it, I found myself describing my classroom experiences with "older boys" like Bert.

"You were a teacher?"

"Yes, for a while after you were born, and for—oh, about eight years before that. All in England, of course, where things are a bit different."

After we said goodnight, Donnie asked for more details.

"Teaching seemed the natural course, as I had always been studious. Before I graduated from university, an offer came for a position close by, and I accepted. I was able to stay at home and ride my bicycle or a bus in poor weather."

"What was it like?" His tell-me-more tone sank any hopes of limited disclosure.

Memories burgeoned once I began, and Donnie's curiosity stoked even more. As he finally grew sleepy, a realization came. As I circled our house under the stars, it grew to fullness.

Since those years, I had grown into an entirely different person with no desire to teach. I wished I had kept those memories stuffed down deep. Some aspects of that former life were better held in port.

Alone in the yard, I allowed them to surface, but only briefly. Images of Victoria filtered through, for her behavior had spelled the end of my career. Her nighttime escapades, noted by the local constable, assured my demise as a public figure in the community, and then she went even further.

Surely, I had let all of this go—left it forever back in Nottinghamshire. Life had become, instead of moving from crisis to crisis, a one-day-at-a-time embrace of work and family.

But under this quiet sky, emotion blindsided me, and I might have been reliving every miserable moment. On the back steps, I quieted myself. Solid old sandstones urged me back into serenity.

Let sleeping dogs lie. Forgive and forget.

Ah, such difficult advice, since forgiving differs greatly from forgetting. I thought I had forgiven all wrongs, since during my last months of teaching, Victoria made life a hellish thing. But on a wayward breeze, yet another bitter tide washed me through.

Though she had been buried all these years, her rashness—whatever the alienists in London hospitals might label it—had destroyed a thing of beauty. Teaching became a work of art as my students and I jostled ideas like a juggler's tenpins. Stirring their young minds and challenging them to prove their untried views had kept me challenged.

Like all of us, they believed what they had been told. Not out to unsettle them unduly, I wanted them to think things through for themselves.

Truth be told, I missed that sort of interaction. After all, this had been my chosen vocation, and I gave it my all. To be torn from my students amounted to a travesty, and that singular accomplishment belonged to Victoria.

Acknowledging this anew strained every cell in my body. In the stillness, individual students came to the fore. Harold Watkins, Tommy Alberts, Winifred Pincher, Mercer Cotton, Elliot Colman. One after the other, their faces paraded before me. Where were they now?

Most likely, they had already passed through training and were serving somewhere on the globe. So young—as young as my father had been when he went off to fight in France.

111

Then something from last Sunday's sermon broke into my thoughts. "Forgiving others means setting ourselves free by letting go of our devastation at another's hand. This new freedom enables us to grow in unprecedented ways and underscores the deep meaning of, 'Unless you forgive others their trespasses . . .'" In English, the message seemed designed just for me.

Suddenly restless, I peeked in at Donnie before circling once more. Never could I forget what Victoria did, but had I truly forgiven her? My image of dear Nottingham smashed by bombs provided a perfect metaphor for the rubble she had created. Yet already, people had begun to rebuild. Bitterness would only hinder that process.

But the *act* of forgiveness amounted to emotional labor no one else could perform. How to forsake the righteous indignation that accompanied Victoria's betrayal, even this long after the act?

Scenes from the fire raged before me, along with another incident even less forgivable. I realized anew that classifying it thus kept me in chains.

What if one desired to forgive, yet found it impossible? This very verbiage contradicted itself. If I wanted to let go of this wrong, it followed that I would find a way.

"I'll pick you up at six in the morning." Norman ruffled Donnie's hair just before he left for home. "Bring a little something to eat for our stop at Enchanted Rock."

"A rock that's enchanted?"

"Yep, a granite mass on the flatland north of Fredericksburg, with caves, hidden pools and creatures we don't normally see. Maybe you and your dad can climb to the top. Would you like that?"

"Oh, yeah!"

Donnie busied himself making sandwiches while I checked on the animals. Strange how attached one gets to a barnyard. We had accumulated miscellaneous ducks, geese, and enough chickens to sell a few dozen eggs a week to the local store.

The cows, a few goats William bought for making goat cheese, the pony Donnie finally named Risk—a story all its own—and a squat hound from Norman shared the barn. Interestingly, the goats arrived on the same day as the pup, Ramshackle by name.

"He wandered onto my land. Named him for the way he runs— his legs get all mixed up. Seems like he's goin' nowhere, but he covers ground in a mighty hurry."

Ramshackle often chased away hungry foxes or stray rabbits. He launched several missions per day and afterward, happily collapsed near the pump. Preventing trouble earned him his keep. Of course, Donnie loved him, and sometimes I heard him murmur to Ramshackle, who followed him like a devotee.

"Don't you worry, boy. The Brits'll get them Germans, I just know they will."

On this evening before the auspicious day when we would leave home overnight, I wondered why I had ever said yes. William would take care of things, but the idea of being absent from our normal daily tasks bothered me.

Waking up to do the chores, walking Donnie to school, checking the trees, digging around any that looked a bit off, fertilizing the soil, working the cider press—simple everyday activities. But they composed my life.

Why leave, even for a day? I suppose recluses staunchly adhere to this principle, so the cycle perpetuates itself.

Forfeiting nearly two days to a German shooting festival seemed a poor choice. First of all, though William had purchased two rifles as soon as we arrived, I had no interest in marksmanship. But I reminded myself that Donnie deserved to know something of the outside world.

When I re-entered the house as twilight slipped into darkness, my reward lay in his excitement. He had packed more food than we could possibly eat and hunched over the map, plotting our course. A few years ago, he had crossed an ocean and half of this wide continent, but this short jaunt would mean far more to him.

Chapter Ten

"This all started in the mid-1800s, when German immigrants formed *schuetzenbundes*, their lingo for shooting clubs. Back then, a man fed his family by hunting, so shooting became an art. Farmers and ranchers aimed to earn the highest mark—a hundred points."

Norman's voice competed with his old truck's engine while dust poured in through holes in the floorboards. Donnie bounced between us like one of those bobble head dolls.

"We'll see all kinds of rifles, some a century old. There's the rim-fire, or falling block action, rolling block, and high-rise. The shooters like to describe their chosen weapons. Sometimes they hold this festival in Grapetown, nine miles south of Fredericksburg, where the very first one was held, or in Tivydale, west about fifteen miles. We'll be in German country through and through."

He went on about the fest's well-defined rules. "Every shooter gets three chances for their best score on Saturday or Sunday. Then the best scorers vie for first place."

Potholes the size of pickle barrels offered considerable resistance to our progress, and even more dust burst in. Donnie and I took turns sneezing.

"In all these years, only a few have shot a perfect round. I think it's three."

"They never missed?"

"That's right. Out of eight or ten shooters with a target fifty yards away, a man with a perfect round always scores highest. Now, about Tivydale, where we'll stay tonight. Population was fifteen in the '33 census, but might be almost thirty by now.

"Used to be called Pumpkinville. That changed to Bunkesville, and then some fella named Tivy donated land for a school, so they re-named the town again. Where we're staying, the owner cooks the best breakfast you ever ate."

Donnie jumped when Norman slapped his hand on the steering wheel. "The Bunkesville Band can sure muster up a polka! Not sure why they kept that name—anyhow, there'll be a lot of dancing right out in the street."

Norman's storytelling held us rapt right up to a great pink granite protrusion. Enchanted Rock. There, he proposed we get out and stretch our legs.

"Came around the long way 'cause I knew you'd like this place. Only eighteen miles left down to Fredericksburg. It's a little more than a mile to the top, but we've only got an hour. Maybe you can get halfway up and back."

Donnie and I climbed fast, to gaze over the hill country from a new angle. My angst about this trip dissipated in the dry Texas air.

"Just think, Da! Indians used to walk around up here. Let's look for arrowheads…"

"I'd like that, but we'll have to come back. Maybe we can find some of those pools Norman mentioned. And look over there—a meadow right on the rock."

"And an oak grove over there!" Donnie gestured left as a horned toad skittered by.

"Listen—I think that's an oriole singing. Can you see him anywhere?"

"Yeah. We must not have any at our place."

"Norman was right—this is a world all to itself, and not far away from Loyal Valley. We'll come back, for sure."

We hurried back down the path. From the moment we got in to the outskirts of Fredericksburg, Donnie took over the conversation.

"Some day I want to go inside that cave we saw way up the slope.

Bet animals live in there, and maybe the Indians used to, do you think? Wonder which tribe—"

Norman slid in a word when he took a breath. "The Tonkawas and the Comanche left us a lot of legends. Some might even be true."

At this, Donnie turned wild-eyed. "What legends?"

"One tribe claims a band of warriors, the last of their kind, defended attacks from other tribes on Enchanted Rock. The others finally overcame them, and ever since, their ghosts have haunted the place."

"Wow! Did you see anything up there, Da?"

"No, and nary a shiver went down my spine."

"Then there's the story of an Indian princess who watched her people get slaughtered and threw herself off the rock in despair. They say her spirit haunts the place still. Then there's an Indian chief who sacrificed his daughter, and for punishment had to walk forever up on the rock—the indentations on the summit are his footprints."

"Sacrificed—but why? Oh, Da, we've gotta come back. Can you imagine—"

At this point, I added my opinion. "That last one strikes me as a bit difficult to believe."

"There's another one about a white woman taken captive by the Indians. She escaped and lived up inside the caves. They say you can hear her screams at night."

"Wow. I gotta tell Anton about this."

"Absolutely. He might not have heard, even though he's always lived in Texas."

Norman quirked his eyebrow. "You sure 'bout that?"

"As far as I know."

"You mean the teacher's boy? I wouldn't be so slap-dash sure."

I wanted to ask more, but the city limits came into view and Norman stopped at the Eckhardt Orchards peach stand. There, I learned the difference between cling and freestone peaches, something Grandfather had never mentioned.

Our open windows provided a preview of the festival. Polka music, distinct and loud, rained down. The mish-mash of noise from people all together in a relatively small area joined the repeat of rifle fire in the distance.

"Where do they do the shooting?"

"Over there." Norman gestured as he parked the truck. "They've got a big range and ten stanchions for the competitors. But you could spend a few hours here and never even go near the shooting. If you're hungry, the bratwurst is out of this world."

"Maybe later—Donnie's sandwiches filled me up for now."

Scrambling over my legs to get out, Donnie ran ahead a little. Sometimes, right in the middle of something, you realize it's a pivotal moment.

This qualified: he would be running ahead of me from now on. Of course I knew this already, but this weekend might help me let go just a little more.

The town's residents had certainly decorated every nook and cranny. One would be hard put to find a corner without bright swaths of bunting, and flower boxes adorned every window in sight. Pots of flaming red geraniums marched up and down the steps of houses and public buildings.

The band Norman mentioned, along with many others, divulged polka music as powerful as the scents in the air. All manner of sausages, Weiner schnitzel with broad homemade noodles, sauerkraut, home-baked dark bread, and potato dishes arrayed long wooden tables to tempt passersby. Women and men toted heavily loaded platters and trays to outdoor tents, with children engaged as helpers.

Around every corner, horses awaited their masters, single or in pairs tethered to carts or buggies. The smell of horseflesh had become like the smell of the forests in Nottingham, always present. Plenty of automobiles lined the side streets, as well, many of them bubble-tops like Norman's.

After we wandered around and watched some of the shooting, Norman suggested we drive over to our rooming house and eat

117

dinner. "Won't take long. We'll come right back, and this way, you'll see more of the countryside while it's still light."

Mrs. Friesen, who managed English with a bit of a roll, showed us to a table laden with goulash, German potato salad, and trays of Weiner schnitzel. We arrived in time to join six other guests around a massive table. They were discussing area history, and we took our seats just as one of them launched into a description of Civil War times in these parts.

"Some men from Gillespie County joined the unionists when the Confederates imposed martial law on this part of Texas. Back then, patriots from Kerr, Gillespie, and Kendall counties organized what they called the Union League, a secret group supporting President Lincoln and the Union.

"Two of them from Grapetown named Hoffman and Rausch, plus about sixty more, called themselves conscientious objectors. They fled south in 1861 to avoid being harassed by the Confederates."

"A group called Duff's Partisan Rangers took up arms for the Confederacy and overtook the Grapetown men at the Nueces River. Killed thirty-four on the spot. Others, they took prisoner and executed, but Hoffman and Rausch survived and hid in the hills."

Before the subject turned, Norman interjected, "Nothing in Texas history has been easy."

Donnie whispered to me, "Just like England."

An hour later, we returned to Fredericksburg for the last round of shooting. As we neared the range, someone started yelling.

"Donnie! Donnie! Over here!"

There stood Anton, so loaded down with boxes we could scarcely view his head. His mother followed a few steps behind, carrying twice as much. They caught up with us and she panted, "We're helping my grandfather. He's in charge of—" The rest came out in German. She set her load down and we chatted a few minutes. Norman retreated a few feet and kicked at some stones.

Donnie pulled on my hand. "Could I help Anton, Da?"

"I don't see why not. Actually, maybe we both should help you. What if we join you a little later, Norman?"

"Sure enough." He went on his way as Donnie and I hefted some boxes.

"Oh, thank you. We do this over and over, but things seem to get heavier each year." Mrs. Bultmann led the way to a warehouse where we set everything down on a long wooden counter.

"This is my Grandpa's building, full of merchandise for several stores in town. Why don't you get Donnie a treat, Anton?"

"C'mon, Donnie. Opa has the best—"

"Just one, all right? And be sure to latch the door." Mrs. Bultmann wiped her forehead with a hankie.

"So you grew up here?"

"A few miles away, but I've attended these festivals since I was a babe in arms."

"Quite the community effort."

"Yes. Somehow, though, each August seems hotter than the last. With jobs like this, one never gets to retire."

"Hmm . . ."

"Are you enjoying yourself?"

"Oh, yes. It's our first time away from Loyal Valley, so Donnie's quite excited. We gleaned some history lessons along the way."

"Enchanted Rock?"

"Yes, Norman has no end of tales to tell."

The boys banged through the door, each with a piece of hard candy.

"Time for us to get back to the shooting, Donnie?"

"Would he like to come along with us? Anton and I have more chores, but doing them with a friend would make it easier."

"Da?" The intensity in Donnie's voice could not be denied.

"All right. Shall we meet back here?"

"We'll be out in front in about an hour for the parade and dance. You might want to visit the *Vereins Kirche* over there." She gestured with her head. "It's the heart and soul of this place and our ancestors. You'll know it when you see a building with eight sides. When the first settlers came, it served as a church, school, and meeting house. They tore it down in 1897 but in '35, our historical society built a replica as a museum."

"Vereins ..."

"It means Society Church. The founders were Lutheran, but they built the kirche so people of all faiths could worship there."

They were off then, leaving me with a glorious evening sky. The sun slipped toward the horizon, creating a breathtaking masterpiece. Last night, the moon had been almost full, and tonight promised another unobstructed view of the heavens. Even against all these lights, the stars would stand out.

The heavenly expanse seemed even more vast than normal as I strolled to the edge of town. After our enormous meal, my digestion, like Grandfather's, called for a walk.

Orderly streets, swept clean, lovely old stone houses, and window boxes full of flowers greeted me. I might have been in Germany, back when Grandfather and I visited one winter. The pine boughs dipped with heavy wet snow at that time, but the feeling remained the same.

Perhaps anywhere you spent time accompanied you when you left, to resurface some day. Having a grandfather here seemed idyllic, and questions filled my mind. Did Anton and his mother come here often? And why had his father gone to Germany? Most of all, what would become of him as Herr Hitler tightened his noose around his own people?

Wandering back to the *Verein Kirche*, I noted that the Civil Works Administration had helped complete the building, filled with artifacts from the first pioneers. No matter where I went, I learned more from their stories, and every new tidbit highlighted their tenacity.

Some time before the shooting ended I found Norman, and we veered downtown for the evening festivities. Such dancing in the streets! Anton and Donnie imitated flag-toting young men goose-stepping in the parade behind last year's King of the

Shooters, a man in his thirties. And the horses—oh my! Arrayed in fresh flowers and shiny harness sets, they added a regal flair.

Surely, a force of workers must be tasked with cleaning up after them, for not once did I spy—or smell—a warm pile of droppings.

When I turned my attention to the dancing, one woman in particular caught my eye. In the typical native costume with a ribbon in her hair and a bright apron, her eyes sparkled like the stars. Graceful, lithe and seeming much younger, Mrs. Bultmann flitted through traditional moves, linking elbows, taking hands, clapping and being twirled through the air by muscular townsmen.

The whole time, her dark eyes glittered like gems. I had never noticed her smile before, most likely because she always concentrated on her students at school activities.

Norman knew someone on every corner and quickly engaged in conversation with a long, lean Texan, so I simply stood and stared. The music seemed to bring out the best in everyone, pulling pleasure from them no matter how far down they had tucked it. All the while, one unique laugh out of many drew me.

This wild rhythm was created for letting loose, and unfettered by daily cares, Mrs. Bultmann responded. As usual, nothing about her appearance stood out, but her every move captured my imagination.

Alarm zigzagged my spine. I had experienced this once before, when Victoria's fine features held me in a daze. But that strong physical attraction seemed quite different from what I was experiencing. All those years ago, my enchantment rendered me incapable of imagining life without Victoria, while this was different.

Even tonight, Mrs. Bultmann's strength stood front and center. A woman left alone, perhaps by mutual consent, to care for their son. But she also executed a full-time teaching position.

One fact, though, stayed with me even after we arrived home. At this celebration, she allowed herself to let go. Even with her challenges, she found a way to enter this annual festivity, a sign of wholeness in spite of her situation.

The trouble with life is that you receive no warning when

something unexpected will present itself. Norman was still talking with another bystander when I emerged from the mad polka's spell. Not far off, Donnie and Anton still marched in their own parade.

Like a man waking, I shook myself. All I wanted was to watch this singular dancer, could have watched her forever, though I had never even heard her first name.

Smitten, perhaps, might best describe my state, yet I had no longing to take my son's teacher in my arms, no romantic designs as with Victoria. No, this surpassed that sort of *smitten*. For one thing, I had sworn I would never again fall prey to a brutal allure that might upend my life.

No, this amounted to a singular desire to know someone—to converse at length, to explore her world. Whatever had occurred, my mind still managed to work, as had proven untrue with Victoria. Donnie, happily engaged in being a boy, remained at the top of my priorities. Besides, this vibrant woman had a husband.

Once I had entered into a union irrevocable except by death, and discovered unutterable misery. Despite my present emotions, my escape from those tentacles left no craving to return.

Chapter Eleven

September 1941

"*T*he ability of Londoners to maintain their composure had much to do with Britain's survival during this trying period.*"

"What does he mean?" Donnie was forever asking questions as we listened to the radio. Every night, we turned on the news report after closing up the house for the night and snuggled into our voluminous armchair.

"Edward R. Murrow is describing how British citizens have stuck with their determination to fight off the Luftwaffe, no matter what. Remember that one night at William's? Mr. Murrow mentioned not showing their hand…"

"Yeah, he said, 'This is London—'"

"Quite. What a terrible siege the people there have endured, but if they had sloughed off, it would be like someone throwing in their hand during a poker game. That can even mean to lose intentionally."

"Why would anybody try to lose?"

A difficult question to answer, but I had probably chosen this very tactic with Victoria. After a while, our battles became a never-ending repetition, so why not let her do as she pleased? I never won, anyway—why keep fighting? Tantamount to losing intentionally, since the struggle had lost its meaning.

"Sometimes a fight seems hopeless. Someone is being beaten so badly that they simply give in."

"But not England?"

"No. Mr. Murrow applauds her citizens for their fortitude."

On the thirteenth of the month, President Roosevelt expounded in his Fireside Chat upon the Greer incident. Because a German submarine had fired on an American destroyer in waters near Iceland, he argued for more intervention in the war. He called the incident an act of aggression and ordered escorts to protect Lend Lease convoys and shoot German submarines on sight.

In the spring, air raids over England had ceased for all practical purposes when Hitler began massing his forces near the border of the USSR. Along with our countrymen, William and I breathed sighs of relief. For the time being, thoroughly engaged with the Russians, the Nazis had cast aside thought for our Isle.

At the same time, no one doubted that Herr Hitler would once again turn his attention on Old Blighty, so our defenses remained at the ready. Hopefully, by the time the Russians had finished fighting his troops on the Eastern Front, his punch would possess far less power.

Harvest was upon us, so once again we engaged in end-of-the-season work. Listening to reports from the vast reaches of the Russian empire disturbed us far less than the accounts of destruction in London last year at this time—a momentary reprieve.

Nearly three years had passed since we arrived in Mason County, and life overflowed with hard work and growing satisfaction. Enlarging the basement shelves to accommodate more apple cider and jam brought a sense of fulfillment. Our intuition—mostly William's—had proven accurate. This land could provide a living.

Three stores now bought our cheese, jam, milk, and cider. Every Monday I hitched Risk to the wagon for short delivery trips. I say *our* products because it never occurred to me to divide our earnings. Eventually one of our products might suddenly come into higher demand and require more alteration, but so far that had not occurred.

A coffee can we stored in Grandfather's safe held profits from the vegetable and fruit stand Donnie and I manned. William and I built the small structure at the end of our drive, but he insisted we separate this money from the rest.

"Someday Donnie will need funds for his education." More than once, William also suggested we divide our cider and jam earnings from his cheese and milk profits. "After all, you bought the land, and keep my cows."

"But you buy the grain and hay, and supply all we can eat."

"Still, the land is yours."

"But we found it together, and you helped us settle in, built the barn— Besides, I never would have made the decision to come without your support."

I could have gone on. When Donnie was born, William helped with everything—cared for him while I taught school, summoned the doctor when Victoria lost control. He kept watch when she turned erratic and wandered about in the night—I shuddered to think how much sleep he had lost during that terrible time.

And then during the fire—who could say enough about his service? He saved what could be saved, and in the aftermath, saw to Victoria's funeral arrangements.

Through it all, he became my confidant—in a word, took Grandfather's place. As I recalled Grandfather's great interest in visiting the United States, I finally mentioned the idea. William confirmed my thinking, and shocked me by saying he would accompany me. His summation perched in my memory like a signpost.

"Whatever would I do here without Donnie and you?"

In a word, we were family. Now William had found Lillian, and little Abigail had become an adorable sprite crawling everywhere. Donnie spent most of our visits making her giggle.

Just last Sunday, he *walked* her across the room to me. She lurched into my arms, clutching my fingers even as she pivoted so as to not lose sight of Donnie.

"Little one, your grip is in fine fettle! My, but you have grown strong!"

Abigail completely ignored my attempt at conversation and

called for Donnie. He came to her rescue, as always, and they tod-dled off across the room. That crystal moment solidified something in me, a fortification that had been growing stone by stone since our visit to Fredericksburg.

Life was good *as is*. Whatever opportunities might come, our simple country existence had grown into something beautiful, and my fleeting attraction to Mrs. Bultmann at the shooting fest had been just that.

School interested Donnie as much as ever, although he brought home more tales concerning Anton. Being the teacher's son would call forth a certain amount of harassment, I allowed. But the older boys' attitudes had more to do with his father. I wondered about him, too. What could be holding him in enemy territory for so long?

The boys insisted he was fighting for the Nazis, and if so, might eventually be in battles with family members from the States. This could happen, indeed. Accounts of cousins fighting cousins in the Great War still circulated. At that time, three heads of state had actually been cousins—King George V, the son of Queen Victoria, Tsar Nicholas III, and Kaiser Wilhelm II.

But an American fighting for the Germans? The very idea sounded reprehensible, yet just five years ago many Americans risked all to join the Spanish battle against fascism. More than 30,000 volunteers from upwards of forty nations registered for the International Brigades to defend Spain's Republic.

The Americans who fought there called themselves the *Abraham Lincoln Battalion*. This conglomeration of over a thousand steel workers, miners, longshoremen, and students sailed to Spain to meet with other internationals. Though the British government deemed such service illegal, beginning in '36, many Englishmen also traveled to Spain to take up arms, as well.

Poets and intellectuals like George Orwell and W. H. Auden fought alongside working class men against the military uprising led by Franco and supported by Germany's rising star, whom most now acknowledged as a madman. These volunteers, mostly in their twenties, joined the Republicans in standing for the common man and a legitimate government.

In '37, when Hitler unleashed his Condor Legion on Guernica, the cultural heartland of the Basque people, he did so on market day when women and children flooded the city. Reports of this atrocity still burned in my mind, especially that of war correspondent George Steer:

"On Guernica loosed their venom,
Hammered helpless men and women
Into pulped and writhing earth.
Thus they brought the blitz to birth."

Those Englishmen who fought for freedom in Spain presaged the future, the horrific London blitz. To comprehend an American-born man of German heritage fighting for his mother country took a greater leap of the imagination, but a strong cultural connection still remained. The *Schutzenfest* had evidenced this first-hand.

Had Anton's father fallen for Nazi propaganda while in Germany with family? Perhaps his relatives had joined the party, and he felt it his duty to follow suit. With the world in such turmoil, this scenario seemed peculiar, yet entirely possible.

One day, Donnie handed me a note in perfect script. I saved it to read while he helped William with the cows and goats. Mrs. Bultmann merely noted Donnie's progress. When he asked about the note at supper, I told him as much.

"School is going well, isn't it?"

He confirmed the note, and described an assignment for his English class, an exposition on an ordinary useful item. No one would know what each student described when they read their essay aloud and would have to guess the object. The work would be due on Friday, giving him tonight to mull over his subject, something we used every day.

He glanced around the kitchen. "Like the teapot—but people would guess that right away, 'cause we're British."

"Maybe one of the tools in the barn? Or we could drop in on William and—"

"Oh yeah! He uses a special spoon to stir the milk into the churn when he's making curds."

"All right. Off we go."

In the end, he decided on William's trusty skimmer, a slotted bamboo spoon that had been handed down to him, and Lillian provided a notebook for Donnie to begin on the spot. Meanwhile, William told me about a letter that arrived today.

"It's from a fellow named Colman. Says you taught his younger brother, who wants to get in touch with you."

"Elliot?"

"I think so. Take it along so you'll have the address."

Later that evening, I read this brother's request.

"Mr. Herring, you may remember my younger brother Elliot from your class in Nottingham School. He would have been about fourteen then, and now is deployed with the BEF. I include his latest address and ask that you write him.

"Our mother would have written him every day, but he left home three years ago, and she has since passed. Elliot seemed so weary on his last leave. I do what I can, but our factory has us working double shifts.

One day, I happened to meet his former classmate, home on leave. He said Elliot got on right jolly with you and suggested you two might correspond."

Elliot had always been a good student, and now and then, we enjoyed a long chat. Throughout the past year, I had considered what I might do to help England, and this seemed ideal.

My letter took but fifteen minutes, telling about our life here and asking after Elliot's service. Donnie penned a short note too, and I suspected that our topics would matter little to a beleaguered foot soldier. The important thing was to receive some mail.

128

Mid–October 1941

The news centered on Moscow, where citizens—mostly women, children, and the elderly, for the fighting men had gone to the front—were building 5,000 miles of trenches around the city. As Nazi troops prepared to attack, most officials fled, taking Lenin's body with them. Boys not much older than Donnie armed themselves to fight.

This unthinkable scene haunted me. Sometimes I wished for a script of the news reports ahead of time, so I could block out what might trouble Donnie. Ah, but those children in England his age—weren't they right in the thick of danger?

The RAF continued bombing Germany, and the Japanese Prime Minister resigned. General Tojo Hidecki, a member of the Imperial Japanese Army and previously the military attaché to Germany, took his place.

Here in the States, President Roosevelt asked Congress for permission to arm the Merchant fleet. Adhering to the Neutrality Act in the face of "unscrupulous ambitions of madmen," he noted, could no longer continue.

Unscrupulous was an understatement. William received details that sickened us. The plight of Jewish people in Poland was painful to ponder—families separated like so many steers, torture and mass slaughter. The misery of war ground on, like an irreversible disease that continually spread.

On a clear day in the midst of all this, Donnie brought home another note. At the beginning of this year, I had taken to waiting for him out at the road instead of right outside the door, so my only conversation with Mrs. Bultmann occurred on the day after I received her first note.

That had contained good news—Donnie was now using the fourth grade reader.

I expected more of the same in this fresh envelope, but found an invitation instead. The function? Next week's spelling bee.

Dear Mr. Herring,

Our students look forward to the local spelling bee next week. We need parents to act as readers, judges, and supervisors. If you are able to help, please join me and other volunteers after school on Wednesday.

Sincerely,

Mrs. Bultmann

The meeting proceeded smoothly, with three mothers and me in attendance. Armed with our tasks for the auspicious day, each of us exited the building. I held the door for the others and left last, but as I stepped over the threshold, Mrs. Bultmann raised her hand.

"Could I trouble you for another minute, Mr. Herring?"

"Of course." I turned back, and she approached.

"Something has come up. I have been—" Her hesitation sent a warning down my spine. "Someone will come to question me on the same morning as the spelling bee. I—that is, my husband—"

Her hand trembled as she swept back a heavy dark wave that fell over her eye. "The government is investigating him."

Surely my jaw dropped. All I could say was, "Investigating?"

"Yes, the Texas Rangers." Her voice thinned to a whisper. "It seems some local citizens have alerted them that Johann might be an enemy alien."

"Why are they talking with you?"

Her sigh rent my heart. "For information about him, I suppose. I can't think of anything else I have done, unless this is about attending the *Schutzenfest*."

I almost laughed. "If they investigated everyone at the festival, their task would take years."

But Mrs. B saw nothing humorous here at all. "Johann went back to Germany several years ago, and—"

Stifling my questions proved daunting, but I waited. One of them was, "Why are you telling me this?" That one, she answered straightaway.

"I don't mean to impose on you. I wouldn't feel comfortable telling any of the other parents, but since Donnie and Anton are friends, I—"

Warmth rushed my chest—she trusted me. Exactly what I had yearned for with Victoria.

"I wouldn't have said anything, except for Anton. I don't want him to know about me being questioned, or to miss the bee, but the meeting is that morning and—"

Her sharp sigh revealed anxiety and foreboding. "They might also ask me about my sister—my twin. She married a man up in Wisconsin and lives there. The F.B.I. has quizzed her about being active in an organization with ties to Germany. Even though I know almost nothing about their meetings or her role, she has warned me to be prepared.

"If you could—I would be most grateful if Anton could spend the night before the bee with you and Donnie."

"Tuesday night?"

"Yes, he could go home with you from school, perhaps? I hope to be back for most of the bee, then. I would be—" The shudder that passed over her called up other shudders I had known. "—So relieved."

At long last, my brain kicked into gear. "Of course. We would love to have him. Donnie will be beside himself with excitement." I should have stopped right there, but blundered on. "He has mentioned some of the older boys—"

Her skin paled. She glanced out the door into the distance.

"Children can be so cruel. I used to—" I nearly slapped my hand across my mouth. I had come close to giving away my teaching past. "I—know some boys like that."

"Fortunately, most of the students have parents who know better."

"Mmm. So we will expect Anton after school on Tuesday next."

With another deep sigh, she bit her upper lip. "I appreciate this so very much, Mr. Herring. I'll send some extra clothes with Anton."

"The boys can practice their words for the next day. I may keep this under my hat until the day before, though, or Donnie might not be able to concentrate on Monday."

"I understand. A good plan for us, too."

I turned to go, but her sigh caught at my emotions. "If—I would greatly appreciate you keeping my situation in strict confidence."

"Of course. Have no concern about that."

Out in the yard, the boys engaged in a pick-me-up baseball game, and on the way home, Donnie chattered about Joe DiMaggio scoring in the final match-up of the World Series. "I sure like that Charlie Keller—if he hadn't driven in Henrich and DiMaggio, the Yankees might've lost."

"That hit made a big difference, didn't it?"

"Yeah. Burton Biggs says his dad jumped up and whooped so loud when Keller smacked the ball, he knocked over—"

The times my mind wandered off on our walk home were as rare as encouraging war news. But this afternoon, wander it did.

An FBI investigation—what *had* Johann Bultmann been up to over in Germany all this time? Without doubt, the boys who taunted Anton gleaned their prejudice from their elders, but did these local suspicions have any grounding in truth?

Scenes from the *Schutzenfest* flashed before me—such a wild sea of cultural activities laced with German culinary specialties. But stronger than everything else floated the lasting image of Donnie's somber schoolteacher, wild and free as she danced in the street, never missing a polka beat.

Muss I den, muss I den...

My German, sufficient enough for a weak translation, came through: "*Must I then, must I then, from the village, must I then... And thou, my dear, stay here?*

How could she bear having her husband gone for so long? And now, all alone, she faced an interrogation. No wonder her voice trembled.

As we rounded the curve toward home, William hailed us, so Donnie ran straight to the barn.

"—something to show you—come over here."

The orchard beckoned me. Such an ideal place to muse. I must get the frightened look in Mrs. B's eyes out of my mind, or when we turned philosophical, as happened of an evening, Donnie would detect something amiss.

Chapter Twelve

Over the weekend, my questions mounted, and found partial answers on Sunday. After church in Cherry Spring, Anton ran up, and Donnie begged to go outside with him.

"Yes, but stay close." Before the words left my mouth, Anton's mother approached.

"Could we speak somewhere?"

With parishioners all around, I considered. William and Lillian were showing chubby Abigail off to an admiring circle, so I gestured toward the side door. Eight or ten urchins skipped rocks into a nearby rivulet as we started in the other direction.

"Just for a few minutes, Mr. Herring. I know you have things to do."

"Could you please call me Everett? And I don't even know your name."

"Emmaline. Yes, that would be better." She pulled a folded paper from her purse. "I should have told you more the other day. That was unfair, so here's a little more of the story."

We slowed down, and her voice seemed measured. "You see, Johann's parents lost everything—their land and home in Ohio— when the banks failed. They started over again, but felt they could never trust an American bank.

"When things were so miserable in Germany, a call came for workers from America to return and help her rise again. Johann's parents decided one of their sons should go, and he was the youngest. Two of his brothers were working hard to regain their farm, and one was studying to become a lawyer.

134

"When we married, I had no idea they thought it still made sense to send Johann, but they wanted him to stay with cousins there for a year or so. By then, the financial situation in Germany had improved, so they thought someone from the family ought to see for himself and report back."

"Johann could not say no to his parents. Anton was almost six when he left. Soon, he wrote that the banks were solid because a new political leader had revolutionized the system there. Things looked bright, so he advised his family to turn their savings into gold and let him deposit it there.

"His parents did just that, but the year passed and Johann stayed on. About two years ago, he wrote that he had earned his passage home. We all expected him to arrive, but he never did. A cousin finally wrote that at the last minute, the government summoned him for some service. I thought perhaps as a translator, but—"

The children's voices carried to us, and bird chatter testified to a welcome rain during the night. Emmaline paused, and we turned back toward the church.

"I know it sounds strange—mysterious even. I might have given up on expecting to hear anything more from him, but—" Her eyes fixed on the boys scuffling in the churchyard—as much as their Sunday clothes and shoes would allow.

"Anton has waited so long for his father. I can accept that something beyond Johann's control must have happened. We may never know exactly what, but Anton deserves—"

"How did you meet Johann?"

"My grandmother's sister lived up north in the same community as Johann's family. They were members of a *bund* there. She fell gravely ill, and mother wanted to visit her, so my sister and I went along."

Donnie saw us and ran over—my deliverance from having to respond. I had scarcely heard of a *bund*, but at least recognized the word, and how dangerous it might seem to the authorities at this point. Anton pulled Emmaline to look at something down by the

135

creek, and we went our separate ways. But my thoughts whirled with what had become of Johann Bultmann.

After dinner at William and Lillian's, Lillian and Donnie took Abigail for a walk. I told William a little of the story, thinking he might have heard something about the German banks.

"Others did the same thing before Hitler turned so antagonistic. Someone told me their relative over here had put their money into some coins minted in 1907. Quite rare, they said, and just before '33 when President Roosevelt made it illegal to own more than a hundred dollars in gold, they sent the coins to the Bank of England. I imagine it might be the same with people of German ancestry."

"Hmm. '33—that was when the Nazis burned down the Reichstag, blamed it on the Communists, and Hitler seized absolute power in Germany. Interesting."

"An underhanded matter, that. Utter deception of the people, if you ask me. I recall your Grandfather's friend writing that he saw that act as the beginning of the end. If there had been enough men like him who would have stood up, perhaps our world would be in better shape."

"What do you think about Johann never coming home?"

"Odd, but perhaps not that uncommon with a long-seated national loyalty. I have read that the Great War produced such anti-German hysteria here, even toward immigrants who had emigrated at least fifty years ago. Maybe because those of German descent clung to their language and customs, they seemed a threat."

"But the anti-Hun sentiment only strengthened German-American communities. Not so different from what happened in Scotland when our ancestors got on their high horses and tried to snuff out their culture."

"The language difference must have had a lot to do with creating this climate, don't you think?"

"Right. English families settled near each other too, but spreading out was easier because they had no language to learn. German immigrants, always industrious, stuck together and built up places like Fredericksburg. Even during our short time there, the architecture made me feel as though I were in a German city."

"Quite, and it makes sense that a group would cluster in an area because of their language. Good thing we didn't have to deal with learning a new one."

William chuckled. "Although some think we sound hoity-toity, and don't mind letting us know."

"Someone I know?"

"I doubt it—a woman in a store one day when I delivered cheese. If stares were knives, hers would have shredded me to pieces. I can only imagine how much harsher that stare would have been if my accent had been German."

Secrets have a way of disturbing things. They're hidden, supposedly, but by their very nature can wreak havoc long before we realize anything has happened. Sharing daily discoveries with Donnie, I might have replied, "I don't know" or "I don't recall," a time or two when he asked about the period before his birth or his first years of life. But he rarely asked, so secrecy seemed unnecessary.

In retrospect, his mother shared such a small amount of my inner life that it took little effort to keep those years at bay. The foundations of what we might have built together began to crumble from the very start, although I missed the signs of steady destruction for many months.

On the contrary, the foundations of our life here solidified by the moment. Even when William married Lillian and moved to town, our plans continued undisturbed. The orchard, the cider, the cheese, the fruit stand, and the animals—all was well, and not a day passed that gratitude failed to well up.

Sometimes when we all sang a hymn in the simple stone sanctuary at Cherry Spring, this gratitude evoked a flood of emotion. Coming here had been a good decision. This community had blessed us, indeed.

So it was that genuine surprise filled me when Donnie inquired on Monday evening, "Something's wrong, isn't it?"

"What makes you think so?"

"You're so quiet. Are you getting old?"

"Old, you say? Maybe we ought to chase around a bit outdoors. What say?"

He blinked, tagged my shoulder, and raced out the door with me in hot pursuit. Half an hour later, I panted up the back stairs and collapsed on the porch floor.

Donnie joined me and raised an eyebrow. "Ready to read?"

"Absolutely, after we wash up. But maybe you ought to start out tonight, to give this *old* man a bit more time to recover."

The merry light in his eyes told me I had convinced him.

These evenings, it seemed right to forego the war report. Dwelling on the misery in and around Moscow brought up unthinkable images. In North Africa, two failed attempts to relieve Tobruk left the Eighth Army abashed and reconnoitering. On another front, the Italians had beaten the Greeks, who were being divided like sausages on a plate.

Was Elliot Colman among the Queen's disheartened troops near Tobruk? Daily, I prayed for his safety. Would a reply to my letter ever arrive?

In the meantime, Donnie and I plunged into an all-American adventure. After he heard about Huck Finn and Tom Sawyer in school, I ordered those volumes and another about life along the Mississippi. Samuel Clemens' skill made that time and place appear idyllic, but I surmised this romantic backdrop would most likely lead to some dire circumstance.

We looked forward to traveling to the wide Mississippi again each night, and imagined taking a cruise up the great river. The author brings to life a season in this country's history never to be replicated.

In the hottest hours, we often took a book along to the spring — our oasis, we called it—where a giant live oak overshadowed all. Here, imagining a handmade raft on the mighty Mississippi came easily.

Huck's friend Jim seemed too strong and wise to remain captive to any man, yet slave he remained. Tom Sawyer, and Tom's Aunt Polly—each character took on magnified proportions in this make-believe world.

Before we lolled about with Tom or Huck after supper, we studied the Scripps National Spelling Bee winning words since 1925. Donnie faced this long list undaunted: *gladiolus, cerise, luxuriance, albumen, asceticism, fracas, foulard, knack, torsion, deteriorating, intelligible, interning, promiscuous, sanitarium,* and *canonical.*

One morning he mentioned seeing word lists in his sleep, and I experienced the same phenomenon. A time or two, he caught me on a meaning.

"Da, do you think the *whilom* folks who lived here would like our garden?"

For a moment, his question stymied me, but I used the context to discern the meaning. Donnie's words took up much of our evenings, but even mastering these spellings and meanings seemed a sort of leisure.

On days when working the cider press rendered me exhausted, a bit of tea and our evening pottage sustained me. And then came the delightful literary journey with Donnie. Always, the energy for learning prevailed.

The bee began at nine, and by eleven o'clock, Donnie stood an excellent chance of victory. Half an hour later, he had spelled himself into the top four third-grade competitors, one other boy and two girls. By twelve o'clock, with the field down to three, I estimated the bee would soon be over.

With my duty of organizing the words complete, I sweated out every word assigned him. He tackled each like a tempting sandwich. Last night, he and Anton quizzed each other endlessly, and Anton was doing well today, too.

Before bedtime, I had them check the animals and run around

the house a few times so they could sleep. Once they settled in, they chatted a bit, but not for long.

Listening to them murmur with a nervous ear, I thought of Emmaline having to answer for her husband's absence. Could she help that Johann obeyed his parents' wishes, or had not managed to return? And what local citizen alerted the F.B.I. in the first place?

Not unlike the situation in England, with spies on every hand. William's friend wrote, "We trust no-one these days. The man you pass on the street might well be a Nazi cozy with Uncle Adolph. Last week, ministry officials paid a visit to a local music professor who emigrated fifteen years ago. Now he has been taken to a detention center, no matter that he taught piano and violin to most of our children, and we consider him an upstanding citizen."

William also heard that the Nazis had killed untold numbers of innocents in occupied France. Many fled their homes, and saying the wrong word might mean death as the invaders overwhelmed their villages.

Mr. Fletcher, who took Emmaline's place this morning, pronounced *chlorophyll*, and I jerked back into the schoolroom. In Donnie's age group, only he and one girl still faced off. This word could mean the difference between victory and defeat. Donnie seemed composed, unflappable, while I held my breath.

If I could muster this much anxiety over a simple spelling bee, what must people be feeling in all the occupied countries of Europe? Poland, Belgium, Holland, France— The tension must be excruciating.

I clutched the notebook I brought to record the words Donnie spelled today. He opened his mouth and started out. *C h l o*—

October 30, 1941

Reading "The End" and closing the cover of *Tom Sawyer Abroad* last night, I asked Donnie about his favorite scene. His eyes lit up as he thumbed back to chapter ten. "Right here—'But, on the other hand, Uncle Abner said that the person that had took a bull by the tail once had learnt sixty or seventy times as much as a person that hadn't, and said a person that started in to carry a cat home by the tail was gitting knowledge that was always going to be useful to him, and warn't ever going to grow dim or doubtful.'"

"Oh, that's my favorite, too. What would you say about this if Mrs. B asked you to write a book report?"

"That it's funny, 'cause they'd get hurt bad, and wouldn't be too smart. But Mr. Twain makes it sound like they are, 'cause they learn a lot."

"How?"

"The hard way, that's for sure."

"I suppose it counts, though, that if we do something ill-advised, at least we never forget what it taught us?"

Closing his eyes, Donnie leaned against my arm. "Yeah. Like Bert, when he—"

I waited, but his voice trailed off and he fell asleep.

Perhaps Bert's latest exploit was better left unsaid.

Nearing the end of another arduous spelling bout, Donnie appeared as energized as at the beginning of this second bee. At almost eleven o'clock, the sun broke through the clouds and streamed in on the children seated in slat-backed wooden folding chairs ranged across one end of the Mason public school gymnasium.

Anton had known victory until the last round, when he was foiled by a word that would have challenged me, too—*logorrhea*. I had to wonder why it contained a double *r*, which is what threw him. And why wouldn't *loquacity* have worked just as well? Did we really need three ways to describe extreme talkativeness?

At any rate, Anton would not be going on to the county level, but would never again misspell this particular word. Not that the occasion would ever arise.

Today he sat with his mother, cheering for the girl who had won his level, and for Donnie. Between them and me, William and Lillian attempted to corral an ever-wiggling Abigail. To spell them, I paced the edge of the large room with her from time to time. Completely happy to be moving about, she engaged anyone not intent on the spelling. A woman leaned down to poke her forefinger into Abigail's dimple.

"What a healthy-looking child! How old is she?"

When Donnie's turn came, I plopped down beside William and handed over his little cherub. Something must be said for having children when you're young and fit. Poor William was enjoying every moment of fatherhood, but admitted being hard-pressed to keep up with this active tyke.

My audible sigh followed the success moving Donnie on to the next round. Intriguing how much energy his efforts cost me! Emmaline seemed completely absorbed in the contest, with her students representing her, in a sense. Anton, too, stayed focused on the ever-increasing drama. But between Donnie's turns, the question that had troubled me since the last bee weaseled through my mind.

When Emmaline appeared near the end of the morning, I showed as much interest as I thought appropriate. She shook her head when I asked how the meeting had gone and turned her full attention to Anton. If I knew her better, I might have realized that headshake, which sent her gorgeous wave cascading over her right cheek, meant her interrogator had sworn her to secrecy.

But it could just as well have signaled that I ought to mind my own business. Ah, well. As best I could, I put the whole scenario out of mind, but still wondered how she had fared. When I picked Donnie up from school, she engaged with other parents or pupils. Was she avoiding me on purpose?

In the meantime, our luscious crop of apples and another bad cold for William gave me plenty to do. Fifty gallons of cider already mellowed on our fruit cellar shelves, but we were nowhere near finished for the season. Taking over the milking and deliveries left me rushing to the school at the last minute each afternoon.

Donnie might have walked home on his own—I knew him to be fully capable and trustworthy. My own selfish desire kept me running back and forth. Loath to forfeit that time with him each morning and afternoon, I operated under a simple principle: nothing could be as precious as these golden moments with my son.

This habit, long engrained by Grandfather faithfully appearing to walk me home after my school day ended, was not to be denied. What would I exchange for the talks we shared back then?

Donnie was growing so fast, we now ordered his trousers, shirts, and shoes from the Montgomery Ward catalog, and within two months, had to send another order. He came up to my chest now—a long and lanky fellow whose freckles and winsome smile still reminded me he was but a youth.

He allowed me to tousle his hair on our way home or before bedtime, and still climbed into our bulging armchair for our evening read. But this could not last forever.

Besides, after hours at the cider press, my body ached, and walking with the sun on our shoulders provided a respite. Donnie worked his way through the significant events of his day, and we sometimes discussed the state of our harvest. The pecans had been picked, the peaches eaten, sold or made into jam.

But these late ripe apples must not be wasted—Grandfather rarely threw one out unless damaged by insects or badly bruised. After finishing the chores, Donnie and I scrounged through the trees, searching out neglected windfalls. Earlier, we had done the same with the peaches and pecans.

Looking back over the years, William's foresight often came to mind. Having been at Grandfather's side for so long, he knew exactly what we would need and had searched out an iron cider press cast in the mid-1850s, just like the one Grandfather used.

While we waited in New York, he scanned East Coast newspapers until he found the perfect match.

The heavy contrivance added considerably to our luggage weight—as much as Grandfather's safe, no doubt. But already, it had proven more than worth the extra cost.

Every year, Donnie was able to shoulder more work, from the first ripening of the season through the final pressings. His help after school and on weekends made things go faster, and his bright spirit dissipated any sense of drudgery.

Had Grandfather felt the same about me as a lad? I like to think so, for he never showed a tinge of impatience, and for my part, working with him meant more than I could put into words.

Season after season, the process repeats, with a rhythm of its own. After we wash the apples, we turn a crank on the side of the hopper that guides them through a set of iron teeth to cut the fruit. Next, the fruit enters the press, named descriptively, for our weight against an auger attached to a circular flat iron mashes the pieces into juice.

This reduces these chunks to a mixture of peelings, seeds, and meat. Under the press sits the wooden receiving container, something like a keg. We keep it lined with cheesecloth, and the resulting juice runs down into a large bowl as we lean into the press.

A workout, indeed. Between cranking and bearing down, my work shirt, already a size larger since we emigrated, is straining at the shoulder seams again.

In the same way as cider-making winds down, life's conundrums eventually settle. But today, there was no *eventually*—only the present moment mattered.

With sunshine flooding his shoulders, Donnie's spotless performance stirred this sizeable audience. Determination showed in his very bearing, a bit forward in the shoulders, ready for anything.

A hush took the crowd as his competitor failed to spell *agoraphobia*. After mastering it, he conquered his final challenge. *Conquistador*.

As with many of life's challenges, this one amounted to far more than winning. Through the entire bee, Donnie had given his best effort. This experience centered on determination and focus, and what a celebration we enjoyed a few hours later! Lillian had slow-cooked Donnie's favorite, pot roast, followed by a luscious dessert she called peach cobbler.

Between bites, Donnie asked, "Why do they call this *cobbler*?"

"I have no idea, dear." Lillian patted his head. "But between you and William and your father, I've no doubt you will find out."

Chapter Thirteen

November 1, 1941

As twilight descended, a cool breeze cavorted with the kitchen curtains. Donnie and I tuned into the evening report, and from near the barn, Ramshackle alerted us that a suspicious scent had reached his nose. Most likely a coyote or ringtail looking for an easy meal, but he would handle the intruder.

Navy communications report a U.S. destroyer escorting a convoy has been torpedoed off the coast of Iceland. German U-boat torpedoes have sunk the USS Rueben James (DD-245).

The sudden attack took the lives of an undisclosed number of sailors who perished in icy, oil-slicked waters.

On the seventeenth of this month, the Navy suffered the loss of eleven sailors on the USS Kearney—again, a U-boat was responsible. These deaths, plus the injury of twenty-two other young men in that incident, saddened our nation, but now we must absorb even more dire news.

The Rueben James, a Navy destroyer was named after a brave boat-swain's mate who took a sword attack for his Lieutenant on board the USS Philadelphia in Tripoli during the Barbary pirate days of the early 1800s. The Rueben James began convoy duty in the North Atlantic this fall.

Unfortunately, our nation's neutrality offers no protection from war-ring vessels, with deadly German U-boats trolling the ocean in search of Allied ships.

The Reuben James had joined five other destroyers in escorting more than fifty merchant ships in a convoy, many flying the Union Jack. Only one destroyer possessed radar able to detect U-boat presence. Sailors could only use their binoculars and listen at the side of the ship for submarine noises.

We must ask whether we can rightfully consider sending our destroyers into such danger from now on. On September 4, when a German U-boat attacked the destroyer USS Greer en route to Iceland, a precedent was set when it counterattacked with depth charges.

At that time, President Roosevelt ordered the Navy to shoot on sight any Axis warship found in waters "the defense of which is necessary for American defense." The North Atlantic assuredly falls within this scope.

At this point, we ask one question: Will this great loss officially draw the United States into the battles that have raged for two years in Europe and elsewhere? Congress has come as far as approving the Lend-Lease Act proposed by our President, allowing ships a supportive role, but will the isolationists now back down and allow a declaration of war?

This had become the impelling topic of our times. In any case, we send our sympathies to families all across this great country. With you, we mourn the loss of your loved ones, and will update you as soon as a new report comes through.

"Do you think we'll go to war, Da?"

"I cannot tell. England surely needs us, that goes without saying. But war is always a last resort, the final choice remaining to us when pressed to defend ourselves."

"A hundred sailors—upwards of, that means at least that many, right?"

"Quite."

"That's an awful lot, don't you think?"

"I do, and what a horrible way to lose one's life."

"President Roosevelt wants us to go to war, doesn't he?'

"It would seem so. Did you hear someone say that?"

"One of the girls at school. She says her older brother wants to enlist, but he's only seventeen, though, and her mother cries when he mentions it."

"Mmm, thoroughly understandable. We shall have to observe how President Roosevelt finagles his way through this one."

"Finagles?"

"Yes. The word may imply scheming or using trickery, and can be spelled several different ways. But it also means bending or twisting in order to accomplish something. Perhaps like I had to do the other day, when we had to cross that fence and I nearly put my back out wiggling into the best position."

"The President has to twist and bend?"

"Definitely. I doubt any politician has had to contort to this extent to accomplish his mission—at least not for a long time."

"Since President Lincoln?"

"Quite. At least since then."

On a glorious mid-November Saturday, we thoroughly cleaned and oiled the cider press for winter before wrapping it in a thick tarp. William insisted on using walnut oil, following Grandfather's mode, and then we stored the massive contrivance in the far corner of the barn.

The moment I unscrewed the lid of the first bottle he ordered, memories deluged me. This unique odor compelled images of Grandfather's fingers stained as brown as the earth. He rubbed and rubbed and rubbed his mill, spending days going through the gears and between the teeth until every inch glistened.

In the evenings, Grandmother teased him, "You have stroked your mustache today." Indeed, brown stain had striped the white.

"Closer to the way we looked when I came a-courting?"

A flush rose on Grandmother's cheeks, for she still recalled those days. In brief moments like this, their love for each other shone so clearly. Arthritis might have disabled her in recent years, but she still saw to the little things that "warmed the cockles of his heart," as Grandfather would put it.

When the cider was working its way through the press, a sound like a brook emanated as it reached the juice receptacle. Uncannily, that resonance accompanied my cleaning efforts too, like an echo. Today, this gentle timbre immersed me in thought as Donnie jumped on Risk and went off for a ride.

No sooner had he left than my thoughts turned to the war. Word from the halls of Congress and the Oval Office proceeded in mixed jargon—isolationists and interventionists at it again. Without doubt, the President wished to provide far more aid to England, but the opposition consistently strong-armed him. Still, on the first of this month, he announced that the U.S. Coast Guard would now operate under the auspices of the U.S. Navy.

Norman noted that this only occurred during wartime—he could smell our entrance into the fray just as he knew snow was coming. Even with William healthy again, I had absented myself from the gas station for months. Each day still brought plenty to occupy me, and Norman stopped by with an update once a week or so.

Over a cup of tea that he never refused, we batted about the ins and outs of the political situation. Clearly, he leaned toward intervention, and scowled when repeating some of Mr. James' arguments.

"Mighty glad for my Czech roots on Mama's side, way back before the Czech Republic. Why, a relative of ours, a Lemsky, played in the Texas band at San Jacinto. Most of our people settled over there, but my Granddaddy moved on. When he first came over, he settled in Ross Prairie, a town founded by Germans.

"Story goes that somebody told 'im he had to speak German, so he got a few other folks together and they headed out to start a new town. The next generation married in with the British."

His attitude struck me as an oddity. I had yet to meet anyone around here with such concern over their origins. Although I was curious about how Norman had ended up here, I left my questions unspoken. As I walked him to the edge of our property, his volume increased, as if he held a personal grudge held over from his ancestors. Could that be true, like the Hatfields and the McCoys I had read about in Kentucky and West Virginia?

November 26, 1941

Over eight hundred British sailors perished when German torpedoes sank the British ship Barham off the coast of Crete.

Donnie and I sat at the kitchen table shucking pecans. Days before, the Axis had renewed its Anti-Comintern Pact for five years. Signatories included Italy, Spain, Croatia, Bulgaria, Romania, Hungary, Slovakia, Denmark, Finland, Manchukuo, and the puppet government in Nanking, Japan. They agreed to fight against Communists, mainly targeting the U.S.S.R.

The newscaster turned next to Erwin Rommel's attempt to outflank the British in North Africa. He met with failure, and the Allies had captured the key supply depot of Gambut, Libya. Also, Congress had approved expanding the Lend-Lease Act to include the French living outside Nazi rule.

Like a storm picking up speed, the escalation moved on. On the twentieth, Donnie and I discussed Japan's ultimatum to the United States, demanding American noninterference in Japanese relations in Indochina and China.

That evening, I beat Donnie to the punch. "What do you think President Roosevelt will do?"

"He'll say, 'the heck with 'em!'" His language grew more American by the day.

"And what exactly does that mean in terms the Japanese can understand?"

The thought lines in his forehead ran deep. "He'll say they have to stop interfering with us in the Pacific."

"Where specifically?"

"The Philippines, for sure."

"True, but an unlikely possibility."

Donnie's expression might have been a billboard for the chaotic stalemate in Washington, D.C. We pulled out our maps, and he turned back to the situation in North Africa.

"Why didn't the British commandos kill Rommel when they raided his headquarters? Shouldn't their plan have worked?'

"Carrying out the raid at all shows great progress, with seven British divisions against ten for the enemy. Operation Crusader marks the first counteroffensive her Majesty's troops have been able to launch in North Africa. That sounds like a victory, eh?"

"Not if they didn't get the *Desert Fox*."

Hearing my son refer to a German general by the nickname earned from his sneak desert attacks gave me a queasy feeling. But it also reminded me that keeping war news from him was impossible.

After school today, I had waited near the building as some of the boys piloted make-believe Messerschmitts against Spitfires flown by an opposing group. What a sight they made, jinking broken branches in hair-raising air battles. What had happened to their baseball games?

How sad to have them tossing around grim war facts and figures. Certainly not ideal, but even in this isolated locale their world altered, and change sometimes flies on unfriendly wings. Now, with Donnie mentioning Rommel as the hated *Desert Fox* who always seemed to get where he planned without giving a hint to our brave soldiers, I kept my composure.

What good would it to do belabor the topic? Besides, full evening had descended, the one time he and I could ward off the world with a turn of the pages.

"A new book arrived for us today." Oh, how I loved seeing this announcement light up his eyes!

"What is it?"

I reached to the bookcase where I had set the volume this morning. Donnie tore it from my hands and read the full title aloud.

"*Kidnapped: Being Memoirs of the Adventures of David Balfour in*

151

the Year 1751: How he was Kidnapped and Cast away; his Sufferings in a Desert Isle; his Journey in the Wild Highlands; his acquaintance with Alan Breck Stewart and other notorious Highland Jacobites; with all that he Suffered at the hands of his Uncle, Ebenezer Balfour of Shaws, falsely so-called: Written by Himself and now set forth by Robert Louis Stevenson.

"Wow—have you ever seen such a long title?"

"The longest ever."

"What does *Kidnapped* mean?"

"Remember when we visited the cemetery near the school and saw Herman Lehmann's gravestone? His family lived here when he was a boy, and he was captured by the Indians."

"Wow." Donnie nestled closer. "A long time ago, right?"

"Yes, in the 1860s, I believe."

"Did Herman's family ever get him back?"

"Yes, but he lived with the tribe for about nine years. Before he died, he published his autobiography, because people all over the United States were quite interested in his experiences."

The lamp highlighted the portrait of Grandmother and Grandfather we had hung on the west wall as Donnie considered. Finally, he suggested, "Could we visit his grave again."

"Yes, perhaps even tomorrow. Now, shall we clean up and begin our story?"

Donnie raced to his bunk and pulled out one of the drawers underneath—William's efficient carpentry ploy soon after we arrived. Three large drawers held most everything a boy could need, all hidden beneath his bed.

As long as a steady supply of books came his way, Donnie rested content, and this seemed a perfect time to immerse ourselves in the fates of a boy from long ago. Surely we would want to spend more time with this new hero—perhaps I should order *Catriona*, the sequel, for Christmas.

Wistful business, leaving Tom Sawyer and Huck Finn behind, but here came David Balfour to the rescue. A journey over the wild ocean and to the Scottish Highlands could not have been more timely. At bedtime, Donnie peppered me with questions.

This new author supplied so much to stimulate the imagination: Why was David kidnapped? Are the Highlands like the hills around here? Who are the Jacobites? So David's Uncle Ebenezer was not truly his uncle?

Ah, the pleasure of embarking upon a fresh adventure, perfect for our perilous times.

Circumstances seemed bound to worsen, with pressure mounting between Japan and the United States. *Those dirty Japs* could be heard out in public now. As William noted, the United States and Japan lay one incident short of war.

One day, I broached my questions about Norman with Lillian. "Do you know much about Norman Landers?"

"No, but I have met his wife—she used to come to church with another lady." She hesitated. "Edgar mentioned Norman a few times, but never in a very good light."

"Really?"

"Yes, they got off on the wrong foot when Norman first came here. Edgar never really trusted him. He always said, 'In every school of fish, there's a bad one.'"

A warning coursed my spine. Out of all the people in Loyal Valley, Norman was the one I knew best. Had I fallen into another situation I would regret? My next thought, that he seemed to fit in well with the men at the station, only produced more questions. Did they merely tolerate him?

That night, a lustrous one at the end of November, I woke to utter silence. My pulse throbbed in my ears as airy silver streamed through the window. An almost-full harvest moon owned the night.

Outdoors, all fell silent. I listened again at the open window to make certain. Indeed, the continuous scratching of insects had disappeared and all around, the first hard frost glistened. From a hill, a coyote yelped and a reply echoed from even farther.

A *whoosh* came from the top of the live oak. Probably an owl swooping upon its dinner—at least something showed signs of life.

Donnie turned over in his bunk, his regular breathing spelling comfort. Together, we had watched the grass turn yellow and orange, the shift of the shadows against the barn wall, the drying of leaves, the completion of the harvest, and alterations in the animals as they anticipated colder weather.

But now, the turn of the seasons had arrived without question, for frost shone white on the pump house roof and bathed the grass along the path.

The first noticeable difference, though, was the lack of sound. Ah, the great silencing.

No more cicada songs, no more insects threatening the trees. This resembles what happens to us in grief, an unnatural state inducing fright. We wander in its void, unable to think or feel.

But the whirr of the owl's flight sustained me. Frost meant no more growth for the season, at least none visible to us. But Norman's honeybees had been at work preparing for this, as had the squirrels. No surprise for them in this occurrence.

They recognized an alteration in the air. Like the creatures, we also scrounged for the days ahead. After leaving Donnie at school this morning, I stripped the last of the dried bean pods. Stacking the stems on a pile brought satisfaction—on some windless evening, we would roast frankfurters over a bonfire.

By day's end, my pile had grown, heaped with wizened tomato and squash vines. Inveterate weeds that hid under leafy plants through autumn met their fate at last.

More than any other seasonal phenomenon, this first frost crept into my bones. Such a welcome arrival, since summer's heat lasted into the fall months here. And yet, something deep within me tensed.

William might call it a premonition, for a few days later, as Abigail, traipsing around stiff-legged in her first walking attempts,

154

regaled us all of a Sunday afternoon. Donnie asked if he could take her out in the back yard before his Sunday school Christmas program practice. Lillian said yes, Abigail needed some fresh air, and helped with the child's coat and hat.

She held the door for them, and William switched on the radio as she returned. Why, I cannot say. Normally we merely talked after Sunday dinner.

But within minutes, the announcer's voice became terse: "We interrupt this broadcast to bring you this important bulletin . . . News Flash. Washington, D. C. The White House announces Japanese attack on the American Navy base in Pearl Harbor. Stay tuned for further developments."

Lillian reached for William's hand, and he grasped hers. His somber dark eyes reflected the seriousness of this news.

"Pearl Harbor? Where is that?" Lillian bit her lip.

"In Hawaii, I believe. The American Navy has air bases there."

Shortly, Lillian ran out to get the children, and as Donnie entered, the announcer stated that West Coast cities now feared being bombed by the Japanese, too. Donnie blinked and looked my way.

"What's happened?"

"One of our Navy bases in the Pacific has been bombed."

"It's them Japs, ain't it?"

I let his grammar go and nodded.

"Can they fly this far?"

"Texas is a long way from the West Coast," I offered as he wiggled in next to me on the sofa. Lillian hugged Abigail close, too. Foreboding drew us all together, and Donnie dared to voice his aloud.

"Good thing we're not in California."

We mused, mostly in silence, while the newscaster shared tidbits about the bases involved in the bombing. At such times, imagination takes over and runs with whatever information we have.

I walked Donnie to his ride to Cherry Spring for practice. Since school started, he wanted to attend church every Sunday. Anton was there, and Donnie's growing skill in German warranted a spot in the program. My language skills left much to be desired, but why not learn more?

After he and the other children left, I stood with other parents bemoaning the attack. Some confabulated the worst. "My brother's son is stationed over there. Wish I could remember the name of his ship."

"This'll mean war. Roosevelt's wanted it for a long time, and just like that, it's come to us."

"After this, Mason County won't have a young man left."

When I fetched Donnie after the practice, everyone was on edge to hear the latest. By then, Lillian had coaxed Abigail to sleep, and William promised he would hurry back from milking. His long stride challenged Donnie and me to stay abreast, and we remained in the barn until he finished. Then we walked him halfway back home, as if we feared allowing too much distance to those dear to us.

After supper, Donnie looked into his homework for tomorrow, and then we listened to Mrs. Roosevelt speak to us. Somehow, her address alarmed and calmed me all at once. I must admit, I felt as though the Queen Mum herself might be on the air.

"Good evening ladies and gentlemen. I am speaking to you tonight at a very serious moment in our history. The cabinet is convening and the leaders in Congress are meeting with the President. The state department and Army and Navy officials have been with the President all afternoon. In fact, the Japanese ambassador was talking to the President at the very time that Japan's airships were bombing our citizens in Hawaii and the Philippines, sinking one of our transports loaded with lumber on its way to Hawaii. By tomorrow morning, the members of Congress will have a full report, and be ready for action. In the meantime, we the people are already prepared for action. For months now, the knowledge that something of this kind might happen has been hanging over our heads, and yet it seemed impossible to believe. Impossible to drop the everyday things of life and feel that there was

only one thing which was important: preparation to meet an enemy no matter where he struck. That is all over now, and there is no more uncertainty. We know what we have to face, and we know that we are ready to face it. I should like to say just a word to the women in the country tonight: I have a boy at sea on a destroyer, for all I know he may be on his way to the Pacific. Two of my children are in coast cities on the Pacific. Many of you all over the country who have boys in the services who will now be called upon to go into action. You have friends and families in what has suddenly become a danger zone. You cannot escape anxiety, you cannot escape a clutch of fear at your heart. And yet I hope that the certainty of what we have to meet will make you rise above these fears. We must go about our daily business, more determined to do the ordinary things as well as we can. And when we find a way to do anything more in our communities to help others, to build morale, to give a feeling of security, we must do it. I'm sure whatever is asked of us, we can accomplish it. We are the free and unconquerable people of the United States of America. To the young people of the nation, I must speak a word tonight. You are going to have a great opportunity. There will be high moments in which your strength and ability will be tested. I have faith in you. I feel as though I was standing upon a rock. That rock is my faith in my fellow citizens. Now, we will go back to the program which we had arranged for tonight."

And that, ladies and gentlemen, was our President's wife, straight from Washington D.C. We hope her words will lead to a better sleep for you tonight, even as we stay alert, ready to convey our next report.

Mrs. Roosevelt's voice carried into our stone house like balm. All across the nation, people in even more remote areas were listening, too. Sons of fighting age would lie awake this night, and daughters vowed to do their part, as well. I could almost feel their pulses, their need for the consoling tone of Mrs. Roosevelt's voice. She spoke a dialect quite different from the Americans we had met here, but her measured phrases issued comfort.

Bless William once again for his foresight in seeing to our radio set. The President's wife exuded hope, stirred emotion, and offered calm in this sudden storm. Though my urge was to stand and applaud at the end, we both sat back quietly for a time.

Then Donnie exclaimed, "Wow, her son's on a destroyer."

"Yes."

"Do you think it's headed to Hawaii?"

"Depends where it was to begin with, I imagine. But the troops in Pearl Harbor certainly need help right now. It must be terrible there."

"All those ships burning and sinking, and maybe some of the bombs hit hospitals and people's houses, too. What do you think will happen now?"

"We cannot know yet. Tomorrow will tell us more."

I meant Donnie and me, but also people across this vast land who bent their ears to the President's wife tonight. Both interventionists and isolationists, Democrats and Republicans, everyone tuned in. Tens of thousands of plain folk gleaned this news in remote farmhouses, hundreds of thousands in large cities.

Locale meant very little right now. Citizens all over the nation quaked in their beds. The war had stolen up like a prowler, bringing uncertainty and dis-ease.

"She said people's sons would be called to go into action. Does that mean the President will declare war?"

"It seems likely, but we never want that. Sometimes, though it cannot be avoided, as with England. And I do believe we are the only country who can help her now."

"So it's a good thing. Not the attack, I mean, but we'll be helping England."

"You might have gotten it just right. We live in a mixed-up time when something can be bad and good at the same time. I think the word *ambivalent* fits, when something is bad in one way but good in another, and our feelings get all mixed together."

Donnie thought for a while, and I waited in silence. Today's stunning news had rendered me slow of words.

"Maybe it's like what Mrs. B said when somebody wrote bad stuff about Germany on the schoolhouse window, and the older boys snickered about it. They had to wipe them off, and she said, 'Our ancestors all came from somewhere else, Spain or Italy, China, India, South America, Russia, Sweden or France.

"Every country had good and bad points, and right now, the Nazis are showing something very bad about Germany. But no country's perfect—every single one has some things we wouldn't like. We need to be careful not to judge the people of a country by their government."

"I tried to think of bad things about England, but—" Donnie's partial statement made me laugh out loud.

"Oh, she definitely has some."

"Old Blighty?"

"Absolutely. In the 1700s we acted terribly toward the Scottish people. Our Parliament passed the Scottish Dress Act, forbidding Scottish men from wearing their tartan plaid."

"Why?"

"Because we wanted Scotland to become more like us—their kilts stood for their differentness. Parliament stupidly thought banning them would kill off the tradition. Of course, that didn't work."

"I bet it did just the opposite."

"Right you are. If I had been a Scot, I would have rebelled, too. We have so much reading to do on that era in history."

"But this is history too, isn't it?"

"Indeed. We're living in the midst of it, and I want you to remember this day. A hundred years from now, people will still be discussing this Pearl Harbor attack."

Solemn, Donnie nodded, and I tucked him in with an extra prayer for those stricken in Hawaii. Long after we retired, phrases from Mrs. Roosevelt's speech rang in my mind.

She appealed to all of us, but especially to mothers and the young. Queen Elizabeth, the Queen Mother—her face wafted before me in the darkness—what an indomitable stronghold for England thus far. Would Mrs. Roosevelt become a similar symbol for this country?

159

This evening, I felt as American as Lillian or anyone else born and reared here. I imagined battleships exploding in flames, carrying their occupants to the bottom of the harbor, and survivors struggling to save whomever they could from burning, oil-infested waters.

British or American, the knowledge that we were all in this together lay hard about us this night. Things would never be the same. Perhaps this event would change things for Mrs. B and Anton, too. Maybe those know-it-all older boys lay wide-eyed right now, realizing that a brother would soon be off to war.

Could they see that they, too, might be called up in a few years? And could they glimpse the ambivalent truth that people and nations might be a mixture of good and evil?

Chapter Fourteen

"**D**a!"

Probably Donnie hadn't meant to use the British term of endearment for one's father in public, and would take some ribbing for it tomorrow. But on this cold early December afternoon, his excitement knew no bounds.

"Somebody brought us a radio, so we got to hear President Roosevelt speak today. Did you, too?"

Before I could reply, he continued. "He declared war! What do you think about that?"

"Did you discuss this in class?"

"Sure. The older guys used bad words about the Japs—somethin' worse than *bloody*."

"And what did Mrs. Bultmann say about the President's speech?"

"She showed us Hawaii on the map and said so many sailors were killed that President Roosevelt had to do something. *A day that will live in infamy*, she had us all memorize that, and said infamy means being famous for being terrible. One of our spelling words this week is *dastardly*, and she said that describes the attack.

"The Japanese lied to us." He gasped for breath. "We don't know how many men they killed yet, but it's a lot—over a thousand, probably."

"Yes."

"And she said all over the country last night, people got together to pray, just like during Dunkirk."

"She mentioned Dunkirk?"

161

"Yeah. The British prayed for their whole army to be rescued. Did you know a third of a million got surrounded by the Germans at Dunkirk?"

"Yes, William and I followed the story closely, and prayed for them to be rescued. Do you recall how our congregation prayed, too? It was late May, and in England, King George VI had called for a national day of prayer."

"And the soldiers were okay, 'cause everybody brought their boats and worked together."

"Indeed."

And now, Mrs. B says Americans'll have to sacrifice. Will we have to sacrifice, too?"

"I would think so. The government may ration our tea supply, or our sugar. Would you be willing to go without?"

Donnie scrunched his forehead and hesitated. Then he blurted, "You bet! We gotta win this war."

Donnie's thoughts burst out in every direction. Somebody at school had said children could help by scrounging for scrap metal and rubber, like children in England. Would I mind if he searched the attic and basement?

I agreed, and we gathered a few items. During our pursuit, I considered a secret plan. Tomorrow, why not order another large supply of tea from the grocer?

Before we went to bed, another event surfaced from Donnie's day. "Mrs. B has changed her name. She only uses one *n* at the end now. Anton told us that's because it's German."

"She told everyone?"

"Yes, and she wrote her name on the board so we could see."

Not the first instance of local folks changing the spelling of their names. Later, I found myself wondering what might possibly impel me to remove an *r* from *Herring*, which had served our family well for centuries.

162

February 1942

Folks, we have a new song by Woody Guthrie, who wrote this piece immediately after the sinking of the U.S.S. Reuben James last fall. Some Americans had friends on that destroyer, but far more of us have relatives who perished on the Arizona, the U.S.S. Oklahoma, or elsewhere at Pearl Harbor.

When the death total is complete, we will know how many of our boys died on that Sunday morning over two months ago. And we shall never forget them.

Sitting in the gas station around the stove, Norman and I warmed our hands. This morning, the talk contained more speculation than facts. At one point, an older chap quipped, "Be better off if Texas became a republic again, I say."

Another replied, "Tried that. Got pretty bad shot up."

All the way home, the chorus of Guthrie's song, ran through my mind, and I wondered, what *were* their names?

So much had happened since the attack at Pearl Harbor. Two weeks ago, on January 19th, a great snowstorm affected much of Britain, and this month looked to be one of the ten coldest Februarys on record. The severity of this weather was still causing a great deal of hardship to our convoys across the North Atlantic, already being interrupted by more U-Boat attacks.

With thousands of troops leaving for one coast or the other, local news seemed trivial. Construction projects were going on all over our state to prepare new Air Force and Marine bases, since our climate lends itself to pilot training. Men and women are finding jobs all over Texas.

But one development hit me almost as hard as the attack on December seventh.

On the first day of school in January, Mr. Fletcher took Mrs. B's place greeting the students, and beckoned another parent over as I handed Donnie his lunch. I overheard only a few words.

"She's being interviewed again."

163

"Do you think she . . . ?"

Another parent greeted me, and I mumbled something appropriate. Heading toward home, my heart sank. Another interview —why? All day, I thought about Emmaline and Anton, and later, Donnie said that he had missed school, too.

No doubt this all harkened back to Germany's declaration of war on the United States on December eleventh. On that day, I waited outside for Donnie after school, and Emmaline had hurried out to speak to me.

"You have heard?"

"The war declaration? Yes."

"I wanted you to know one of the parents brought a radio today, and we discussed the situation as much as possible." An older boy walked by, and she paused until he was out of hearing distance. "But some of the students—"

Donnie came running up, so she stepped back. "I'm sure Donnie will tell you about it. Thank you, Ev . . . Mr. Herring." She hurried away and Donnie took over.

"Tell you about what?

"What happened when you were talking about the war today."

"The one with Germany. Da, can you believe we have two wars now?"

"Barely. We have a lot of work ahead of us—but tell me what happened at school."

"Bert called Mrs. B a filthy Hun and then Tobias said, 'Yeah. Your husband's a Nazi.'"

"Oh my—"

"Yeah, and Mrs. B's face got real red. Then Bert stood up and yelled, 'Our GIs're gonna beat him and all them other Germans. They'll be sorry they started this mess.' He got real close to her and lifted his arm like he might hit her. But then he changed his mind and he and Tobias ran out."

"What did Mrs. Bultman do then?"

"She turned to the blackboard for a little while."

I could see myself doing the same thing in similar classroom situations. At such times, Thomas Jefferson's advice occurred to me—"If angry, count to ten before you speak. If very angry, count to an hundred."

"Everybody got real quiet, and pretty soon, she started talking about the war again, just like nothin' had happened. She drew a big map on the chalkboard and showed us all about Germany, how it got divided after the Great War, and the way it is now."

"So you understand the geography?"

Nodding, Donnie hurried on to another exciting topic. "Guess what? We got to play baseball even in the cold, and because Bert wasn't here, I got to be the catcher, and got somebody out at home."

"That's wonderful."

Thankfully, the war had not totally obsessed him. He could still enjoy sacrificing out in the cold for the sake of play. Even so, the bit about the young bully fueled my fury, and I allowed a nasty thought: sending him off to fight the Germans might not be so bad. At any rate, since the second semester started, I had heard no more of this kind of thing.

Another wind of change blew in with the winter air. On February seventeenth, Joe DiMaggio exchanged his salary with the Yankees—a $43,750 annual fortune—for $50 a month from the U.S. Army. Donnie and I discussed other players who had been drafted or signed up. If anything manifested patriotism, it was these players' sacrifices.

Last March, Hugh Mulcahy became the first major league player to enlist, followed by Hank Greenberg and Bob Feller. But something about *DiMag*, the *Yankee Clipper*, registering for the draft made an extra impact on Donnie and his classmates.

"What'll happen to the World Series now? Joe's been the majors' Most Valuable Player twice in seven years, and he's won six pennants!"

"I expect the Series will survive. Don't you think it's fair that every man does his bit, regardless of whether he's famous or not?"

"Well…"

"In England, even Prince George, the Duke of Kent, serves with the Royal Air Force. He's the younger brother of King George VI, but he doesn't get off."

The stardom afforded baseball players seemed almost on a par with the British adulation of the royal family in my homeland. At one of our Sunday dinners, William added another fact worthy of consideration.

"Have you heard about the government taking away Joe DiMaggio's father's fishing boat? Maybe it's temporary, but in some quarters, Italians are almost as suspect as the Japanese."

"Is Joe's dad a citizen?"

"I guess not, so he comes under West Coast restrictions for enemy aliens being in waters off the coast, even though he makes his living by fishing."

"That old saying, *All's fair in love and war.*" Lillian added her two cents while making sure at least some of Abigail's food entered her mouth.

"Da, you and William are aliens, aren't you? Am I, too?"

"True, we have yet to become official citizens."

"So they could come and take everything away from us?"

William took his turn. "I suppose so, but we emigrated from a friendly country. This is the way of war—everyone with a connection to the enemy becomes suspect."

"But what about Mrs. B? She and Anton were born here. They'll be okay, won't they?"

Had he heard something more at school? I waited, but he required an answer, and now. Lillian gave the obvious one.

"I should think so, honey. But all the way around, war can be unfair."

"Do not be anxious about tomorrow; tomorrow will be anxious about itself," William added. He rarely quoted Scripture, and only at dire times. Grandfather's Chinese proverb came to mind alongside this advice: "When we talk of tomorrow, the gods laugh."

On our walk home, Donnie kicked a rock the entire way,

immersed in his own thoughts, but Grandfather's voice kept me company. I could almost hear him say, "The gods laugh not at *us*, but at our audacity. They laugh because we're human—we think we know so much—but the future is impossible to predict."

What had been the circumstances? I wracked my brain to no avail, and resorted to what I did know about Grandfather. He awoke every morning ready to embrace whatever came his way, moment by moment. Nothing alarmed him, as he took everything in stride.

He always reminded me, "The past is past, it wasn't meant to last." The first few weeks after the fire, this advice taunted me. Visiting the cemetery seemed to help some people, but seeing Victoria's grave only plunged me deeper into regret. Why had I ever fallen for her charms in the first place? And how could she have humiliated me so?

In the end, what possessed her to carry out such an evil deed? Her rash actions turned all of my plans into literal ashes. Why did she hate me so much, and what could I have done to change the course of her behavior? Worse, she risked our son's life and William's, too.

As always, I landed squarely on the baffling premise that none of these questions would find answers in this life. The past was not meant to last, but without sorting it out, without some form of resolution, how could it not? Still, wallowing in these quandaries and the self-pity they engendered amounted to even more waste.

At some level, I knew this, yet continued to wallow. William steadfastly reminded me I was not alone. Once, he even quoted from James Russell Lowell—"One thorn of experience is worth a whole wilderness of warning."

The challenge, of course, was to put the past behind me where it belonged, although it fought to stay foremost in my mind and heart.

At about that time, Donnie began to discover words, and once he did, he never stopped. Before age two, he carried on full conversations with himself, and each fresh utterance rang sacred to me.

Oh, the wonder of utterances melding with meaning in a young mind, wisdom straight from the lips of an innocent.

In retrospect, his propensity for language went a long way toward saving me. Each new evidence of the intimate connection between ear, eye, and brain filled me with wonder. I might not understand the workings of Victoria's mind, but here was Donnie, developing his own ability to think and make sense of the world around him.

During that time, guidance came from many quarters in a mix of dreams and memories, a potpourri of need and pain, hope and trust. But most of all, our future path clarified through Donnie's new words.

Discovering something every second, he toddled before me, always trying out a new sound, a living testament to goodness itself. In the shadow of Victoria's hatred and malice, he shone like a star, vibrant, full of courage, and so very verbose.

Gradually, shame receded as I focused on what needed to be done each day, for Donnie at first, then for myself as well. And as the present gradually overcame the past, a peculiar thing occurred. The future opened up.

One day, William brought Donnie in from a walk. I had just received a visit from the headmaster, saying that in light of the circumstances, my presence would no longer be required at the school, and would I be so kind as to come directly to retrieve my belongings? After hours, that is, so as not to intermingle with my former students.

Of course—hadn't I stayed away since that awful day when Victoria sealed my fate? I had become adept at skulking in the shadows. Still befuddled and in shock, I had no idea of the belongings to which the headmaster referred. Pencils? Ink pens? Perhaps a notebook or two?

"I kept very little in my desk. Perhaps I shall leave it there."

"But you have taught for years. Tonight, we shall go together. After we get Donnie ready for bed we shall stroll him over in the pram and I shall wait for you outside." So said William, always insightful and practical at the same time.

I agreed, and afterward, was glad for our foray. Three students had slipped messages into my desk drawer, saying they missed me. "Especially in English literature. Your substitute only knows how to lecture."

Reminiscing all the activities we had shared to bring literature to life brought a smile. In that classroom, with the memory of the most humiliating day of my life, these messages went a long way toward healing. I left the building with a lighter heart. If I could survive this, then life might still hold some surprises.

William had been right about the need to return, because gradually after that, each day grew a bit easier. Then one evening as we let Donnie tire himself out on a walk, William made a declaration.

"I have been thinking, Sir, about the United States. What is to keep us here? Why not gather together the information your Grandfather accumulated about that country and move there? If we search out an already established orchard, I can start a herd of milk cows, and we might give it a go."

His admission stunned me, but in honest moments, this proposal beckoned like a fresh-brewed cup of tea. Our temporary quarters had sufficed, Mrs. Tilman continued to be most gracious, yet we must find something else, something more permanent. And so we began our research. Months later, we arrived here.

On this late afternoon as Donnie and I approached our home, I surveyed our orchard, "Do not be anxious . . ." fell over me like a benediction. A horrendous war was underway, producing constant disastrous news, but life here and now still must be lived. And despite the war, each day offered fresh joys.

Ah, that was the secret—Grandfather's, William's, and mine. To live each day with no thought of the past or the morrow. To dwell in the present moment. I might have no power to control my wayward emotions, yet the power I did possess—to control my thoughts—meant far more.

Having succeeded in scuttling his rock all the way home, Donnie drew near as we rounded the curve.

"What have you been thinking about, Da?"
"Oh, this and that. How about you?"
"Joe DiMaggio. And his dad and mum."

What a cold morning this was! In Russia, temperatures of -52 Centigrade had recently been recorded. As the German army pressed on Moscow, bitter weather killed more soldiers than combat. Freezing to death—what a horrid way to leave this earth.

For Allied convoys braving the North Atlantic, severe storms brought great danger, and across the whole of Europe troops and civilians alike suffered. On January nineteenth, a great snowstorm dislocated life across Great Britain. Picturing men and women out in the impossible elements bade me draw Donnie closer under the afghan while we listened to the evening report.

Coming here had proven positive in so many ways. Not the least was missing this record-breaking winter cold. The wood-burning half of our stove fulfilled its destiny, keeping us pleasantly warm in these months.

The war was making its mark on our state, with heavy involvement in civil defense. Down by the Gulf of Mexico, incidents of foul play regarding aliens occurred, and Governor Stevenson called on former Texas Rangers to set up a Texas Defense Guard. The legislators had thought ahead and passed a measure last year, in case it became necessary to federalize the Texas National Guard.

One day, Donnie related tales of Nazi torpedo U-boats in the Gulf of Mexico and spies lurking along the coast. "Traitors hold lights to guide them, Da. Who would do something like that? And the coast ain't so far away at all." Surely, these details of intrigue had come from his schoolmates, not his teacher.

My first reaction, to protect him from living in fear, led me to spread out our Texas map. We peered at the terrain, and he was all ears.

"See Alpine way over here in West Texas? Norman told me a

former Texas Ranger named Phil Moore lives there. The Adjutant General has commissioned him to raise a mounted battalion of at least one hundred men up to the age of sixty-five to protect Texas from invaders."

"Mounted? They ride horses?"

"Yes, the Rangers were always cowboys, and Mr. Moore is patterning this organization after the Frontier Battalion of the 1870s. They will serve along the Rio Grande River. Moore wants them to wear cowboy boots and hats rather than the normal regulation uniforms."

"Wow! D'ya think we'll ever get to see 'em?"

"You never know."

"Somebody at school said her daddy's uncle used to be a Ranger. Then he was a highway patrolman, but now he's a state investigator. He's doing something about cattle rustlers."

"Really? Norman would know about that. I'll have to ask him."

"Will you?"

"Most likely."

"So, you think Ranger Moore knows about the U-boats and spies?"

"Righto. I do, and we can rest easy."

As it happened, Norman stopped by again the next day. More than happy to oblige, he supplied a great deal of information that I relayed to Donnie after school.

"The Governor has expanded the Department of Public Safety into a whole new state police agency, mostly due to the Rangers' handling of a shooting back in '37, before you bought your place. Over in an old riverboat town in East Texas, someone shot the Marion County Sheriff.

"Just after that, the New London school blew up—a gas leak that killed 300 students and teachers. They were just startin' to use natural gas to heat big buildings and something went wrong.

"The Rangers kept law and order there until martial law was declared. Truth is, if the Rangers hadn't corralled our ancestors into law-abiding citizens throughout the years, Texas wouldn't be what she is today. You've prob'ly heard of Benjamin McCulloch up around Brady. He commanded one of the Twin Sisters for Sam Houston at San Jacinto." Norman stopped for a moment.

"You know what they were, right?"

Fortunately, Donnie and I had recently read about those cannons, so I could give an honest nod.

"Anyway, the rustling still goes on, 'cept nowadays the thieves transport stolen animals in trucks, so the Department of Public Safety developed a new system. When Colonel Carmichael was the director, he knew what he was about. After he died in a car crash, the Assistant Director took his place.

"Homer Garrison's his name, from Lufkin. Even though Governor O'Daniel had cut everything in the budget but the telephone cord, the Rangers kept on."

"He didn't support them?"

"You know how things can be—it was all political. He wanted the police force to operate under the Adjutant General's office. Still, the Rangers managed to get car radios and their own radio station, KTXA. Long story short, when Coke Stevenson, a real rancher, replaced O'Daniel in the governor's chair, the Rangers finally got some recognition. Stevenson enlarged the department and the budget. Sure am glad he took over, and just in time.

"Now we've got good men in there—most of 'em have been county sheriffs or deputies before. Sure am glad they're all set, 'cause we really need 'em now. Did you hear they've launched a search for Fifth Columnists down in Galveston?"

"No."

"They seized short-wave radio sets, photographic equipment, ten pounds of gunpowder and firearms. Picked up more'n seventy people, and discovered aerial photos of a black plant, maps of the port, and a Very gun for flare shooting. They sent eleven of 'em off to the immigration authorities."

"Do they believe the Japanese might come up through Mexico instead of attacking the West Coast? That's a lot of area to cover."

Norman shrugged. "Somebody smarter than me must consider it a possibility."

Later, I pondered his response. How much of what he said was fact, how much conjecture? William and I discussed this, but I thought better of passing all the details along to Donnie. We needn't tiptoe about, afraid that Japanese soldiers would sneak up on us in the orchard.

Instead of dwelling on what might or not come to pass, this would be an ideal time to learn more about the history of the Texas Rangers. I searched the library for resources. Norman took note and brought a book for us to read. So it was that on these cold winter nights, Donnie and I immersed ourselves in Walter Prescott Webb's, *The Texas Rangers: A Century of Frontier Defense.*

While England survived the coldest temperatures on record and extremely heavy snows, Texans shivered, too. But every evening, we feasted on tales of wild doings all across Texas Territory in the old days. And wild they were, from belonging to the Republic of Mexico to becoming a state of the Union, to seceding in 1861, to being occupied by Union troops, and finally back to official state status once again.

Through it all, the Texas Rangers kept law and order. What courage they showed, riding out after vicious outlaws! Donnie uttered the word "Wow!" over and over each evening.

Were we reading lore, legend, or truth? There was no way to tell for sure, but we learned how deeply Texans believed in the Rangers, and the Rangers in Texas. As with Robin Hood in the forests of Nottinghamshire, the story mattered most, and somehow through it all, some manner of justice prevailed.

When we closed this book, Donnie made one sleepy comment. "I'd give anything to meet a Texas Ranger, Da."

"I wouldn't mind meeting one myself."

Chapter Fifteen

O n a promising day a few weeks after FDR's war proclamation, Donnie informed me of an auspicious visitor to the Loyal Valley School.

"A speaker came to talk to us today, and he's a Texas Ranger!"

"Did he wear boots and a cowboy hat?"

"Yeah, and he's been a Ranger forever. Didja know the Rangers kept order during the hurricane in Galveston way back in 1900? And now he's showin' a film all across the state about detecting gas and teachin' people to wear gas masks. Oh man!"

"Oh my. Tell me more."

"He was one of the sheriffs that chased after Bonnie and Clyde. Didja know they came through Loyal Valley?"

I certainly did not, but Donnie plunged ahead without waiting to find out.

"Yeah, they stopped at the filling station for gas—can you b'lieve that? They were that close to the schoolhouse! Anyhow, the Ranger said Texas is about 750 miles wide, that's about half of the way to New York City, and right now we have a five-step defense plan, so we'll all be okay if any of the enemy comes here.

"We've got private guards at the big factories, and the Rangers can always step in if the police can't handle somethin'. Then there's the brand new Texas Defense Guard, and if that don't work, they can call the United States Military. That's the Coast Guard, Army, Navy, and Marines."

"If that *doesn't* work. And the Air Force, too?"

"Yep. About half a million soldiers are training in Texas right now. There's a shell loading plant and a powder plant and petroleum refineries and a TNT plant, too. And a steel mill, and Army bases and Navy ports.

"The Germans want to shut down all of this stuff. And we got an Army camp at Tyler, and they're building an Air Force Training School out west somewhere, and we have to watch the Gulf for German U-boats, too, like Norman said. Mrs. B says the Texas Rangers sure do have their work cut out for them."

"I should say so. What is this about wearing gas masks?" I had just received a letter from Elliot, who wrote while awaiting his unit's departure.

He could not disclose a destination, nor whether he would travel by air or ship, but I presumed the British Expeditionary Forces had tapped him as an infantryman. He shared some of the sights that impressed him during his time in London.

Sacks of sand piled in front of every store, in case an incendiary struck nearby. Underground sleeping stations holed out everywhere, even under the public parks. British children, very young ones, wearing gas masks as they skipped rope or played conkers.

Now, here in the United States, my son was describing the same type of mask. Perhaps we were not so isolated after all.

"We might have to wear 'em some day, so we gotta be ready. The Rangers are teaching air-raid wardens to recognize enemy planes, and we can help, too. If we spot one, we gotta run to the local police station. Ranger Ted said so—it's our duty."

"Ranger Ted, eh?"

"Yeah. He was named after Teddy Roosevelt 'cause his father rode with the Rough Riders! Can you believe that?" Donnie's eyes could not have opened wider.

"He thinks maybe they'll start a Junior Texas Ranger unit. If they do, Ranger Ted said we'd get to be sworn in just like the real Rangers, and our job would be to collect stuff for the war effort. They need all the tin foil and paper, metal and iron and cardboard we can find."

His exuberance carried us straight to our orchard, and I learned that no actual gas masks had been shown at his school, only the film concerning them. As if emerging from a trance, Donnie glanced around. "Wow, we're home already!"

I ruffled his hair. "Indeed. What an interesting day you have had. Your visitor shared several things I hadn't heard before. But most of all, your wish to see a real live Texas Ranger came true."

The picture Ranger Ted painted for the students alerted them to all kinds of change. Soldiers, pilots-in-training, and munitions factory workers would soon flood our state. In recent months, William kept relaying tales of challenges faced by constables back home, with troops there amassing from nearly every corner of the earth. It only stood to reason: add thousands of young men to the populace and watch the crime rate rise.

Later, I lay in bed listening to Donnie's peaceful breathing. Hopefully, not many of these aberrations would filter down to our sheltered abode. But the possibilities unsettled me, and after a restless hour, I got up and re-read parts of Elliot's letter.

This next operation might include hand-to-hand combat with the enemy. Can't say I'm pleased about that, but a soldier hasn't a choice. Who could have imagined things would come to this? I remember you said in our history class that after all the destruction and loss of life and limb in the Great War, surely modern countries would find a better way.

Most of what we talked about rings true, but we guessed wrong about the nations, didn't we? They're not as smart as we thought. Enough about that. We must take things as they are.

Please tell me about your life in Texas. How did you decide where to go, and what difficulties did you experience? My best regards to your son. I should like to hear more from him, too, and hope he can grow to manhood in a world free of war.

I recalled Elliot as a slightly built, fine-boned fellow. To think of him contending with a well-armed and trained Nazi soldier gave me the fidgets. Like the 30,000 Hessian soldiers hired by the British government to fight in the Revolutionary War, they approached war-making as a full-time occupation.

In the morning, we would write to Elliot. Donnie could put his exuberance into words on paper, and we would seal and send our messages with prayers for his safety.

On a sunny Saturday morning, the war encroached on our space. Our sky space, at any rate. Out along the path, Donnie and I were trimming the grass midway up my work boots. Yes, we should have gotten to this task much earlier, but the weather was fine, and our scythes swished back and forth. I had just expressed my gratitude for his diligence and reminded him to watch for snakes.

" . . . makes this job go so much faster."

From a distance, a low hum began and increased in volume. I glanced up, and Donnie had already trained his eyes on the spot. But the spot, a mere pinpoint at first, grew until we hardly had to squint at the sun.

Such a clear late December day, but a cloud seemed to be forming. Before I realized what was really happening, Donnie yelped.

"Da! This has to be a training exercise. The air force is gonna have a mock dogfight right over our land!"

And so it was. After gaping for some minutes, we found a seat on a shaded rock and simply gawked at the airplanes whizzing across the sky. Every dive and turn brought exclamations from my son, and when one plane dipped low enough to see its markings, he burst forth.

"Oh! See, they marked that one like a Messerschmitt. See the black cross on the back? Ooh! That one over there's a Messer, too. Sure hope our guys knock him out."

I agreed, but not for real. Not here, not now. The heavens turned black with airplanes, and the same sensation I experienced with an encroaching summer storm flooded me. For the most part excitement, but also a helping of common sense alerting me to potential trouble.

But for Donnie, jubilation alone flushed his cheeks. He maintained his seat for a few minutes, but soon stood to punch the air in a victory symbol. For the rest of the show, he ran around mimicking pilots' maneuvers, all the while cheering on the American forces.

"It's a Curtiss P-40 Warhawk! Go, 40, go! All the way from Buffalo, New York—didja know that's where they make 'em, Da?"

Two minutes later, "Wow! Look at that guy swoop—ooh, he sure got that Messer, didn't he?"

So it was. From now on, not a day would pass without glancing up to see if another air show was coming our way.

Years ago, I realized my tendency toward obsessive thinking. I can analyze till the cows come home, as they say, and sometimes still fall into that trap. This terminology came straight from William, who pointed out the mental muck and mire I kept falling into after the fire.

After another almost sleepless night, he sat me down. "You know, Everett, the kind of circles you turn in your mind might be just as dangerous, in their own way, as Victoria's behavior. Donnie is your responsibility now, all the more reason to inspect your thinking. I experience my own challenges in this area, and your Grandfather was faithful to alert me when I went astray."

At the time, I could not imagine William doing anything of the sort. He must have detected disbelief, because he rephrased the same concept.

"There was a time in our lives when he pointed out the dangers of dwelling on a thing too long."

"How did you stop?"

"I learned by looking back at previous experiences. Certain topics from the past had power to take me hostage. But your grandfather said that at more than one crossroads on that downward slope, I could draw a line and say, 'No more.' I have a choice how long I allow a thought to engage me and the power to turn it around.

"I realized that thinking about those subjects always led to a dead-end. Your grandfather gave me examples—he also had a tendency to over-think things at the factory.

"So I saw my choice: not to toy with certain thoughts, not to even *begin* thinking about them, since they spiraled into doubt or fear or anger. What a dreadful waste those musing were, but once I made this decision, my perspective improved."

His advice served me well. Paying attention to my thinking when it grows wayward became a habit, though this is not to say I am no longer vulnerable.

Every once in a while, this old habit still draws me, and it did just that after Donnie told me about the Texas Ranger's visit. Seemingly reasonable questions presented themselves as if they deserved my full attention.

"What if enemies come to the hill country? What if we discover that moving here was a mistake after all?"

These unanswerable questions were unworthy of my attention. Declaring this was half of the battle. Losing a few hours of sleep is better than losing a whole night, and several times, I caught myself after tossing and turning.

"So this is all about my age-old concern, *Have I been a fool?* Have I made a wrong choice and must somehow pay for it? Will I be put to shame even though I have done my very best?"

I talked to myself as William might: I was not the center of the known world, and had no power to, by a single sincere decision, irrevocably hurt my son. Of course I would never want to, but the voice in my head insisted my choices might lead to disaster. After all, had this not occurred with Victoria?

If I followed this line of thinking, I became chief of all sinners, to quote the Apostle Paul. As the worst, I deserved the most severe punishment, and not just now, but forever and ever. Thus it went—a never-ending descent ending in unwillingness to take any risk. But I had ferreted out the basis of this thought line, its false, self-defeating tenets. It rested on the concept of unworthiness: I am unworthy of love, incompetent, ill-motivated, and lacking in common sense.

"No," I told myself after reading Elliot's letter. "No, no, no! I am a human being, imperfect, yes, but no more than any other. Still, God gives me the right to choose my way. This doesn't mean everything will always go as I think. Things beyond my control may occur."

Beyond my control— My cheeks still burned at the memory of Victoria somehow making her way past the headmaster's office one afternoon and the scene she had made in my classroom. But I had nothing to do with her behavior—had never even dreamed her capable of such a thing. Moreover, her actions made a statement about her, not about me.

To anyone hearing my monologue, I might seem a lawyer making his case. And that would be true, for I sat in the defendant's seat in a harsh court of justice. With such a kind grandfather, and Grandmother indisposed much of the time, I sometimes wonder how my bent for self-criticism evolved.

At any rate, the final point in my argument involved Grandfather and William, who knew me well and still thought highly of me. Based on their evaluations, certainly I might turn a deaf ear to the taunts of darkness.

They issued from merely one season of my life, an error in judgment. Even so, I had done my best with the consequences, and above all, the precious child sleeping nearby proved that good could come from our worst blunders.

To the casual listener, I fancy this appears rather weak-brained, but so be it. I offer these specifics only because of what happened the next morning.

If you visualize William as the quintessential butler, you are correct. Never brusque or curt, his demeanor might be described as poised. Even on the night of the fire, when so much lay at stake, his character remained true. Organized, straightforward, calm, thoughtful, far-sighted. Yes, even then.

Thus, when he waved me into the barn after I returned from

walking Donnie to school, I expected nothing of what transpired. My long-time mentor and ally sank onto a hay bale. He had moved the cream can to the corner, yet it sat uncovered. The cows were out to pasture already, for even though the morning rose brisk, the sun shone, and a little frost did nothing to dissuade their hunt for nourishment.

At nearly nine o'clock, the pasture still glittered, with Risk busy tearing off winter growth near the fence line. A perfect day for cleaning out the barn, and later, I thought to mend a potential break in the fence. That was the way of it, always something to address.

Normally, William would have met me *en route* from the school. But clearly, he had been waiting, and his very posture spoke distress.

I claimed a nearby bale. "What is it?"

His eyes showed signs of a sleepless night. He dropped his head into his hands. My heart leapt into my throat, but there was nothing for it but to wait. After perhaps a full minute, he began.

"Lillian is expecting another child." His voice came from a dark cavern, but though I was surprised, this seemed like good news.

"The doctor says she needs to stay off her feet now, but I must find a good-paying position."

"I thought all was in order."

"Yes, but this changes our needs. I must reconsider the future. Having two children means double of everything—two educations to save for, and—" The rest of his statement drowned in a sigh. Relieved that nothing untoward had happened to Lillian or Abigail, I waited for him to continue.

"Kenneth needs help at his hardware. He offered me a position months ago, but I thought taking a job unnecessary. Working there would mean purchasing a vehicle, for one thing."

"I would need to stay there at least one night a week. Even if I only worked three days, gas will soon be rationed, so I would have to limit my trips."

"And Lillian would need help with Abigail while you're gone."

"Especially now, in her condition. Oh, I don't see how this can possibly work." He clutched the worn brim of the leather beret he had sported ever since I could remember.

"Hmm." I could never have voiced my first reaction—this challenge was no more than those he had faced in the past, and he always found a way. Something else must be bothering him, something that skewed his thinking.

"I— Please understand, I don't expect you to come up with a solution."

"Does Lillian understand?"

Another sigh fraught with distress. Not out of confidence in my response, but because I had no idea what to say, I waited once more. Meanwhile, my mind swam with possibilities.

Loyal Valley offered few positions compared with Fredericksburg or Mason, but perhaps some local might need William's expertise. Certain workers were being drafted, and what about ranchers? Norman had recently hired a man named Bernardo.

My next thought was that we could set up a year-round store. Folks turned toward town at our corner, so we might take advantage of this. Our produce and fruit stand had reaped far more profit than I ever imagined, almost as if this community had been waiting for us.

But something told me to hold off spouting ideas. In this dark mood, William might not grasp the potential of any notion right now. Better to allow him some time.

And allow myself some, too, to weigh the pros and cons of building a bigger shed. Always one to run with a thought, it heartened me to recognize right off that enlarging our roadside stand would require considerable expense, not to mention possible complications. Would we irritate the grocer in town? If we added cheese and milk, would he stop purchasing our vegetables and eggs?

William straightened his shoulders. "Thank you. Why has this befuddled me so?"

"Your news came as a surprise, didn't it?"

"Quite."

"What does Lillian say about all of this?"

"She desires security for our children, of course, but something I cannot quite grasp is going on between her and Kenneth. It's as if he holds sway over her."

I angled my head, which was all William needed.

"After Edgar died, she worked for Kenneth for next to nothing. He exercised control over her, I believe. She—she is overly—overly intent on pleasing him. Not *pleasing* exactly, but she despises conflict, so—"

"So Kenneth is the problem?"

The breadth of William's sigh answered for him. "I doubt I could work with him for long." Not one for deep sighs, William let go another long one. "And I fear people are going to think—"

Had this man ever been one to mull over what people would think?

"What might they think?"

"At our age—you know I have turned past fifty and Lillian is—" William fidgeted. "People will look at us and think—"

Always a look-you-in-the-eye sort of fellow, he changed before my very eyes. He seemed to physically shrink.

"When Abigail was born, Kenneth took me aside. I shall never forget him saying, 'At your age, a man ought to practice some self-control.'"

"Truly, he said that?"

"Yes, but out of Lillian's hearing."

Remembering our two-hour stint with Lillian's brother at Thanksgiving, I knew there simply had to be an alternative for employment. Kenneth would wear anyone down, even stalwart William.

"How would he know? He has never had the fortitude to marry! Besides that, what you do is none of his business."

"Quite! Yet how do I tell him, when Lillian seems wholly set on pleasing him?"

"Have you checked for employment here?"

"No." Such uncharacteristic dullness in William's tone—I longed for the right words to cheer him.

183

He turned toward home. "We shan't solve this today, but thank you for lending me your ear."

Any other time, I might have quipped, "Friends, Romans, countrymen…"

But William was far too downhearted, and as I observed his glum figure heading back toward Loyal Valley, one of Donnie's spelling words came to mind. *Perseveration: Continuation of a thought or action to an extreme degree or beyond a desired point.*

How had my personal William the Conqueror suddenly slipped into the debilitating thinking that mirrored mine at the worst of times?

The envelope looked as though the Pony Express had toted it across the Rockies and through a raging Colorado River. On this April day, I set it aside to open when I was alone, and was glad I had.

March 28, 1942

Dear Mr. Herring,

Presently in a makeshift hospital north of London for rehabilitation, I thank you for your latest letter. The United States seems quite far away, but I met a GI from your state, a lanky fellow with a drawl. I believe 'twas the city of Amarillo. Are you near there?

My memory may fail me, as that meeting occurred before I was injured. Fortunately, the evacuation hospital doctors operated on me straightaway, and held out hope that in a hospital back here, my leg might be saved. But such was not to be, and thus the nurses here guide me through a regimen of salt baths and exercise.

Fortunately, the rest of me remains whole, so I will be able to return to some form of administrative duty, like many other amputees. The nurses here are helpful and kind, except one who sees it as her duty to oversee my every move. She puts me in mind of our headmaster, never a laugh allowed.

All in all, things are going well. My father was able to come down for a short visit, and I will be granted leave to go home after being fitted

with an artificial limb. Father spoke of winter's ravages in Notting-
ham—several of our old trees fell prey to February's severe cold.

A week ago, I assumed my unit would no longer have need of me, but
that shows my ignorance. With so many fronts to cover, I ought to have
surmised they would find a suitable desk for the likes of me. Thankfully,
you instructed me well concerning careful record keeping, as that lot
will surely fall to me now.

No matter, as long as they don't return me to North Africa. I have
had quite enough of that continent.

Hopefully, this war will reach you and your son only through the
news reports. May you stay well and content.

Sincerely,

Elliot Colman

Mailed from London, the letter had taken three weeks in transit.
Perhaps Elliot had been wounded in Libya. He neglected to say,
most likely by design. Who would have thought British troops
would still be fighting the Germans in North Africa?

But American forces had little to brag about, either. The situation
in the Philippines looked disastrous. The bravado of local boys
as they left their families at the station would take some time to
translate into victories on land and sea.

In January, Hitler had reinforced his Arctic Convoy routes. In
February, Singapore fell to the Japanese. William's contacts were
still in shock—simply impossible to believe that fortress had fallen.
Not a great deal to chortle about these days, for in every direction,
our high hopes kept being dashed.

"Catastrophic," was William's comment when he made a special
trip over to inform me about Singapore, and Prime Minister Winston Churchill agreed. "Worst disaster" and "largest capitulation" in
British history summarized the situation in his eyes. I could hardly
fathom the voices on the airwaves—80,000 Commonwealth troops
taken prisoner after only seven days of defending the "Impregnable
Fortress?" Could this possibly be the case?

Then on the nineteenth, over a hundred Japanese aircraft attacked

Darwin in northern Australia, killing 240 people. A week later, in the Battle of the Java Sea, the Allies failed to stop Japanese attacks on Java. To make matters worse, early in March the Dutch East Indies surrendered to Japanese forces.

A few days later, President Roosevelt ordered General MacArthur to leave the Philippines for Australia. But as the Japanese bore down, the General left behind tens of thousands of American troops. Disease took an enormous toll, as supply lines were cut off by the enemy. Only a matter of time before the Imperial Army's superior forces would defeat the remaining force.

Next, the Germans began an all-out aerial assault on Malta, over 800 Axis Aircraft pitted against 140 planes defending the island in heroic, but futile efforts. Finally, earlier this month, the Allied forces on Bataan surrendered to the Japanese and the Philippines fell.

Picturing 78,000 Filipino and American prisoners of war forced to march sixty-five miles through highland jungle in the Bataan Death March stirred newfound rage, and my American acquaintances revealed a heretofore latent side. First Pearl Harbor, now this, after everyone had bid their sons good-bye with such fervent hopes!

On April eighteenth, 1942, countenances brightened a bit as sixteen B-25 bombers launched from the *Hornet* carried out the first air raids on Japan. Such an embarrassment to the Japanese high command! Even though the raid inflicted little damage on intended military targets, we all breathed a bit easier.

I say *we* because it was our young men going off to war, like those in Great Britain, which had already suffered defeat on so many fronts. But given Texas history, citizens saw fighting against great odds as necessary at times, and this definitely qualified.

Warriors like Sam Houston had been thoroughly ensconced in their minds at a young age. We learned that later in life, having been called a fraud, this veritable U.S. senator had beaten a member of the House of Representatives over the head with a hickory cane on Pennsylvania Avenue. Years before, as a military leader, he had

186

gained superiority through retreating, though his troops disliked this tactic.

But then they whipped General Santa Ana's forces at San Jacinto—in eighteen minutes. All of Houston's maneuvering finally paid off. Donnie's apt comment summarized the lesson to be learned from this bit of history.

"He stuck with his plan even though everybody disagreed. He didn't let anybody hold him back."

Had not the Cherokees named General Houston an honorary member of their nation? And what other American had served as governor of two states? It was difficult to overestimate the effect of this man on the state of Texas, and today's descendants of hardy pioneers held high expectations for their sons to use their brawn and wits to bring a quick end to this war.

Even with the unlikelihood that many present commanders' expertise could compare to General Houston's brilliant military prowess, I entered into my fellow citizens' hopes. Joining with them as they saw off their sons united me with them in a new way.

On most days, William accompanied me, and we both filed our naturalization papers. But what painful disappointments awaited us all.

Chapter Sixteen

"**X**erophilous."

Donnie carefully wrote down the word while I wondered why anyone should ever have opportunity to employ it. Besides learning his spelling list for the week, he must now learn each Greek root and meaning, plus write an example sentence.

"*Because we were working out in the desert, we carried more water in this xerophilous habitat.* How's that for a sentence?"

"Perfect. Even with so much that's green part of the year, the cacti on our hills declare our area semi-desert. Do you recall the names of some of them?"

"Prickly pear, with those bright yellow blossoms, and horse crippler—the one with dark pink blossoms behind the barn. Those little pineapple ones already flowered. And the yucca—at night, I used to think the blossoms looked like ghosts with their big white petals."

"So did I. During our first spring when I walked outdoors, the moonlight made them look exactly like that. William commented on them, too."

Xerophilous was the last word on Donnie's list, so he started his mathematics homework. Mrs. Bultman, like any conscientious teacher, gave her students plenty of work.

My thoughts returned to William's dilemma. Today I had spoken with Norman, in general terms, about jobs in town.

"You're thinking of getting a job?"

"No, just checking around." I had noticed lately how he often

188

sought more details before supplying answers, and set my mind to disclose no more.

A few days had passed since William revealed his troubles, and things had not improved. If anything, his outlook declined even more. But Norman needed to know none of this.

William's assessment made sense. At some level, Kenneth held Lillian in thrall. When she worked for him after her husband died, she stayed in a room above the hardware and caught a ride to check on her house from time to time. Perhaps Kenneth got too used to having her at his beck and call and expected the arrangement to last forever.

About the time we arrived here, the business needed extensive carpentry work, so Lillian returned to Loyal Valley to catch up on things. William first met her at church, and then spied her at work out in her yard. He stopped to chat with her, and over the fence, romance worked its magic—such a lovely story.

England had always interested Lillian, so his proper British pronunciation and formal ways ignited her curiosity. A tale straight out of Jane Austen, but not everyone saw their relationship through loving eyes.

Things went poorly with Kenneth when Lillian explained she was about to wed and would no longer be working at the hardware. Because they had co-inherited the business, he felt she owed it to her parents to keep working till death did them part—William's tongue-in-cheek summation.

Their rapid courtship and marriage surely shocked Kenneth. This, I could understand. The suddenness surprised me, too, although I realized how quickly love could strike. One moment you went about your business, a normal person. The next, you became stricken, as it were. But Kenneth, who had never even courted a woman, felt betrayed by Lillian's decision.

From the very start, Lillian and William discovered such happiness together, but their newfound joy was lost on Kenneth. Now, he threatened to contest their parents' will. On Thanksgiving last

November, he finally paid them his first visit, after giving Lillian the silent treatment for so long.

With all of the war construction, the hardware business was thriving, so he truly did need another worker. Instead of hiring someone from his town, he pressured Lillian to come back, in complete disregard of her needs, not to mention William's and Abigail's. When Lillian refused, that left William.

One element remained a mystery. Who had come up with this idea? Surely, Lillian realized that the logistics could never work, especially considering her pregnancy.

The solution seemed simple. Say no, stick by it, and let the chips fall where they may. These old sayings coin the truth quite well, but fall on deaf ears when one is in the thick of it.

No one has to tell me how complicated family ties can become or how difficult it is to say *no* to a family member. You don't want to hurt their feelings, and in this case, wouldn't want to upset the finances of the thing.

Thus, William felt obliged to work for Kenneth, but Lillian and Abigail needed him at home in the evenings. I would have thought him capable of standing up to Kenneth on principle and taking whatever consequences resulted. Stalwart, steady William, always in charge and self-sustained.

This only goes to show that no matter how well you know someone, surprises may still await. When William divulged these details yesterday, the torment in his tone took me aback. He loved Lillian, wanted her to be happy, and loathed the thought of disturbing her. At the same time, fury against Kenneth raged within, but William's long history of holding anger in check also surfaced. Enveloped in emotion, his perspective suffered.

Anyone could see he belonged right here beside Lillian through these potentially trying months before the birth of their second child. On the other hand, if he refused Kenneth, and his brother-in-law carried through with his threats, this little family might lose some rightful resources. Also their protector and provider, this troubled William greatly, and no easy way out presented itself.

Re-thinking his conundrum, I came to the same conclusion that occurred at the outset. William must find good-paying work close at hand. Who cared, in the long run, about Kenneth's anger? He operated on some outdated set of family rules and had lost sight of Lillian's best, if he ever possessed it.

Once I set my mind to it, several job possibilities came to light. Word had it that an orchard owner might need help, and a fellow employed by the gas works had gotten injured last week. Perhaps a temporary position there might lead to permanent employment.

With William caught up in this web, I set my mind to search out suitable employment for him. Hopefully, something fitting would turn up, and Lillian would see the wisdom of the plan.

"Actually, I need a manager. The government called our son to supervise building a prisoner-of-war camp up at Brady. He was with the engineers in the Great War, and the Army's going to need plenty of space for prisoners."

"Brady, north of here?" Ah—the origin of William's bull.

"About an hour, up in McCulloch County. They're fifteen miles from the geographical center of the state, so they call themselves the Heart of Texas. The camp'll be a couple of miles out of town on 360 acres, about 200 buildings in all, to house up to 3,000 prisoners. And they're building a hospital with a 150 beds.

"Of course, it's costing a lot, but for Clayton, it's good work. When we start to win, we have to put the prisoners somewhere, don't we? The Army aims to activate everything in September, so you can imagine the long hours our men are working. There's a big dairy up there called Gandy's. They'll supply the camp, but Clayton says I can find extra business on the fringes. That's the way of war." Mr. Grunkle sighed, and I wondered if he had gone across in the Great War, but held my question.

"To make matters worse, now our grandson's been called up. I had hoped—" Under the glaring light from a bare bulb in his office, he appeared quite haggard.

A *manager?* That word stood out above all the rest of what he said, and when he paused, I almost leapt over the desk at this fellow I had seen at the Cherry Spring church but never gotten to know. We were visiting in what had developed into a creamery on his land between Loyal Valley and Cherry Spring.

"Yes. My father brought this trade here eighty years ago, and I've carried it on, first with just our family. But then people began buying cheese and butter instead of making them, and—well, you see the result."

His business had grown into a warehouse-like shed obviously newer than most of his farm buildings.

"Heaven only knows the demand will only increase with new airfields going up, too."

"I may have a tip for you concerning a manager."

"Really? Someone local?"

"Yes, and experienced. Mature, a solid worker, utterly reliable."

"Can he drive?"

Visions of William chauffering Grandfather throughout England paraded before me as I replied in the affirmative. What a royal British ride he would give Mr. Grunkle's products, once he learned to steer from the left side of the vehicle instead of the right!

"Tell me who it is, man. Someone I might know from church?"

"Yes, William Parker. Better yet, shall I run and fetch him? Is this morning a good time for you?"

"The sooner the better. I needed help two weeks ago."

A few minutes later, like a boy who just won a ball game, I burst into William and Lillian's quiet abode. Lillian, reading to Abigail, looked paler than normal, and I realized I hadn't seen her in a few days.

William was just entering from the back yard, so I raised my voice. "I don't know if William is interested, but I have learned that Mr. Grunkle needs a manager at his creamery."

Lillian's eyebrows advanced toward her widow's peak. William dashed in, ducking his head for the low arch between the dining and living rooms.

"Manager? Edward Grunkle, you say?"

"Yes. The government called his son to help build a camp up at Brady, and now his grandson has deployed. Mr. Grunkle has a big new contract pending with the Army Air Force, so he needs—"

"Oh my goodness—right here in Loyal Valley." An undeniable spark laced Lillian's voice.

"Yes. And right up your husband's alley."

Speechless, William used a dishtowel on his dripping hands.

"He expects you straightaway."

"Now? Oh, my. What do you think, Lillian?"

I grabbed Abigail and took her to the window to watch for a roadrunner. She had read about them, but seen none, and you never knew when one might appear. And any excuse would work.

Her parents reached consensus quickly. Of course, William ought to find out more, even if this meeting failed to produce a position. What would be lost?

After a brief talk and a tour of the premises, William found himself hired. His countenance mirrored shock and delight—what a happy duo, since his cheery smile had gone missing. My heart fairly burst at this new connection, though I had waited outside during the preliminaries.

After William informed me, his new employer gestured him to an anteroom and bade him change into a work uniform. I walked with him to the door, and his calm request settled over me like balm.

"If you wouldn't mind stopping to tell Lillian?"

I nodded like an over-eager youngster. "Of course. Yesterday's sermon is proving true for you, I daresay."

His quizzical expression brought forth the merest description. "Remember the fourth Psalm we read aloud? The writer pleads with the Almighty and notes past answers to cries of distress. Then he begs in the present, 'Have mercy upon me . . . hear my prayer.'"

"Ah, yes—recalling past deliverance during present troubles. We talked about that at dinner. How could it have slipped my mind?"

"Easily. Even a few minutes ago, you were still in distress. And then, *Whamo!* as Donnie would say, you're right in the middle of the answer!"

"Indeed, I should say! I can hardly believe Mr. Grunkle's offer—sixty dollars a month!"

"More than Uncle Sam is paying Joe DiMaggio, old chap!"

"Plenty to set aside for the future, so we shan't have to worry. Now, no matter what Kenneth schemes against us, all will be well. Everett, how can I ever thank you?"

"You might teach Donnie your cheese-making methods, as you may need someone to take that over. Is he old enough to tackle it?"

"Certainly. We may have several things to work out."

When I spoke with Lillian, I started off with the verse from the sermon, for arguing with Scripture often proves difficult.

"What? He's hired? Already? But—"

"Yes, he won't be home until after five." I chose to ignore the *but.*

"But Kenneth—"

"Yes? Is there trouble?"

Keeping an eye on Abigail out in the back yard, Lillian shook her head. "My brother—oh, you have no idea how difficult that man can be!"

Waiting seemed advisable. Perhaps if she chose to reveal more, I might offer something to help redirect her thinking.

"Sit down, won't you? Would you like some tea?"

"Perfect. I can peek out at your little sweetheart while I wait, or put the pot on if you like. William said—"

"He told you about the doctor's advice to be careful?"

"Something like that—I believe he mentioned doctor's *orders.*"

"Well, don't believe him if he says I need bed rest, all right? He's so solicitous, but really, we managed just fine with Abigail, and I'm only a couple of years older now. Everything will go well. It's just that—I think William was so surprised this time."

"Mmm. He is one to plan things out."

A relieved sigh escaped as Lillian set the water on to boil. "You realize that about him?"

"Surely. If he hadn't been that way, my life would have been so much more complicated. For one thing, our transport from England to here—I truly can't imagine having made that trip without William in charge. He thinks of things that never would occur to me. He foresees what could go wrong, you might say."

"But yet, he has such solid faith."

"Oh, indeed. More than I do, when it all comes down. He's simply more detailed than some people—thinks things through, but always leaves room for further guidance."

"Hmm." Lillian's shoulders shifted. Adding a bit more about William's temperament seemed appropriate.

"You see, when he worked for my grandfather, he bore a great deal of responsibility. Grandfather was like me, rather more impetuous. I have no idea how much trouble William saved him throughout his life, but he kept me from plenty."

"Really?" Lillian left the pot to heat and sank down across from me. Out in the garden, Abigail probed the depths of her sandbox with a short branch and sang a little ditty. Years ago, someone with foresight had planted a lovely willow to shade this side of the house, and what a difference it made.

"The soul of kindness, William also has an inborn bent for organization. I could list numerous instances of him watching out for me as I grew to manhood. He was always there, just behind the scenes, encouraging and warning me, too, if needful. A time or two when I strayed, he still supported me.

"I can't imagine you straying."

"Ha!" I shook my head like a watered-down dog. "Oh Lillian, I may not stray often, but when I do, I proceed right to the edge of the cliff."

She retrieved the whistling kettle, poured a pot to steep and delivered it with two cups. "Sometimes I wish I had known William for years like most women do with their husbands. And you, too—tell me more."

"All right, but this is just between you and me. I wouldn't want anyone else to know."

Her nod sufficed. The question in her eyes begged me to continue.

"I married too young. My heart was smitten with the very first girl who evinced interest in me, and our marriage amounted to one big mistake. Except for Donnie's birth, of course."

My first sip of tea fortified me. How had I gotten into this, anyway?

"Young love can be such a two-edged sword."

"Indeed. Grandfather asked me if I was sure about Victoria, and of course, I thought so. I believe William had reservations, as well, but knew better than to press the issue. Looking back, I think he saw right through into my so-called new love. From the start, he seemed to realize how much she might require of us all.

"At any rate, we married, and from the first, I discovered it impossible to please Victoria. Nothing I did suited her. Even now, I have no understanding of what she truly wanted. But I will say that Donnie's birth quite undid her.

"I shall never comprehend it, but that experience caused an irrevocable change. From the first moment she failed to—that is, she never took to him."

Lillian's heartfelt sigh rolled over me, along with an old emotion newly unearthed. "I still find it difficult to say the words, but 'tis true. Donnie brought no joy to Victoria, and at the same time, she constantly conjured ways to make life miserable for me. Perhaps she blamed me for her state of motherhood.

"How sad."

"Finally, she—" How to say this? "She interfered with my work. I was teaching at a boy's school, and intended to continue." I glanced around. I had forgotten all about Abigail, but Lillian was keeping watch. "Oh my. No one here is to know I trained as a teacher."

"Nothing you say will leave this room." Lillian leaned forward

a bit, and through the window, sunlight shed a shimmering veil over her light hair.

"At home, I gave in to Victoria about nearly everything, but she wanted more. One day she came to my classroom. I still can hardly fathom her audacity, but—" My face was flaming like the fire pit in Norman's back forty acres when he burned a month's trash.

"I—perhaps it might be best to leave this story here. Victoria humiliated me beyond the telling, in front of my students. And my headmaster. I knew I could never again face those young fellows, not to mention him."

"Oh, my. I'm so sorry."

"A long time has passed. Forgive me, but talking about it brings back the exact feelings from that evening, as strong as ever. For weeks, I moved about in a trance, while William managed our daily affairs and helped care for Donnie."

Another sip of tea helped dissipate the lump welling in my throat. "If I live to be one hundred, I doubt I shall ever live down the shame of that day."

"It was Victoria's shame, not yours." Lillian pressed her hand over mine. "Something like that becomes like a cloud over you. You may learn to ignore it, but you can never forget."

"Quite." What a sensation, to know someone understood. I allowed for this gift to wash over me. "You must have experienced something similar?"

She looked away. "Yes, with Kenneth when we were much younger, but he still holds it over me today."

I waited, but she disclosed no more. Not an uncomfortable silence, though, more like the silence between fast friends.

"I hope you can overcome it. When Victoria set the house on fire—William has told you about that, hasn't he?"

"Yes. How terrible—she must have lost her mind. But I wonder—" Lillian scrunched her forehead. "Did her action set you free in any sense?"

"One might say that, but only because William remained there to shield me through that awful time. I became free to leave Nottinghamshire and begin again."

"Maybe Victoria sought power over you. Some people have that strong desire."

"Yes. But I failed to comprehend it at the time, and I saw myself as a miserable failure. Every moment, I asked myself, 'Why can't I make her happy?'"

"Some people invoke those feelings in us—they enjoy seeing us powerless. Maybe they don't even realize what they're doing."

"That is as close as I've come to grasping what went on between us. William saw it all along, I believe. Grandfather had been gone for some years by the time Victoria died, and William stood by me every step of the way."

Lillian stared out at Abigail, still content with her stick and her song. "There's nothing like one faithful friend in time of need—a good mate, I suppose you say in England. I'm afraid I can never be completely free until Kenneth— It's awful to think like this, but I can't imagine him changing. He always brings up the past, as rigid as a fencepost—sees things today as he did thirty years ago."

"Mmm. But you have grown and changed?"

"Yes, so much. Edgar and I were happy, although we wanted children in the worst way. But now, William and I—I do hope you understand how grateful I am to be expecting another baby?" She took a deep breath as I nodded.

"I know William means well, but my independent streak— Anyway, this complication with Kenneth—how can I explain it?"

The clock marked time, ever moving onward.

"You see, I made a promise way back when Mama died. How I wish I had never made it. Kenneth and I would keep the store going, I vowed, so after Edgar died, I went back to work with him, but—"

"Did you work well together?"

Lillian's rueful chuckle waved over me like an evening breeze. "Not at all. Well, I suppose Kenneth thought we did, because I constantly did his bidding. But now—"

"You have a husband, a daughter, and another child on the way."

"Yes, so to keep Kenneth quiet, I—" She sighed as deeply as William had the other day. "I suggested maybe William could work for him. Such a lamentable mistake. I should never have voiced the idea."

"William would do almost anything for you, but he dreads spending time away from you and Abigail."

"Right. It was silly of me to mention—impetuous. I said it to give Kenneth some hope. I've always tried to rescue him, but when he gets an idea in his head—"

"If your mother were living, do you think she would hold you to your promise? Would she want to make life difficult for you and William?"

Sudden light filled Lillian's eyes. "Never. Of course not. I know she wouldn't!"

"Then why should that promise give Kenneth any power over you?"

"Because he heard me—but the promise was to Mama, not to him." She angled her head as recognition dawned, and her eyes shone like gems.

"Oh! I can tell him I know in my heart Mama has released me from my vow. Maybe then he will finally see I'm a grown woman with a life of my own."

"And that he has a right to a different life, too?"

"Yes—that's it exactly."

"But he still may not understand. He sounds quite set in his ways."

Dashing down the rest of her tea, Lillian fingered the ruffles on her apron. "You're right. Crazy, isn't it? I'm a grown woman with a husband who loves me, and Edgar did, too. Yet I haven't been able to stand up to Kenneth, although I know I need to."

Outside, Abigail hummed *The Yellow Rose of Texas*, and Lillian groaned. "Oh my. That song sends a message in itself. William calls me his yellow rose."

"And so you are. He never dreamed he would meet someone like you."

199

"Likewise. A few days after he first happened by, he asked me if those were yellow roses out beyond the fence. I said, 'No, they're buttercups, or some of them might be Texas Lonestars.' He squinted in that direction and said, "'They look like roses to me—and so do you.'"

Lillian's sigh came from deep down. "But we were talking about Kenneth. He's like a poisonous snake in the well house. I know better than to go in there, but still do, because I feel so guilty. His accusations haunt me, although I know his opinion shouldn't matter this much. I've allowed it to complicate our lives."

The wheels of comprehension were whirling. I could almost see them cutting new track for her to follow.

"Maybe it's because Kenneth and I were so tied to Mama after Papa was killed."

"How did that happen?"

"An accident. He was delivering a load of supplies to a mine—" Sometimes sparse details suffice—she had lost her father in such a violent way, and then Edgar. In the shade, Abigail still sang her tune, and Lillian's color improved by the second.

Through my shirt, sunlight warmed my back. Nothing compares to a second cup of tea on a bright Texas morning, especially with someone you have come to trust.

Chapter Seventeen

William became our area's chief cheese maker, and not just for his family and a few customers. Best of all, Donnie learned the skills William's father had passed down to him.

"How many people can say they make curds from a centuries-old recipe?" Thus William introduced his lessons. "Maybe one day you will share this process with others, but for now, let this be our secret."

"Your boss might not like it?"

William laughed outright, a lovely sound that for some time had grown rare. "You certainly have thought this one through, young man. Yes, although Mr. Grunkle's business has grown so fast, he might not even notice."

Caring for the cows fell to us entirely now, and William paid Donnie for his work. As usual, life found a new rhythm in the midst of change. Who knew how this first job might color Donnie's future? On the practical side, waking early to do the milking, tending to the curds with great care, and making deliveries taught responsibility and reliability.

With the military forces building up *over there*, some in our congregation suggested a weekly or biweekly prayer service. One fellow expressed more doubt than belief. "This has gone beyond anything we can do." I understood his argument, but his point argued *for* praying, not against it. His fear threatened him into helpless inaction.

I was no stranger to such a generalized sense of alarm, which can be so difficult to overcome, because we may assume that our own confusion speaks for the entire universe. But most people had recently seen their sons off at the Brady depot or taken them to training centers here in the state. They longed for the comfort inherent in prayer.

Our pastor's simple comment settled the matter. "Our boys in harm's way need our help. We may not be able to measure the effect of our prayers, but neither could the early disciples."

A bit later, William brought up the story of Dunkirk. In 1940, we had lived and breathed this saga as reported from London, when thousands prayed day and night for deliverance. Back then, William had asked the church members to join in, but a reminder could not hurt.

"Remember when congregations all over England prayed night and day from May twenty-sixth through the evacuation at Dunkirk? You recall the outcome? Our seemingly small gathering can make a difference."

I interjected, "Even the Prime Minister, not known for his faith, called the rescue 'a miracle of deliverance.'"

Observing the order of the universe placed me solidly on the side of beseeching Heaven. This war might have metamorphosed into a *world war*, but the earth's established patterns still remained. They surrounded and nurtured us, had we eyes to detect them.

Cows needed milking morning and night. The sun still rose and set in orderly fashion. Toting Donnie's fresh curds to the cool shade of the side porch, we noticed how much the grass, with no fanfare, had grown overnight. Whatever might befall, a steady cadence undergirded creation.

Staring up at the constellations when I woke in utter stillness, I considered that far across the Atlantic, Elliot Lardner might have observed these celestial figures a few hours earlier. When I watched a sitting mother duck or goose nurture her young still in the shell, the connection between all life seemed so obvious. Despite war raging on many fronts, nature's irrevocable *order* continued.

Through plagues and floods, conflicts and other manifestations of human greed, this earth perpetuated human life. Here, my studies of the ancient and not-so-ancient past stood me in good stead. This oneness with all who had come before and those who would follow, though much still remained a mystery, quelled my anxiety like nothing else.

By day swallows dipped in the sky, red-winged blackbirds adorned fence posts like sentries, and meadowlarks warbled their earnest songs over placid cows munching in the pasture. In the shade of tall pecan trees, squirrels reared their young, and along the fence line, a red fox skulked, hoping for a chance at our eggs.

Coyotes, black bears, raccoons, prairie dogs, and countless other creatures played their roles hidden from our eyes. Where once buffalo and wild horses roamed, cattle claimed their sustenance from the land.

Cows, goats and sheep grazed. People tilled their gardens, seeds entered the earth and produced after their kind.

Wildflowers preceded the peach and apple blossoms, and though I had never viewed a pecan blossom up close, I had no doubt they existed. Without petals, the female flowers or small nutlets hidden way up there in the trees, like spikes on the side of shoots, would develop into nuts as they were pollinated and fertilized. The process would take seven months, but one day, fruit would come of this annual cycle.

Seen or unseen, this was the way of things, the sequence of growth and fruit bearing. Disease and drought might threaten, but by-and-large, pecan flowers gradually transformed into the hard-shelled nuts we gathered.

In winter, we sat at our table and cracked their smooth shells, securing the edible inner portion in a bowl. Pecan meats provided protein and added texture and flavor for our stuffing, cakes and pies.

Replete with tragedy and chaos, even war could not change this earth's systematic foundation, no matter how devastating the reports over the airways, or how desperate my homeland had become. In Grandfather's Nottinghamshire orchards, this same reliable progression persisted, and his voice, in which I first heard the laws of seedtime and harvest, drummed from these very different hillsides.

"While the earth remaineth, seedtime and harvest, and cold and heat, and summer and winter, and day and night shall not cease."

Of course we would pray—plead with all of our might for an end to the evil stalking the earth and the return of local boys. How could we *not*? Though the Maker and Sustainer of all already knew our concerns, voicing them brought us solace and solidarity, and somehow, those who prayed naturally in German blended in with those of us who used English. Donnie, Anton, and several other children came along with their parents, and Donnie learned some phrases. If only the world at large might work this way!

The clime and form of this remote hill country, though unique, evidenced a ready connection to the rest of the world. We would lift our concern not only for the sons of this locale, but for each soldier and sailor, every hurting family around the globe.

Frederick Douglas called freedom of speech "the dread of tyrants." Doubtless, open prayer had become unwelcome in Herr Hitler's Germany. Voicing both fears and faith flew in the face of such a taskmaster, but we would stand against him in this one small way.

As heat continued to bear down, Lillian's feet swelled almost beyond recognition. This baby, scheduled to appear in late December, had chosen a lovely time to enter the world, but the temperatures of summer caused Lillian to remark, "I can feel the heat sucking the energy out of me before the day even begins."

No doubt even the most stalwart of grizzled ranchers in these parts looked forward to the arrival of cooler air. But for now, our relentless weather required endurance. Donnie and I had enlarged our garden, and toted water to the far corners. We discussed how we might extend our irrigation troughs next year. Planting as early as possible seemed the best insurance, as well as choosing our seeds with care.

This we did every winter, from the seed catalogs that came in the mail. If *drought-resistant* appeared in a description, we ordered that variety, and also put to use our recent experience.

Root vegetables, we had learned, managed the heat better than others more fragile in constitution. Through neglect or drought, one might harvest a much smaller version of carrot, but a carrot would manifest, nonetheless. Peas, cabbage, and spinach took the least water, so we planted them farthest from the pump. All the while, we played a game.

If given the choice, which plant would we be? I chose the turnip or beet. Since we eat the majority of the plant, its energy goes not into foliage and stems, but into viable food.

Donnie chose tomatoes, since they enjoy a longer growing season and the water they use spreads over an extended period. He noted, "But mostly, it's 'cause they smell so good, even the leaves, and people could eat me raw or cooked."

This diversion saw us through some laborious hours One day, the aftermath of Dunkirk preoccupied me while we worked, and I thought how carefully Mr. Churchill had worded his "We shall fight on the beaches" speech.

Only one month into his new office, the poor fellow faced stalwart enemies. Barely avoided, the Dunkirk debacle could hardly qualify as a success. A miracle, yes, but as the Prime Minister quipped, "We must be very careful not to assign to this deliverance the attributes of a victory. Wars are not won by evacuations."

Carefully chosen words, indeed. While the populace jubilated at the return of over 300,000 British soldiers, Mr. Hitler prepared to invade England. Despite the evacuation saving our troops and buying us time, Mr. Churchill realized the British people must again be rallied for the war effort.

I couldn't help but wonder—presumably, such an avid reader as he would glean much from literature during these trying times. In the midst of a restless sleep, did he waken suddenly with a word from the ancients instructing him? Aeschylus seemed especially appropriate these days—"From a small seed a mighty trunk may grow."

Now that a year had passed since Dunkirk, war-weary troops had become even more exhausted and in need of deliverance. In his private moments, did the Prime Minister consider the attack on Pearl Harbor another miracle?

Lillian and William grew accustomed to Kenneth's continued attacks. I had to admit to that wiry fellow's prowess. He struck in their most vulnerable spots—do the emotions get more delicate than with an expectant mother already caring for a toddler?

But like our garden, Lillian became stronger through this added hardship. And hardship it proved to be, in the form of Kenneth's poorly formatted notes decrying her lack of love for their deceased parents.

His raging proved that he saw life in black and white. Either Lillian devoted herself to the business their parents had founded, or she hated them. No alternative existed between the two.

Hearing his latest underhanded tactic, I nearly laughed at the obvious irony. *Selfish*, he called Lillian. He lived alone while she poured herself out for Abigail and William.

Uncaring, he added. His list went on, and each adjective could so easily be turned back upon its sender. I found myself pondering why some people turn on family members at times like this. They desperately need what only family can provide, yet drive away their relations.

One positive effect of all this was a growing kinship with Lillian. She might share Kenneth's latest antic when I stopped by with the mail. As the weeks wore on, his ploys became more ridiculous, and I developed a certain sympathy for him. In truth, he had become pathetic.

Of course, I kept this well hidden, and as the weeks passed, Lillian's countenance changed. Perhaps this ruddy refulgence on her cheekbones rose from her condition in such merciless heat. But as Kenneth's accusations became more far-fetched, a little nipping began at the sides of her mouth, like a grin being born.

Watching this heartened me no end. With each bit of power she reclaimed, her eyes brightened. Her step, though heavy with child, showed spirit.

William noticed this, too. "How does she do it? That Kenneth's a rapscallion—puts me in mind—" He glanced at me before continuing. "— of Victoria. He's so sure he's right. But Lillian is realizing the hold Kenneth has had on her."

This marked the first time he ever mentioned Victoria's character. Always, he had kept his judgments to himself, so I tucked this omission away as a special insight.

Finally one day, Lillian giggled aloud while reading Kenneth's latest note aloud. He had outdone himself this time, calling her a hard-nosed bully. That caused me to burst out, too, and we laughed until tears coursed her cheeks, and she held her growing middle.

"Oh my! What good medicine you are for me, Everett."

"It's Kenneth who deserves the praise. He has a way of bringing out the best in us, don't you think?"

She chuckled again. "Oh, my, I really shook this baby up! I can't believe he would say I never cared for Mama at all. He must have forgotten how I nursed her to the very end." She peered into my eyes. "This means something, doesn't it? I can't recall when I've laughed this much."

Sprawled on the couch beside me, Abigail looked particularly angelic. Something in me whispered, *time to listen.*

"I've always been so sure Kenneth's misery was my fault, but he's done this to himself. Now, he even makes up facts to support his point."

"Perhaps he has begun to feel desperate."

Lillian leaned back in her chair. "Yes, maybe, but I can laugh! It's not necessary to take him so seriously, or myself, either. What a wonder to be able to see things differently than we used to—everything always seemed so deadly serious."

"Perhaps your capacity for joy is growing."

"*Capacity for joy*—I like the sound of that."

"I learned about mine through losing it for a time. Finally accepting that I could never meet Victoria's expectations gave me a start. But here, my ability to enjoy life has flourished in a new way. All it takes is a sunrise or an evening star."

"Oh, I know what you mean! I'm seeing the world as if for the first time, all through Abigail's eyes. She notices the smallest things, and each discovery holds so much meaning. Now, I get another chance to do all it again with this second child."

"I understand. Donnie's sense of wonder still astounds me."

We shared a few quiet moments, and of course, cups of tea. These times had the feel of something precious. Lillian was fast becoming the sister I'd never had, and truth be told, my first real female friend.

Maybe she sensed this too, for she asked, "Do you think you'll ever marry again?"

"I have learned not to make unequivocal statements about the future, but I have everything I need right now." After a moment, I added, "Perhaps I made enough mistakes with Victoria to last a lifetime."

"You've never told me what she did."

Nor had I ever told anyone except William. But on this autumn morning, a quiet assurance overcame my reticence.

"She had grown ill. Her mind had—" Not a good beginning. After all these years, could I still not put the scene into words without making excuses for Victoria? As I fumbled, Lillian busied herself fetching pound cake and pouring more tea.

"You don't have to say, Everett. It's all right."

How glorious to feel comfortable in revealing nothing at all, if I wished. This in itself made me want to finish.

"One day Victoria came to my school—right into my classroom.

She stood in the back and started to disrobe." Seeing Lillian's cheeks flame gave me pause.

"First she removed her coat, then her sweater. She called to me in a wheedling tone. Of course, the boys turned to stare at her. Then she left her shoes and ran barefoot to me, flung her skirt to the floor and started to unbutton her blouse.

"'Evvy!' Her cry brought me out of my stupor, but I stood there helpless. I can still hear her yelling that nickname she called me in private." The long-denied image became so real, I felt I could reach out and touch Victoria again.

"What did you do?"

"I simply gaped. I couldn't have moved an inch if my life depended on it, but there was no need. By then, the headmaster had followed her trail. 'Madam—' The look on his face sent a queasy sensation through me. He kept his voice controlled, but his eyes bulged. When Victoria turned and addressed him, the prominent vein in his forehead threatened to pop.

"'Want to see more?' She unbuttoned the last button and removed her blouse. In her camisole, she started for him, but he grabbed her wrists and dragged her out screaming. I stood dumbfounded, with the boys shushed to silence."

Sickness washed over me even now. "I had tried so hard to please her. Tried to make her happy in every way possible, but—"

Innocent in slumber, Abigail stirred.

"In the weeks leading up to that terrible day, she kept asking why she couldn't come to school. By then, I should have realized how her mind worked, but I never dreamed she would try it."

Between Lillian and me stretched an interlude, serene and unfettered. Abigail stirred again, but Lillian kept her seat.

"How awful." It was a statement, not an exclamation. "She wanted complete control of you."

I knew she was right.

"And you felt responsible. You kept bending to her wishes."

The backs of my eyes burned. No need to agree aloud, for in her own way, Lillian had traveled this road, shouldering responsibility for Kenneth, succumbing to his every demand. Oh, the sweetness of knowing another human being comprehends your very worst moment!

Abigail mumbled something. Still, Lillian stayed immobile.

"So then, you gave up teaching?"

I let our newfound understanding communicate my answer. I might have been conversing with William or Donnie, for we spoke wordlessly, too. When Abigail slid to the floor and her small feet pattered the living room floor, Lillian ran to reassure her nothing had changed during her nap.

But something *had* changed. Putting the story into words with Lillian loosed something in me, like opening the door first thing in the morning and breathing deep. We spoke no more of this, but focused our attention on Abigail, who drank her milk and dived into a piece of cake with gusto.

Perhaps you had sleepwalked through a nightmare. Perhaps you had battled relentless forces. But like nature's rhythms, this foundation of family grounded you through it all, and you knew it would suffice through whatever lay ahead.

On May seventh, the Allies took Tunisia. German and Italian troops surrendered in North Africa on the thirteenth. On the sixteenth, the RAF commenced an air raid on the Ruhr. On the twenty-second, Admiral Donitz suspended U-boat operations in the North Atlantic, and on June eleventh, one of Hitler's henchmen, a fellow named Himmler, ordered the liquidation of every Jewish ghetto in Poland.

As school let out, Donnie and I gave ourselves to the garden. Late during the first week of summer vacation, an unexpected visit from Norman lightened our load.

The offer came as he exited his rattletrap bubble-top pick-up. Like a fallen peach, though bruised and marred, the vehicle still had something to give. In fact, it had carried us to the *Schutzenfest* and back home again.

"Ho there, Donnie boy! Helping your dad today?"

Donnie replied as he hefted a bucket of water from the pump. Then Norman spotted me, as well.

"Brought you somethin' that might help around here." Norman pointed his chin toward the bubbletop. "Bought m'self a new truck yesterday. Got a great deal, and don't have room for this old bone-shaker at my place."

I leaned on the fender, wondering about the price. Learning to drive couldn't be that hard, could it? Meanwhile, Donnie turned his big brown eyes on me. He knew better than to voice his desire, but I could almost hear him beg, "Say yes, Da. Please?"

Norman took my speechlessness for interest and spewed more details. "I figure this old jalopy might be worth a bed load of your cider and jam. My wife loves your apple butter, too—she still can't understand how a man puts out such good eats."

"You want to make an exchange?"

"If it's all right with you."

"This surely would help with deliveries."

"And with watering your trees. This old girl's used to carrying water, believe me."

I turned to those big brown eyes. "What do you think, Donnie?"

"Can I learn to drive?"

"I expect you will, and so shall I."

And that was that. Norman had hauled over enough gasoline for a month—he didn't want to unload the barrel from the truck bed, he said. Swallowing my pride came easier now, since we had continued our talks from time to time through the winter and spring. Whether or not our jam and cider equaled the truck's value remained debatable, yet impossible to figure.

Norman said it did, so I accepted his estimation. Having ridden to Fredericksburg in this very cab, Donnie and I already felt at home inside, so when Norman gestured for me to take the wheel, Donnie piled in the back with Ramshackle.

With Norman beside me, I jerked the column. On my second

try, the gears sprang into motion and we rode around the orchard in a mix of awe and laughter from Donnie, with Ramshackle barking for good measure. When we jerked to a stop near the house, Norman bade me back up, turn around, and park again. Then he jumped out.

"So that's done. I'll head home. Bring your payment whenever you're ready. If I'm not there, Bernardo will be. He won't be gone again till shearing time next spring—did I ever tell you he's the best shearer this side of the border? They call 'em *tasinques*. Livin' up here, he can make a little money during the off season, too."

"He sheers sheep?"

"No, mostly goats. Angoras. The need for Army blankets and uniforms has quadrupled the demand. A *tasinque* like Bernardo fleeces a hundred goats a day, at three cents per animal. Not much to feed a family on, but now he's got a decent place to live. Better store that gasoline in the shade. They say it'll soon be rationed."

"We can give you a ride."

"Nah. This way I can check on a few things between here and there. A man my age gets used to ridin' everywhere. The walk'll do me good."

We no more than waved him off before Donnie let loose. "Wow! We have a pick-up—we won't have to walk to Loyal Valley to catch a ride to church. Can't believe it!"

"Neither can I. Let's load it full this afternoon for our first trip over to Norman's."

"Didn't he say one load?"

"Yes. But I'd rather pay a bit too much than not quite enough."

212

Chapter Eighteen

O n the Sunday before July Fourth, someone posted a note at the filling station about a community picnic. Word spread, and everyone brought their food to the Tabernacle, where the surrounding grassy area between there and the school served as a park. A good time was had by all, if discussing the war can be considered a good time.

Someone had saved a few fireworks from last year, but most people agreed we would have to forego them from now on. Lillian had no idea of Great Britain's history with fireworks, dating back to 1486, when King Henry VIII enjoyed a display for his wedding. William took pleasure in regaling us with the story.

"Her Royal Highness, Queen Elizabeth I, became quite fond of them, and appointed a fire master to see that royal fireworks displays went to plan. Of course, you have heard about the gunpowder plot?"

"Yes, but I forget the details."

"In 1605, a dastardly plan supposedly fomented by one Guy Fawkes was found out—a plot to blow up the Houses of Parliament. This led to celebrating "Bonfire Night" every November fifth."

"But not now?"

"Definitely not—the blackout prevails."

Donnie had gone to play baseball with some boys, or more questions would have arisen. I wandered through the small crowd, and a week later, still pondered the conversation I overheard. By then, the Allies had landed in Sicily, and word had it they would soon bomb Rome. I could only hope they captured Palermo more quickly than they drove the Waffen SS from North Africa.

William walked home with us while Lillian took Abigail home for a nap. On our way, another memorable incident occurred. With no warning, a splendid creature crossed the path right in front of us, keeping its frame parallel to the ground and using its tail as a rudder. It had the look of a bird, but—

"Oh man! It's a Great Roadrunner!" Donnie's bugged-out eyes most likely matched my own.

"Upon my word!" This was all William could muster.

We had yet to see one of these up close, and the sight left us awestruck. We kept our eyes on our feathered friend as it rushed off on some intense mission, and stood aghast even after it disappeared against the horizon.

Born to run, this bird could outrace a human being. From its sturdy bill to the white tip of its tail, its body measured two powerful feet. It could kill a rattlesnake, and its bushy blue-black crest and mottled plumage blended with this country's dusty shrubs and rocks.

We had read all about the Roadrunner, but why had it taken this long to see one? Would we ever see another? The visitation happened so quickly it stunned us, and we each took a few moments to catalogue the unique sight.

Something akin to this reaction recurred that evening as I rehearsed a conversation I overheard at the picnic. I hadn't intended to listen, but after ingesting far too much fried chicken and watermelon, had taken a stroll to aid my digestion.

Lillian had taken Abigail home, and William went off to observe a fundraiser for the war effort—people paying a dime for a chance to dunk someone into a tank of water.

A few men gathered between there and the gunnysack races, and their discussion drifted my way as I meandered along San Antonio Street.

"You're sure?"

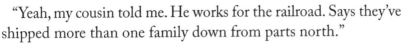

"Yeah, my cousin told me. He works for the railroad. Says they've shipped more than one family down from parts north."

"Germans?"

"Um hmm. From those conclaves in the Midwest and up in New York state. I think this one came from Wisconsin. They're members of a German *bund* led by a guy named Fritz Kuhn. He says what Hitler did to get Germany out of the Depression would sure help us here.

"He's even met with Hitler and his henchmen over there. Then there's something called the Silvershirt Legion, led by somebody named Pelley. They believe the Jews control our economy, and that's what caused the Depression."

Like a criminal, I clung to my position without moving. Only one voice seemed familiar.

"Hitler hates the Jews and so do these folks. You get some committed fellas like that together, and things can turn dangerous. That's the kind they're shippin' down to the camp at Crystal City. Some might even be spies."

"Who is *they*?"

"The Federal Bureau of Investigation—here, the local authorities take care of cases, or the Rangers. Can't have spies around here with all these military bases goin' up."

"The Gulf's so close—too close for comfort. Wouldn't be that hard for an enemy U-boat to spit out some spies in the dead of night, would it? Didja hear our teacher has connections up North, too?"

"And she changed the spelling of her name."

"What's the story on her husband? Thought I heard something 'bout him goin' to Germany?"

"Yep. He's from up north, Ohio, wasn't it? Or maybe Wisconsin. My connections say all of a sudden, he left for the Old Country. Never came back. Mighty peculiar."

"Yeah. And she's gone now?"

"Up and disappeared. Her landlord, old Elmer Stone, really took a liking to her boy. Probably gave her low rent 'n all."

What I knew about Emmaline flashed through my mind like that speedy roadrunner. Her family lived in this area, but her husband came from somewhere up north.

And she had been questioned. Twice. That was the extent of my knowledge, except that she knew how to teach children and had won Donnie's heart. Glad for the low mesquite tree between the men and me, I lurked a bit longer.

"They're bringin' lots of 'em down to Crystal City. Got a German school there. Some of 'em want to go back to the Old Country, so they'll be exchanged for American prisoners of war."

A cold finger traced my spine. The government would deport American citizens, even children?

"You don't say?"

"That's what I hear. Keep it to yourself, though. Can't be too careful these days."

"Just think—might've had a spy right here, teachin' our children."

"Raises the hair on the back of your neck, don't it?"

"Bein' on the school board, how'd you ever let this slip by?"

"Nobody raised a question. We knew she was from around here— from good stock down around Fredericksburg, where everybody dates back to the 1800s. But I guess some of these Germans up north came over after the Great War and can be slippery. Word has it that her sister married into their kind."

Two of the men wandered off, and the remaining ones switched topics. But their discussion left me breathless and aching with questions.

Who in their right mind, German heritage or not, would want to go to Germany right now? Something else chilled me—the identity of the speaker who offered the most information about this subject. No mistaking that voice. It was most certainly Norman's.

Once when I mentioned him in passing, Lillian had said, "Norman Landers? That man's got a cousin in every corner of the world that you can name. Sits on every board in the county. Bet he even has a cousin in Nottinghamshire."

We chuckled about that, but Norman did seem to know people everywhere, and a great deal about multiple topics. He had taught us so much about the hill country, but this was different. More than what he said today bothered me—excitement and intrigue filled his voice. He seemed pleased that Emmaline and Anton had disappeared, and oddly energized by this camp called Crystal City.

Perhaps I would take him some more curds and jam in the morning, even though he said we already paid too much for the bubbletop. I had no doubt that Emmaline was entirely innocent, but this sort of talk highlighted my immigrant status—far be it from me to owe Norman a thing.

In August, King Albert's brother, Duke of Kent, perished in a plane crash *en route* to Iceland. He shared his passion for aviation with his brothers Bertie and Edward, and thus joined the RAF. Like the King, George flew to air bases to help boost morale, and his plane crashed near Caithness in Scotland.

As William put it when he brought the news, this marked the first time in 450 years that a Royal Family member lost his life on active military duty. Along with the King and Queen and Princesses Elizabeth and Margaret, the British people mourned. Donnie took it all in as William and I discussed the intense pressure on the King.

"Wait a minute. I thought George VI was King?"

"True. But in 1861, after Queen Victoria's husband, Prince Albert, died at an early age, the queen decreed that no one after her would ever again rule under the name *Albert*. So our present-day Albert, who had never wanted to be king, chose to be called George the Sixth."

"He didn't want to be king? Why not?"

"Only one son or daughter of a king inherits the crown, and Albert's brother Edward had been preparing for this since childhood. He was crowned but soon abdicated. Albert had never planned to assume the throne."

"Abdi—" Puzzlement showed in Donnie's expression and I offered a bit of help.

"The word comes from the Latin *abdicatus*, meaning to disown."

"Edward didn't like being King?"

William took over again. "Righto. His rule lasted only about a year in 1936. He abdicated in December, and then King George was crowned. Rather a shy sort, he still took up his duties and has ruled admirably."

Abigail tugged at Donnie to play with her, so we left it at that. Another history lesson barely begun.

"Wish I could ask Mrs. B, but she and Anton didn't come to the picnic. She always explains things so well."

"Yes, she certainly does." I withheld further comment and resorted to my own inquiries. If Emmaline and Anton were indeed at that camp, would their stay be temporary? What could she have done to raise suspicions? Moreover, could she be proven innocent and released?

One day on a mission in town, the temptation to stop by Mr. Stone's house nearly overcame me, but Donnie accompanied me at the time. No use disturbing him.

The next day, he stayed to help Lillian for a while, so I detoured by the house where Emmaline and Aaron lived. Closed shutters revealed no sign of life. What a sinking feeling. So what I had overheard was true, Emmaline and Anton had left Loyal Valley.

The same sensation enveloped me as when I discovered some baby robins missing from their nest last April. Donnie and I remarked that the mother built it awfully low, in a mesquite tree not far from our back door. This made it easy for us to observe her goings-on, but dangerous for her helpless fledglings.

Soon, three beautiful turquoise-blue eggs appeared. The Mama dutifully cared for them, keeping them warm during early summer storms. She even stood and stared me down one day when I peered through the branches. Soon after, a tuft of feathery white appeared through a crack in an egg. The miracle had begun.

We kept as close watch as possible, while still giving this feathered family their privacy. Faithful and true, the Mama flew back and forth from the creek to feed her young.

But a few days later, utter quiet alerted me. The hollow lack of sound struck me as I passed the tree. Three babies—they ought to be cheeping to be fed.

Later, I stole a brief glance. Sometimes silence and emptiness deliver the strongest message, and that same message came to me as the closed shutters on the house Emmaline and Anton had occupied.

September, 1942

On this rare fall day, perfect shirtsleeve weather, one might forgive our climate for the ravages of summer. So much had happened since school started, my mind whirled. These quiet mornings gave me time to process everything in the war, and also in our little world.

As always, we kept abreast of the war's several fronts, the very least we could do. I wanted Donnie to understand its broad scope, since when the final shot had been fired, his generation would inherit the remains. Yes, even in our small corner of the universe, the effects would be noticeable.

Strange how we refer to where we live this way, as if Earth's land mass were drawn out in linear fashion, with measurable dimensions. Even with unbelievable horrors occurring all around us, we still focused on this particular spot.

Meanwhile, Lillian's midsection expanded even more than during her last pregnancy. Donnie remarked on this during our most recent visit. "Are you gonna have more than one baby this time?"

She burst out with laughter. "I should, don't you think? Despite the heat, she maintained her steady constitution, sewing volumes of new play clothes to last Abigail through the winter and spring. She also continued to produce the best bread this side of the Mississippi, and reveled in her role as housewife and mother. We stopped by one day after school, and Donnie burst into the house to seek Abigail. Down on her hands and knees scrubbing the kitchen floor, Lillian motioned him toward the back door.

"She's just around the corner. She'll be so glad to see you!"

He raced out, and Lillian gave me a look that could only be interpreted as a warning. If I told William we had caught her doing such strenuous work, she would never speak to me again.

Much of the time, she and Abigail joined in a lovely duet, a unique rendition of "The Yellow Rose of Texas." Privately, she told me that the yellow rose in the song referred to a woman, not a flower, but the tune was catchy—flower or woman, who cared?

William hurried home to a happy household, but also enjoyed his first raise at the creamery. He delighted in his work and could scarcely believe his pay. Even better, he had relaxed. For him, that is—I wager a former butler never fully lets down his guard.

One Saturday while making deliveries in our jalopy, Donnie and I lovingly christened the old girl Hazel, since we were discussing the pecan crop at the time. Hazelnuts entered into our dialogue and Donnie exclaimed, "That's it. How about calling our truck Hazel?"

I instantly agreed. As we bumped along toward our next destination, he patted the dusty dashboard and turned quiet. Returning from our deliveries, he fell asleep, and I rehashed the enormous alteration William had undergone in the past few years. Now a contented American employee, he had functioned largely on his own back in England.

Grandfather's rather loose rules—guidelines, I should say—left great leeway for personal choice. That proved true in my upbringing, and also with the household's everyday needs. I doubt Grandfather checked on the details of his affairs, all managed by his butler and closest friend.

He followed the same plan with his estate, which in the end made matters quite simple. I daresay many a butler enjoyed a far less trusting relationship with his employer.

The only time I ever saw William in tears was the day Grandfather passed from this world. His eyes glistened when he gave us our first glimpse of Abigail, but at Grandfather's funeral, he broke into unabashed weeping.

Through his friendship with William, Grandfather also bequeathed him another inheritance. Me. By the time Grandfather passed, I was grown, but in the ensuing years, William revealed how seriously he took his guardianship.

We might have rebuilt after the fire, but instead, he spoke of crossing the Atlantic.

Perhaps I would never understand his thinking, but here we were, fulfilling Grandfather's treasured dream. And the decision had proven fruitful.

Fully invigorated by his position with Mr. Grunkle, William fairly beamed these days. As for me, a sense of contentment often descended as I went about my daily chores. Then one day, William alerted us about a program on the BBC. Last year, one of his British friends, a Vicar, mentioned talks being broadcast from Oxford—the BBC had recruited a don named C. S. Lewis to speak to the British people.

"Remember that sermon my friend heard at St. Mary's church? This is the same speaker. Maybe we shall be able to tune in this time." The Vicar had sent William copies of *The Listener* and *Radio Time* so we might get the scheduling right, but with the difference in time and airwave interference, we had been able to hear only bits and pieces of what became a series of twenty live broadcasts.

More recently, William's friend sent him a little paperback called *Broadcast Talks* containing the first two sets of chats. We found them down-to-earth and practical.

The talks still continued, and for some reason, we managed to catch one entitled *Beyond Personality,* in which Lewis tackled the topic of prayer. He said that many people question how God can possibly attend to so many requests at once.

At this, Donnie's eyes brightened. He had asked the same question recently, and why prayer only seemed to work sometimes. If we were meant to trust, wouldn't answers be less random? I made a poor stab at an answer, but this talk surpassed my reasoning.

Mr. Lewis noted that one of our assumptions about the Divine might be askew. Because Time maintains such a hold on earth, we think the same must be true in other realms, and believe Time governs God. But some things are not in Time at all. We think in terms of past, present, and future, but in Eternity, neither past nor future exist.

In that realm, all moments are present. So, with infinite attention to give, God attends to each of us when we call, as if we were the only individual in the world.

When the broadcast ended and led to some gay fiddle music, we listened a bit longer before readying for bed. How wonderful that this Oxford professor took time to address my countrymen—at such a time, what encouragement he must have offered them. And perhaps he had no idea his instruction reached us here.

The specific timing of catching this broadcast signaled the very Divine care he emphasized. Through listening and our conversation afterwards, Donnie realized the universality of his questions. His concept of the world enlarged, and so did mine.

But in our community, summer of 1942 brought an overnight change. In August, a bespectacled, rather muscular young man accompanied Mr. Fletcher on his annual visit. Introduced as Mr. Kidney, lately arrived from eastern Texas, the new teacher seemed instantly at ease with Donnie, who made known his ardent desire to learn as much about airplanes as possible.

A letter sent to all parents forewarned of this alteration and had alerted Donnie, so he already grieved losing Mrs. B and Anton. When Mr. Fletcher presented Mr. Kidney, Donnie was ready.

"Nice to meet you, sir." Mr. Kidney had barely exchanged niceties when Donnie burst out, "Say! Have you heard about the Grumman F6f?"

Mr. Kidney's first words laid claim to this student's devotion. "Have I ever! The Hellcat. I certainly hope it lives up to its name and helps bring this war to a speedy end. I would be flying one myself, were it not for my weak eyes."

That did it. The school year beckoned on bright wings, but the transition contained a bit more pathos this year. My *whys* concerning Emmaline and Anton simply refused to be stifled, and inquiring of Mr. Fletcher provided no help.

"She and Anton had to move away."

"Have they gone back to their family near Fredericksburg?"

"Farther, I think, but that is not for me to say. Official business, you know, Mr. Herring." He remained tight lipped until he and Mr. Kidney went on their way.

His verbal dance only increased my curiosity. Why hadn't Emmaline brought Anton to bid Donnie farewell?

Early in September, with Donnie's after-school exclamations over Mr. Kidney's classroom expertise and his baseball gamesmanship, I rested easy about our new teacher. Spelling work marched on as before, and this new instructor seemed especially apt at science and mathematics, my weak spots.

Freed of concern over my son's education, my curiosity focused on Anton and his mother. Where had they gone, and why? The question niggled at times and nagged at others. How might I discover the specifics? I did stop to speak with Mr. Stone about his lost renter, and he divulged the little he knew.

"Heard a ruckus one hot night back in July, so I came out with my gun. Thought maybe it was critters after my sweet corn, but saw a car over t' the rental house. When I walked up, one of the men pulled out his identification—Texas Rangers.

"That shut me up right fast, so there was nothin' to do but stand back and watch Mrs. Bultman leave the house. Anton, too—little sleepy-eyed fella still in his nightclothes. Wish't I coulda done somethin', but I just stood there.

"She left a lot of her things. Oughta get 'em to her somehow. You don't happen t' know where they went?"

"No, but if I hear anything, I will let you know."

Emmaline had sent the remainder of her rental payment, he allowed, but with no return address. He produced the note she included and shook his head as if still trying to grasp its meaning.

"I regret having to leave so suddenly and without any notice. Please do what you will with our belongings. Thank you so much for your many kindnesses to Anton and me."

No hint of her destination, only regret about the circumstances. I patted Mr. Stone's shoulder. "Perhaps another renter will happen along soon."

"Shouldn't be hard with so many folks movin' about." He shook his head. "But I did take to that young'un, such a smart little fella."

Weeks later, still no answers. Though I hated taking the time, I stopped in at the gas station one morning, hoping to hear something. But that day, the men must have been busy elsewhere. Considering the overheard Fourth of July conversation, I avoided the temptation to ask Norman outright.

And then an idea occurred. Why not speak with Emmaline's grandfather? I could make a run down there easily and get back before school let out. We did the morning milking early, anyway.

Like a slow-baking plum pudding, this plan stewed in the back of my mind. The route remained clear from our *Schutzenfest* jaunt— not far at all, and I had gotten my license.

So it was that midway into September, I dropped Donnie by the school on my way, keeping my intentions quiet. Better that way, especially in case of ominous news.

I stopped at Mr. Stone's and asked if I might haul any of Emmaline's things to her family. He hurried to a small outbuilding, and after we loaded a few boxes in the truck bed, I headed south.

Several miles down the road, a general sense of foreboding, like a man sensing a heart attack coming on—or so Grandfather testified—enveloped me. To no avail, I attempted to shrug off the feeling

By the time I pulled up across the street from Opa Bultmann's warehouse, the unpleasant sensation grew in spite of my easy drive.

As if I were a random customer, I entered the establishment and looked around.

Of course, the warehouse clerk noticed a stranger and made efforts not to stare. Hadn't Norman said these German communities stuck together? Perhaps visitors arrived only during their celebrations, or more likely, the current tensions had heightened suspicions.

Full shelves offered a fine array of useful items to peruse, and I asked if individuals might make purchases. Donnie could use a thick sweater, and I added an extra wool blanket, two things to delete from our Montgomery Ward order.

Some heavy denim overalls caught my eye, just the thing for cider making. After three seasons, mine remained usable, but in sad shape. And then I spied some long Johns, a set for Donnie and one for me would do well.

Pleased I had brought along enough cash, I approached the counter and made my purchases. The clerk, a cheerful sort, made small talk about the weather, and we conversed a bit. A door shut in the back room and someone coughed. Then came some shuffling. Could that be Emmaline's grandfather?

As if to produce a quick reply, an older fellow burst in with a request in German. I understood the gist: "Henrietta, would you mind running over to the post office? That package we ordered last Monday should be here."

The clerk hurried out, leaving me with the proprietor. On second look, a family resemblance showed through clearly enough. High brow, dark hair, strong posture, eyes both wise and searching.

"Good day, sir," I began. "Are you related to Emmaline Bultman?"

His eyes pierced me. "Who asks?"

"Oh, forgive me. Everett Herring here. My son Donnie is a friend of Anton's, and his mother taught his classes at Loyal Valley. We came to last year's *Schutzenfest,* so they showed us your store."

His shoulders sagged as he glanced around. Fortunately, no one else had entered.

"They have moved south of here."

"Do you have an address? My son would like to write to Anton."

He shook his head. "Not yet." He looked around again. "Our granddaughter, Emmaline's twin sister—she has been taken for an enemy alien."

"But they were both born here in the States, weren't they?"

He sank a worn elbow on the wooden counter. "Yah. Our daughter says maybe Emmaline is teaching at the German school where they took Hulda now."

"Oh?"

"Yah. They asked her about Johann's father and about the banks. Some years back, he heard the money was going better in Germany, so he bought *reichmarks* for his father. His father turned them into gold and returned them to deposit over dere." He gestured vaguely eastward.

"Before the border closed, Johann booked passage on a ship. But they must have been turned back." Mr. Bultmann rubbed his beard. "Emmaline thinks he might be working in a labor camp now."

At the risk of troubling him even more, I ventured, "Do you know where Emmaline and Anton went?"

"Yah. To a place called Crystal City."

"Have you heard from them?"

"Our daughter did. She says maybe she can visit them some day."

"Is Anton in school?"

"Yah. Strange, he studies now in German."

"Indeed?"

He lowered his voice even more. "My daughter, she is afraid Hulda and her husband, even the little ones, will be taken to Germany. A neighbor up North reported dem to the authorities because they went to a meeting."

"A meeting?"

"Yah, of a *bund*." He scratched his head. "Yah, always like two peas in a pod, Emmaline and Hulda, and my wife took dem with her when she visited her sister years ago. Hulda fell in love with a

Northern boy and never came back. If only they had moved down here. Now she and her family are with her husband in—"

Opa's voice trembled. He closed his eyes for a few moments. "Her uncles—my sons—fought for our country in the Great War. Who vould ever tink our letters to her would be censored now?"

"So Emmaline and Anton went to the camp. Do you understand why?"

"My daughter, she tinks because Emmaline can speak German. They have a school dere, and this was Emmaline's way to see Hulda. Otherwise, maybe they might never have met again on this earth."

"Oh, my. I wish I could—"

Mr. Bultman leaned heavily against the counter. "Hulda has done nothing wrong. At the meetings, everyone saluted the American flag she said." With thick fingers, he gestured to the one hanging out front. "Ve have alvays loved America. Our daughter's heart is breaking, and she says 'Why, oh why did Mother take us along when she went up to see Aunt Meta?'"

In this establishment filled with all manner of everyday necessities—pots and pans on shelves or hanging by their handles, canned goods, lamp oil, candles, utensils, tools for outdoor work, barrels of flour and corn meal, another barrel of pickles, clothing and yard goods galore—a large wall clock ticked away the hour. No doubt brought from Germany, packed away in a wooden crate nearly a century ago.

Opa's parents had crossed the Atlantic with hopes as high as the ones William and I cherished. He had built his business on honesty and hard work and been a good citizen. Now, his granddaughter was suspect and held in government custody. And her twin—who could know what had gone on in Emmaline's mind when she heard about her sister?

Our eyes locked in absolute helplessness. Footsteps sounded, and soon Henrietta set down a basket of mail at the counter's end.

Opa Bultmann drew himself up. "Vel." That one syllable said it all.

Chapter Nineteen

The European world has become a network of spies. Reports of intrigue in the Scandinavian countries arrived over the wireless, and William's contacts write about much the same afoot in England—coppers always on the alert for black market operators, or spivs, as they are labeled. Or worse. *Worse* refers to German nationals who manage to sneak across the Channel and make landfall.

One never knows when something might be misinterpreted, so discretion is urged in public places. Someone under a brown Fedora might be listening, intent on sending information to the enemy.

When the stores and movie houses closed, people stayed home, or those on errands traveled like specters, by moonlight or in the shadows. Reports pictured the entire populace with collars turned up, faces averted, although knowing the British as I did, this simply cannot be the case. No one likes a good chat with a stranger as much as a British citizen.

But everywhere, posters remind them to withhold the whereabouts of their sons' military units, troop movements or any other information that might be of interest to the Nazis. William's correspondent sketched out several of these posters. One depicted a suckerfish with the message, "Don't be a sucker. Keep your mouth shut!"

He said that posters with "Loose lips sink ships" could be seen all over the place. Another showed a human hand with an obvious ring putting together a jigsaw puzzle and the warning: "Bits of careless talk are pieced together by the enemy: *Convoy sails for England tonight.*"

Yet another boasted a caricature of Hitler with an enormous ear and the message "Mr. Hitler Wants To Know!" But the one that caught my attention was a cross with a soldier's helmet hanging from one bar. Above it appeared: *A careless word.* Below it: *another cross.* Words have become a danger.

Though far away from England, as I spoke with Emmaline's grandfather the other day, the same need for secrecy reigned. He put a thick arthritic finger to his lips and whispered, "Keep all of this to yourself."

I agreed, and as Hazel hummed her way toward Loyal Valley, a puzzle piece gradually slid into place. Hulda and Emmaline were close twins, so perhaps the Rangers had explained that Hulda might be deported, and out of love for her sister, Emmaline decided to apply for a teaching position at the camp.

But what of this middle-of-the-night departure? I had no idea, but her motivation made sense. She must really love her sister.

Before I left Opa, I asked, "If my son sends a letter to Anton here, could you get it to Emmaline?"

"Yah. My daughter will make sure he gets it."

When I asked if I could drive the truck out back to unload Emmaline's boxes, he seemed relieved at the change of subject. We shook hands before I left, and his eyes glinted as he thanked me.

Censors. That word taunted me as I drove. An American-born citizen held captive with her entire family. As for Emmaline, if Johann had tried to get back home before the war, that certainly ought to make a statement to the authorities. In the meantime, she had been forced to make her way alone, and Anton remained fatherless.

What should I tell Donnie? How could I possibly explain? Enamored with warplanes, excited about all the air bases and pilot training going on close by, even some in Mason, and doing well at school, he faced each day with the hearty exuberance of youth. He reached almost to my shoulder now, and soon would match me in shoe size, but was still very much a lad.

No country is perfect—of course not. I once thought England

as close to perfection as nations come, but even a surface explo-
ration of her imperialistic sins would douse that belief. Still, I
respected what she had accomplished in certain areas, and my
heart thrummed to *God Save The King* (or Queen).

With the United States, I had no false beliefs to overcome,
having entered her shores as a well-read adult. The devastation of
the Indian tribes and slavery marred her history, but both traced
straight back to my own ancestors.

Here, Mexican, English, German, and Czech immigrants had
tamed the land, and in the process, the native population declined.
In the decades since war and disease ravaged many of the tribes,
immigrants from many other locales had settled here and developed thriving enterprises.

The first time I heard the phrase *melting pot*, I admired the
image. But this melting took time, perseverance, and tenacity. The
Italians had suffered cruelty as immigrants, and the poor Irish, oh
my! They suffered terribly in Europe, and cruelly here, as well. But
as time passed, the pioneer dream still wooed many and people
sacrificed to emigrate.

Back to the question of what to tell Donnie about Anton. A
few times, I almost began. My reticence reminded me of Hazel,
grinding out movements in fits and starts. One day, she might
refuse to cooperate at all.

The night after my trip to Fredericksburg, the moon draped
the orchard with silver as I wondered what I might say to Donnie.
And, as is often the case when my mind travels a well-worn path
with no resolution, finally I launched a feeble prayer.

"Please show me."

The thought of Anton locked up in the Crystal City camp
troubled me most. What a waste! One letter from a friend on the
outside might do him untold good. Still, I hesitated.

When the answer arrived, I had nothing to do with how it came
about. Occurrences like this have done much to convince me of
the unseen resources available to us all.

Even through my years with Victoria, I had always believed. But each time a specific, well-timed answer became clear, I tucked away the evidence to recall during periods of doubt.

The same Creator who formed us cares about specific situations in our lives. This I believe, because I have experienced it. The Maker of All is concerned with our foibles, efforts, and hopes. No other concept heartens me more, and more than once, this deep knowledge has held back despair.

This time when the answer appeared, I could have wept with gratitude.

"Da! Guess what I heard today?" Donnie's after-school reports became a bit less effusive as the year progressed, but not today.

"Mrs. B's teaching in a prison. The girls were talkin' about it, so I'm pretty sure it's true. One of their dads knows a man who's a guard there."

"What did Mr. Kidney have to say about this?"

"He didn't hear. It was recess time and I was waiting to bat. The girls were playing hopscotch, and Mr. Kidney was pitching and umping at the same time. Angelina said Anton and Mrs. B went down south someplace. Her dad knows for sure 'cuz he's on a war board with Mr. Landers."

"Norman?"

"Yeah."

I had not frequented the library recently, and those times of Norman being such a kind neighbor seemed distant. He hadn't stopped by since—when was it? The day he brought us Hazel, perhaps. His boards must be occupying a great deal of his time now.

"Did Angelina say where Anton and his mother are?"

"No." We had reached the barn, and Donnie petted Risk's neck. "But I really miss him. If he'd been here, our team woulda won today, I just know it. He plays shortstop, and always gets the ball to first base quick as lightning."

"Mmm—I can try to find out something more."

"You gonna talk to Norman?"

"Probably not. If he's a member of this board, as you say, he most likely can't speak about what's going on."

"Yeah, but you'll find a way. I know you will."

What a thrill to hear your son express confidence in your abilities. We both fell silent through the milking, but ideas already churned in my head. As we strode toward the house and a late tea, they crystallized into a plan.

"Do you have any homework tonight?"

"Not too much—just spelling and math."

"Well, how about writing out your spelling list twice and when I find an address for Anton, we'll mail one copy to him, along with a letter from you? Surely he misses you too, and all the goings-on at school."

"Yeah. I doubt he can play baseball at a prison."

Writing to Anton excited Donnie so much that he almost gulped his supper. While he started his lists, I walked through the orchard in the cool of twilight, considering how things had worked out. Once Donnie shared what Angelina had said, divulging at least part of what I knew had been simple, and would pave the way to share the rest.

There was a time when I borrowed Grandfather's faith. After he passed, I borrowed William's, especially through Victoria's betrayal and the fire's aftermath. But in spite of what some might call a second-hand belief, somewhere along the way, a conviction had settled down in my soul.

No matter what occurred, I knew all would be well. I never had defined exactly how this belief developed, but as the sun hastened to waken the other side of the world, the answer came in a recollected image from long ago.

In fact, I had forgotten this drama played out years ago, with Victoria shrieking at the top of her lungs. It was late and everyone else had gone to bed. But she liked the night and wanted company, no matter that I had early classes in the morning.

Her screams resounded in my ears again now, as harsh and

full-bodied as if she repeated them here. That night, as I often did, I simply stared at her, but for some reason, my silence encouraged her hysterics. By that time, I had learned that nothing I said or did would calm her.

There would be no peace until she fled the house. Hours later, she would return "clothed and in her right mind," like the Gerasene demoniac. But on this night she paused. Hair seemingly on end with fury, eyes wild with hatred, she spat at me.

That single act seemed more violent than her slaps or her fingernails clawing my arm. I considered our baby, innocently asleep in the next room, and reached for her, caught her elbow.

"Do you really despise me so much?"

Fierce light shone in her eyes, along with calculating comprehension. I realized Victoria knew exactly what she was doing.

No more words passed between us, but in that very moment, a sense that all would be well overtook me. How utterly improbable, yet I would have staked my life on this truth.

In an instant, she left the room and clacked down the stairs like someone possessed. In that indescribable interlude, something stirred in me, a nesting of sorts. What better way to put it? My spirit nestled down. Some might say, on the contrary, that I gave up hope.

But nothing remained to try with my wife, no new strategy I might employ, no tactic that might assuage her ill will. Accepting this produced an inner quietude I had lacked for months.

The next day on the way home from the school, I stopped by to speak with our physician, who had long since described what I finally could consider. Perhaps I had been unready to embrace this solution before—sometimes we must try every possible angle before we accept reality. The physician's response clarified this principle even further.

"Ah. At last, do you see, Mr. Herring? Coming to this realization takes a certain amount of time for most people. Human nature avoids the conclusion that our loved one may never change." He peered at me over wire-rimmed glasses that slid halfway down his thin nose.

"If you wish, I shall make an appointment for you with the entrance officer at the psychiatric hospital. None of us seek this end, but sometimes it becomes our only alternative."

By then, I had become professional at standing and gaping. But I must have managed to utter agreement.

"Excellent. My secretary will inform you of the admittance date."

The admittance. I could scarce imagine Victoria's reaction. Three days later, the letter arrived. The appointment had been set for Tuesday next.

That night, Victoria set the house on fire. I would forever wonder if she had some sort of premonition.

As for me, could anyone be prepared for such a life-shattering event? Facing her death and the destruction of our dear home, the only one I had ever known, took every energy I possessed. Yet that moment when Victoria spat in my face had paved the way. I might be shocked, stunned, altogether numb, but whatever happened next, I knew I would survive.

As Donnie worked in the house, I discovered an apple sapling in need of staking. Why hadn't I noticed this by day? Bending to inspect, all alone out in the gentle quiet, an inner strengthening enveloped me. Impossible to describe, perhaps akin to an herbal syrup coating a sore throat.

When I returned, Donnie would have finished his letter to Anton and be getting ready for our nighttime reading. Deep into the history of baseball, we looked forward to each new chapter.

Risk nickered as I passed the barn. Though he could not see me, he sensed my presence. Crossing the expanse to the house, I embraced the same kind of assurance—I was not alone. Who can explain such a thing?

R. W. Emerson put his hand to it and succeeded as much as anyone. "All I have seen teaches me to trust the Creator for all I have not seen."

An invisible essence can make a powerful impact. An intangible foundation—for instance, faith—cannot erase life's baffling questions. I daresay I still entertained as many as ever, perhaps even more. But at the same time, what *I had not seen* lacked power to eradicate all I *had* seen.

In plenty of time before Christmas, Donnie and I prepared a package for Anton. I had begun corresponding with Opa Bultmann, and the day before Thanksgiving, he sent a note that only Emmaline's mother would be allowed to visit.

Our boxes included tinned meats, along with butters and jams, warm scarves and hats. Donnie thought of a tin of tea for his teacher, since she had told the class she relished one on cold days.

In a separate box, we packed books. Donnie gave up his much-loved copy of George Washington's biography, along with the story of Sam Houston. As he packed that volume, he reminded me how Sam had lost his young wife early in their marriage, not to death, but to another man.

"Yes, I remember."

"Like you," he added. The concern in his voice ran deep.

"But Sam survived and became a great general." I decided to inject a bit of lightness. "Perhaps I, too, shall become a great general one day!"

Donnie chuckled, and we returned to our work. He wanted to send along his sketches of the latest airplanes, but we feared the censor would throw them out.

"Can you imagine having somebody read our mail before we do?"

"Our letters from Elliot Lardner have been censored, since he serves in the British Army."

That gave Donnie pause. "How can you tell?"

"When we have finished here, I'll show you."

"You must really like him, to spend fifteen cents to send him letters."

"Elliot was always a good student, curious about everything. I'm sure our letters mean a great deal to him. If I were with a fighting unit, I would long for letters. I was spared, but only because of moving here."

"You would've had to fight if we had stayed in England?"

"Most likely. The draft goes beyond my age."

"So I would be staying with William?"

"I expect so."

For a moment, Elliot's face juxtaposed with Donnie's. In such a short time, he would be of *fighting age*.

"You know, you remind me of Elliot. He was one of my best students. I surely hope he makes it through the war."

Donnie's eyebrows rose, but he said no more.

We popped some popcorn to cushion our gifts, and I smiled at the thought of Anton opening the box addressed to him in Donnie's handwriting. Hopefully, this gift would spur a little joy during the Christmas season.

The first week of December, I hauled our boxes and some letters to Fredericksburg. Opa's voice faltered when he mentioned Hulda, her husband and children. His daughter had told him their ship would leave New York Harbor in January. By now, I had learned a bit more about the camp, and others like them.

All over this nation, people had been interned as enemy aliens. Japanese-Americans and Italian-Americans like Mr. DiMaggio and his family. The Italians had been freed, though, but Japanese and German-Americans were still held. Who could stand against the President's Executive Order and the F.B.I?

On the trip home I held the steering wheel with an iron grip, as if Hazel might opt to pull away. But the thought of Emmaline making this difficult choice out of love for her sister calmed me. True, who might stand against the government, but at the same time, who might stand against this kind of love?

That day, William had hired me to run an errand to an establishment close to Fredericksburg, so I accomplished both goals at once. In past weeks, he sent me on several delivery missions for the creamery, which provided an even better picture of our environs in all directions—so many possibilities to explore.

But seeing Emmaline's grandfather dampened my interest. My questions ballooned as I neared home.

Some of Donnie's recent spelling words haunted me. *Travesty, injustice, intrigue, discriminatory, prejudice, partiality, bias.* He said it best when I supplied a few more details that evening.

"They're shipping Anton's aunt and uncle to Germany? Can't we do something?" The flush on his cheeks made me wonder whether I should have kept this information under wraps.

"I wish we could think what it might be."

He stormed around the house expressing my exact sentiments. Then he stopped mid-stride. "This means they'll never come back here?"

"We don't know that for sure, but Mrs. B must have thought it a possibility. If she hadn't gone there to teach, she might never have seen her sister again, or Anton his cousins."

He turned quiet. "What if we— Do you think we could drive down and visit them after Christmas?" Such a hopeful expression lighted my son's face.

"Anton's great-grandfather said only Mrs. B's mother can visit. I doubt very much the rules will change."

"But after her sister leaves, will she keep teaching there? I might never see Anton again, either."

"Perhaps not for some time, but at least we can stay in touch." Donnie's stormy expression told me I offered him little comfort at all.

Before our goodnight hug, he whispered, "Sorry, Da. It just makes me furious about Anton."

"Not at all, Son. It upsets me, too."

By now, Elliot surely had returned to active duty somewhere on the continent. Hopefully in England, but he might be sent elsewhere, as the Army always had paperwork to do.

This seemed as certain as anything else these days, but my last letter had been returned with a **MISSING IN ACTION** stamp. What could this mean? I could only hope that when he was wounded and evacuated, his permanent papers had mistakenly been marked MIA.

Strange to receive your own letter back, and even more peculiar to imagine such a lively young chap, already physically diminished by the war, now missing. William had not heard from Elliot's brother either, so we entered the limbo of not knowing.

Every night, Donnie and I prayed for him, and Donnie added a singular plea for Anton and Emmaline. In the shadow of innocence battering Heaven with a heartfelt plea, I added my similar requests.

As Christmas neared, Donnie asked again if we might visit the Bultmans. I had no desire to bring up the subject with Norman, but this seemed the only possible course, since I had no idea how to contact Angelina's father. Telling Donnie I had done my best meant the world to me.

Raising my ire takes considerable effort, but Norman had accomplished this feat back on the Fourth of July. Since then, I had determined not to allow him a glimpse of my displeasure. If only someone else had pertinent information about Crystal City, other than the local sheriff.

No matter how American I felt with my fresh naturalization papers, I had no desire to visit the Sheriff's office with a question connected to enemy aliens. Even Opa could not see his daughters and grandchildren before the ship left, so who did I think I was?

But that night when Donnie brought up the idea of visiting Anton, his last words had been, "This is what I want for Christmas, Da." My heart sank. I muttered something about how we don't always get what we want, especially in wartime, but he clung to his desire.

So I must make one last attempt to discover what I could about visits to Crystal City. With so many connections, Norman probably knew someone with access to the information.

I worked on my phrasing, thinking how P.M. Churchill must have labored over his speeches to encourage, motivate, and—yes—strike fear into the British citizenry after Dunkirk. My quest, seemingly trite in comparison, centered on Donnie, but something vital was at stake.

How would he view the government once this war ended? Would he comprehend that some of what occurred originated in wartime paranoia on the coasts and in some northern states? And that officials did sometimes change their stand—hadn't they deemed Italians once again acceptable, even thought they were declared enemy aliens after the Pearl Harbor attack?

Donnie knew this because of Mr. DiMaggio, of course. Mr. Kidney shared the information with his baseball-enamored students as soon as it became public. But since then, several more internment camps for Japanese citizens had sprung up.

Had we lived elsewhere in the nation, we likely would never have heard about Crystal City. But we *had* heard. Would Donnie's concept of justice be jaded by these aberrations of a nation at war?

This question carried great import. Though I had given him no reason to hope, I knew I must do my utmost to grant his wish. This fact, however, did nothing to prevent me from stalling when it came to approaching Norman.

Chapter Twenty

"Did you drink tea as often before you and William married?"

"No, but my uncle loved green tea and believed it medicinal. My mother often enjoyed a cup with him. I think he acquired a taste during the Great War through contact with some British soldiers."

"Aha, those were good men, spreading our tastes!"

Lillian set her steaming teapot between us. "Didn't Jane Austen write, 'But indeed I would rather have nothing but tea?'"

"Ah, yes. When I was young Grandmother used to quote Kipling around teatime:

We had a kettle; we let it leak:
Our not repairing made it worse.
We haven't had any tea for a week.
The bottom has dropped out of the universe.

Had we been deprived of our teatime for a week, something like that drop might have resulted."

"Mmm. Such good memories. What was your Grandmother like?"

"Strong. Severely arthritic toward the end, but she never let that stop her from being active. Her circle of lady friends went about doing good and gained a reputation in Nottinghamshire. Grandfather said the rural Women's Institute united them early on, and they stayed loyal to each other and community projects throughout life. But Grandmother made it a point to always be home by teatime."

"Wonderful. I don't know how I did without my daily tea all those years before William and I met."

"An Englishman without his tea would be difficult to locate, I daresay." I glanced behind the house, where Abigail lined weed stems in a row on a big flat rock. With great care, she arranged them from shortest to longest.

"She already shows some of William's penchant for organization, don't you think?"

"Yes, and his perseverance. When one stem proves uncooperative, she could throw it out and pick another. But she sticks with what she picked and fits them into a pattern."

"Or forces them." Lillian rubbed her swollen ankles. "I wonder what this next one will be like. After church, a lady foretold a boy. She could tell by the way I'm carrying, she claimed, and seemed so certain. William thinks she's relying on old wives' tales, and so do I."

"It won't be long before you find out."

"Yes, and Mr. Grunkle told him not to worry if the baby comes on a workday. He's to take as much time as he needs."

"What a fine man. It's as if he and William have worked together forever."

"Yes, William calls this his hidden blessing—here he was needing work, and Mr. Grunkle had no idea what he had to offer. I'm so thankful you thought to speak with him."

Abigail ran into the house and raced for Lillian, who leaned toward her with open arms. The petite urchin developed ringlet curls in the humidity, and grew more delightful every time I stopped in. But she had difficulty finding space on her Mum's lap, and sometimes turned to me.

"It's gratifying to know my ideas sometimes work to good ends."

Abigail pulled her mother to the kitchen, where Lillian washed her hands and face and gave her some cheese and crackers. Between bites, the little charmer sent coy smiles to me across the table.

Of course, she still looked for Donnie when I arrived with the mail, but I was better than no visitor at all. One morning I happened to find a bit of chocolate in my pocket. That day, Lillian looked rather frazzled—I had not seen her like this before, and she never disclosed the reason.

With that piece of chocolate, I wooed Abigail out for a walk. Lillian seemed relieved, and after ten minutes, Abigail's short legs grew weary. Oh the bliss when she accepted my offer of a lift! I had longed to hold her, but she always veered away.

Our relationship altered further as she succumbed to a snooze in my arms. I enjoyed this when Donnie was a babe, and relished half an hour sitting outdoors while sweet Abigail slept. After that day, she ran to me when I knocked.

Later, I described the scene for Donnie, and his comment warmed my heart. "Slow and steady wins the race, Da. Now Abigail sees you like I do."

"At least I make a suitable second-best to you."

"Do you think the Prime Minister thinks, s*low and steady wins the race?*"

"I think he might add *intent* to complement slow and steady. Slow, steady, and intent on the goal. But definitely not *slow* in airplane production."

A horse possesses no capacity to vomit. I learned this from the veterinarian one night in November when Risk refused to eat and locked his hooves on the barn floor. Throughout the day, he stood there still-legged. Norman's description of this friendly creature's pulchritude had proven accurate—he never acted this way.

Had he somehow eaten too much grain? I checked the storage area, and that seemed implausible.

Nothing changed by the time I went to get Donnie, so I stopped by the vet's, who agreed to come before evening. By then, Risk, still frozen in place, showed signs of obvious distress. Donnie stood close, rubbing his distended belly.

"Could he have eaten any extra grain lately?"

Focused on Risk's midsection, Donnie gave no answer.

"Son?"

"I—last night I gave him an extra handful for a treat."

"Mmm. Just last night?"

"And the night before." Donnie stared at his boots. "Just a little every night."

"Didn't William say any more than his usual portion could be dangerous?"

"But it was only a bit each time." Donnie buried his head in Risk's hide, so I could hardly make out what he said next. "I didn't think—"

"We'll see what the veterinarian says. Hopefully he can help right away."

"You don't think Risk'll die?"

Risk kept nosing his middle, a sure sign of pain. Thankfully, the sound of a motor and automobile door opening stalled our conversation.

The veterinarian palpated Risk all over, checked his hooves, shone his flashlight into his eyes. Donnie kept a hand on the halter, while I hung back a little. Truth be told, prayers ascended with every thought.

Awful things were happening to children in my homeland, who faced far worse than this. But how would Donnie ever surmount his guilt if Risk were to succumb?

"He hasn't foundered. That's a good thing." At this pronouncement, Donnie took a full breath.

"Have you been giving him water?"

"Yes, all day long."

"Good. Keep that up. And withholding feed?"

I let Donnie answer that one. "Yes, sir. He hasn't eaten since last night. Right, Da?"

"Right."

The vet squatted to survey Risk's front hooves again. "I'm going to administer a dose of mineral oil and leave some for you to give him every four hours. His feet aren't hot. Heartbeat is only slightly elevated, but it would be good to let him stand in the coldest water you can find as soon as I leave.

"Keep him there for ten minutes, and repeat this after the next two doses of oil. This might be a long night for you. Let me know tomorrow if he doesn't improve. If he does, hold back feed for another day, but give him plenty of water and continue the cold water baths."

I held the vial of mineral oil while he positioned a tube down Risk's throat. The whole time, Donnie petted the pony's nose and whispered in his ear.

"Mild-mannered—sure doesn't put up much of a fight. Or else his gut hurts even more than this tube." When the vet removed the tube, he asked, "Think you two can repeat this in four hours?"

"We'll manage." I eyed Donnie, who nodded.

"All right then. Rinse out the tube gut and return it tomorrow if this works."

"How will we know?" Donnie's voice sounded a little stronger.

"By a great big pile of manure on your barn floor, even stinkier than normal."

That prophesied pile of manure became the highlight of our week. Donnie, who faithfully helped with the late night and wee hours' medication and went with me to cool Risk's feet in the spring water, yelped at me midmorning.

"Da, come see! Oh man, does the barn ever stink!"

Busy with the same peach tree that had required so much attention these past weeks, I hurried over. Donnie's screwed-up face radiated joy in spite of the putridity.

"Looks like he'll be fine now, right?"

"Indeed. Let's get this cleaned up right away." I grabbed a shovel, but he took it from me.

"I'm the one who fed him too much."

"True. But you learned your lesson, righto?"

"Yes, sir."

"That's all that matters—it's what mistakes are for. What say we both tidy up this answer to our prayers, and then you can return the tube?"

Soon after Risk's ailment and recovery, I finally spoke with Norman. I had gone to his place twice, but each time, Bernardo said he had left for the day. Never a sign anyone was home, and I wondered about Norman's wife. These visits provided a chance to practice my minimal Spanish, and Bernardo proved a patient teacher.

Then one day I checked on the war news at the library. Deeply engrossed in an article, I looked up to note Norman standing beside the table.

"Ho there. Haven't seen you around for a while."

"Nor I you."

"That old Ford workin' all right?"

"Yes, just fine. Are you on your way out?"

"Yep. Got a meeting at ten. Discussing some of the goings-on due to increased espionage. Enemy aliens right here in our midst." Shocked that he disclosed so much, I returned the newspaper to its wooden bar and followed him outside, where I blurted my question without employing any of my well-planned techniques.

"Do you know anything about the internees at Crystal City?"

Norman rocked back on his heels. "How'd you hear about the camp down there?"

"Donnie brought home something from school."

"What do you know?"

"Not a great deal, but I'd like to find out if visits are allowed."

He pushed his Stetson back on his head. "Still eyein' that German teacher, are you?"

My cheeks heated, and I bristled. What did he mean by *eyeing*, and *still*? "Mrs. Bultman is an American citizen, and she's married. Besides, I have no intention of *eyeing* anyone."

"Is that so." He enunciated this as fact, not question. "A fella has to pay attention who he associates with these days."

"Donnie learned so much from her, especially about American

history, and is friends with her son. He wants to visit Anton over the Christmas holiday."

"You don't say." Norman's horse pawed the rocky earth. "Well, I s'pect those folks down there'll be mighty busy during the holidays."

"I'd merely like to know the rules. How might I?"

Norman pursed his lips. "Son, we may do things differently here than where you're from."

"The British War Ministry transports suspected aliens to a prison on the Isle of Mann, but most of them are not English citizens. And I highly doubt they are allowed any visitors."

"That so? Well. You'd do well to remember this is wartime here too, and the U.S. government does what it has to do."

"Of course."

Touching the brim of his hat, Norman pursed his lips. "Don't have an answer for you, but I do have a suggestion. Mind your own business." He turned on his thick heel and mounted while I stood there watching.

To say I fumed and fussed the remainder of the day would be an understatement. His condescension incited me, probably because it reminded me of a certain headmaster in my past. The way he jumped to conclusions infuriated me, and told me how closely he watched me.

Worse, now I must tell Donnie we had no hope of paying Anton a visit before he left the country. All those prayers he prayed—

The conversation with Norman went round and round in my head. What might I have said differently? Nothing, and I knew it. If he did know anything about the camp, he had no intention of telling me.

Finally, I retreated to the house and dug about for a book by one of Grandfather's favorite authors. A figment from G.K. Chesterton, only a short phrase, had come to mind as I worked and fretted. Something about living in small communities, but what was it exactly?

It took some time to locate the passage. Just before I had to leave for the school, I found the quote, as rich and comforting as I had imagined.

"The man who lives in a small community lives in a much larger world. He knows much more of the fierce variety and uncompromising divergences of men… In a large community, we can choose our companions. In a small community, our companions are chosen for us. Thus in all extensive and highly civilized society, groups come into existence founded upon sympathy, and shut out the real world more sharply than the gates of a monastery. There is nothing really narrow about the clan; the thing which is really narrow is the clique."

By the clan, Chesterton made no reference to the Ku Klux Klan, which Lillian had told us still lived and breathed in our state. No, he referred to any group that isolated itself because the members thought themselves better than outsiders.

Two phrases instructed me, …*lives in a much larger world…our companions are chosen for us.* How true. We scarcely could have found a smaller group of people with whom to associate, and among them, Norman stood out.

Like all of us, he saw the world through a certain cultural lens. Now I knew that his lens allowed for my presence, yet not my opinions, should they differ from his. If we lived in London, we might pass on the street hundreds of times without ever interacting.

There, in New York, or even Dallas, I might avoid him entirely, and even consider him an example of virtue if he tipped his Stetson when we passed on the street. I might think his high hat a bit ostentatious, had I not known that John B. Stetson created "The Boss of the Plains" to provide insulation from the elements.

But because we lived in Loyal Valley, Norman and I were likely to tangle. Bound to, I might say. Here, I must accept him as he is, for removing myself completely could never be.

A great weight lifted as I headed to the school. I envisioned our existence as hermit-like, and had never intended to broaden my scope. Outwardly, it would seem our realm had narrowed, but today proved exactly the opposite.

Reflecting on our run-in, I discovered reason for gratitude.

Have you ever opened a door in the morning, when being shut up for the night has tightened the air in the house? We open the door or window, and our closed-in feeling fades. In sweeps freshness, along with the scents of our locale.

These depend upon the season, and may include a waft of wisteria or a touch of sweetness from honeysuckle or roses. My first whiff usually includes a tinge of wildflowers, especially in early spring with the bluebonnets abloom. Lillian says they have no aroma at all, but others, William and I included, note a heady scent, almost sickly sweet, like lilacs.

This initial early morning air also contains an element from the barn, unless the wind has turned. We might smell a neighbor's burn pile, or the hole where they bury their garbage. In a city's close quarters, these scents would co-mingle, with specific ones difficult to trace.

Back in Nottinghamshire, the forest always presented itself first-thing, with verdant texture and color, but also a foundational aroma honed through the centuries. Back in the land of my birth, surely that one rich fragrance filled my senses.

Moldering leaves from thousands of towering veteran oaks and the fleeting bouquet of grasses and wildflowers intermingled with small animal scents—all would make their mark. Not far away, the South Forest would reveal a distinct bovine odor.

Here in the hill country, opening the door before the sun rises brings a hint of fruit from our trees, along with welcoming coolness that bids one enter a new day. If a breeze blows from the spring, one detects a vernal twinge, even in winter's cold.

This protected haven, cool even in the ravages of summer heat, exists separate from all else. How fortunate we are, and how blessed our garden, for once we made its discovery, William made haste to extend its life-giving properties.

Trenching an underground passage and installing a pipe under the drive proved well worth the effort—now we enjoyed a hydrant mere feet from the vegetable patch. If we let the water flow gently in the evening, the furrows Donnie and I dug kept it contained and guided it past the first two rows. In extreme heat, we still might need to tote pails to the farthest reaches, but far less often.

Opening the door for the first time each day reminds me of change, that persistent companion we often detest and push away. But accepting its inevitability allows us to let go our efforts to influence the future. Instead, we focus on present gifts and embrace whatever good comes along, even as we release our concept of *normal*. This elusive entity keeps altering, and normalcy for the cat equals terror for the mouse, does it not?

Perhaps this opening of doors means so much because I barred my internal house for so long in an attempt to keep things as I imagined them to be. But Victoria breathed her own air, so different from mine.

Early this morning, with Donnie fast asleep but the birds wide awake and chattering, I walked toward the spring. Somewhere a rooster crowed, and from the opposite direction, a donkey brayed as he butted against his tin-roofed enclosure. People would soon awaken and tend to their chores, but I cherished this solitary time, this sense of being awake, all alone in the world.

Not far down the way in Loyal Valley, William would soon rise and ready himself for work. Lillian hopefully slumbered on, preparing for her great upcoming labor.

Surrounded by charming scents, I squatted beside the spring and cupped my hand in its delicate flow, a fitting image for trying to fight change. At best, one clenches the palms together with the smallest finger outside the rest, hoping a small amount stays intact, but soon, all is lost.

December had come, but fulfilling Donnie's wish to see Anton appeared as impossible as retaining water in my grip. At times, change allows only one viable option—acceptance.

I breathed deep of this new day, even as the moon slipped farther away. Grandfather called his morning walk a constitutional, the single action that grounded him for whatever he might confront before sunset.

Once again, I pictured the Crystal City camp. What must it be like for our friends, knowing their dear ones would soon leave for enemy territory? Even my fertile powers of imagination failed me, and I could only lift them up to our Creator.

Even as I did so, in moonlight still filtering through high branches above, footsteps sounded. Definitely boots grinding on rock. In the shadows, I froze. Who could that be, out before dawn? I waited, hoping Donnie still slept soundly.

Whoever it was—a large enough fellow from the sound—proceeded toward the road, so I slipped from shadow to shadow in pursuit. From my refuge under a low-hanging branch, the intruder's objective became clear: the sign Donnie and I had fashioned and nailed to our post.

Tall and broad-shouldered, the chap bent down, his Stetson shadowing his face. Something metal glinted, but I could hear nothing. A few seconds passed, though it seemed an hour.

He stood tall. Something made a *click* and he wiped his hands on his pants before striking out. The pre-dawn light had changed a bit, and I knew the gait was the unmistakable booted ramble of Norman himself.

Hardly daring to exhale, I waited until all was silent. When I inspected the sign, I could detect nothing amiss. Just when I needed it, the moon absconded, but I determined to return for a better look in daylight.

Chapter Twenty-one

One Saturday after we closed up our vegetable stand, Donnie hailed me. He had wandered off to search for insects while I finished securing the premises.

"Come here, Da! Something you gotta see!" He held up something shiny.

"What have you found?"

"It's a knife—somebody's jackknife, and it's a humdinger, don't you think?"

Looking closer at the sign, I still found no alteration. "Hmm. Somebody must've dropped it when they were walking by?"

"But why would they be standin' way over here?"

"I have no idea. Quite a puzzle, don't you think?"

I thought I had learned most available information about John Meusebach before Mr. Kidney assigned Donnie a report on this Texas pioneer. He requested that parents aid their children with this assignment.

Delving into the story of John Meusebach provided special pleasure. What a tale we discovered! For a solid week, Donnie and I spoke of almost nothing but this man who had made such a difference in Texas history. Donnie's desire for accuracy increased when Mr. Kidney announced that several students would read their essays at a public gathering before school let out for Christmas.

How Donnie labored over his outline, and then paragraph

-by-paragraph, created his masterpiece. He practiced reading it aloud until we both had it memorized.

Baron Otfried Hans von Meusebach became involved with emigration to Texas in February of 1845 when he became commissioner general of the German Adelsverein, or aristocratic association, also known as the Nobleman's Society. Born in Prussia, the well-educated Meusebach sacrificed a baronship to help more than 7,000 Germans settle in the United States.

The Society for the Protection of German Immigrants in Texas sought to establish a presence in the Territory of Texas, soon to become a state. With this in mind, after his ship docked in Galveston, Meuseach traveled to New Braunfels with a hardy group of pioneers.

From there, he set out on horseback to explore a land grant 150 miles north. In 1846, he began a community on the Pedernales River and named it Fredericksburg in honor of Prince Friedrich of Prussia.

In October, Meuesebach and thirty-five others surveyed a wagon road between New Braunfels and Fredericksburg. On May eighth the next year, John led twenty wagons with 120 settlers further into the territory.

The peace treaty he instigated with six Comanche chiefs opened up the land between the Llano and Colorado Rivers, part of the Fischer-Miller Land Grant. John married a much younger woman named Agnes and they had eleven children. Four of their daughters died when they lived in Comanche Springs.

His election to the Texas Senate led to his appointment as Commissioner of Land Grants. He granted over 700 colonists a total of 324,160 acres for settlement. During the Civil War, his family lived in Fredericksburg and operated a mercantile.

They also owned land at Waco Springs on the Guadalupe River near New Braunfels. You can tell they came from a place where there was no land to buy!

After a tornado and a flood, they moved in 1869 to Cold Spring in the south part of Mason County, on the overland stage route to El Paso. Meuesebach built a mercantile and horse-exchange stop, and served as postmaster and notary public.

During the Civil War, he changed the name of Cold Spring to Loyal Valley, because people had been so cooperative. Also, he wanted to express this community's deep loyalty to the Union cause.

Meusebach realized the soil in Loyal Valley was fertile, different from the thin topsoil layer covering rock in much of the state. He developed a fruit orchard with sixty kinds of peach trees, thirty–two varieties of pears, and fourteen kinds of plums. With starts from all over the world, he grew fourteen varieties of grapes.

He also grew a garden with asparagus, cauliflower and other vegetables. Besides all this, figs, pomegranates, apricots, apples, and cherries flourished under his care.

He also built a Roman-style bath and planted lovely wisteria, crape myrtle and hedges of jujube plums, otherwise called Texas dates. Roses? Meusebach nurtured over 200 varieties. When we come across certain trees and vines that grow nowhere else in Texas, it's likely that John Meusebach brought them here.

A scientist at heart, he experimented with oil-producing trees like the olive, always seeking more commercial endeavors for his fellow immigrants. He became friends with noted German scientists, a geologist and a botanist, and created a large rock collection.

He also collected sixteenth and seventeenth century German literature. A former steam boater often visited the Meuesebach family. This man, Captain Charles Henry Nimitz, is the grandfather of Admiral Chester Nimitz, who now commands the Pacific Fleet.

In his later years, John Meusebach weakened. When he died in 1897, his family buried him in the Marschall-Muesebach Cemetery at Cherry Spring, following the tradition of royalty to provide and care for their own cemeteries.

The words on his gravestone describe his life: TENAX PROPOSITI, meaning *"tenacious of purpose."*

We cannot begin to measure how much modern-day hill country citizens owe this intrepid pioneer.

The day of the reading, William took an hour off from work, since Donnie had been chosen to share his essay. Lillian felt too

253

restless to sit for an hour in a public setting, so William bundled Abigail for our outing. Her weary mother looked more than grateful.

All went well, as expected. Norman even made a point of congratulating Donnie, and after the successful program, the audience enjoyed hot cider. William and I chatted briefly with Mr. Kidney before Donnie and I walked home.

By eight o'clock that evening, little William Everett Parker entered this world. A few weeks later, on January seventh, 1943, and the new pastor pronounced him, an able specimen, for he made quite a fuss when the water touched his head. As his sponsor, I *got an earful*, as they say.

Kenneth did not attend, and we avoided any mention of him. Mr. Grunkle joined me as the child's other sponsor, but William placed his son in my arms for the ceremony. Adorned in Abigail's long white baptismal gown, William Jr. looked as pleased as Ramshackle with a cactus spine in his snout.

Having dealt with squalling young saints in the past, the pastor simply projected his voice. "How good to celebrate a new member of our family. The women have brought pecan pie for us all after the service."

William beamed down at his son, Lillian gathered their infant in her arms, and they led the way. At Donnie's baptism, it had been William holding him and Grandfather beaming. Had Victoria been present for the ceremony? I could not recall.

This was an auspicious time for war events also. In November, the Red Army had surrounded the German forces in Stalingrad, and defeated them in February. The two armies lost a million men fighting over this already-destroyed city when the Russians refused to surrender, and block-by-block fighting ensued.

More significant military advances occurred, as well as some tragedies, but in Donnie's view, the Grumman Hellcat topped them all. William's exuberance matched Donnie's, and he called the aircraft "A good sign for *Old Blighty*, indeed."

"Why do you call England that?"

"Some British soldiers corrupted the Indian term *Bilayati*, meaning *foreigner land*. I suppose a soldier misinterpreted it to mean England specifically. Perhaps at that point, the natural English brilliance gave way to humor, also a trait of our fatherland."

"Why do you call it fatherland?"

"We might say motherland as well, or mother country—simply a manner of speaking. At any rate, this new airplane could make all the difference in this war."

This conversation occurred during an evening visit with William and Lillian. Donnie and I toted along ham and potatoes. *Berkshire* ham, no doubt. The winter term of school had begun, and baby Willie provided a fresh focus for Donnie. Since his birth, he mentioned Anton less frequently.

As war reports came through, I could only imagine how the fighting would multiply in the coming months. With such heavy Nazi losses in Russia, surely the people of Germany would suffer even more. Johann and I had never met, but in line with my New Year's resolution, I kept lifting him up, along with his forlorn little family.

Human beings become attached to their homes. Be it ever so humble, there's no place like home. This has nothing to do with the materials used in construction, though I had been overjoyed to know a stone house awaited us here. Having lived in one for thirty-odd years, and now in this one, I attest to the peculiar power a place holds.

Why should our small acreage create the same tranquility I once felt in Grandfather's house? Why, indeed? The answer that occurs to me is *family*. Here, Donnie and I have forged a life, and what we share reflects the very meaning of *home*.

No great moments, such as visits by the Queen and King of England, take place here, but hundreds of small ones make up the essence. I expect one day when Donnie goes off to college, this place will follow him, as Grandfather's—the house, the garden, and all we shared there—accompanied me across the Atlantic.

Though I rarely think of Donnie leaving, that day will come, and all will be well. Perhaps he will never return here permanently. That will be up to him, but if my life is any model, the comfort of hearth and home—snuggled into our big chair of an evening, reading away the time, operating the cider press, cooling ourselves by the spring or mucking out the barn—all these will abide with him as unique comfort.

Cold weather strengthens the desire to belong, to stay close, and winter's depths stir the longing for spring. This year, the season has gone back and forth, inattentive to the human desire for constancy. One week we see our breath when we step outside, another, we barely need a jacket. But as a backdrop for either one, the picture of our boys *over there* or *down there in the Pacific* arises and feeds our perspective.

Starting back in January, the Japanese reputation for brutality had increased when stories leaked out about the fate of 20,000 American troops in the Philippines, along with more than 60,000 Filipino soldiers. We had heard about the Bataan Death March, but now, newscasters and articles included gruesome details told by a few escaped GIs.

For hundreds weak from hunger and Dengue Fever, a forced sixty-six mile march up the mosquito-infested island of Bataan meant certain death. Once the survivors reached a train, their captors crammed them into stifling boxcars. Many more died standing, en route to a POW camp in the mountains.

The Japanese captured American nurses, too. Something about women suffering quickens the fighting spirit, even beyond the reality of thousands of men in captivity.

If we hadn't been determined enough to defeat "those lousy Japs" before, this fresh news rekindled the rage pursuant to Pearl Harbor. The Philippine atrocities now coming to light occurred two years ago—since then, how many more Americans had lost their lives in prisoner of war camps?

Wherever I went, every face reflected one purpose—victory at all costs.

The realm beyond Time that Mr. Lewis referred to in his radio broadcast resurfaced in our church service more than once. Today, Donnie brought it up as we returned from another lovely Sunday dinner at Lillian and William's.

The concept brought a bit of comfort concerning Emmaline and Anton—if Time exists only in our present earthly realm, perhaps this is true of suffering, too. Perhaps,

Unbeknownst to us, some solace reaches beyond the circumstances in Crystal City. In sacrificing for her sister, Emmaline may have gained a gift beyond our knowing.

Little W. E. Parker grew so much between visits, and revealed his personality in lusty yells for food. Lillian lived at his beck and call, as ought to be, at least for a time. Watching her reminded me of how much Victoria missed with Donnie at this age—for his first few months of life, William searched out a wet nurse to take her place.

Meanwhile, life in the country continued. Soon Daisy, one of his cows, would calve. This situation had evolved like a scene in a good book. One day William, who had been scheming to purchase a bull, had been down at the filling station when a rancher stopped to fill his tank on a trip from Brady. William engaged him in conversation and discovered a treasure close at hand.

Mr. Richards was hauling a few of his prize bulls to a buyer near Fredericksburg. He described their intriguing bloodlines—his grandfather, Colonel R. G. Shannon, hailed from Ireland on the famed river Shannon, and received his first cattle as a gift from Queen Victoria, shipped to New Orleans. When the Colonel passed, Mr. Richards' father continued to breed fine livestock, and now carries on the family tradition.

"Queen Victoria? You are quite sure?"

"Indeed. Impressive, eh?"

I had heard the truck and hurried in from the orchard just in time to glimpse its dark green paint flash as it left the yard.

"You saw his new truck leave, didn't you? That and his expensive hat and belt buckle confirm his success. Think of it—his bulls trace their blood lines back to England. When I asked the price of one, Mr. Richards allowed he might be willing to sell on the spot."

"Just like that?" William always found a way, but this time, I marveled.

"Just like that. Surely, this was meant to be. How often does one meet a man toting a valuable bull through Loyal Valley?"

Who could argue with this reasoning? And so it was that we spent an extra day fencing a portion of the pasture to contain this powerful creature until the appropriate time for his services. William had planned out the dates and alerted us that though it was still early for Daisy to deliver, one never knew.

So we observed her most carefully these days. Then one morning, she distanced herself from the rest of the cows. By the next day, she showed signs of agitation, so William summoned the vet. Our challenges with Risk had taught me that this white-haired fellow never minced words.

His long years of expertise instilled trust. One got the sense that he had seen about all there is to see. But this time, he scratched his head.

Donnie could no more contain his anxiety than a cactus might grow without spines. "Do you think she'll be all right?"

The old vet set his hands on his hips. "Sure hope so. How about you fetch me some fresh water and we'll see if we can get her to drink?"

Donnie raced off, and I hovered near William during the assessment. After fishing around inside the cow's body, the vet removed his arm, covered in blood above the elbow.

The way he shook his head made me bite my lip. When William had this cow bred last winter, having a newborn calf seemed delightful, but as with many of life's undertakings, complications may arise. The second plunge of the veterinarian's arm into the cow's backside certainly looked like complications to me.

"Her stomach is twisted, but the calf seems all right. Sometimes when a cow tries to get up, her stomach gets turned—we call it twisted gut or a twisted abomasum."

By this time, Donnie returned, and his eyes lighted like fireflies. Doc noticed, and offered more details. "We also call the twisted part the maw, rennet-bag, or reed tripe. It's the fourth and final stomach compartment and secretes rennet, which is used in making cheese." He patted the Daisy's side. "Awful tight, gal. Is she normally out in the pasture?"

Concern lined William's countenance. "Yes, we just brought her in because I thought she might be in labor."

"Mmm. This might resolve itself before she calves. She's not twitching her tail or pacing, and her pulse seems normal. Let's turn her out again and if she gets agitated, call me again. We'll roll her over, and hopefully that'll do the trick. There's also a surgery we can try."

When Donnie and I discussed the situation afterwards, he turned somber. "I sure hope she doesn't lose the calf. I already have a name picked out, and William will be so sad."

During those next two weeks of keeping close watch, we discovered the potato bugs. Several showed on some leaves one morning, and by late afternoon, the number multiplied. Dozens of khaki colored, black-striped insects gnawed on leaves left and right.

We removed them one-by-one and squashed them with our boots. We worked through twilight, when darkness forced us to give up the fight.

"This stuff on my hands is yucky. Where'd these bugs come from so fast?"

"I'm not sure, but we'll find out." Later, I turned to my trusty botanical encyclopedia, complete with sketches, and had Donnie read about them.

"Hey! They lay orange eggs under the leaves. Gotta get rid of them too, or a whole new generation'll start to eat in a few days. Can't let 'em mess with our mash." It warmed my heart to hear him refer to the dish so dear to me. Americans cooked mashed potatoes, and we enjoyed them, too. But for our palates, mash with its special vinegar sauce, held first place.

"We shall start early in the morning."

Donnie woke before me and had the tea brewing. We downed a hasty breakfast and hurried out to our long potato rows.

"There's so many. Do you think we can win?"

"Absolutely."

"But they've been layin' eggs while we slept."

"No doubt."

"How can we ever get 'em all?"

Thinking of the war's ever-growing complications, I hesitated a bit. "Remember the meaning of your name. I think we stand a good chance."

Working against this insect hoard gave me pause. Such a multi-tudinous enemy, but if we applied the same principle to the war and many other exigencies, we might face them with the same determination John Meusebach employed.

Or so I felt at the beginning of this endeavor.

Two hours later, Donnie mentioned old John as we washed off disgusting reddish-brown slime at the pump. "Do you think Mr. Meusebach had potato bugs on his vines?"

We discussed this for a while, and what remedy he might have used. Then it was time to check on Daisy.

Out in the pasture, she raised her tail and turned in a circle—*agitated*. We haltered her and led her to the barn where she panted, trod across the stall and back again, and twitched her tail like the windshield wiper on Norman's newfangled truck.

"She's scared." Donnie plied her with water, and she drank but a little.

"I'd better drive to town for William and Doc. Will you be all right alone with her?"

He shrugged. "Of course, Da. I'm gonna be a veterinarian some day, you know."

Chapter Twenty-two

Williams's healthy baby calf, now weeks old, came into the world without ado. Apparently Daisy's stomach had untwisted by itself, so Doc saw no need to roll her. Donnie christened the perky little creature Pokey, an ideal choice.

Out in the pasture now, the little tyke nosed around close to her food source. Donnie made frequent trips to report on her as I wrestled with recalcitrant fence posts.

"Do you think Pokey really oughta be outside? She's so young."

"A healthy little one needs fresh air and sunshine."

"Remember how Mr. Meusebach worked with cattle?"

"As I recall, he mixed Texas longhorns with—what kind was that?"

"Holsteins. Mr. Kidney says Holsteins originated in the Netherlands about 2,000 years ago. People crossed a black breed from the Batavians and a white one from the Friesians to create a new breed."

"Did he say who the Batavians were, or the Friesians?"

"The Friesians were Dutch. The Batavians—I forget."

"They were Germans. How did you get on this subject?"

"One of the boys said his family lost some steers last night and thought it might be cattle rustlers with a truck, like that Texas Ranger said. Wouldn't that be somethin', right here in our neighborhood?"

"Mmm."

"Mr. K says if we want to study animal science, Texas A&M has a good program."

"Indeed?"

"Yeah. Betcha John Meusebach would've gone there if he'd been born later."

I looked up from twisting a wire, and Donnie's earnest expression suggested this desire might develop into more than a passing whim. So far, he had considered being a teacher, or as Anton's situation developed, studying law.

Meanwhile, the potato bugs returned like the Luftwaffe and bombarded our helpless plants with orange splatters. Violet Trueblood from church said she swore by Neem oil. That afternoon, she demonstrated how to spray the plants, covering the top and underside of each leaf. Leaving us with instructions for reapplying the deterrent, she accepted our offer of a ride back home.

Next year, we should plant our potatoes somewhere else, she instructed. Her preventative horticultural advice: sow some catnip or tansy with them to ward off insects.

"But be sure to watch the catnip. It'll take over your whole garden if you let it."

"Won't the smell attract cats?" I was thinking mountain lions, for though we had not yet spotted one, they roamed this country unseen.

Violet got my message, and her bright eyes stopped me short. "Certainly not *big* cats." She cocked her head toward Donnie, who was bouncing in the back of the truck. "Big cats have plenty to eat up in the hills. Lots of rodents out there, you know."

Just the sort of information I needed. I had come to think of my early morning sighting of Norman beside our sign in the same way. If not, the belief that he had intended to carve something there would have overwhelmed me.

But what? My worst imaginings gave ample room for conjecture. But why let anger gnaw me thin, as it did with Victoria years ago?

Every time I spotted his knife sitting on the shelf above our sink, I let go of that moment anew. Whatever he had intended, he had not completed the action. Whether that moment stemmed from his grandfather's rebellion against speaking German or not, such a deep-seated hatred might be unconscious. Called out, Norman would employ denial and become even less likely to come to grips with it.

Besides, my immediate concern was Donnie. The day he found the knife, he exclaimed, "This is like what them older boys used when they carved something in the windowsill at school, and Mr. Kidney made 'em draw it on the blackboard for everybody to see."

"What did they draw?"

"A swastika. Mr. Kidney explained how it was a Greek cross with the arms extended, and what it meant these days. Then he asked why any patriotic American would want to draw something like that?"

"What did the boys say?"

Bert said, "I was gonna put a X over them both, but then you walked in."

"An X over them? Now that makes some sense, at least."

Their faces had turned awful red, and they just stared at the floor. Mr. Kidney made 'em stay after school to sand down the wood. The next day, they had to stay after again and varnish everything real good."

"Sounds like a reasonable consequence."

We talked about what good—or evil—might result from a particular action. In this case, Donnie's class learned the symbol for the Nazis. How many times he had seen it before, I could not say—from time to time, newspaper articles used it in a photo, but not often.

Here in Loyal Valley, patriotism ran high, and a swastika signified our common enemy. Mr. Kidney had handled this situation well, and no doubt the boys' parents added to their punishment.

One day, a letter came from Opa Bultman. His few carefully written words revealed the amount of effort he had made, and the note he included from Emmaline, along with one from Anton for Donnie, had the same effect.

Dear Donnie and Mr. Herring,
Mother brought us your lovely package. I cannot describe
how much it heartened us. We have adjusted to our new
circumstances here and hope all is going well with you.
Mrs. Bultman

Anton's letter gave a few details about his studies, but not a word concerning the future. Of course not—his mother had warned him about the censors.

Emmaline's brevity hovered over me like a cloud. She wrote nothing about hopes for the future, and very little about the present. Such an intelligent woman, and so brave—would I have made the same sacrifice for a sibling? I assumed she felt needed at the school, and her teaching must be going well.

As summer's heat encased the hill country, I noticed more details this year. Certain colors once had seemed superfluous, since brown, grey, black and crème had made up my world. Solid wooden bookshelves, floors and desks grounded this conservative color scheme, as did tall echoing hallways. Subdued colors, hues to instill quietness and scholarliness.

Tweeds and woolens, silk cravats, leather caps, black umbrellas and overcoats, everything worked together to create the monotone of a teacher's existence. Who gave thought to purples or rose or yellow, much less the flamboyance of orange?

But here, bright shades finally caught up with me. The seeds William so carefully packed for our Atlantic journey produced far more than lovely flowers. Their influence spread down into my soul.

On the path to the barn, the hollyhocks displayed a veritable insurrection of color. Blossoms from burgundy to pink to pale yellow danced in an errant breeze, and intermingled lavender plants cast their royal hues. Along the fence line, salvia, snapdragons, and morning glories splashed rose and red, yellow and purple.

Even during long dry weeks when Donnie and I often took our midday meal at the spring, color burst forth. Tiny wildflowers ran rampant in patches like quilt work, and dusky greens and rusts displayed humble glory in simple musty lines on fallen logs, rocks and tree trunks.

Donnie's inquiries as to species and type received vague answers—these plants simply *were*, and my efforts with the encyclopedia often failed miserably. But as we basked in this lushness, a thought niggled. No prison camp boasted flowers. Did everything seem so much brighter in contrast to the dullness I pictured for our friends?

We often referenced a book of botanical listings made in the last century by a Dr. Lindheimer whom, we learned, became a comrade of John Meusebach and made many of his observations on Meusebach's property. He collected specimens for a Harvard University doctor, and over thirteen years, catalogued lists of 1,500 species.

Old John M. seemed destined to enter our world time and again, and Donnie and I often discussed his wide influence. As for Mr. Lindheimer, as a young man he taught in Germany and campaigned for governmental reform. One of the Dreissinger refugees, he came to the United States with intellectuals and others from across Germany, after the failed Frankfurt-Putsch rebellion in the 1830s.

Donnie went wild when we read that after living in Mexico for a year, Mr. Lindheimer left for this country and was shipwrecked off the coast of Alabama. We revisited Robert Louis Stevenson for some time before moving on to Lindheimer's arrival in San Jacinto the day after the final battle for Texas independence.

"Can you believe that, Da? There still would have been bodies, wouldn't there? And blood, plus plenty of vultures and other carnivores?"

"I expect so." I quickly returned to ferreting out the names of those tiny wildflowers we recently noticed near the spring.

So it was that we ascertained several species' identities, and learned that Dr. Lindheimer had been credited with at least twenty specific discoveries. Donnie allowed as how every species in the States must surely be labeled by now.

"I would think so, but one never knows. It depends if we consider the territories."

"Alaska and Hawaii? Do you think botanists are working there like those old Germans did here a hundred years ago?"

"No doubt, except both territories have become key to the war effort, so scientists may have had to postpone their work. But where something remains to be explored, people will always do so. I can't imagine that only those *old Germans* possessed that sort of curiosity, can you? Remember the Englishman who named the Lacey Oak."

"For sure."

The wind whistled through the chimney and the clock chimed nine. Tonight would bring little relief from the heat, but perhaps in the wee hours, cooler air would blow in.

After Donnie slipped under his sheet, I touched his forehead. So many profound thoughts in this boy's mind, I could almost sense them churning.

Before I turned off his lamp, he murmured, "Do you think we can go to Alaska?"

"You never know—we have many trips to take, don't we?"

"Yeah. Alaska would be great—a lot cooler than here. We oughta make a list." After I thought he had drifted off, he added, "First we have to go back to Old Blighty, righto?"

"Absolutely."

Springtime sniffles had descended upon William and Lillian, so Donnie and I spent Sunday afternoon on a lark. In Mason, our county seat, we visited the old Army fort up on a hilltop overlooking town, and discovered this had been Robert E. Lee's last command post in the U.S. Army before the Civil War.

This, of course led to exclamations—"Wow! We're walking on the same dogtrot where General Lee did, Da!"

"Righto. And these stones around the doorway—see the scars?

I can almost imagine privates in the U.S. Army hefting them into place back in 1851."

Later, we drove Hazel down the James River Road south of town, crossed at a low mark, and launched our canoe on the James River. This lazy wet pathway sparkled in the sun, and oh, what a relaxing hour we shared. We left the canoe to pick up and hiked back to Hazel, who faithfully navigated the way to the bat cave.

Someone had told me it was on land owned by the Eckert family, and well worth the effort to get there as the bats emerged for the night. So we waited, and our reward came in a great rush.

As daylight waned, without warning, black winged creatures filled the air. The deluge came so suddenly, for a moment they epitomized the evil assaulting this world. But as the cloud dissipated, I shook off that image—no need to ruin a glorious day.

Our short trip offered a respite from a week filled with work. Most nights, darkness fell as we came in for supper. Sundays always provided a reprieve, but today, our explorations stretched the afternoon like a lovely silver thread.

The next day, back in our routine, the potato bug war raged on despite our faithful Neem oil applications. A full-scale re-infestation seemed underway, so I considered spraying the whole patch with the formula I used for weeds, a vinegar, salt, and water mixture. But that would have killed the potato vines, too, and as Donnie reminded me, they nourished the potatoes, hidden under the earth.

"It's photosynthesis, Da. We mustn't kill off the plants!"

This fight had become exasperating, but Violet predicted we would still reap a crop. I imagined the beleaguered potatoes down there, like Londoners bunking in underground tube station tunnels, side by side in the darkness on a night of bombing.

Always, the evening newscasts prodded us to the bigger picture—our potato bug war became mere trivia in the light of a German plane sinking the British ship SS *Erinpura* in the Mediterranean, killing nearly 800. On the same day, May first, SS

General Hanns Albin Rauter declared the removal of all Jews from the occupied Netherlands.

But also on that day, we saw progress as German troops vacated Jefna, Tunisia. On the thirteenth of the month, the North Africa campaign officially ended, having been waged since September of 1940. After two and a half years of defeats and victories, and at such great cost, our troops finally reached their objective.

Always, this interplay of bad and good news played with our senses. On May fifteenth we gave no thought at all to potato bugs, and less than normal to the war, because the Cincinnati Reds' Clyde Shoun no-hit the Boston Braves 1-0. Very rare, but not as unique as a perfect game, according to Mr. Kidney.

If I were to write a book about 1943, it would be called, *Willie and the War*, since the Sicily campaign coincided with Willie learning to crawl from the kitchen to the parlor at record speed. In July, good news from the battlefields cheered us. On the twenty-second, we heard that the Allies captured Sicily.

In autumn, they landed in southern Italy, or as Winston Churchill called it, "the soft underbelly of Europe." But that soft underbelly proved not so soft, after all, and the march toward France seemed interminable. By Donnie's tenth birthday in November, our troops were suffering terribly in their attempt to drive out the Germans. Bitter fighting from hill to hill took place in miserable winter weather.

Back in the summer, the RAF had launched a bombing raid on Hamburg. The destruction of munitions factories brought exquisite satisfaction to many in England who had survived the Luftwaffe's devastating attacks. The evening report a day later told us so, with *hurrahs* in the background.

"Do you think they'll run out of cities to bomb, Da?"

Donnie's question stymied me. In other words, would thi *tit-for-tat* business ever end? And if it did, what would be left of the world?

When the newscaster announced the arrest of Benito Mussolini, he admitted this still was rumor. "But if it proves true, we most likely are observing the fall of the Italian Fascist government. The question is, will Marshal Pietro Badoglio take over? And will he negotiate with the Allies?"

"What do you think, Da? Will he?"

"Yes, I think he will."

On August seventeenth and eighteenth, nearly 600 RAF bombers had targeted the Nazis' rocket factories on the German island of Usedom, the most populous island in the Baltic Sea. There, Nazi forced labor built V1 and V2 rockets that Uncle Adolph launched across the Channel into England. At the same time, a diversionary force of Mosquitoes dropped flares and small explosive loads over Berlin to distract German defenses.

Donnie leaped up when this description came over the airwaves. "Attaway, boys! Knock 'em out! Give 'em the old one-two!" He sounded more and more like any other American boy.

"Do you think any of our boys helped out the RAF, Da? Do you think any of 'em might have practiced right here in one of those mock dogfights we saw?"

American forces also celebrated major triumphs over the Japanese. On the island of New Guinea, they ambushed the airfield at Wewak, and Air Force planes destroyed 150 enemy planes, an entire bombing formation.

In August on the Island of Kiska in the North Pacific, they launched an amphibious assault to seize the last enemy strongholds on U.S. soil captured by Japanese forces in 1942 on Kiska and Attu Island. As it turned out, our troops reclaimed Kiska from no one at all—thousands of Japanese soldiers had been evacuated weeks earlier.

But the booby traps and mines the enemy left behind took the lives of far too many American and Canadian troops, and caused confusion that led to friendly fire losses. How I hated to hear those words! At least we could now use the islands for our bases—some commanders called this whole scenario a good training experience.

On a bright note, underground sources reported that the

Luftwaffe chief ended his life over failing to defend Nazi Germany against Allied bombing raids. Official word denied this, of course, but one way or the other, he would no longer head the organization.

Meanwhile, German forces were clashing with Italians in Lju-bljana, Slovenia. Donnie and I looked that one up for preciseness, as he reminded me Mrs. Bultman would do. We considered the location of Bulgaria, also, since King Boris III had died following an audience with Herr Hitler. Had he been assassinated? No one knew for sure, but speculation circled the globe.

At the end of August, the Danes sank most of their naval fleet to prevent it from falling into Axis hands, as had their king, Christian X. In the same news report, Washington put Berlin on notice concerning German atrocities against the Poles—the day of reckoning would come, and war crimes would be punished.

This long-awaited announcement heartened the free world, but most likely brought little comfort to the Polish people, who had suffered so dreadfully. For them, it surely rang hollow—too little too late.

But William nearly chortled as he told us about a new naval fighter plane developed and first used last year. The Grumman F6F Hellcat included improvements on the Wildcat, and aero-buffs held high hopes for its use, especially against the Japanese. With Donnie all agog, I searched the newspapers for more information.

On Donnie's auspicious day, William and Lillian invited us for dinner, and Lillian baked a cake. Somehow, she managed to depict an entire baseball team on the top, with only a dribble of frosting here and there, due to sugar rationing.

Unadulterated delight overtook the guest of honor. "Why, you even made the pitcher throwin' a strike! Wow!" And so she had, using various sized buttons and cardboard cutouts for players. Abigail and Willie joined in the festivities, making a royal mess of their clothing as we ate. But Lillian simply shrugged, as if to say, "It's just a shirt and a dress, and I can wash them."

The whole day, recollections flooded me. How could this

towering youth be the same helpless infant I carried out under the Nottinghamshire stars to explain the meaning of his name?

As far as I could ascertain, he was indeed conquering his world, and I looked forward to seeing him continue. Would he become an airplane pilot, a botanist, a veterinarian, or choose some different path entirely? Time moved so fast, I would soon know.

His gifts from me were books. As I ordered them, I kept in mind Mr. Kidney's latest comments. These arrived in a note he delivered into my hand one day after school, as Donnie engaged in a virtual dogfight with his mates on the playground.

Always an exemplary student, Donnie helps younger children when the opportunity arises. His curiosity will take him far, but his mind will soon need stimulation beyond the boundaries of our classroom. I foresee him completing his high school work two to three years ahead of schedule.

Recently, Mr. Kidney made a point of mentioning his own accelerated schooling, for his college studies began at age sixteen. He also said Donnie would begin studying Latin next fall. "He's nearly fluent in German—that can only help."

But one phrase stuck in my mind: *two to three years ahead.* The idea boggled my mind, so I released it for the time being. Let Donnie enjoy being a boy as long as possible.

Watching him collide with another supposed pilot there in the schoolyard, he yelled, "My P-38 can beat your old Messerschmitt any day!"

"Oh yeah? You 'Mericans don't know what you're talkin' about. The Luftwaffe ain't done with you yet, you yella-bellied GI!"

Ah, for the good old days of baseball. This war could not end soon enough.

Perhaps William longed for the good old days, too, since he and Lillian presented Donnie with a professional-looking leather baseball glove. He immediately started using it with Abigail, tossing a ball of yarn back and forth.

"Keep it on the floor, now. Only on the floor." Lillian touched

Abigail's shoulder to reinforce her instruction. "Willie wants in on the game, too."

Giggling and clapping, Willie made known his jubilation as that bright ball whizzed back and forth. He pulled himself to a stand, hanging onto William's leg.

Suddenly, William cried, "Look, everyone—Willie's just taken a step!"

"Oh my, Daddy!" (Lillian had taken to calling William *Daddy*, since he answered to that most often, anyway.) She clapped her hands. "Such a strong boy you are, Willie!"

Then she turned to Donnie. "What a milestone, and on your birthday! It won't be long, and he'll be running around with you."

1944 brought change to our church, since Pastor Bergner died in October of '43. I suppose, realizing his age, many parishioners were not surprised, but his sudden passing caught me unprepared. I had grown used to his preaching, which steadily improved my German. His loss marked a first for Donnie, and led to long talks.

As he processed this new experience, and I considered finding an English-speaking congregation. But our Sundays had become such a comfortable routine, church with Lillian and William, dinner, and time together in the afternoon. Donnie understood a great deal of German now, and our midweek prayer group had bonded, too.

When Pastor Brunatte came, we transitioned easily. I suppose some might have though it peculiar for British expatriates to worship in German, but the situation worked out well for us, not that different from Roman Catholics using Latin for their services.

Our new pastor had a way of linking present events with ancient ones, and in one sermon, he used the Surprise Hurricane that struck Galveston back in July in conjunction with a New Testament story. This launched Donnie and me into research about the hurricane that struck Galveston in 1900, a violent storm that killed 8,000 people.

"Back then, they didn't have much warning, right?"

"Perhaps none at all."

"But they call this one the Surprise Hurricane. Why did it come without warning?"

I reminded Donnie that our radio friend had answered this. The reason had everything to do with the war.

"With all radio traffic being censored for fear of a German U-boat picking up a signal, this storm sneaked in on our unsuspecting citizens with a vengeance."

"They'll never do that again, will they?"

"One would think not."

"What does the *U* mean?"

"Undersea boat. *Unterseeboot*, wouldn't you think?"

"Mrs. B would know for sure. Or Anton."

Ah, so he still missed them.

On Sunday, June fourth, William read us a letter from London.

Something big is about to happen down at the coast, and already has begun. You can bet on that, with so many soldiers and sailors from every place imaginable stationed between here and there. Indians and Belgians wander the streets with Aussies and Poles, French, Canadians, Greeks, New Zealanders, Americans and others.

I can't help but notice the noise the Americans make. A few rowdies make a big difference in our attitudes, and some people have lost patience already. Parents who see them after our young women tighten their lips at the mention of GIs.

But where would we be if they hadn't come? I keep reminding people of this. One of my neighbors says they act like they own our country. Probably because of Eisenhower's position—after all, we made him the Supreme Commander a year ago, didn't we?

We hear of some wrangling high up in the ranks, and I think, 'Monty, do set your pride aside. We must end this war. Forget who gets the glory, man!'

But mostly, everybody's working together. Whatever is about to take place has made this island a mighty crowded place—scarcely standing room on the train to Portsmouth the other day. You would never believe the number of troops, and the harbor is just as crowded.

Not a room to be had due to the numbers, and also to the Luftwaffe, which has taken out building after building. I talked a pub owner into letting me sleep on the floor. He was used to this, and can hardly keep enough food on hand.

He made a few choice comments about the Americans, too. Then he noted we have to remember they're quite young, and homesick. But no matter, he is glad they're here.

Mr. Churchill had much to do with that, and for us, he will always be number one. Last year, my neighbor saw him out in the East End, no less. With tears on his cheeks, surveying a bombsite.

Now isn't that a true hero? He has brought in the best scientists to work on enemy codes, and will see us through to victory, rest assured.

The King and Queen have been visiting bombsites, too. I never imagined we would hear about them out in the boroughs with everyday folks, did you?

On this quiet afternoon, Donnie kept Abigail occupied with some paper dolls while little Willie napped. When the letter writer mentioned the American soldiers, Lillian let go her usual composure and stood up for them.

"Most of those boys have never even been away from home before. They're probably scared to death, too. The Brits had better keep that in mind. And I'm sure they're profiting from all of the business!"

William and I exchanged a look and left well enough alone.

Two evenings later, early reports of Allied landings on the Normandy coast painted a clearer picture. The newscaster's voice went hoarse as he outlined various beach landings and commanders. He also mentioned the entrenched German forces waiting for our boys as they stormed onto beaches through fierce gunfire.

But mostly, we heard about this invasion's positive impact. Though fraught with danger and sacrifice, it promised to make all the difference and hasten the war's end.

As the Allies fought their way across northern France, our prayer service continued in earnest, and we often mentioned certain harsh struggles to liberate specific villages. Each evening report brought news of some heretofore unheard of locale where the Germans put up yet another venomous fight. Donnie and I marked each location on our map, and I kept a list to take along to our meeting.

One evening, the news included the recent loss of Theodore Roosevelt Junior in the Utah Beach landings. By now, even the "other Roosevelts," Teddy's clan, were supporting their Democrat cousin in the election.

As summer progressed, those who assumed the invasion would lead to instant victory realized they had been sadly mistaken. The reports listed a cruel amount of casualties, and we acknowledged that each soldier or airman came from someplace like Loyal Valley, where a family longed for their son to come home.

In our simple requests and remembrances, the overall anxiety borne by our little segment of this nation found a resting place of sorts. I likened the effect to our hens at roost in their nesting boxes every evening, their anxious scratching for nourishment and day-long cackling ceased.

Similarly, our fears and hopes settled down in the small sanctuary where we met to lift our concerns to heaven. A difficult concept to explain for someone with no experience or desire for such, but nonetheless valid.

We followed the troops through savage battles, and finally they liberated the besieged city of Paris near the end of August. Vicious fighting still continued as other Allied troops threaded north through the western foothills of the Alps. Continuous bitter battles multiplied the constant casualty counts.

One day Norman stopped by unannounced again. As if nothing had occurred between us, he sauntered over to where I was working.

"Haven't seen you around the library." His accusing tone struck me the wrong way. Bathed in sweat, I had been struggling with a stubborn fencepost for over an hour.

"No. I have been quite busy."

"Drove up to Mason yesterday. Got a friend there who was notified of his son's death in Normandy. The Nazis mowed him down with two other buddies in the battle for some little town over there."

"How terribly sad."

"That's all you can say?"

I pushed back my soaking cap. Fortunately, Donnie had gone to help Lillian this morning, but in the oppressive heat, my mood left a great deal to be desired.

"What would you like me to say?"

"You Brits better be grateful we're helpin' you out of this fix, giving our sons for the cause. That's all I know."

His words impacted like a slug to the chest. I took a step back from the post and stared at him.

"Did you hear me?"

"How could I not? I think you can rest assured that the British nation will always be thankful the United States entered the war."

"Well, just so you know. We're payin' for your peace with our blood, like we did in the last war."

"Yes. And so are the Polish, French, Dutch, and many more. Thousands have died in Europe, and so many more in the Pacific Theater. My father sacrificed his life in France during the Great War—I never even knew him. I wonder, have you heard about the way Hitler is killing the Jews?"

I allowed no time for him to jump in. "It's horrendous. Beastly. Evil unleashed on this earth like never before, and we all have to work together to win. Don't you think it's time to realize we all are sacrificing, and set aside this sort of talk?"

One part of me awaited rebuke. At the same time, I wondered what troubled Norman so deeply. Under his brash exterior, some-thing must be agitating him constantly, or why should he come after me like this? What did he hope to gain?

Whatever it was, I would not know at present. Without a word, he walked on.

He reminded me of a testy adolescent trying to stir up a fight. My instinct was to run after him and grab him by the collar (except he was taller by a few inches.) I would ask him about his intentions that morning when he dropped his knife near our sign.

But to what end? Visions of arguments with Victoria returned. They had produced similar results, a wildly beating heart, and no resolution in the end. Perhaps one good outcome was my presence of mind. I could suffer being falsely accused without accusing in return.

With my forehead dripping, I took a deep breath. Being free of conflict had been one gift in coming here, and despite the heat, outdoor work brought its own satisfaction. Now, though, with William working full-time, I was hard-pressed to finish everything that needed doing.

As Norman's figure faded into the distance, a great sigh swept me. I had no energy to waste attempting to figure out my neighbor. Of course, this did not mean I stopped trying to do just that, or that this scene failed to rob me of sleep—but only for a night. I had Victoria to thank for this—she had taught me that no amount of fretting on my part could change the unchangeable.

When my normal pattern returned, I dreamed of Elliot. Months had passed since our epistolary communication, but at times, his face still appeared in the darkness. My dream had me young again, and suddenly robbed of a limb.

I wakened thinking of this young soldier. Would I ever hear from Elliot again, or in this case, did *MIA* mean *missing forever*?

The shelf in my mind for unanswered questions had grown in length and depth. Elliot occupied space there, along with Victoria, Emmaline, and Anton. Now, I slipped Norman onto that shadowy ledge where clarity escaped me. In the process, I realized something positive.

Norman had not even mentioned the national election, in which Thomas Dewey, the GOP candidate opposing Franklin Roosevelt in his bid for an unheard-of fourth term, came off as pompous.

FDR's daughter pigeonholed him as the "little man on the wedding cake."

Recently, the President rode in an open car through all boroughs of New York City in the rain, and an estimated two to three million citizens came out to greet him. Who else could lead the United States to the end of this awful war?

Down at the station, Jerrold would have something to say about this. No doubt, he would note that a fourth term would produce a dictatorship, not a democracy. But Norman remained a staunch devotee, and as predicted, the President won hands-down.

Late in October, just before the election, newsmen hailed the Japanese Navy's defeat in the Battle of the Leyte Gulf. During this massive naval battle, possibly the largest in history, Americans witnessed *kamikaze* pilots in action for the first time.

Via Donnie, Mr. Kidney's opinion came home. Though we won a massive victory, effectively destroying the fighting capability of the Japanese Navy, pilots like these would be responsible for many American deaths before the war ended. And according to a newscast, many of them were no more than boys.

Chapter Twenty-three

One Sunday afternoon in late November, Violet Trueblood, our potato bug ally, informed us about Norman's wife. According to Lillian, Violet ranked as the kindest woman who ever lived, and when she knocked on William and Lillian's door after our noonday meal and burst in, her voice trembled.

"I'm afraid Doris Landers has lost her mind. Someone found her in the middle of the night, halfway over to House Mountain. This has happened a few times before, and Norman's fit to be tied." Dabbing her eyes with her hankie, Violet sniffled.

At the time, Donnie was outside with Abigail, and Lillian invited Violet to sit down. She waved off the offer and stood clenching her twisted hankie.

"Doris has always been timid—we grew up just down the road from each other, you know. She used to ride along to town with Norman, but for the past few years, no one has seen her out at all. Oh, I wish I could do something."

After Lillian walked her out, we mulled over the news. A short, fine-boned woman—that was all I recalled from my glimpse of Norman's wife when Donnie and I hauled over our payment for the truck. She had hurried inside from the long front porch as we entered the yard.

"Violet and I will take some food out to them. I'll talk with her tomorrow. Seems she and Doris were as close as sisters for years, but then Doris stopped leaving home."

Later, on our way home, evening stillness prevailed in Loyal

Valley. To the East, House Mountain rose like a giant creature in the twilight.

Donnie had heard Violet and Lillian talking outdoors and voiced his concern. "That lady was halfway to House Mountain—so many snakes and coyotes out there at night."

Ah, good—he had not heard exactly who Doris was. "We can be thankful they found her alive."

The next day, Lillian provided a bit more insight. "Poor Doris—I can't stop thinking about her. Edgar had some business dealings with Norman over the years, and I doubt he knows how to deal with this."

"What do you mean?"

"He has little patience when things don't go his way. This situation with Doris can't be fixed easily, and now it's out in the open. That will really bother him, and I've also heard he's been all worked up about enemy invaders lately." Then she added, "I wonder if he has any true friends."

"Enemy invaders? What have you heard?"

"Not much, really. Just that he's been stirring up talk with no good reason. Someone said he got into a row with one of the men down at the gas station, too. Years ago, Edgar told me that when Norman moved here during his school years, he caused trouble for the teacher, but as an adult, he fit in pretty well, I thought, until this past year. I suppose the war sets certain people on edge, and yes, there have been sightings of U-boats along the coast."

"But everyone around here is American through-and-through, and we know we can trust each other. We may honor our German heritage, but I've never heard of one person being anything but loyal to the United States. Just look at all the local men who signed up right after Pearl Harbor, or even earlier."

Quite a speech for Lillian, who usually spoke her piece succinctly. Now, she returned her attention to the situation at hand. "I imagine Norman's already called Doc out there. Sure hope Doris doesn't have to be put in an institution."

Images of a different doctor and an institution from long ago swirled in my head. "Mmm. The last two times I've seen him, Norman has acted less than friendly. This might explain his behavior, at least in part."

"So you've noticed? I wondered how long you could put up with him. He's so—"

Lillian left her sentence hanging, and I kept further questions to myself. But clearly, her sympathy extended more to Doris than to Norman.

That night, Donnie and I ate supper with William and her, and on the way home, the grand bowl of the sky teemed with stars. Arriving at home, we circled the orchard to observe them from various positions, and as we craned our necks, the dark bulk of House Mountain reminded me of Doris.

What had it been like for her, wandering out there in the night? Had she tried to find her way home, or in her state of mind, did *home*—the one place we ought to feel comfortable—no longer exist?

Before going inside to read, Donnie and I lingered on the porch steps to gaze at the heavenly spectacle. Cicada songs surrounded us. From the barn, Risk whinnied, and Donnie petted Ramshackle. "You're such a good old dog. Yes you are!" warmed my heart.

Some time later, Donnie yawned. Reluctant to go inside, we finally knew the time had come.

Questions plied me as I lay considering what Norman was experiencing. What might I do to be neighborly without offending him? Seemingly nothing, but perhaps if I spoke with Bernardo, he might give me an idea.

In the aftermath of the Liberation of Paris and the Allied advance through the foothills of the French Alps, whole divisions now prepared for a final confrontation with Germany. But in Italy, our troops still slogged toward victory. In late August, they had begun to penetrate the Gothic Line defenses on the Fifth and Eighth Army fronts, but made no decisive breakthrough.

Since two Italian governments existed at this point, what

amounted to civil war skirmishes kept breaking out. Because of the Nazi scorched-earth policy, women and children were now starving to death. The power-hungry leadership had created an intolerable plight for its citizens.

With the entire world's fate at stake, the worst of human nature kept rearing its nasty head. All around us, those with loved ones in harm's way on various fronts continually held their breath.

When I stopped by with the mail, Lillian was as upset as I had ever seen her. She motioned me into the house, where Abigail entertained Willie with some building blocks.

"When I went out to hang up the washing, I found Doris Landers in the far corner of our back yard. She was all hunched up, with no jacket, and barefoot. Her arms and face were bruised and she was shivering. When I approached, she bolted into the street. I couldn't leave the children, but she took off toward Doc's street. Hopefully he saw her running by." Lillian shook her head. "That poor woman. What are they going to do?"

"What are the alternatives?"

"Keep her under lock and key or hire someone to stay with her, I suppose. I've heard of a sanitarium near Dallas called Timberlawn. Things can't go on like this much longer, or I'm afraid Doris will come to a terrible end."

The image of flames engulfing Grandfather's house came to mind, and Victoria's body lying alone in the carriage house. A terrible end, indeed.

"I'll talk to Violet again soon. She's known Norman since childhood. Actually, I think she mentioned that he once tried to court her, but Violet showed no interest. Anyway, maybe she and Doc can speak with him."

What could it hurt to take some cider and jam to Norman's house? By now, they had surely run out, and hopefully no one would even see me. Chances were, he would be making his rounds in his new truck, checking things out, and if Doris were inside, she would be in bed. Probably, someone was staying with her, so I would leave the items on the porch, and that would be that.

I thought it over some more, and just after noon, skulked the back way through the brush near the spring. The countryside bore a fulvous hue now, as Donnie had mentioned last week.

Fulvous, another of his vocabulary words, complete with connections to a certain duck found in England. Had I ever seen this species, he wanted to know—a sort of yellow-brown with extra long legs? I could not recall such a sighting—something to check with William.

Our creek had dwindled to the width of one large step. The cider jug jiggled in my backpack, but safely, since the jams, wrapped in newspaper, cushioned either side.

As always, the lacey oak reminded me of our good fortune. Near the springs, ground cover remained green even now. Perhaps we might make more of this area one day, when the work slowed down—clean out some of the brush and level the ground.

Striding over the hill through a triangle of land belonging to another neighbor I knew fairly well, my thoughts darkened. When Norman saw these things, he would know who had visited, and perhaps find fault. Aware that our small token of concern might be taken the wrong way, I had no way of gauging his reaction.

But what good comes of ignoring our better impulses? It only makes sense to listen to these urges, even when they involve a perceived risk.

Ah, the complications of life. I increased my pace and found the Landers's yard quiet except for a mongrel too old and weary to bark. The sight reminded me of Norman's kindness in our first years, when he had sent both Risk and Ramshackle our way. And Hazel, still faithfully carrying out her duty.

Steeling my resolve, I crept to the porch, shuddered off my pack, and took out my offering. Not much, but something, at least.

Almost back to our mutual neighbor's fence line, I heard someone tramping behind me. My neck hairs stood on end as I turned to see Norman coming my way, pale and disheveled. Without his Stetson—definitely a first. He seemed so much shorter, and a bald spot showed on the crown of his head.

"Didn't have to do that, you know."

"We heard—" Dare I say it? "—about your wife. If we can do anything to help, please let me know."

"Nothin' anybody can do."

"I am so sorry."

Aware of small movements in the sparse ground cover between us, I waited—probably mice searching for sustenance, while Norman appeared to be searching for words. I might mention my extensive experience with an illness similar to his wife's, but Lillian had advised me to avoid anything that might be taken as advice.

As I made to go, his voice turned so quiet I could scarcely make out his words.

"—was wrong about you, Herring. No Communist woulda done this."

Like cottonwood fluff caught in a breeze, his admission rode the air between us. Then he mumbled something else, so I leaned closer.

"May have made a mistake about—" He stared off into the distance. "—that German teacher, too." He flinched when I lifted my palm, and all utterance died in my throat. Then he turned back toward his house, and I wondered if through one of the windows, Doris might be watching.

October had brought another hurricane to Florida, killing eighteen people. The storm also hit the Carolinas and Virginia. Braced for a similar event, our Gulf Coast found a reprieve this year.

During November, the evening news had made guesses as to what would happen next on the Western Front, but reports of specific battles ceased. As we prepared for Christmas, Lillian heard from Violet that Doris had been sent to Timberlawn. Her comment offered a modicum of comfort: "I don't know what it's like there, but I hope she'll be safe now."

"Makes me wonder—Violet said *sent*. It's none of my business, but I'd sure like to know how she got there. Did someone drive way out here to escort her? I hate to think of her being dragged out of the house and constrained by strangers."

Always full of information, Norman must have turned quiet about this news. Violet offered a speculation at our prayer meeting that week, but no one seemed to know for certain.

Our humble festivities this year would center around the children, of course. The approaching holidays seemed muted by the knowledge that the respite in Europe had ended, and our troops presently engaged in a horrible nightmare called the Battle of the Bulge.

Record cold magnified misery into grinding agony for entrenched Allied soldiers, with German panzers bearing down on their positions. The enemy had surprised us once again—our commanders had become convinced the Germans could no longer launch an offensive.

Lillian kept knitting socks "like crazy," as Donnie put it. "'Cause our soldiers have got the Trench Foot somethin' awful."

William shook his head at this. "Wouldn't you think after the terrible suffering from that in the Great War, our military would have prepared better than this?" He rarely spoke of the past, but glanced at Donnie. "I remember your grandfather writing home about Trench Foot when he was fighting."

My father—I had never heard about this before. Visions of soldiers with frostbite, some with toes missing, passed before me.

A full year had passed since Emmaline and Anton entered Crystal City. I should go down to Fredericksburg and see what news Opa Bultmann had heard, but kept putting it off. Grim reports brought to us each evening played a part in my procrastination. The war and its far-reaching effects had a paralyzing effect.

Herr Hitler enjoyed a tactical advantage in what he called "The

Watch on the Rhine." Allied commanders had aided him with their enormous error. GIs had been preparing for winter camp, and Hollywood stars even flew to the Ardennes to entertain them.

On December fourteenth, Marlene Dietrich sang for high-spirited troops in the little town of Bastogne, France. The next day, the Giants' outfielder Mel Ott and other ballplayers visited First Division Headquarters in Belgium, from whence many officers had gone to Paris on leave. They had no idea that Uncle Adolph's final great offensive was at hand in the Ardennes Forest.

Fighting began on December sixteenth, when three German armies consisting of a million soldiers broke the Allied defensive line and headed west toward the Meuse River. If they reached Antwerp, the main Allied supply port, how would we ever recover?

Each new broadcast heightened the tension stretched like electrical wires from coast to coast. Lillian noted that her fingers had gotten stiff and sore. Of an evening, William joined her, for he was one of many Brits who learned to knit during the Great War. Donnie tried his hand, and so did I.

Comic relief came in Abigail's winsome expressions as she took up an old pair of needles and mimicked our motions. All the while, Willie eyed us with wonder. Often, we ventured to their house after supper, so as to avoid enduring the demoralizing evening report alone.

For a break, Lillian took up reading *The Mystery of the Blue Train*. William had always enjoyed Agatha Christie's novels, and developed a full bookcase. To hear Lillian's attempted British accent, "Hercule Poirot: the world-renowned, moustachioed Belgian private detective, unsurpassed in his intelligence and understanding of the criminal mind, respected and admired by police forces and heads of state across the globe—" brought a chuckle from us all.

"That novel looks to be a classic, my dear. Published in '28 and still widely read." William patted her hand. "Mrs. Christie's writing provides a unique diversion these days."

Ah yes, a diversion much needed after Christmas and into the

New Year. After six dreadful weeks of fighting through frozen forests in Belgium and Luxembourg, our GIs covered the territory from Elsenborn Ridge in the north to Diekirch, Luxembourg in the south.

We all wore our hearts on our sleeves for them. I don't know how many times I heard the phrase—*our poor boys*—during this time, and each utterance issued from the heart.

Hearing Prime Minister Churchill's speech to the House of Commons on December eighteenth helped a bit. "Care must be taken in telling our proud story not to claim for the British Army an undue share of what is undoubtedly the greatest American battle of the war, and will, I believe, be regarded as an ever famous American victory."

The full account of his address carried by the newspapers showed his deep understanding of what the horrendous losses at the Bulge meant to the American people. Reading it reminded me of his own American roots.

"I have seen it suggested that the terrific battle which has been proceeding since 16th December on the American front is an Anglo-American battle. In fact, however, the United States troops have done almost all the fighting and have suffered almost all the losses. They have suffered losses almost equal to those on both sides in the battle of Gettysburg. Only one British Army Corps has been engaged in this action. All the rest of the thirty or more divisions, which have been fighting continuously for the last month, are United States troops. The Americans have engaged thirty or forty men for every one we have engaged, and they have lost sixty to eighty men for every one of ours. That is the point I wish to make."

Gettysburg—over 50,000 soldiers died in that one battle. Donnie and I had not yet delved into the American Civil War, but it remained on our list. Once again, my sense of belonging here surfaced. Though he had never lived here, did the Prime Minister feel the same?

Because of this immensely costly battle, the reality Allied commanders wrongly assumed at the outset had become true at last. The

Nazi machine lay depleted, with no resources for another assault. As winter turned to spring, we knew the war in the European theater simply must end, although entering and overtaking Germany still posed plenty of challenges.

Donnie drew a new map—this time of Germany. We followed the reports of our troops' determined progress across wide rivers, fighting the enemy at every turn.

And then on April twelfth came the news of President Roosevelt's death.

As the same Pullman cars that had transported him to Warm Springs, Georgia throughout his presidency traveled north to Washington, D.C. with his body, thousands of mourners lined every stop along the route.

Even Lillian, a lifelong Republican, shed a tear. "He's been our President for so long. How sad he won't get to see the war end."

At long last, victory was ours. Who could ever forget this momentous day, May 8, 1945, or President Truman's proclamation? Mr. Kidney obtained a copy, which Donnie wrote out in longhand to bring home, and read with great aplomb in our living room to our supper guests.

A Proclamation

The Allied armies, through sacrifice and devotion and with God's help, have wrung from Germany a final and unconditional surrender. The western world has been freed of the evil forces which for five years and longer have imprisoned the bodies and broken the lives of millions upon millions of free-born men. They have violated their churches, destroyed their homes, corrupted their children, and murdered their loved ones. Our Armies of Liberation have restored freedom to these suffering peoples, whose spirit and will the oppressors could never enslave.

Much remains to be done. The victory won in the West must now be won in the East. The whole world must be cleansed of the evil from which half the world has been freed. United, the peace-loving nations have demonstrated in the West that their arms are stronger by far than the might of dictators or the tyranny of military cliques that once called us soft and weak. The power of our people to defend themselves against all enemies will be proved in the Pacific war as it has been proved in Europe.

For the triumph of spirit and of arms which we have won, and for its promise to peoples everywhere who join us in the love of freedom, it is fitting that we, as a nation, give thanks to Almighty God, who has strengthened us and given us the victory.

Now, Therefore, I, Harry S. Truman, President of the United States of America, do hereby appoint Sunday, May 13, 1945, to be a day of prayer.

I call upon the people of the United States, whatever their faith, to unite in offering joyful thanks to God for the victory we have won and to pray that He will support us to the end of our present struggle and guide us into the way of peace.

I also call upon my countrymen to dedicate this day of prayer to the memory of those who have given their lives to make possible our victory.

Even Willie sensed the solemnity of this occasion, and sat beside Abigail with his hands nicely folded. When Donnie finished, William saluted him.

"A fine rendition of an even finer proclamation. My high hope is that this will lead to victory in Japan very soon."

On the afternoon of Victory in Europe day, Mr. Grunkle provided fresh-churned ice cream at the creamery. He invited the whole community and played an admirable *founder of the feast*.

His younger grandchildren came, so our little ones enjoyed playing with them as much as they did slurping their cold treat.

Even wild Willie, into his third year now, made his first new friend that day.

Donnie, who dropped Abigail off on his way home from school of late, had come running in with Mr. Grunkle's invitation. Outside the creamery, I noticed Norman deep in conversation with someone sporting a Stetson as impressive as his. But even protected by that massive brim, he looked pale, and the next time I looked, he had disappeared.

Our celebration was tinged with anxiety for those with sons still deployed in the Pacific. After we bit our nails through the battles for Iwo Jima back in March and the almost four-month long fight for Okinawa in April, May, and June, the *Los Angeles Times* still estimated we would lose one million more men if we invaded Japan proper. Knowing that the war in Europe had ceased only increased our longing for peace in the Pacific.

Through the summer of 1945, this desire remained uppermost. Even as parents and wives received family members back from the war, everyone awaited the next announcement: *Victory in Japan.*

But on August sixth, the flight of a Boeing B-29 Superfortress shocked us all. Colonel Paul Tibbets named that Superfortress the *Enola Gay* after his mother. He and his co-pilot, Robert A. Lewis, took off from North Field in the Mariana Islands and flew six hours to Japan. There, they dropped the first atomic bomb and nearly obliterated an entire city.

Of course, Donnie brought home these details about the bomber and the attack. This was the first I had heard, and he gladly offered more. Bookended by exclamations—"Wow! Man! Can you believe…"—the specifics of the raid might almost have been lost as his mind ran amuck.

"Think I'll ever get to see a B-29 in person," Da?"

"This has gotta end the war for sure, don't you think?"

"Mr. Kidney says …" He finished this sentence several times with various specifics his teacher had pointed out. The class had pored over a large wall map of the area the Superfortress covered in its flight.

"This was a *flight of destiny*, Mr. K said. The world will never be the same."

"The bomb destroyed an entire city?"

"Yeah."

"Do you recall its name."

"Starts with an H. Something like Hero— Boy, that Colonel Tibbets sure is one, don't you think?"

Later, William filled in the spelling of *Hiroshima*, and I began our research. In the days that followed, reports revealed such devastation in the Japanese homeland—surely, surrender must be at hand.

A little over a week later, V-J day finally arrived. Now the *whole* war was over! Mr. Grunkle renewed his invitation to Loyal Valley and environs. This time, relief lined every face, and the talk centered on the surrender, on a U.S. Navy Iowa-classed battleship in Tokyo Bay.

Mr. Grunkle chortled, "That's because a naval vessel is considered sovereign territory for accepting a surrender. My grandson's been in Okinawa a long time now—says he won a hundred Japanese yen, or $6.67 in a poker game last October, betting on the Tigers to win in the last game.

"Anyway, he wrote his folks that President Truman made sure the USS Missouri was used for the surrender, 'cause that's his home state. The Japanese big-wigs had to travel all the way across the harbor and climb the stairs like ensigns."

"Yeah, and the Missouri flew Commodore Perry's flag from way back in 1845 when Japan was forced to open up to the West. A hundred years ago—now, what about that?" Norman offered this tidbit.

Someone broke into applause, and he came close to smiling. This afternoon, he seemed more like himself.

Over the summer, I glimpsed him a couple of times from a distance. Each time, my quiescence surprised me—not a hint of anger or recrimination. How encouraging to move ahead without making moral judgments on Norman—or on myself. Hearing him as much as apologize was far more than I had expected during the heat of our conflict.

One morning, Donnie and I took down our sign for a fresh coat of varnish. I gave little thought to Norman, except to wonder if he noticed.

Perhaps my distress with Victoria had taught me something, after all. I only know that growth, in whatever form it occurs and through whatever circumstances, brings such a sense of satisfaction. I knew myself far better now, and chose to care about someone if they had hurt me. I could look past their immediate action, value their personhood, and even sympathize with their situation.

As folks milled around outside the creamery, another man added, "Nimitz is one of our own, right proud of him, aren't you? That fella knows his history. Anchored the Missouri on the exact spot where Commodore Perry did, and chose an honor guard all over six feet tall. Besides that, the Japs stand right under the gun turret during the surrender. Nothing like rubbing it in."

At the mention of Admiral Nimitz, Norman flinched. Everyone knew the Admiral had grown up in Fredericksburg, with German-American roots through and through. Did Norman sense this irony?

Whether he did or not, it was enough that the war had ended. What a relief, yet still no letter from Elliot. How many of my former students had survived the fighting? Had any of them made what the newscasters called *the ultimate sacrifice*?

And what of Emmaline and Anton? Donnie rarely asked after them any more, and with the creamery needing me less for deliveries now, I procrastinated a drive down to see Opa Bultman.

Great sorrow still lay in store for many families, as the final casualty lists had not yet reached them all. But oh, the release washed out in tears and hugs on V-J Day, and the gratitude lifted to Heaven!

Immersed in the heady aroma of Mr. Grunkle's rich ice cream, our local citizenry repeated the sentiments voiced after the Great

War. "Never again a war like this. Surely, this was *the war to end all wars.*"

As Hazel chugged toward home, thoughts of Grandfather brought him especially close. Without doubt, he had uttered these words back on Armistice Day. Having lost his only son—his sole child—grief must have clouded his joy.

As autumn deepened, the aftermath of war continued to monopolize our news, and what reporters missed, Donnie brought home from school. Did I know that a Texan scout had navigated a clear spot over Hiroshima to drop the bomb? Had I heard that the Texas *Lost Battalion* had finally been freed back in August? These were the men who helped American POWs build the bridge on the River Kwai in Burma—why were we only learning this now?

"Wow, Dad, besides Admiral Nimitz and General Eisenhower, Colonel Oveta Culp Hobby was from Texas, too, and so was a pilot named Houston Lee Braly, from up north at Brady. And another guy from Brady—James Earl Rudder. He's the one who led the attack at Pointe du Hoc, and he came back and became the mayor.

"Did you know that over 750,000 Texans served, and a million and a half men came here for training? And thirty-three Texans earned the Medal of Honor. Audey Murphy got the most medals of any GI, and Commodore Dealey's the most decorated naval officer.

"Mr. Kidney read to us about a fella named Rawlings, too. He flew sixty-one missions in a B-26 bomber and never got shot down. Aren't you proud we live in the Lone Star State?"

If Mr. Kidney felt badly that he had not been able to serve, he certainly made up for it by honoring those who did. One fact went unmentioned, though. A total of 22,000 Texans had given their lives for the cause. Stories would be filtering from this immense war for decades.

Among them would be those of young men who perished quite close by. Twenty-one instructors and pilots in training died in plane crashes on and around Curtis Field in Brady. Perhaps at one time or another, they flew over us in practice missions.

During the war years, our trusty radio brought news from afar, but also reports of these accidents. The Brady *Standard-Herald* provided more details.

Near Big Spring—Curtis Field Field Cadet Dies in Accident—Brady Standard-Herald—Sept. 15, 1942

He was on a solo cross-country flight from Brady to Westbrook, Mitchell County. Kastelic's nearest of kin is his father, of Erhaut, Penn.

The body will be sent from Big Spring to his hometown for burial, with aviation student Joseph Peck accompanying.

After the nightly news carried these details, William moaned. "They are all so young. Such a tragedy."

Earlier that year, in February, he had noted the death of another young pilot who crashed on the Richards Ranch. "Why, that must be the man who sold me our bull."

As the war continued, more devastating stories followed.

Crashing in a pasture 20 miles southeast of Big Spring, Lewis J. Kastelic, 20, aviation student from the basic flying school at Curtis field, was killed Sunday, (Sept 13, 1942)

January 18, 1944 Cadet William R. Curl, member of Class 44-D in basic training at Curtis Field, killed in a routine training flight accident at the field Tuesday afternoon.

. . . Both airplanes were returning to the field after completing scheduled student training flights. BT-13A #42-41920 landed squarely on top of BT-13A #42-42583 just as it was touching down on the runway. The propeller of BT-13A #42-21920 smashed through the cockpit of BT-13A #42-4258, killing A.C. Carl instantly.

The airplanes remained in the "piggy-back" position as they rolled down the runway, coming to a stop about 400 feet from the point of collision.

Nothing quite so sobering as these news reports. Our younger boys might play at dog fighting, but the sad truth of this war came home to them over and over in the evenings. Nothing to do but talk it all over together and pray for the victims' families.

As autumn faded, we celebrated birthdays and looked forward to a delightful holiday season, with Abigail and Willie starry-eyed at its very mention. In the winter semester, Mr. Kidney was transferred to the Mason school and a female teacher hired in his place.

She started a debate group with the older students, so Donnie stayed after school three days a week, and Abigail, in her first school year, insisted she would be fine walking home with a classmate. Heaven forbid another war arose when Abigail came of age, but if so, she would find a way to serve.

The end of the school year brought dubious news. Our local school would be closing, so students would be attending classes in Mason. I discovered that Mr. Kidney had been aware of this when he agreed to transfer, but was sworn to secrecy.

Some students lived between here and Mason, so the distance would change little for them. Over the summer, one father purchased a used Lincoln seven-passenger Brougham. He figured eight children plus him equaled seven adult passengers, and each family gladly paid a little for gasoline. That settled the matter.

This news set anger churning against the powers that be. On an impromptu visit one evening, Norman spouted his disgust. Realizing an adult shared his views heartened Donnie. Though we all knew enrollment had declined, accepting the state's decision took time.

On the last day of school, the old stone building's irrevocably scarred doors closed for good. It seemed we ought to hold a ceremony, but time moved on. One bright spot shone for Donnie in all of this—in the Mason school, he might have Mr. Kidney for a teacher again.

"You just never know what'll happen, do you, Da?"

My agreement ran deep .In the midst of change, he found something to anticipate as his Loyal Valley school memories entered that nostalgic, never-to-be-repeated realm. Perhaps it was my imagination, but every time I passed the building, an air of sadness seemed to permeate the small structure.

Some day, I suppose, Donnie will meet old friends, and in their memories, nothing will have changed. They will recall four friendly stone walls, Mrs. Bultman's geography lessons, discussing airplanes and playing baseball with Mr. Kidney, and always, the lingering aura of chalk dust.

But word had it that opportunities abounded in a larger school system—chances to compete against other towns in sports and on debate teams, plus a wider variety of classes. All in all, Donnie took the alteration in stride, and I lagged along behind, aware that this marked only the first of many turns in his path.

Chapter Twenty-four

Winter 1947

Going over the past, I might opine, "If this had not happened, then—" If the Great War had not taken my father— If Mother had not contracted the influenza— If I had not married Victoria— I always stopped there, because then there would be no Donnie.

But I could go on—if Grandfather had not left us amply supplied, William and I might never have left England. And of course, had the house stayed intact, we would never have considered emigrating.

We all do this, since life travels in circles. One thing leads to another, and sometimes our most trying experiences, even the most devastating, forge our next steps.

So it was on the day before Thanksgiving in '46. The Sunday service at Cherry Spring had ended with "How Firm A Foundation." Grandfather hummed this hymn often, and said Robert E. Lee loved it. During the Spanish-American War, Civil War veterans who had fought for both the North and the South sang it together on Christmas Eve—Teddy Roosevelt, rowdy warrior that he was, must have taken thought to honoring the Savior's birth.

In our peaceful little sanctuary the Sunday before Thanksgiving, with bird chatter just outside the window, I could never have guessed how I would need this hymn in the ensuing week.

"What more can He say, than to You He hath said
to you who for refuge to Jesus have fled
I'll strengthen you, help you, and cause you to stand . . ."

By now we had all adapted to the war being over. Many of those who came here as military trainers returned to their homes, but quite a number settled in. Some air bases had been closed down or used for storage. Others became small municipal airports or developed into larger ones, as with Love Field in Dallas.

Willie would soon be four years old, which seemed impossible. With Mr. Grunkle's son and grandson home, William made all deliveries himself, giving me opportunity to catch up with work I had let go.

On Tuesday during his milking, William praised his employer. "Never a more generous soul—this job appeared at precisely the right time. We already have a good bit saved up."

"Did Kenneth ever find a good worker?"

"We have never heard. At least Lillian will still inherit half of the store—so says our lawyer. Kenneth's bark is worse than his bite." A while later, William lowered his voice to make an odd request, and his tone perked up my ears.

"If anything should happen to me, you would watch out for Lillian and the children?"

"Of course, as you would for Donnie."

"Indeed." He went on about the three children being like brothers and sisters. Donnie came in then, so I never asked what spurred his request.

Soon, an answer arrived, in a way that could not have shocked me more. The next day, I stopped by to talk with William, and within seconds found myself out in the yard, kneeling beside him on the rocky soil. The color had drained from his face and blood pooled beneath his head.

I had scarcely knocked when Lillian pulled me here. "Going for the Doctor—Abigail should be home any minute—Willie's down for a nap." She ran out the gate and down the street.

Unable to accept William's lack of response, I crouched there, following my training for school emergencies. Check airways, stop the flow of blood. Check pulse. Keep victim undisturbed. All the while, I blurted, "Where does it hurt?"

But William's lips, a translucent shade of blue, remained still. Staring up at the gutter he had been cleaning and the tall wooden ladder askew on the earth, I pieced together his fall.

There, was that a faint pulse in his neck? As the doctor opened his bag, Willie called from inside the house. I flew to the lad's bed—the bed his Da had so carefully made for him—and took my first normal breath.

Through the front window, we spotted Donnie and Abigail coming home and went out to the front room. But through the open back door, Willie noticed Lillian and the doctor. "Daddy fell down?"

"Yes. You and I will stay here until the doctor helps him. Let's get you some water." Much calmer at this age than he had been at two, Willie took my hand.

Information drifted in. "Still with us, but barely . . . struck his head on this stone . . . quite a deep gash . . . bleeding has almost stopped."

"Will he be . . .?"

Silence.

" . . . to the hospital fast. Send for the ambulance."

At that, I hurried to them, handed Willie to Lillian and raced out. Ah, Donnie and Abigail. I motioned Donnie over and asked him to keep Abigail inside for a while.

Clearly, Doc's wife had maneuvered the large ambulance before. Solemn and efficient, she backed as close as possible to the front door as I ran to tell the doctor.

But the expression on his face sickened me. The ambulance was no longer needed. Lillian's sobbing carried into the house, where Willie stood and gaped. When he saw me, he pummeled into my arms and hid his face.

The doctor leaned near Lillian. "I believe he passed without pain, Mrs. Parker. Probably a heart attack."

Clenching Abigail's hand, Donnie drew near. "What's wrong?" My eyes filled.

"Oh my." I sank into a chair. "I'm afraid William took a fall."
"Is he all right?"
"No. He has—I believe the fall has stolen him away from us."
"Stolen him? You mean . . ."
"My daddy died?" If anyone could vie with Donnie for verbosity, it was Abigail. "Like that soldier named Freddie?"

Instantly, she connected this with a local boy whose remains finally arrived home for burial last month. We all went to support the family when his father drove his son's body home.

"Yes, like that."

Her face crumbled, and she ran to Lillian.

Willie clung to my neck and Donnie grasped my forearm as we squatted beside Lillian and Abigail, whose tears splashed on the part in William's hair. With leaf debris and blood staining his work clothes, that perfect part stayed as he had combed it this morning. Even his expression remained dignified.

My mind went numb. This simply could not be happening.

Then Lillian caught my eye, and her anguish broke my heart. Doc said something about taking William to his office, since he acted as the local coroner, but the words sounded like so much porridge bubbling in a pot.

Not until we buried my dearest friend that Saturday did my inner vacancy give way. The dribble of dust on stark pinewood opened a torrent inside me. Then came those dreaded final words, *ashes to ashes.*

One vital difference separated all past grief from this. William had always stood beside me to share the abhorrent resonance of dust sifting onto wood. At my father's burial, William was there, and with mother, Grandmother, Grandfather, and Victoria.

He was meant to live forever, and his passing sentenced me to a hazy no-man's land. How might I ever accept his absence?

For the children's sake, life went on. Though crushed, Donnie and Abigail kept occupied with school. Meanwhile, I helped Lillian with Willie as much as possible.

The next weeks became a blur, with offerings from every quarter. People brought sweet potato casseroles, enough home-baked bread and roast beef to freeze for the future, and of course, pies, turkey, and sage dressing.

Managing it all gave Lillian a focal point. William's foresightedness in purchasing freezers, or *the deep freeze* as we called them, brought fresh tears as I toted a load of food to ours.

"International Harvesters," he had announced when he heralded these grand inventions. "They will last forever."

Each night, Abigail burst into sobs at bedtime, and tummy aches ailed Willie for weeks. When Donnie and I helped put them to bed, we drove home in silence or spoke quietly about William. Our memories brought indescribable solace, and often by the time we reached home, I hummed the tune that had carried me through this time.

"For I will be with thee to comfort and bless,
and sanctify to thee thy deepest distress."

Some nights as Hazel bumped along the dirt road, we sang the verses together, and Donnie asked about the meaning of "sanctify to thee." My skill with words failed me. The closest I could come was "Somehow, in the long view, our troubles may draw us closer to God."

"Our confirmation book says sanctify means *make holy*. Do you really think that'll ever happen with us losing Uncle William?"

"It surely doesn't seem that way right now." My voice rang hollow in my own ears. Gradually, I realized that nothing had ever hurt this much. Not the fire. Not losing Victoria. All the losses I had known piled up together at the doorway of my soul. This inner agony manifested as a physical ache in my chest, and more than once I questioned whether my heart might stop.

Things would never be the same, and pretending was futile. Through the Christmas holidays, William was everywhere we looked, yet nowhere at all.

"He's in a better place," or "He will always live in your heart," ring empty. I hated going anywhere people gathered. Not that they lacked sincerity—William, the quintessential butler, had found a place in their hearts, as well.

On weekdays, I kept to myself, but even then, his death slapped me in the face. Each twenty-four hours crept by, and I longed for nighttime, when I could retreat into silence. But sleep refused to come, so I longed for morning.

Out in the orchard one day, the toe of my boot caught on a gnarly root and I fell smack on the cold, hard earth. For a few moments, I lay there stunned. A precise metaphorical image of my emotional state.

Something warm trickled down my temple, and I reached up. No, not blood, but furious tears. I picked myself up and carried on, playing the strong one for Donnie, Lillian, and the little ones after school. But my insides churned, and refused to be stilled.

Starting in January, the worst winter weather since 1895 struck Nottingham and all of England. It seemed that England's frozen countryside, buried under twenty-one inches of snow for six long weeks, mourned William along with us. Word of his passing gradually reached his mates who had missed corresponding with him, and inquiries arrived, along with descriptions of the most debilitating storms in living memory.

Someone enclosed a newspaper clipping of icicles the entire height of a brick tunnel at Sherwood. I had walked under that very tunnel with Grandfather, and most likely with William. One massive icicle looked as thick as a strong man's arm. I could barely believe my eyes.

What a harsh setback for our people, still trying to recover from the war. When had we ever seen tractors with snowplows in the streets of our city? Fuel lines froze, piles of snow blocked roads, schools closed, and needful repair work halted. Stopped in its tracks, William's friend wrote.

Exactly the way I felt, but I kept moving. At the same time, my soul stayed stuck.

Since he started working for Mr. Grunkle, William and I had spent fewer hours together, but our companionship always felt like home. Losing him left a ghastly crevice.

My wordlessness shocked me as much as anything. The children were bound to ask after William, and dreaming up answers stymied me.

"Did his good suit get all dirty when those men put him in the ground?"

"Can he see us now? Can he hear our prayers?"

My answers verged on those uttered by well-meaning people. One day I heard myself respond, "Your daddy will always be with you." But Abigail needed a stronger image.

"Like Jesus in my heart?"

"Mmm. Sort of." She had heard this at Sunday school, but a child like Abigail rarely accepted things easily.

Then and there, I decided to replace my impotent answers with questions. Who was I to define the way William would *be there* with her?

The next time Abigail asked a question, instead of saying something trite, I waited. Sometimes she required no reply.

Asking, "Do you sense him with you?" allowed her to put words to her emotions. Still imperfect at best, yet that is the way of grieving.

Lillian, on the other hand, had her own quiet way. Only when she brought up his name did we speak of William.

One rainy day, though, as I oversaw Willie's building endeavors on the floor, she stood at William's bookcase. After fingering a full row, she carefully pulled out a volume—*The Murder at the Vicarage*. Would reading about death, about murder, be helpful?

But then I recalled Miss Marple's introduction in '27 in *The Tuesday Night Club*. Somewhere I read that Agatha Christie had no idea this new character would rival Hercule Poirot in the public's affections. Three years later, at the publication of *The Murder at the Vicarage*, Miss Marple surprised her creator with immense reader response.

Just then, Lillian caught my eye. The lift of her brows seemed to say, "Why not? This may be the diversion I need."

Now thirteen, Donnie internalized his emotions more than in the past. Milking William's cows brought us both an odd mix of comfort and pain. Once, we looked up at the same time, and Donnie's heartfelt question wrenched me.

"Why do you think God allowed William to die?"

The rafters produced a *hoot* from our pet owl, and we both glanced upward. Finally I shook my head. "I don't know, Son." Later, as we walked back to the house, Donnie draped his arm over my shoulders.

"I love you, Da."

"And I love you."

Chapter Twenty-five

February 1948

"With this ring I thee wed."

Tears glistened in Lillian's eyes, full of hope and joy and sorrow, all three. Around us, the children formed a circle. Abigail held a dried wildflower bouquet from our cottage garden, and Donnie guarded Lillian's ring while taming Willie through the short ceremony.

When I slipped the ring over Lillian's knuckle, a vast weight lifted. A man committing his life to a woman with two young children might notice intense responsibility falling upon his shoulders. Not so—that, I took up immediately after William's passing. From this moment on, Lillian and I would share the load in a new way.

As with so many other circumstances, our bond blossomed over these years and resulted in this surprising culmination. Never would I have visualized us as man and wife, because I had long ago cast aside the idea of marriage.

But after fifteen months since William left us, this step made perfect sense. Not that love must be logical. Lillian and I had already faced pure misery, knew each other so well and enjoyed a solid friendship.

After the funeral, days jam-packed with the animals, work in the orchard, and Donnie's activities hushed my emotions. His pastimes grew to include basketball. His lanky form proved ideal for lunging toward the hoop with the ball and foiling opponents' scoring efforts. On winter nights, cheering on his team provided a release.

Another boy from Loyal Valley played, too, so we collected him before the games and took him home afterwards. Abigail and Willie loved the excitement, and often fell asleep on the ride home. At times Lillian joined us, or enjoyed a quiet evening.

Whenever I could, I attempted to ease her load. As she said, having an energetic four-year-old would have been much easier twenty years ago, or even ten.

Through the years, I had heard mention of women's intuition, but now learned about it firsthand. Aware of her feelings for me long before I had any inkling, Lillian guarded her fledgling knowledge.

As spring sprouted around us, Donnie and I often supped with her and the children. Reading to Abigail afterward seemed quite natural, and Donnie did the same with Willie. On those evenings, Lillian often slipped out for a walk under the starry sky.

Summer's advent held a bittersweet tinge. I cleared some brush on ten more acres William had added to our total just weeks before he passed. With each swing of my axe, I thought how excited he would be to join me.

The advent of the fireflies brought my first hint of a fresh connection with Lillian. We had gone out one late June evening to watch these unique insects light up the hillside like miniature stars. The children collected them in jars, watched them glow from their beds, and set them free in the morning.

Donnie made sure Willie captured his share, while Abigail proved herself quite capable on her own. Every few minutes, one or the other would show us their catch, and Lillian and I exclaimed appropriately. Perched on the rail fence at the back of her lot, we drank in sweet scents on the breeze and cicada song all 'round.

Perhaps twenty minutes into this adventure, Lillian gave Abigail a wave, and her fingers brushed my arm. She touched the spot again, and the lavender scent she always wore caught my attention. Something stirred in me, but just then Willie raced over.

"Mommy! Mommy, look!"

Lillian attended to him, and I wandered off to applaud for

Abigail. But when Donnie and I took our leave that night, a new light shone in Lillian's eyes. I surmised her equilibrium had returned, giving her joy in simple things once more.

But far more was afoot. After some months, she confessed this during the harvest. Certain scenes need not be detailed, but by this time my awareness had increased as well.

Oh, the talks I had with William on those evenings as I checked on the animals while Donnie did his homework. On each occasion, William's last request came to mind. *Would I take care of Lillian and the children?* Everything within me answered *Yes*, and during the winter holidays, Lillian and I began to make plans.

We kept our intentions quiet, but midway through January, Donnie asked, "Are you and Lillian going to get married?" He eyed me over a cow's back as we sat milking of an evening.

"I believe we might."

"Oh, good. When?"

"Sometime soon, maybe. What do you think?"

"You mean when? How about next weekend?" His approval swirled in my head. Most likely, he had known for some time.

After we said our vows, Donnie and I moved a few things into Lillian's. I could easily drive or walk to the country every day, but the school shuttle left from town.

On weekends, though, we stayed at our stone house and began to consider how we might enlarge the structure to accommodate us all.

Lillian allowed that William loved this place, and had sacrificed to move to town when they married. She sold her property and relished working in the garden.

The stoneworkers, I daresay, grew weary of my so-called help, but I learned even more about the scars created when masons saw and file and rub stones for a perfect fit. Without the marks made during this process, much would be lost.

Our structure would stand as strong and welcoming as ever, but with more spaces for each of us to claim. Lillian remarked of an evening how this appealed to her—places to go, nooks where one might pause in solitude for a bit.

By September, our rambling abode boasted two new bedrooms, and off of ours, a small library. Abigail moved into the other room, Willie took over Donnie's old haunt, and Donnie transformed the upstairs into his bedroom and his study nook.

Building deep shelves for my library and placing each book brought such satisfaction. I worked alone after the children left for school or had gone to bed.

When all was settled at last, I stood back to observe my desk, complete with Grandfather's letter opener. Shelves full of books, most of them Grandfather's, backed the chair Donnie and I had used all these years. Later, I added William's cache, smoothing each spine and recalling how he rescued Grandfather's library and fastidiously packed each volume for our Atlantic crossing.

Each day, he and Grandfather made themselves known in myriad ways. But I harbored no doubt that here in this room, their presence would waft even stronger.

September, 1950

"Donnie comes across as several years older. He's passed out of two freshman classes, Everett. We can't hold him here forever."

That had been Mr. Kidney's analysis at term's end. "Never have I known a lad his age so well read."

I argued that college requires far more than that. Donnie possessed a never-ending desire to learn and the determination to succeed, yes, but I simply could not send him away—not yet.

So it was that Mr. Kidney opened up his personal library. A few weeks later, his father, a professor at Texas A&M, also began sending reading material. Donnie's desire to become a veterinarian had blossomed, and on Saturdays, he learned hands-on with our local vet. At his end-of-year tests, he passed another college course.

During the summer, a growing conviction that he could handle this vast change decided the matter. He would enter the university in the fall—sixteen going on seventeen seemed far more acceptable than fifteen going on sixteen.

His belongings filled one of our trunks that crossed the Atlantic, and witnessing his tearful good-byes to Willie and Abigail gave me pause. But as Donnie and I drove toward San Antonio, where he would catch the train, he squared his shoulders.

A few weeks earlier, we had taken the train to visit the college, so he knew his dormitory. We even met his dorm "mother," who pointed out the rules—silence in the hallways, a ten o'clock curfew, lights out by eleven.

Tonight, I would stay over. Tomorrow Donnie would be on his own. As with the "Wabash Cannibal" he once chortled, change moves ever onward.

During the past year, his direction became even more obvious through working with our local vet, and Mr. Kidney had been so helpful. In the process, I gained a true friend, and meeting Mr. Kidney's parents in College Station relieved my reservations. They issued Donnie an open invitation and said they expected him for church every Sunday and dinner afterward.

Best of all, Mr. Kidney, Senior welcomed Donnie into his expansive library. The sparkle in my son's eyes declared his delight. Perhaps Grandfather experienced this odd mixture of excitement and reservation when he left me, not much older than Donnie, at university to ride the train back to Nottinghamshire.

So many exhausting leave takings in the ebb and flow of life. The Greek philosopher Heraclitus expressed this sentiment well. "There is nothing permanent except change."

One day, Donnie would graduate, find a post to fill, marry and have children. In the first weeks after William's death, I had wondered how life could proceed, and the ensuing years provided the answer. Now, Donnie was setting out into the world.

From such a distance, nearly 200 miles, how might I remain

an effective father? Letter writing. Of course. Tonight, I would commence, and faithfully send two letters per week, honoring Grandfather's practice when I attended university. Knowing his letters would arrive, even knowing the day, had stabilized me during those years.

The next day as I neared Loyal Valley, my thoughts turned to the Bultmans. Would our questions concerning them ever find closure? I had written Opa a few more times, but he replied only that Emmaline had taken a government translating position during the closing months of the war. He had not heard from Hulda and her family.

Emmaline and Anton moved out East, but Opa failed to mention the city. A few months later, Donnie heard from a classmate that Emmaline had contracted a serious disease. Weeks passed, but we heard no more.

Something our vicar said during my confirmation came to mind. "Your questions always challenge me, Everett."

The particular one he referred to was "Who folded the linen napkin that covered Jesus' head, and why was it left separate from the grave clothes?" Inquiries like these had instituted that *unanswered* shelf in my brain.

Recent years only multiplied its contents. I never heard from Elliot or his brother again. William's sudden demise left me baffled, as did Norman's behavior during the war. Emmaline's condition and Anton's whereabouts added to the list.

Our recent sermons centered on the fortieth chapter of Isaiah, and one verse resounded:

> *"Lift up your eyes on high, and behold who hath created these things, that bringeth out their host by number: he calleth them all by names by the greatness of his might, for that he is strong in power; not one faileth."*

"In this context, the word *faileth*," our pastor explained, "means *goes missing.* Not one of those God calls by name is missing." Yet for us, so many had gone missing. Texas Hill Country passed by, and I considered all the young men absent from their families because they had crashed here during their pilot training.

House Mountain stood in the distance, but its stark beauty was lost on me. Through all of the wartime chaos, it remained, through the War Between the States, the War for Texas Independence and untold battles between various Indian tribes and then with the U.S. Cavalry. In all of these, how many people had gone missing?

The Indian boy reared in one of House Mountain's caves—where was he now? That older fellow who predicted the weather as he passed during our early months here—had not trekked by for years.

Lillian noted that during the last century, Catholic priests and sisters founded an orphanage near Dallas to care for children orphaned by Indian bands, virulent diseases, childbirth, fires, or any number of accidents with horses or guns. Hundreds of frontier children grew to adulthood without even knowing their origins.

But none of this decreased my curiosity concerning Emmaline and Anton. I parked and sat for a few moments before Willie discovered I had returned. So many questions—like those bats Donnie and I had viewed exiting their cave one Sunday afternoon long ago.

Then, in the stillness, a consoling thought rose, almost an audible whisper. "Missing to you, but not to Me."

Christmas 1951

The house fairly burst with energy as I left to fetch Donnie, who had caught a ride to Fredericksburg. During Thanksgiving, he stayed with the Kidneys to study. Abigail and Willie wrote him each week and could scarcely wait for him to arrive.

Hidden away in the cellar or the attic, the barn or the new garage we built a few months ago, homemade gifts also awaited his arrival. Lillian had the children baking cookies and breads, industrious all. Tomorrow, Donnie would lead us on our annual search for a suitable Christmas tree, cut it down, tote it home, and help Abigail and Willie dress it for our Christmas Eve.

When I spied Donnie outside his friend's house, he was talking with a tall fellow. Donnie noticed me next to our new Ford Fairlane. He approached, and his companion walked over with him.

This stranger's gait stirred a vagrant memory. His dark hair, fringed around the ears with grey, gave him a distinguished look. Some new acquaintance from school, I supposed.

Embracing me soundly, Donnie stepped back. "Do you recognize this fellow?"

I started to shake my head, but then the tall chap held out his hand. "Hello Mr. Herring. It's been a long time." Where had I heard this voice? The young man shuffled his feet, and something about that movement spurred recognition.

"Anton? Is it really you? How did—"

"Anton's going to A&M, too, Da. Can you believe it?"

"I'm afraid I'm just a freshman. It took me some time to make it there."

"But you succeeded—how wonderful! You came to see your great-grandfather?"

"No, he passed last year. I'm visiting my Grandmother."

"Oh my. I got to know him just a little these past years. My condolences."

Clouds gathered in Anton's eyes. His sigh, though controlled, spoke volumes. "You may have heard that Mother passed, too." He looked away. "In Spring of '46—they told me she contracted lockjaw."

Tetanus, what a horrible death. Had the doctors out East no medicines to give Emmaline?

"Well, then. I should get my luggage and call a taxi."

"Do you need a ride—your grandmother lives in Grapetown, doesn't she?"

"That's out of your way."

"Oh, but not by much, and we're in no hurry."

313

"All right. Thank you."

The two of them took off, leaving me to ponder. Emmaline would be in her mid-forties. For some years now, certain treatments had been efficacious for tetanus.

Had Anton, all alone with her and far from his family, witnessed her death? My questions multiplied.

For now, hearing him and Donnie converse would have to be enough. We left him with an invitation to come see us, and he said he would sometime during the vacation. On our way home, Donnie had little to add about the Bultmans' years of exile—he and Anton chatted mostly about school and classmates, he said.

"I could tell he'd rather not discuss the rest, but he did say why he started studying so late. He had to work more than one job to save enough money for college."

Perhaps this wartime mystery would remain on my *unanswered* shelf forever.

Potato bugs paid us another visit, the first recurrence since our original battle. I kept rotating the crops and planted ample catnip, in obedience to Violet. But this season, something went wrong. Yet another mystery.

When I noticed the first bug gnawing away at a leaf, I had just finished re-reading Voltaire's *Candide*. Having included all possible human complications, he gave simple instructions at the end: *Il faut cultiver le jardin*. Over the centuries, students made much of his statement, insisting on various metaphorical meanings for his advice to work.

But I wondered. After all *Candide* endured in this tumultuous world, tending a garden made sense. His travels across Europe and to Argentina included multiple disappointments and taught him the priceless value of the present moment.

Why, at the end, should Voltaire not encourage us to focus on what lay at hand, to make the most of *now*? Why *wouldn't* his hero turn to his gardening? Old John Meusebach might well have offered the same advice.

Instead of Donnie playing nearby, Willie tromped in the rivulet from the creek. His frequent shouts revealed a noisier personality than Donnie's, more inclined to kick or pound on things.

I envisioned him as a baseball catcher, down on his knees with balls flying at him, loving every rough-and-tumble moment. Soon, I hoped, Willie would labor at the cider press with as much gusto as he exhibited in his play.

Now almost twice as large as when we first arrived, our house meandered south, creating a courtyard of sorts. Shielded from wind and sun, this area developed into a pleasant bower accessible from my library. Lillian and Abigail, weeding and deadheading flowers there right now, helped with its upkeep.

As for our early plantings, William would say, "Against all odds, a veritable cottage garden has developed. I daresay we can be proud of our work."

But my aging joints protested when I weeded our vegetables or worked at the cider press, though such efforts led to blissful sleep. As the years flowed on, an important alteration had occurred. My tendency toward morbid introspection nearly died out. In those instances when it surfaced, I simply said, "Here we go again."

Something else changed. Donnie and I had rarely entertained visitors, but Lillian often invited Mr. Grunkle and his family or some other friends from church. These old stone walls absorbed a great deal more noise and laughter these days.

In fair weather, Norman sometimes stops by to plop in his favorite spot and watch me work. In a rusting metal chair, the kind with a bounce in the seat, he seems content. Having Doris enter the hospital mellowed him, and when she died last year, he disappeared for a time.

His voice seems even lower now, his opinions pared down. Once in a while he stays for supper, and Willie has become his favorite. Recalling how my struggles with Victoria subdued me, I realize that not so much separates us. Each of us lives with problems and joys—what makes us distinct is the personal path we travel.

When Donnie comes home, Anton often does too, and their chess games last into the wee hours. No young men ever engaged in deeper discussions, although Anton remains insular about his past. Even after he realized horticulture was not his bailiwick and decided to pursue a degree in law at the University of Texas, he and Donnie have maintained their friendship.

As for Emmaline Bultman, may her memory be honored. Many Loyal Valley children, now grown to adulthood, gleaned much from her determined, patriotic spirit. This I say, still hoping that one day all wrongs will be righted and all grief assuaged.

So our life goes on, full of puzzles and challenges, but also common pleasures. Busy with day-to-day concerns, we have yet to visit Old Blighty. I rather imagine Donnie will see to this himself, and perhaps in our later years, Lillian and I may tag along.

In the winter months, my bookshelves bring William and Grandfather close. At other times, in the garden or out in the orchard, a breeze toys with a branch and casts a shadow near me. I glance up, expecting to see William approach with a fresh insight or notion to ponder.

"Perhaps we ought to lay another line of pipe from the spring next fall, Everett. What do you think?"

"A good idea, as usual, and the spring offers an endless supply. But thanks to you, our cottage garden already has all the water it needs."

As he turns to go, I notice something like a shadow beside him, almost a phantom. Could this be my old enemy? A multitude of alterations parade before my mind's eye, all of them endured, survived, and leading to my present happy estate.

I lean in for a better look. In that fraction of a second, the truth becomes clear. Throughout all the twists and turns of this life, it has been not change itself, but my dread of it that brought such distress.

The shadow melds with William's form, and in another instant, fades away.

In His hand are the deep places of the earth; the strength of the hills is His also.

Psalm 95:4

Book Club Discussion Questions

1. How did Everett's experience with Victoria affect him?
   In what ways did he do his best to help her?
   What can we take away from his decision never to teach again?

2. What significance does William have in Everett's life?
   How does he fit (or not) with your mental image of a British butler?
   Describe what, if anything, surprised you about William.

3. Which events back in England trouble Everett and William the most?
   From the perspective of history, which troubles you the most as a reader?

4. What role does Mrs. Bultmann play in Everett and Donnie's experience of their new home?
   How do you feel about what happened to Emmaline's German-American family during the war?
   Most of us have heard about Japanese-American and Italian-American internees, but usually not German-Americans.
   Why do you think this is so?

5. What effect does Donnie's progress through childhood/youth have on Everett?
   What do you think of the way the author brings Lillian into Everett's life?

6. Discuss how Everett processes the immense grief he experienced before he emigrated to the United States.

He refers to several life lessons he learned through it all. Which impresses you?

7. Describe Everett's reaction to Norman's experience with his wife's mental health.

Discuss how this situation alters Norman.

During this era, women had few alternatives for support—how do you think the outcome might have differed if Doris were living today?

How did the news about Doris affect Everett's perspective toward his relationship with Norman?

8. As the driver who takes Everett, Donnie, and William from Fredericksburg to Loyal Valley, he offers them ample information about their new home. What else do his comments supply about the area in general?

Special Thanks

A word of thanks to so many kind Hill Country folks: Charles Eckert at the Mason County Public Library supplied valuable information about early German settlers, and Tony Plutino of Llano River Region Adventures shared a wealth of geographical wisdom, plus insights into the area's plant and animal life.

Rancher John Byerley provided a day tour of Loyal Valley and House Mountain. He also introduced me to Billy Henke, a member of the last class at Loyal Valley School, and his wife Agnes. Interviewing Billy also revealed a very close look at a *long* Hill Country snake that soon met its demise. Thank you so very much for bringing Loyal Valley to life for this Northerner! Reading *Homeland Insecurity* by Stephen Fox enlightened me concerning the treatment of German-Americans during World War II—thank you for your work, Stephen.

I am also grateful to Evelyn Weinheimer at the Fredericksburg Pioneer Museum, and to Irene Rode Merz at the *Vereins Kirche*— nothing like first-hand information from those who grew up right here in this land. Thank you also to Kyle Moseley at the Brady Heart of Texas Historical Museum, for helpful information about WWII pilot training.

My gratitude goes to historical author Lynn Dean for vital architectural information, and for her patience in driving me around this beautiful area. Michael Barr, I so appreciate your time and encouraging comments, and as always, a great big hug to those who read this manuscript and caught my many slip-ups.

About the Author

Words have always been comfort food for Gail Kittleson. After instructing expository writing and English as a Second Language, she began writing seriously. Intrigued by the World War II era, Gail creates historical fiction from her northern Iowa home and also facilitates writing workshops/retreats.

She and her husband, a retired Army chaplain, enjoy grand-children and in winter, Arizona's Mogollon Rim Country. You can count on Gail's protagonists to ask honest questions, act with integrity, grow in faith, and face hardships with spunk.

Visit Gail online at: GailKittleson.com

35411982R00184